Advance Pr
Pinocchio's Guide to th

Booklife Reviews Editor' ... s richly inventive debut novel proves as enchanting—and as darkly surprising—as the original fairy tale from which it takes inspiration…

It's a fairy tale for adults that doesn't blink at the real world's harshness or cheapen historical atrocities when lacing in the fantastic. Moon's fantasy showcases the heart it takes to stand up for what's best in us all as that evil threatens to swallow the world. …

Takeaway: The surprising story of Pinocchio taking on fascism, written with polish and playful power.

IndieReader: *Pinocchio's Guide to the End of the World* is both an unofficial sequel to Collodi's novel and a rebuttal to his message about the virtues of obedience. …

Yes, he can be impulsive, headstrong, and naive. But Pinocchio is also resourceful, loyal, and willing to risk himself to help others. …It may not be to everyone's taste, but it works. Oh, how it works.

IR Verdict: Eva Moon manages to balance humor, adventure, and drama in *Pinocchio's Guide to the End of the World* and the warm humanity of her characters helps illuminate one of the darkest chapters of the 20th century.

Pinocchio's Guide
to the
End of the World

ISBN: 979-8-9869263-1-5

Cover design by: Patrick Knowles
Library of Congress Control Number:
2022918011

Published by Falling Moon Productions, LLC
Printed in the United States of America

Pinocchio's Guide
to the
End of the World

Eva Moon

Falling Moon Productions, LLC

1

Sure, I can tell you what happened. No one will believe it, even though they all know I can't lie.

It's been so long, nearly everyone who was involved in that business is gone, God rest their souls, and someone should know.

If it's true what those scientists say—that if you wait long enough, dry land becomes sea and sea becomes dry land— then someday, the bottom of the sea might rise up into mountains, and on one of those mountains, a tree might grow that's a little different from the others. Whoever finds that tree might discover what's hiding inside, and then where will we be?

You and I won't even be dust's own memory of dust by then.

• • •

The day she made me a real boy, I was maybe ten, eleven years old. It's not the kind of thing I can be exact about. When would you count from? The day Papa carved me? The day the tree fell? The day the acorn pushed out its first white rootlet?

It was the summer of 1910. The first automobile anyone had seen with their own eyes had driven through our dusty little Tuscan town a month before, and people were still talking about it. The weather was so blazing hot, even the crickets couldn't be bothered to chirp, but I took off running, just for the joy of feeling bone beneath muscle beneath skin for the first time. By the time I got home, she was gone, and it would be many years before I saw her again.

I had promised her I'd always be truthful and obey my Papa. Being truthful was easy. I can't lie. The last time I tried was when Father Matteo asked me if I knew who painted "Kiss Me" on his forehead when he fell asleep in the vestry. My nose hadn't grown more than a pimple since I was changed, but if I even thought about lying, it itched like hell, and if a lie managed to get past my lips, I couldn't stop sneezing until I confessed the truth.

I had no such disability when it came to obedience, but I did my best anyway. I hardly ever skipped school, and I worked in the shop nearly every day before and after. I swept up enough wood shavings to build an army of marionettes and carried enough buckets of water to drown every one of them.

But there were lapses. Mostly thanks to Ludovico, that ham-faced bully. He hated me for the crime of being different. The other boys might have just let it go in time, but with him egging them on, I got into fights almost daily.

It didn't help that he was right. I had been given a human body, but inside I still felt the same as before. Papa tried to tell me it didn't matter, but he and every other person in the world had been made the usual way. No magic could erase the fact that I was more closely related to the chair you're sitting on than to my own Papa.

I never would have survived without my friends, Alidoro and Eugenio. Eugenio's family made the wine that inspired most of the trouble I got into, including the Father Matteo incident. Mostly, we hung out under this big oak tree, talking about the great adventures we were going to have when we grew up. The tree is still there. You can see it if you walk past Paola's café and look up to the top of the hill. It has a nice view of tile roofs and vineyards and offers the hope of a breeze on a hot day.

• • •

I was sixteen when Italy entered the Great War. No one could think or talk about anything else, and we devoured any scrap of news from the front. The grown-ups were mostly against it. They thought Italy should have stayed neutral. We envied the older boys heading off to fight and be heroes. I wanted to enlist, but Papa wasn't having it.

"I can't run the shop by myself."

"You ran it by yourself before me!"

"And I was so poor, the only way to have a fire in winter was to paint one on the wall. Is that what you want for your old Papa?"

So, there I sat, day after day, rooted to my stool, watching other young men pass our little workshop window on their way to adventure and glory. I might as well have stayed a tree.

I was still sitting there when they started coming back—what was left of them. Papa stopped making toys and learned to make wooden legs and arms. It should have put me off wanting to go, but it didn't. Even maimed, they were what I was afraid I'd never be: real men. I'd rather have been dead and buried on a battlefield as a man than buried alive here as a boy.

My wish to go fight wasn't granted until the summer of 1917, when the war was almost over.

• • •

We were sitting under our oak tree passing around a bottle Eugenio had pinched from his father's cellar when we saw someone running our way flat out.

"Hey, Alidoro," said Eugenio. "Isn't that your little brother? What mischief have you been up to now?"

It could have been any number of kinds of mischief, but when Alidoro's brother reached us, red-faced and sweaty, he threw down a damp, crumpled newspaper.

"You're getting constructed!" he shouted.

We crowded around to read the paper. Alidoro smacked the side of his brother's head.

"Conscripted, you idiot."

The government had conscripted all eighteen-year-old males to join the army. Every single one.

I ran all the way home.

"Absolutely not!" Papa crossed his arms and glowered at me. "Counting from when you became a live boy, you're barely seven years old!"

He tried to keep the glower going, but it was such a ridiculous argument, even he had a hard time of it. I grabbed an apple from the bowl on the table, held it up so it stared at him with two wormhole eyes, and gave it a high, squeaky voice.

"Counting from when I was picked, I'm barely seven days old!"

Papa rolled his eyes and sighed.

• • •

On the morning I was to report, I was up before dawn, pacing the floor while Papa tried to squeeze one more wedge of cheese into my rucksack.

"Keep it, Papa."

"Who knows what they'll feed you in the army?"

Outside, my neighbor Rodolfo wrestled with a rucksack even more overstuffed than mine while his mother fluttered around him weeping noisily.

"Hi, Rodolfo!" I called. "Good morning, Mrs. Passerini."

She waved me off and blew her nose into a handkerchief. "What good morning? The two of you are still babies!"

Eugenio and Alidoro were already at the crowded square, along with their parents, brothers, sisters, aunts, uncles, and cousins. Ludovico was going, too. He jeered when he saw me.

"The army must be desperate. For firewood."

He and his buddies just about fell down laughing. I knew I shouldn't let him get to me, but this could be my last chance to punch his lights out. I started for him, but Eugenio and Alidoro steered me away.

We could have walked to our muster point in Florence. But Eugenio's father had some barrels of wine to deliver there and insisted on giving us a ride.

"I might never see you boys again," he said, his voice bleak.

We climbed up and sat atop the oak barrels. He clucked at the horse, and we jolted forward, waving our hats and blowing kisses to the girls while the grown-ups wept. Then I turned away. My eyes were on the future. I didn't even look back to see the only home I'd ever known vanish around a bend.

Along the way, strangers shook our hands or shook their heads, sometimes both. We saluted as if we were already seasoned veterans instead of the greenest of sprouts.

The cart creaked and rattled up and down every hill, but got us there before we detonated with impatience. Country boys like us jammed the transfer point, some loudly ready to slay Austrian bastards and others white-faced with fear and homesickness. Despite the din and confusion, the officers got us all sorted out and onto the train. We chugged north and east all night. I don't think I slept a minute. When the sun rose over the Adriatic, its shimmering sapphire blue felt like a good omen.

The training camp was the first place I dipped my toes in the waters of army life. Weary officers assigned us to units and handed out uniforms, rifles, and horsehair blankets. When I found my unit's sagging barracks tent, I dumped my things on an unclaimed cot and grinned. It felt like a first deep breath after taking off a jacket three sizes too small.

I wish I could tell you how I saved my unit from an ambush or how I single-handedly defeated an enemy regiment, but you don't want the barrage of sneezes that would lead to. The truth is, the epic saga of my career as a hero of the Italian Army wasn't even a short story.

After six weeks of marching around muddy fields and exasperating our commanding officers with our breathtaking incompetence, we were somehow deemed fit to haul our eighteen-year-old hides to the front.

From a distance, the Italian Alps looked like a picture postcard, but up close, they were a stew of rain, muddy snow and ice, all of it well-peppered with Austrian bullets. Six days after we arrived, I was digging a latrine when the world exploded in a red mist.

Things were foggy for a while after that. At one point, I thought I was a wooden boy again, back inside the giant fish with Papa. Sometimes, voices spoke to me, but I couldn't understand them, and for some reason, I thought I was in America. Eventually, the voices switched to Italian and told me I was in the hospital. A splinter from a shell had relieved me of my left leg just below the knee. I would have preferred America.

Alidoro was my most frequent visitor, and he kept coming even though I was pitiful company. Not that he was in a position to offer much cheer. He had two kinds of news: bad and worse.

"Rodolfo's gone. Sniper."

I shuddered. I'd known Rodolfo my whole life. Poor Mrs. Passerini. My eyes filled with tears, and it was a few minutes before I could speak again.

"Eugenio?" I asked.

"Still on his feet. Ludo too, I'm afraid."

"Damn. I guess he's too mean to die."

I said a silent prayer for Rodolfo and Eugenio. And for Alidoro, too. He never once mentioned that he was the one who carried me down the mountain on his back while bullets whizzed past. I heard it from a nurse.

It wasn't the last time he saved my skin, but that's getting ahead of myself.

• • •

The war spun me right back to where I started as fast as a yo-yo on a string. By spring, I was home, though it felt as foreign as the front.

Papa insisted nothing had changed. "Don't the houses still look the same?"

They did, but new ghosts haunted nearly every room.

"Don't spring flowers still bloom?"

They did, but most of them ended up in the cemetery.

"Don't people still buy vegetables at Sabbatini's?"

They did, but where was the sound of their cheerful haggling?

I stopped reading the papers. If anyone spoke of the war, I hobbled out of earshot on my crutches. The news was an abyss of pain, and I had enough of my own. Every week's mail dressed more mothers and sisters in black. In my school class alone, nearly half the boys died on those wretched heights. And for what? To paint an imaginary line on a slightly different strip of land than it had crossed a few months before.

It wasn't just that I was a cripple. Plenty of men got around on wooden legs, and Papa offered to make me one. But I'd gone to war hoping it would make me a man—a real human. Instead, it was turning me back into wood, complete with a stump. Why not lop off my other leg and my arms and my head and replace them with wood, too? Then I could be something useful like a bookshelf or a bench.

I planted myself at the kitchen table and drank. If you could find a new leg in a bottle of wine, I'd have been a centipede by summer's end. Papa shut the door of his workshop and stayed there day and night.

The war ended and Eugenio and Alidoro came home. Eugenio married his sweetheart, Angelina, within a week, and they settled in at his family's vineyard. I'm embarrassed to tell you how rudely drunk I got at their wedding. But he forgave me as always and would come sit with me when he could get away, though I didn't deserve it.

Alidoro wasn't home more than a month before he landed a job with the state railroad. Paola announced that she would host a send-off party for him at the café. I didn't want to go. He was heading to a real job. He'd travel and see new places, while I would be stuck here forever like a nail in a plank. But it felt petty, even for me, to sulk at home and not see him off after everything he'd done for me. I'd go. But I'd hate it.

A week before the party, Papa emerged from his workshop and laid a sacking-wrapped bundle on the kitchen table. He had a glow about him I hadn't seen since before the war. What on God's earth was there to glow about?

"Open it," he said.

I flipped open the sacking without enthusiasm. Then I sat up straighter. I had seen plenty of wooden legs—clumsy, dead contraptions that looked like torture devices. But I'd never seen one like this before. It gleamed in a pool of dusty sunlight, sleek and softly shining.

I brushed a finger lightly along the shin. Smooth as warm water. The foot looked almost real. I ran a finger down the sole, half expecting it to flinch with ticklishness. I flicked a toe. To my surprise, it moved. I pushed it again and the whole foot flexed with a faint hum of hidden gears. I looked closer. The joins were barely visible, no wider than a hair.

Where had Papa learned to make something like this? It seemed to hold energy coiled inside. It was magical.

Heart racing, I slid my hands under it and hefted it. Heavy, but probably no heavier than a real leg. I unpinned my trouser leg and rolled it up. My stump was fully healed now and showed no signs of growing back. I took a deep breath and let it out slowly. There was a thick sock for my stump. I pulled it on and slid the cup over it. It felt awkward and foreign. Papa showed me how the straps worked and helped me snug them up.

He prodded it critically. "The cup will need some adjustments. Try standing."

I gripped the edge of the table and pushed myself up on my good leg. I slowly let the new leg take some weight.

When I pressed the foot into the floor, it pressed back. I gave it more weight and released my grip on the table. With my full weight on it, pain shot through my stump, but I was standing. Without crutches. I bounced lightly, and the new foot bounced along with the old one. I grinned at the clack of my new toes against the floorboards. Time for a step.

I lifted the leg and brought it forward. I wobbled and brought the foot down harder than I meant to. It sprang up and kicked out wildly. I tumbled back, taking down the chair and half a bottle of Chianti with me. Papa helped me to my feet.

"Take it slow, son."

Ha! This leg had no idea how to take it slow.

I ricocheted around the room until Papa begged me to stop before I wrecked the house. I didn't want to stop. I was just starting to get control over it, though you might not have thought so if you were watching. The leg felt like a caged wolf, wild to escape. When I finally ran out of steam and collapsed on the floor, I gaped up at Papa in wonder.

"How?"

"Do you remember when I first made you?"

I nodded. If you read the book, you might recall the log Papa carved me from was already alive. He only had to give me a shape. The minute I had legs, I bounced off the walls of this very room, mad with joy.

"I saved some of that wood. Just in case."

I felt a shiver of the same joy. I might never be a real human. I might be half man, half tree forever. But this leg could go places. I wouldn't be stuck in a dead-end village.

I leapt toward the door, but my new foot tangled with the old one. The straps gave, and I went one way while the leg went the other.

Papa helped me to a chair. "Don't rush it, son."

I wanted to strap it right back on and run as far as I could. But I had to admit my stump was sore and chafed. The leg might be magic, but it needed some very unmagical fitting.

I decided to wait and surprise everyone at Alidoro's party. I didn't leave the house the whole week while Papa made adjustments. I practiced and worked at gaining my strength back and dreamed about where to go. I wanted a fresh start— somewhere no one knew me. Florence? Rome?

On the day of the party, I was still as likely to bounce off a wall as take a normal step, but I wasn't going to wait. I opened the door and bounded out. Next door, Mrs. Passerini stood in her doorway with a watering can. She dropped it when I whizzed past. I might have heard Papa's voice shouting, "Wait!" but there was no chance in hell of that.

Everyone was already at Paola's when I burst in. They all stared, astonished.

"No more crutches for me!" I announced.

I ran a few laps around the tables, only knocking over two chairs. When I stopped, everyone crowded in to have a closer look.

Paola poured drinks all around and I raised my glass. "A toast! Happy travels to Alidoro! And to me!"

Everyone cheered. There were more toasts and claps on the back and requests to see it again—until a familiar and unwelcome voice intruded.

"What's the occasion?" Ludovico swaggered in, puffed out in his new militia uniform, and took in the scene. "Looks like an illegal Socialist meeting to me."

Oh, did I mention? Ludovico also came back. And if he was mean before, war had hardened his meanness into a sharp and heavy axe head. He joined the fascists and set about a relentless program to "bring the country to order." As if a sleepy village where it was news if a horse threw a shoe could drag Italy down into chaos. After he found a Socialist pamphlet in Constanzo the cobbler's pocket and forced an entire bottle of castor oil down the poor man's throat, people just tried to stay out of his way. I did, too, and I was ashamed of it. I watched him abuse my friends and told myself I was too crippled to take him on. Not anymore.

"Get lost, Ludo," I said. "This isn't your party."

Horrified gasps sucked the air out of the room.

His eyes fixed on me and he sneered. "I thought I smelled the stink of rotting wood."

I sprang at him. My unexpected agility caught him off guard, and we tumbled to the floor. I swung my fist, but he was quick and strong. He shoved me off easily and hopped to his feet. People scattered out of the way, screaming and shouting. We circled each other, looking for an opening. Ludo pounced. I leaped aside, and he slammed into the counter. He turned, lowered his head and charged again, but I was nimble as a cricket and spoiling for a fight. I leaped onto his back and rode him like a pony, pounding his head and laughing with the sheer brute joy of finally letting the bastard have it. He threw me and I landed on a table, splintering its legs and sending plates and glasses flying. The room spun, but I shook it off and pushed up, feet crunching in broken glass. A pistol appeared in Ludo's hand. I grabbed a splintered table leg.

Papa's voice rose above the din. "Pinocchio! No!"

Ludo aimed at me with murder in his eyes. My leg punched against the floor like a piston as my arm swung in a wide arc. The table leg struck his head with a crack. He dropped to the floor like a sack of flour.

The choked silence was as sudden and complete as the uproar had been a moment before. I stared at Ludo's inert body on the floor. Get up get up get up.

The silence lasted until a bottle rolled off the edge of the bar and hit the floor with a loud clatter and everyone started shouting and weeping at once. Except Ludo, motionless and pale, blood pooling under his head. And me, rooted to the floor like a post. What had I done? Not even on the battlefield had I knowingly killed a man. Hands gripped my arms and hustled me out.

2

At home, Alidoro pushed me through the door and bolted it. "Come on. There's not much time."

Papa pulled food off the shelves and stuffed it into my old rucksack. He'd sacrificed everything for me my whole life, and even now, he was still at it.

I sagged against the wall. "I've ruined everything."

He shook his head. "It's my fault. If I hadn't made that leg—"

"Papa, no!"

I didn't want to take the rucksack, but he pushed it into my hands.

Alidoro was at the window. "You should go now. You don't want to be here when Ludo's pals come looking."

Papa pulled on his jacket and hat.

"Papa, you can't come with me." If I was caught, as I likely would be, I didn't want him anywhere near me.

Papa stroked my face and looked at me with sad eyes. "I'm not, son."

I winced. Of course, he wasn't going with me. But he couldn't stay here, either. Ludo's pals would be out for blood.

"Don't worry," said Eugenio. "Geppetto has friends."

The words stung like a slap. Of course, Papa had friends. He'd been a friend to everyone his whole life. Had I truly been a friend to anyone ever? For once in my life, I would do the right thing. Not for me. But for him. For everyone. I slung my rucksack over my shoulder. If I was gone, it would blow over soon enough.

We heard shouts in the street. Fists pounded on the door.

I hugged Papa one last time and ran out the back, never imagining it would be fourteen years before I came back home and longer than that before I saw his face again.

● ● ●

I cut through vineyards and olive orchards and stayed away from even the smaller lanes until I was well out of town. I'd spent my whole life sneaking out and knew every gap in every fence by heart, even in the dark. When I reached the crossroads, I stopped.

The night was cold, but the short time I'd been at the front had hardened me to the trials of a Tuscan December. I pulled up my collar and looked at the stars in the cloudless sky. A bright star glinted not far above the horizon, and I thought about making a wish on it. But what should I wish for? To start the day over and stay away from Paola's? To start the year over and avoid the shell that took my leg? To start my life over and run away with the marionette theatre before I could ever be burdened with flesh and bone? No. What was done was done. In the end, there was nothing to wish for but for Papa to be safe and not suffer too much for my stupidity.

I had just killed a man. An officer. How soon would a warrant be out? Where could I go? How could I live?

Florence was too close. Rome? Naples? Nowhere in all of Italy would be safe. I'd have to leave the country.

In the distance, a wolf howled. I shivered. I was as alone as I'd ever been and feeling so sorry for myself that I might just sit down and wait to be hauled off to prison. I needed to keep moving. But where to?

My glimpse of the Adriatic from the army train came to mind. I'd go to sea. It would solve both the problem of where to go and how to survive. I was young and healthy. Surely I could do *something* useful on a ship, even with a wooden leg. Lots of sailors had wooden legs, didn't they? They did in pirate stories. I could almost hear the sharp wind cracking the sails of a great galleon. Did they still have galleons? I saw myself in the crow's nest, gazing through a spyglass toward a distant horizon. Or hauling in fishing nets with my mates, a song on our lips. That was a man's life! Which coast was closer, east or west? I should have paid more attention to geography lessons in school. I had a vague idea west was closer. So, I bid goodbye to the sapphire Adriatic and headed west, and then wherever the wind would take me.

A little ember of excitement began to sizzle its way through the lump of self-pity in my stomach. How many hours had I sat in the workshop, wishing I was off having adventures? Well, now I'd have them. Nothing but adventures as far as the eye could see!

I walked faster. A minute later, I ran. I raised my head and howled at the sky. The wolf howled back, and I grinned. I would be a wolf: alone, fearless, and bold. I was sorry about the trouble I'd caused Papa, but I wasn't sorry I'd killed Ludo. If anyone needed a good bash to the side of the head, it was him. As I passed a farm, I caught sight of a little fox prowling around the chicken coop. I tried my wolf growl on him, and he took off like an arrow. Yes, I would be the wolf.

My wolf run was short. My new leg was a miracle, but my old body was out of shape, and even a miracle leg takes getting used to. I found a broken rake handle to use for a walking stick and hobbled on.

After the sun rose, I ate an apple and a hunk of bread from my rucksack and slept in a wheat field until pelting rain woke me. Why couldn't my wolf life have started in June? I set out along the road, ducking into the cover of wheat fields whenever anyone came into view. By late afternoon I was cold, wet, and so sore I could hardly walk.

Mostly, I traveled at night and slept in fields or haystacks by day. Even without a murder warrant on my head, a lone drifter like me could find trouble anywhere in those days. My hometown wasn't the only place overrun by Fascist Blackshirt thugs. They were multiplying like cockroaches and likely to crawl out of any crack.

By the fourth day, I felt stronger and had adjusted to the leg, but with each day that passed, I was more wary of being stopped. I hitched a ride from a farmer heading for Livorno and gratefully tucked myself in the back of his wagon among the bushels of carrots and beets, under a stretch of mildewed canvas that smelled like burnt sausages.

He left me on the outskirts of the city and told me to follow the canal to the port. I couldn't just stroll along its banks in the open. I kept the canal on my right but dashed from shadow to shadow through the quiet, cobbled streets. Maybe I was not the wolf, but the cockroach.

At the port, I slid into the shadows under a trestle and rested against a piling to wait for sunrise. A few lights silvered the oily water. A large merchant steamer flying a British flag dominated the harbor. Not a galleon, but it did have several tall masts in addition to the smokestacks. Nearby, a scow piled high with coal rode so low in the water it seemed in danger of sinking straight to the bottom. Just as the sky began to pale, a school of small fishing boats swam toward the mouth of the harbor. I thought about asking one of them to take me, but they'd be coming back at the end of the day, and I didn't care to be part of the catch. I needed to be on that steamer. Above the boats and ships, winches on the docks craned their iron necks like guard dogs sniffing out intruders. I ducked deeper into the shadows.

Going to sea had seemed grand and manly, but now that I was here, I knew I was just a green country boy. How do you go about getting a job on a ship when you're an outlaw? What would I say if they asked about my seagoing experience? That most of it was inside the belly of a fish? And while I was pretty sure there were peg-legged sailors, I suspected most if not all of them had two legs when they started out.

I leaned against the piling and absently rubbed at the scar on my wrist. I had lots of scars. Everyone did back then. For me, in addition to the usual kinds from the rough and tumble of boyhood in the country and somewhat rougher tumble of soldiering in the Great War, I had this one on the back of my wrist—just a pale spot. It's not a scar, really, no more than your belly button is. It's wood that didn't change when she made me human. No bigger than an olive leaf, but it goes deep, to the bone. Sometimes, in a wet spring, it tries to grow a twig. One time I let it grow, and it sprouted a leaf before I brushed against a door frame and snapped it off. And it itched—a nagging reminder that I wasn't a natural-born human, and I never would be no matter how many stars I wished on.

Sailors and dock workers started trudging past in ones and twos. Another tramp, like me, stopped in the shadows. He leaned on the next piling over from mine and offered me the end of a cigarette. We smoked in silence as we watched the port shake off the night. He was tall and rangy with a face dark from the sun, ground-in grime, or both. His bright red hair spiked up at angles as if each clump wanted to get as far away from the others as possible. There was nothing threatening or dangerous about his appearance, though I wouldn't say he was entirely sober.

He squinted at me and tipped his head toward the harbor. "You a seagoing man?"

He spoke decent Italian. I guessed he was English.

"Not yet. You?"

"Aye. Took a bit of a break, you could say, but now I find I have an urgent need to make myself scarce."

"I know how that is."

He pointed his chin toward the steamer. "She's sailing today. I'm just on my way to the pool."

"The pool?"

"The Seamen's Office. If you want to sign onto a crew, you gotta go to the pool."

"Think they'd take me?"

"Don't see why not. You look strong enough."

"I've never set foot on a ship."

He shrugged.

I rapped my knuckles on my wooden leg. "And I'm missing a bit."

"War?"

"Where else?"

He nodded. "Well, you've no doubt seen worse than you'll find on any ship then. What can you do?"

"Not much. I worked in my papa's woodshop."

He brightened. "Well, there you go, mate! Chippy always needs an extra hand."

I blinked at him.

"Ship's carpenter's always called Chippy."

For the first time in days, I felt a glimmer of hope. I stuck out my hand. "Pinocchio."

He shook it. "Lampwick."

He translated his name into Italian, and I laughed out loud. With his flaming red hair and sooty face, it was a good fit.

"You're a fine one to laugh," said Lampwick. "With a name like Pinky-o."

"Pinocchio. It means 'eye of pine.'"

"Ha! Shoulda been leg o' pine, but never mind. I'll just call you Woody."

He doubled over laughing at what he seemed to think was a great joke. It took some explaining, but I finally got that it was a play on the words for wood and eye in English.

Just then, we were distracted by the arrival of a pair of militiamen patrolling the dock, asking questions of passing workers.

We ducked out of sight. "Looks like last night's about to catch up with me," said Lampwick.

Or me. As soon as they passed, Lampwick took off down the dock at a rapid pace he somehow made look like a casual saunter. He called back to me without stopping or even looking back. "You stuck there or what?"

He didn't need to ask twice. I grabbed my rucksack and ran. We slipped into a cluster of men milling around outside the Seamen's Office. A weary-faced officer processed us one by one at a small wooden table set up just outside the door. When it was Lampwick's turn, the officer scowled.

"Lampwick, you drunkard. I thought I'd seen the last of you."

Lampwick laughed. "Sorry, mate. I'm like the clap. You'll never be rid of me."

The officer sighed and shoved a form and a pen across the table. Lampwick scratched an X at the bottom.

Lampwick pushed me forward, but the officer waved us off. "You know you're not to bring your pet rats on board."

"You'll want this rat. He's a war hero."

The officer rolled his eyes. "Who isn't?"

"Well, Chippy may have use for him."

The officer squinted up at me. "You know carpentry?"

"You might say I was born to it, sir."

"Any sea experience?"

"None to speak of, sir."

He tapped his pen for a moment and looked over his roster. "You can start as a deck boy." He pushed a paper and pen toward me. I didn't even glance at it. I just signed my name and handed it back.

"Thank you, sir," I said, saluting.

Both he and Lampwick snort-laughed.

Lampwick slapped my back as hard as Alidoro ever had. He might be skinny as a lamp wick, but he was strong. "Come on, then, Peggy. Move it."

As soon as I could breathe, I said, "Peggy? I thought I was Woody!"

"Deck boy's always called Peggy. With that leg, it suits as good as Woody."

I stared up at the ship that would be my home. It had seemed so regal, floating in the harbor at dawn. Now, in full daylight, I could see that it had been dethroned some time ago. Its pocked sides were streaked with rust, and the stacks were black with soot. I gulped. I was trying to get away from hulking brutes dressed in black, but it looked like I'd be answering to one more.

Lampwick was already loping up the gangplank. I trotted to catch up. "Why are there masts on a steamship?" I asked.

"Wind's free, lad," he called over his shoulder.

I only got a glimpse of the busy deck before Lampwick led me down a rattling iron ladder into darkness. We climbed down so far that if there was a porthole, I was sure I'd see the mermaids combing their hair. A few more levels down, when I figured we'd left the mermaids behind for Satan stirring a lake of fire, we arrived in Hell. The crew's quarters were dark, stifling, cramped, and hot. The walls sweated and creaked, and the throbbing engines shook the teeth in my jaw. The men greeted Lampwick with streams of abuse, though they saved some for the new deck boy. It was no worse than the army and better than I figured the police would be.

We were underway before dawn the next day, and I quickly learned how a Peggy spent his time. My main job was to serve food, but I was expected to scrub out the mess rooms, clean up vomit, clear the latrines when they stopped up, make tea all day long and half the night, and run endless made-up errands for the crew's amusement. My bed might have been a loop of filthy canvas, but it didn't matter because I rarely had a chance to use it.

The sailors were from all over the globe and spoke a dozen languages, mainly English, French, German, Spanish, Portuguese, Chinese, and Italian, and they shouted orders at me in all of them. I thought I'd never sort it all out, but not getting clobbered is powerful motivation. Soon, I could jabber well enough in each lingo and get by in a few more besides.

My second day out, we hit a storm. The galley was on the opposite side of the ship from the messroom with no shelter in between. I had to carry six loaded dinner plates at once, three on each arm like a circus acrobat, while the deck heaved beneath my feet. The first time I tried it, I ended up on my back, covered in meat, gravy, and potatoes. I got up and went back for another load. On the third try, I made it to the messroom door before the deck swung down and I flew up. A potato shot out like a cannonball, hit the overhead, and stuck there. I picked another potato out of the gravy on the floor and held it up so it could see its buddy.

"Look at that," I said to it. "You have friends in high places."

The potato tilted its head and regarded his mate. I gave it a low, gravelly voice. "Looks a bit like the captain, don't he?"

"Hmm. I see what you mean. Half baked, hard boiled, looking down on us, and smashed."

The sailors collapsed with laughter. I raised my arm so the potato in my hand was standing at attention. "Three cheers for Captain Spud!" I bellowed.

Everyone joined in and cheered for Captain Spud. We left him there until the steward made me scrape him off. After that, they treated me better, when they weren't hounding me. I got so I could make it from the galley to the messroom in a gale, carrying three plates on each arm and one on my head without spilling a drop. In time, I got to be good enough on my new leg that there was no job aboard that I couldn't manage.

On my third day out, Cook—a terrifying, pox-scarred walrus of a man with black whiskers bristling nearly up to his eyes—handed me a pail filled to the top with potato peels.

"Take this to Hurley." He gave me such convoluted directions where to take it that I was sure it was on some other ship.

"Can't we just throw it overboard?"

He laid a meaty hand on my shoulder. "This is precious cargo, boy."

Hurley turned out to be a short, wiry Irishman, the master of a hidden and illicit still. He let out a firecracker shout of relief when the scrap pail arrived, its bearer green-gilled and dripping sweat. He handed me a bottle.

"Here. This'll fix you."

I gulped down a swig of poteen so strong I spent the next ten minutes coughing while he roared with laughter.

"It's just vegetables, mate," he said. We became instant friends, and I never again hated peeling potatoes.

I did finally get promoted to Chippy's mate and someone else got to be Peggy. It wasn't that I was brilliant at carpentry, but more that Chippy had stiff joints, and it pained him to bend or squat. Even with a wooden leg, my smaller size and nimble footing made me useful for getting at hard-to-reach places.

I spent more years than I should have at sea. I ran copper from Valparaiso, coffee from Rio, coal from Newcastle, rum from Port-au-Prince, guns from Tripoli, and one time a nine-piece brass band from New Orleans. I sailed through the Straits of Gibraltar, around the Horn, and through the Panama Canal. I boiled my brains in the tropics and chipped ice off the decks in the North Sea.

And between times, I caroused in port as hard as I worked onboard. I had my first taste of sailor's liberty in Marseilles. Lampwick took me under his wing, and I couldn't have had a better guide. The night ended in a drunken brawl with a crew of enormous Swiss sailors. Just as the gendarmes arrived to cart us all away, every light in the bar miraculously went out. We slipped away and ran, not stopping to catch our breath until we were blocks away.

"That was a lucky break," I said.

Lampwick winked at me and tossed a handful of fuses into the air. "When all else fails, lad, pull the damn plugs."

I tried that trick any number of times over the years, but I never managed it as neatly as he could.

My sailing days are long behind me now, but the one thing I still miss is the night sky at sea. If you've never seen it, you have no idea how full of stars the sky can be. I only ever saw one thing that surpassed it, but that's a tale for later.

• • •

In the summer of 1930, we were headed for Hamburg with a load of Egyptian cotton when we had engine trouble. There was nothing for it but to drop anchor and wait for a part to be shipped out. Lucky we weren't hauling fish. We were too far from any port to take a dinghy for shore leave. The best we could do was camp out on a barren stretch of beach on the North Sea coast. Not paradise, but better than staying aboard, where work would always be found for idle hands.

Hurley dug deep into his stores of hooch, and we made driftwood bonfires that sent sparks halfway to the moon. The weather was cool but dry, and the local fish were most obliging. If you so much as dropped a line in the surf, plaice and little dabs fought to get on the hook. Tonio, the only other Italian in the crew besides myself, played guitar and had an endless supply of filthy songs in seven languages. With no girls at hand, we made do dancing with each other.

On a brisk, sunny day with a light southerly wind, I walked down the beach alone. I felt restless and unsettled. When I was a boy, I thought if I went out into the world and had adventures like a man, then I would be a man. But inside, I was still the same, still a wooden boy.

I perched on a rocky spit and cast my line into the surf without even looking to see where it hit. The fish must have sensed my low spirits, as they gave the hook a wide berth. After an hour or so, I was about to give up when I felt a heavy pull on the line. I stood and started to reel it in. It felt like something big, but with little fight. Probably driftwood. Another fitting nickname for me, I thought. As I reeled it closer, it broke the surface. Not driftwood, but a tangle of old net.

When I had it close enough, I hopped down to the tip of the spit and pulled the net in by hand. Something large was caught in it. When I had it close enough, I saw it was a dolphin, panting through its blowhole and nearly drowned. He was in bad shape, with a deep gash above one eye like an angry eyebrow. I reached for my gaff. It would be a mercy to put him out of his misery, and he was big enough to feed the whole gang on the beach. But he looked straight at me with his sad old man's eye. I never thought a fish could have a heart, but this one did, and it was breaking.

I pulled out my knife and sawed through the netting. When he was free, he lay still in the water. Was he too far gone? But then he shook himself, and I swear he winked at me. I could almost hear him promise to return the favor someday.

"I'll hold you to that, brother," I said. "Now go on home."

He bobbed his head and vanished under the water. Maybe it was time for me to go home too. Papa wasn't getting any younger, and surely the dust of my misdeeds had settled enough by now that I could slip in. I decided to finish this run and then sign on to a ship heading to Italy. I walked back empty-handed to the jeers of my mates, but I didn't care. My thoughts were a continent away in a dusty little town in Tuscany.

If I'd known then that it would be nearly three more years before I got home, I might have thrown myself into the sea then and there. But I never would have met Serafina. So maybe things go the way they're meant to.

3

After Hamburg, we pulled in at a port on the north coast of France to top off the hold with cases of wine. It was a small port, but wherever sailors stop, bars and brothels sprout like barnacles. We only had one night, but Lampwick, as always, knew where the action was. In this case, it was a club with a burlesque show and a live jazz band. It was 1930. Everyone was hot for jazz.

We were close enough to hear music when a circus poster tacked to a lamppost caught my eye. Nowadays, people think the circus is kids' stuff, but they were a big thing back then. Anyone with a horse, a monkey, and a sack of spangles could slap some paint on a wagon proclaiming the World's Greatest Spanglemonkeyhorse, and people would line up to see it.

Except for sailors on shore leave. After months cooped up aboard ship, you'd have to be crazy to choose a circus over live jazz, booze, and burlesque. But I never claimed to be sane, and in my defense, it was an Italian circus, and I was still feeling a bit homesick. Across the top of the poster in tall, swooping letters was "Circus Grillo"—Cricket. Below it, the usual garish illustrations: a bear, a strong man, plumed horses. No crickets, though. At the center was a woman balancing on a tightrope on one toe and sporting an enormous pair of butterfly wings. Above her head, in curly script, it said LA FARFALLA—the Butterfly. Even though it was just a drawing, something about her hooked me. The half-closed eyes and sly smile made her look like she had a secret to tell only me. When the others noticed I wasn't with them, they came back and peered over my shoulder.

"A little bit of home, eh?" said Lampwick in Italian, with rare sympathy.

Hurley zeroed right in on my angel. "Look at the pair on her!"

"Ooh, watch out for the stinger!" warned Tonio.

Lampwick cuffed his head. "Butterflies don't have stingers, you dolt."

"I was warning *her*."

"Woody's little stinger couldn't hurt a fly," said Lampwick. "Or even a butterfly."

They all roared with laughter.

"You guys go on. I'll find you later," I said, still riveted by the poster.

"You know it's all fake, right?" asked Lampwick. "She's probably sixty, fat and toothless."

When they couldn't get a rise out of me, they gave up and left me there. Lord knows they'd all had stupid crushes too.

It made no sense at all, and I knew Lampwick was right, but something about her just plain called out to me. I had to go, even if I only ended up making a clown of myself.

I peeled the poster off the post and showed it to locals who pointed me in various directions. Despite their help, I found the circus not far from the waterfront. A large tent painted with red and white stripes sat in an open field that was surrounded by warehouses and tradesmen's shops. Smaller tents clustered beside it for the sideshow, concessions, and cages of sad animals. I skipped those, bought a ticket and a beer, and went straight into the main tent. A few scruffy clowns hustled the crowd while a small combo—violin, accordion, trumpet, and snare—lurched through popular tunes. The high wire glinted near the top of the tent under a dark blue canvas sky painted with silver stars. It couldn't be that much harder than walking the spars aboard ship. The wire was thinner but moored on solid ground instead of a heaving deck.

The band struck up a fanfare, the lights dimmed, and the ringmaster strode into the spotlight. He was a big man, barrel-chested with a shiny bald pate above fierce black eyebrows, mustache, and beard. He introduced himself as Maestro Grillo, Master of Ceremonies of the Most Impressive Wonders of Europe. The maestro was more impressive than most of the wonders that followed. The horses were swaybacked but the riders reasonably adept. The acrobats did their tumbling routines with skill but not much daring. Would they never get to the butterfly girl? I thought about getting another beer. The splintery bench was starting to chafe my backside. I tell you, if I ran a circus, I'd put the main attraction at the start of the show instead of the end.

Finally, the lights went dark except for the spotlight on Maestro Grillo. He spread his arms wide.

"And now, ladies and gentlemen! The peerless star in the heavens! One of the true wonders of the world! I give you … La Farfalla!"

His spotlight vanished, and a second one shone on the high wire. La Farfalla was already at the top, standing on the tiny pedestal as if she had flown there. The sound of applause and music faded from my ears like the rumble of the surf when you pull away from the shore. Nothing existed but her and my pounding heart. She was more beautiful than the poster, with big dark eyes, short, wavy dark hair, small red mouth above a pointed chin. And wings. They were magnificent—each as wide as she was tall, shimmering with a cascade of colors in mesmerizing swirls and edged in velvety black. She swept them back and forth and made a full turn to show them off. I knew none of it was real. The straps that held her wings on were clearly visible. But it didn't matter. My heart was hers.

The band began a lilting waltz, and she swept onto the wire on her toes. She danced so nimbly above our heads her feet might have been on a solid ballroom parquet. She used her wings the way I'd seen other tightrope walkers use a pole, to aid her balance. It made sense, but I didn't want to be reminded that they were fake. They shimmered in the light and fluttered when she moved. Whoever had made them had to be about as clever as Papa.

The music crested as she pirouetted faster and faster; her wings blurred into a chrysalis of color. The cymbals crashed, and she stopped, still as marble, serenely balanced on one toe. And then she looked down. Directly at me. Her eyes widened. I could not have been more than a dot in a sea of upturned faces, but I was sure she saw me as clearly as I saw her. Was I dreaming?

Then it was a nightmare. Her perfect balance faltered. She wobbled for a heart-stopping moment, wings flapping frantically, and slipped from the wire. Time slowed. I flew from my seat, shoving people aside as if I could get to the ring in time and catch her.

At the last possible moment, her wings snapped wide and beat downward hard enough to send swirls of dust into the air. It slowed her plunge just enough to avoid disaster. She landed on her feet, staggered, and nearly fell to her knees before Maestro Grillo caught her arm and pulled her upright. Was that part of the act? I went back to my seat, red-faced. La Farfalla and the ringmaster held hands and bowed in every direction. The audience roared their delight.

She scanned the crowd, and her eyes met mine. An electric jolt snapped between us. Her lips parted in surprise. Her wings fluttered, just a little. Then Maestro Grillo tugged on her arm and led her out of the ring.

What had just happened? I tried to tell myself it was my imagination. She hadn't singled me out; it was her job to seduce the audience. But I knew what I felt. And I knew she felt it too. But why? How? I sat there like a rock in a river while the crowd streamed around me.

The voice of one of the circus workers roused me from my stupor.

"Monsieur, the show is over."

I jumped to my feet. "I need to talk to La Farfalla."

He snorted. "Impossible. She talks to no one."

"But it's important! We … she knows me."

He shook his head. "You must leave. We're closing."

I dug through my pockets. Did I have enough to bribe him? I held out a handful of francs. "Please. At least take her a message."

"I'm sorry, Monsieur, but it would mean my job."

I acted resigned, but of course, I wouldn't give up. My ship sailed the next day. It was tonight or never. I thanked him and left the tent.

Outside, I approached a man carrying a stack of chairs.

"Got any work needs doing? I'm your man," I said in Italian.

He shrugged. "You can ask the foreman in the morning."

"I'm here now and willing." I tried to look both capable and hungry.

"Can't do a thing before tomorrow, my friend."

I would have to find my own way in.

Once the crowds left, the fairgrounds were nearly deserted. Unfortunately, this wasn't a big port where a man could be up to something at any hour of the night and no one would notice, so I had to stay in the shadows of the shuttered businesses surrounding the field as much as I could, looking for any clue about where she might be. At the back of the circus, the painted carriages that served as homes for the performers were lined up just inside battered portable fencing. I could see lights in some of the small windows. Which one was hers?

One by one, the lights went out. I heard the clatter of pans. A man cursed, a violin played a sad tune, a lion roared, and then, quiet. And I still had no idea where she was. I turned to trudge back to town but stopped myself. What was I? Some shy wallflower waiting to be asked for a dance? No. I was a seagoing man. A man of action.

I made it halfway towards the circus before I stopped myself again. What did I think was going to happen if I found her? That she'd get drunk in an alley with me like some portside doxy? That we'd run off together and live happily ever after in a little rose-covered cottage? She was an angel. A star! I was nobody. A grubby sea dog. She hadn't singled me out. The obvious answer was she mistook me for someone else.

I walked away. I could still catch up with Lampwick and the others. But when I saw a cluster of sailors near the waterfront laughing at a mate lying in a puddle of his own vomit, I turned around once more.

When I got back to the fairgrounds, a car was stopped near the back fence with its headlights on and two figures standing beside it. A man's voice rumbled, and a woman's voice rose in protest, though I couldn't make out any words.

I slipped behind a horse wagon parked outside the fence.

The man was bald as an egg, and at first, I thought he was the ringmaster, but this guy was grossly fat and clean-shaven. He pressed himself against the woman. When she pushed him away, he raised his hand to strike her face, and I stepped out of the shadows but stopped when she spoke.

"Mark me and he'll kill you!" she said.

"You think pretty highly of yourself," he said, but he lowered his hand, and I backed up, just a step. Then, without warning, he punched her in the stomach. I sprang straight at him, over the hood of the car, and took him down with a fist to the face. It was over in an instant. The man lay on the ground sniveling, blood streaming from his broken nose. I wanted to hit him again, but I heard a soft groan and looked up. The woman stood a few feet away. She was bent over, panting, and clutching her arms around her middle. I went to her.

"Are you hurt, miss? Should I get someone?"

She shook her head, still bent over. Then she took a deep, shaky breath and straightened up. My heart stopped. It was her. Her eyes widened when she saw me, and I had the same feeling I had earlier that night—that she knew me. Or someone who looked enough like me to fool her, even this close. Whoever he was, I'd have done anything to be him.

"I'll live," she said. She poked at the man on the ground with a toe and then gave me a sly grin. "He might not, though."

She looked around, then held out her hand to me. "Come on. Let's get away from here."

I took her hand, and we ran. I had no idea where to go, but I didn't care. If it meant I could keep her with me, I'd run to Shanghai and back. We stopped to catch our breath under a bridge overlooking the harbor. There were no streetlamps here, but the moon was high and nearly full. She stood so close to me in the darkness I could feel the heat of her body.

"Who was that man?" I asked.

She ignored my question and pulled me into the moonlight. This close, I could see dark circles under her eyes. A shadow by her ear might have been a bruise. I touched her face gently. She batted my hand away and peered up at me intently, using her fingers to tilt my head one way and another. She examined my hands and ran her palms up my arms, squeezing and prodding. I had no idea what she was searching for, but I was happy to let her keep at it as long as she wanted. Any second now, she'd realize her mistake, and that would be the end of it, but until then, I was all hers.

Her fingers found the one spot I wished I could keep hidden. She pushed up my sleeve and peered at my scar close up, scratching it lightly with a fingernail. I resisted the urge to pull my hand away. To my surprise, she smiled.

"I knew it! You are!"

"You don't know how bad I wish I was," I said. "But we've never met. I'd remember."

"No, no. I don't know you," she said. "But I know what you are."

"What am I?"

"You're a Blue, of course!"

"A blue what?"

"You're being silly!" She laughed, but when I didn't, her eyes widened in surprise. "You don't know?"

"Not if you won't tell me!"

But on some level, I did. And the thought of it just about knocked the ground from under my feet.

"Is there somewhere private? Where no one will see us?" she asked.

I didn't know this port, but I knew ports in general. Her hand was cool in my feverish one as I led her down the harbor steps to the wharf. One of the boathouses would be unlocked or could be made so without too much trouble. The first two were locked up tight, but the third one had a badly corroded padlock that gave when I smacked it with a rock. Inside was a jumble of nets, coils of rope, pots of paint, broken oars, and rolls of old canvas—all the usual things you'd expect to find in a boathouse with a rusted lock, along with all the usual smells. She wrinkled her nose, and I could have kicked myself. How could I bring someone like her to an old boathouse?

"Do you want to go to a hotel? I have some money."

"No, this is better. But we could use a light."

It took some fumbling around, but I found a lantern hanging from a nail on the wall and a box of matches on a plank beside it. We would have had light in a moment if nerves hadn't turned my fingers into sticks. But eventually, she stood before me in a pool of warm lamplight.

She brought her hands to her throat and unbuttoned her long coat while I tried to remember how to breathe. When she reached the last button, she let the coat fall from her shoulders. Beneath it, she wore a simple white dress that clasped at the back of her slender neck but left her back bare. I was sure they could hear my heart pounding in Southampton. I took a step toward her, but she held up a hand.

And then, she changed my life forever.

Without breaking her gaze from mine, she parted her lips and inhaled deeply. The breath went on and on and on, far longer than should have been possible for such a small body. Air filled the veins and ridges of two incredible and utterly real butterfly wings, raising them until they brushed the wall. I couldn't help inhaling along with her, but in me, the air had nowhere to go, so I held it until I thought I might burst. She gave her shoulders a small shake, and the wings snapped smooth as sails in a fresh breeze. I had to be dreaming, but when she turned to face away, the breeze from her wings caressed my skin and fluttered my hair. She stood relaxed and let me devour them with my eyes. I could see where they joined seamlessly with the substantial muscles of her back. Even in the dim light from the lantern, the colors and patterns were dizzying. The larger swirls were made of smaller swirls, and those were made of even smaller ones. I imagined it going on like that forever, and it made my head spin.

In a long, long exhale, she let her wings grow soft and drape close to her back, their tips just brushing her ankles. Under a loose coat, you wouldn't know they were there. She turned back to face me with a brilliant smile.

"I'm a Blue too. One of hers. Like you."

I was so bewitched that for a moment, I couldn't make sense of her words. Like me? She was so unlike me, where would I even start?

"You were once a toy, a puppet, I think. Right?"

I nodded.

"And someone came and made you real. Someone beautiful and kind and magical."

I nodded again. I might as well still be a puppet, dumbly bobbing my head. But I couldn't speak.

"I was a marionette. A fairy princess." She rippled her wings, though she didn't fill them all the way. "Before the Blue Lady made me real. We're her children. Blues."

With that, my legs gave out and I sat as abruptly as if I had strings and someone had just snipped them through. Why had it never occurred to me there might be others who had been brought to life by the Blue Lady? I must have sawdust for brains. Of course, I wasn't the only one. What did I think she'd been doing all these years she'd been away? Knitting in a rocking chair? But the thought had never entered my head.

La Farfalla sat beside me. "Don't feel bad. If you haven't met another Blue before, how would you know?"

"How many are there?"

"Who knows how many children she has? I've met maybe thirty."

Thirty? Until this moment, I didn't even know there were two. It had been over twenty years since she changed me. In that time, she could have changed hundreds. Thousands.

"I can't believe I never knew."

She shrugged. "You can pass for a Normie—a normal person. That's rare. People think we're freaks, but in the circus, we can hide in the open. There's a boy in the sideshow who has scales and swims in a tank like a fish. Did you see him? Everyone thinks it's a trick."

"Are there others at the circus right now?"

"Only me and the fish boy at the moment. They come and go. Most don't stay long." She picked up my hand and traced the oval scar on my wrist. Then she dropped her chin into her palm and sighed. "You're lucky. You can go anywhere."

"Maybe I have a tail."

Her eyebrows shot up. "Do you?"

I resisted the urge to give a smart answer. "No."

Something didn't add up.

"But you knew! Before you ever saw my scar. How did you know?"

"I can't explain it." She reached up and turned my face towards hers. Her eyes were dark and probing, and a slight flush rose in her cheeks. "When I saw you, I just knew there was something different about you. Something special."

I had no idea what that could mean. So many questions filled my head, I didn't know where to start. I didn't want to waste a minute of whatever time we had before she returned to the circus and I sailed away.

"Farfalla," I began.

"That's just for the act. My real name is Serafina."

Serafina. It fluttered in my chest like angel wings and made me wish my own name was a little more sublime.

"I'm Pinocchio."

She laughed. "Pinocchio? And do you really have eyes of pine?"

"I used to."

"Well, I like it."

"I hope it's not rude to ask, but … can you fly?"

She sighed. "No. My wings are nearly useless. If I try very hard, I can rise a little, but not even as high as you could jump."

She stood and swept her wings back and forth with enough force to raise a cloud of dust, but her feet lifted no more than a few inches off the floor.

"It's a pathetic joke, isn't it? A butterfly who can't fly?"

"But what about when you fell off the wire? You flew up at the end."

Her face darkened. "If I do it right, I can slow my fall just enough. But it's a dangerous trick. Twice I've broken my ankle, and once my arm. It scares me every time, but without it, I'm just another tightrope walker, and we are just a second-rate circus. That's what Maestro says."

"The ringmaster?"

She nodded. "Maestro Grillo. He's ..." Her face twisted in anger for a moment, but she smoothed it and spoke in a quiet voice. "I'm lucky to have a home, work, safety. We Blues don't have real families like normals do. We find them where we can."

Lucky? To risk her neck every show? I was the lucky one. I had no actual father, but Papa loved me like a son. With her coat off, I could see old and new bruises on her arms, pale lines of scars. These weren't the results of occasional accidents, but years of abuse. My anger spiked. I thought of the man who'd pressed himself against her, and my hands fisted. I would rescue her from this. My jaw tightened, and my rage cooled into icy determination.

Serafina laughed.

"Oh, Pinocchio, your face is like a picture show. My life is not that bad."

I touched a scar on her arm. "What about this?"

She twitched her arm away. "The circus is hard work. Everyone gets bumps and bruises."

I tapped her nose with my fingertip. "And what about this? You know what they say back home about lies and long noses. Yours should be out the door."

"Nonsense. I'm the star! You saw the other acts. He would starve without his beautiful Farfalla on the high wire."

I leaned in, fighting to keep from shouting. "And what about that man tonight? What else do you do to save the Maestro from starvation?"

Her eyes flashed, and before I could take back my words, she slapped me but good.

"You know nothing!" she spat. "Everyone in the circus has to eat."

How was the entire circus her responsibility alone?

"Please, Serafina. I only want to help you!"

"You have a passionate heart, Pinocchio. I love that, but don't think you're a knight on a horse who can rescue the maiden from the tower. I have a good life. Everything I need is taken care of. Even if I wanted to leave, what else would I do? Work in a shop? Who would want someone like me?"

More lies. Lies told to her so often, she believed them. I wanted to kill this Maestro with my bare hands.

"*Everyone* wants someone like you. They want to *be* someone like you. How can you not know that? You're the most magical, beautiful, perfect person I've ever met!"

"What fairy tale are you living in? The world is a dangerous place for Blues. Blues who can't pass. At least at the circus, I'm safe."

I gripped her shoulders. "Safe? You fall off a high wire every day with no net and then take abuse from strange men at night and you think you're *safe*? I may be living in a fairy tale, but you're living in a horror story, and you don't even know it." I leaned close and spoke in an urgent whisper. "Serafina. Let me take you away. I have some money. We'll get on a train and go as far away as we can. We'll both start over."

I hadn't planned it. The words just popped out. But as soon as I said it, I knew I meant it. Jumping ship and running away with this woman felt both insane and vital. Tears welled in her eyes, and she opened her mouth to speak. I put my fingers to her lips to stop her from saying no.

"You can be free. Just pack a bag. No, don't even pack a bag. We'll go. This minute."

She turned her face away, and a tear escaped and ran down her cheek. "You don't know him. He'll track me down and bring me back and it will be a thousand times worse. Where could I hide with these wings? It's impossible."

"Nothing is impossible, Serafina. He's beaten you down so low you believe his lies. He's just one small man in a huge world. Bigger than you can imagine. Tonight, you were lucky. But tomorrow, your luck could run out. You could break your neck. I know you must think I'm just saying these things because I want you, and I do. I want you more than I've ever wanted anything. But it's more than that. You're a miracle, and fate has more in store for you than a short life under the boot of a bully. Anyone who knows me knows I can't tell a lie. My ship sails in a few hours. Say yes, and it sails without me."

The words rushed out. I don't even know where they came from. A storm of emotion zinged through my body and electrified my skin. I wanted to keep talking until she agreed, but I bit my tongue. It was up to her now. She'd already had too many men forcing her to do things she didn't want to do. I wouldn't be one more, even if it meant I lost her.

She looked into my eyes for an endless moment. Fear, hope, doubt, and wonder chased each other across her dark irises. Then she took my face in her hands and kissed me, lightly at first and then with growing fire.

"Yes," she breathed into my mouth.

The floor dropped away and left me floating. She might not be able to fly, but right then, I could have flown the both of us around the world on wings woven from that one word.

I slipped my hands around her waist and ran them up her smooth back. The skin where her wings emerged was exquisitely sensitive. When I touched her there, she gasped, and her body melted against mine. Her wings were soft and warm as velvet in a sunny window. When I ran my palms along their edges, she shuddered and moaned, and they fluttered in a way that was strange and magical and unbelievably erotic. For a time, nothing else existed in the world aside from her and me. Not one thing.

And later, when the world existed again, it was an utterly new one. Before, I was the only one like myself in the world. Before, I was all reaction and no direction. Before, I had crushes but never love. Now, I was no longer alone. No longer rudderless. And I was in love. Serafina's happiness was not just more important than my own, it was essential to my own. It was magnificent and terrifying, and it left me breathless.

She gently disengaged herself from my arms. I immediately pulled her back and kissed her. She closed her eyes and her wings shivered, but she kissed me on the nose and sat up.

"I have some money saved. I'll go back for it and few necessities and be back in a wink."

"No. It's too risky. Don't go."

"There's nothing to worry about. He was drinking last night, and when he drinks, he sleeps like a bear until noon."

I peered outside. It was still dark, but the sky looked like it was thinking about morning.

"I'll go with you."

"Absolutely not. Wait for me here. No one thinks anything of it if they see me come in late. But if anyone sees you, there will be trouble."

I tried to argue, but she wouldn't budge. I made the best deal I could. "One hour. I need to get my things from the ship too. If you're not back in an hour, I'm coming for you."

She rolled her eyes. "All right, all right. One hour. But it won't be necessary." She kissed me again and left.

I flew back to the ship, sneaked on board, and stuffed a few things in my duffle. I would have told Lampwick I was jumping ship, but of course, he wouldn't drag himself in until the last possible minute, which it nearly was. I took half the money he kept in a hidden stash and left a note promising to pay it back with interest. Maybe I took a little more than half. I was starting a new life, after all. I snuck past the second mate and ran back to the boathouse.

A quarter of the promised hour remained, and every second was agony. My imagination reeled from one disaster to another. She was being held captive. She got lost. She was injured. Eaten by the lion.

Just after dawn, the door swung open, and I nearly cried out with relief. But it was an old fisherman after some oakum and a bucket of tar. I barely managed to slip behind a net hanging from the rafters. I can't recommend fishing nets as a hiding place, in general. But he didn't look up.

I was done waiting. I took off at a full-out run.

The circus was quiet. No commotion or screams for help. The gates were closed and locked, but a man was sweeping stray candy wrappers from the dirt in front of the tent. I called out to him, and he ambled over.

"We don't open until ten."

"I need to speak to Serafina. To La Farfalla. It's urgent."

"You and every other guy. Buy a ticket at ten."

"Just two minutes and I'll be gone. One minute."

"Get out of here before I have you thrown out."

I shook the gate. "It's life or death!"

He turned away and shouted, "Alberto!"

I took advantage of the moment to jump the gate and race past him, heading for the carriages around back. He took off after me, shouting for Alberto.

I flung open the door of the first carriage I came to. Three acrobats were getting dressed. They shrieked and clutched their robes around themselves.

"Serafina?"

One of them pointed. I started to turn, but a hand like a grappling hook caught my collar and yanked me back. An instant later, I dangled at eye level with Alberto. I recognized him as the circus strongman. He was at least twice my size.

"Gotcha!" he growled.

We quickly drew a circle of curious people in various stages of dress and amusement. I didn't care. I wasn't backing down.

"I'm not leaving until I see Serafina," I said with way more conviction than the situation called for.

Alberto dragged me back towards the gate as if I were a puppy who wet the rug. Our audience trailed after us, no doubt expecting a good spectacle. I struggled to free myself, but I couldn't break his grip or wriggle out of my jacket, and my flailing attempts to kick him fell short of the target.

The gate loomed closer, but Alberto veered off to a section of fence a short distance away, toward a large pile of manure. Swell.

"Just ask her. She'll want to see me! She knows me!"

Alberto grabbed the seat of my trousers in his other hand to toss me over. I closed my eyes.

"Hold on a moment, Alberto."

I recognized that voice. It was Grillo, the ringmaster.

Up close, he was older than he'd seemed the night before but no less imposing. He wore shiny black boots, spotless jodhpurs, and a clean, starched white shirt open at the collar. His face was still pink from a shave. I resisted a suicidal urge to reach out and wipe a bit of shaving cream off his neck.

"You wish to see our Farfalla?" he inquired lightly.

It's hard to be manly and resolute when you're dangling by your collar and the seat of your britches, but I did my best.

"I demand to see her!"

He smirked. "Alberto, please show Signor …"

"Pinocchio."

"Signor Pinocchio to La Farfalla's quarters."

Just like that?

Alberto put me down, not letting go of my jacket, and marched me to a carriage painted with a fanciful scene of Serafina hovering like a fairy in a garden of roses. He dropped me at the door and knocked.

The door opened and I was face to face with Serafina. She looked at me with mild disappointment, as if she'd ordered coffee and I was tea. She wore an embroidered silk kimono that must have been quite rich at one time but was faded and frayed at the edges. She held a cigarette casually in one hand.

"What are you doing here?"

"You didn't come back!"

She flicked an ash from the cigarette and glanced at the crowd of eager witnesses. "Well, you might as well come in." She stepped back and waved me in.

Inside, she shifted a cosmetic case and a pile of sequined costumes from a chair to the bed with practiced ease. The tips of her wings peeked below the hem of her kimono. A shiny top hat hung on a hook on the wall, along with an assortment of scarves and feathery things.

"Have a seat."

I tried to see the woman who had melted in my arms just a few hours ago. Was this even the same person?

"Serafina! I thought something happened to you!"

"As you can see, nothing has happened to me."

"Something clearly has. And I won't leave until I know what it is."

She took a slow drag from her cigarette. "You shouldn't have come here. I tried to warn you."

"I jumped ship for you!"

"That was unwise on your part. Did you really think I would give up everything to run away with a penniless sailor? Excuse me, former sailor."

"But … but you knew I was a Blue from the top of the tent!"

She shrugged. "There are a lot of Blues. It's interesting, but it doesn't make us soulmates."

I sputtered, unable to form words.

She sighed again. "Listen. Pinocchio. You're a sweet boy, and we had a lovely night, didn't we? The adventure! The fantasy! Did your heart pound? Mine did."

She sat back and blew a cloud of blue smoke into the space between us, and for a moment, it made her look hazy and far away.

I leaned forward and whispered, "He's forcing you to say these things, isn't he? Did he threaten you? Just tell me. Nod if it's not safe to speak. I'll put an end to it. I swear on my life! I'll protect you."

She laughed lightly. "Look at you! So serious! There are no threats. No dangers. This is not some cheap novel." She crushed out her cigarette. "I like to have fun. My husband likes to hear about it afterward. It's a little game we play."

"Your *husband*?" My skin felt so tight I thought I'd burst open any second and spatter the walls.

"Honestly! You boys are usually wise enough to play along and not cause trouble."

I was speechless. *You boys?*

"Look. I'm sorry if your feelings were hurt. It was meant to be fun. I thought you knew. Now, if you'll excuse me, I need to prepare for the matinee."

She turned towards her mirror and picked up a pot of lip color.

I lunged forward and got in her face. "You can't just dismiss me like some naughty child. What we felt was no game. It was real and you know it!"

She turned away and dipped a finger into the pot. "Please leave now, or I will call for Alberto."

I grabbed her wrist. The lip color shone on her fingertip like a drop of blood.

"Look me in the eye, Serafina, or Farfalla, or whatever your name is. Look me in the eye and tell me it meant nothing to you. Tell me you're not being threatened. Tell me it's your own wish for me to go."

She sighed like I was a pestering toddler. But she met my eyes and said, "It was just a game. There is no threat. And I wish for you to go. Now."

She went back to her makeup. When I still didn't move, she waved me away impatiently. "If you're worried about running into Alberto, I suggest you go out the back."

Alberto was the last thing I was worried about. Honestly, it would have been a kindness if he'd wrung my neck. I stumbled out, blinking in unreasonably cheerful sunshine. The other circus people were still there, waiting to see if there would be any more excitement. They stared, but no one stopped me as I trudged out the back. The car from the night before was gone. Had I dreamt the whole thing?

I wandered into a squalid underground tavern with no aim other than to drink myself to death. And the drunker I got, the angrier I got. It was a game? Go away? Just like that? I ran out on my shipmates for her. I had another drink and progressed from angry to pathetic. I was the original easy mark. Would I never learn? Why would someone like her—beautiful and talented, a star—want to trade her glamorous life for a poor nobody like me? I was just one of a thousand lovestruck sailors. I wanted to die.

I didn't die, but I got drunk enough to be tossed out of the lowest dive in town.

I drank up my money, and then I drank up Lampwick's money. I drank up my denial and my pain. When I had nothing left but empty pockets and rage, I went to the port. My old ship might be long gone, but there were always other ships. I should have gone home, but I was too broken and bitter and angry for a happy homecoming. I found a ship as broken and bitter and angry as myself—a villainous old steamer called the Albatross that wasn't much more than rust held together with more rust. It was headed for Hong Kong. I signed on as a deckhand without a second thought.

4

I've shipped with some rough crews in my time, but the crew of the Albatross was the roughest.

That suited me just fine. I worked hard on board and drank harder on shore. I avoided women in port, but I was game for a fight anytime. My only goal when I crawled into my bunk was to be too wrecked to dream. I didn't even think about home. Better for Papa to think I died than see me like this.

I almost got that last wish.

It was October, and we were steaming toward Southampton with too much Australian iron ore in the hold. Near sundown, we were rounding into the channel when black clouds stacked on the horizon. The skipper was anxious to make port, so we plowed ahead, hoping to outrun the front. No luck. Soon, the waves rose so high I could have reached over the rail and plucked a fish right out of a wall of water, if I wasn't clinging for dear life to anything I could grab hold of. Even the oldest hands were green with seasickness or white with fear.

I was topside, trying to keep the hatches fast, but we took on so much water the ship began to list. Her ancient sides groaned like a sea monster whose back was breaking. We went nearly vertical as she climbed the black face of the biggest wave I'd ever seen, and it was all I could do to hold on to the rail and pray. She sat on the crest for a horrible moment, then plummeted with the shriek of rusted metal giving way, and I was thrown into the raging sea.

I fought to the surface and clutched a splintered length of oak railing that floated nearby. The ship was gone, but I could hear cries for help. I tried to swim toward the sound, but debris and rough sea made it impossible to do anything but cling to my bit of rail. Near one end of it was a neat, finger-sized rectangle of darker wood where I had patched a gouge not a fortnight back. I knew exactly where it had been on the ship and for some reason, seeing it broke me. I wept for that little patch of wood, lost out here in the sea where it didn't belong. And then I wept for my mates. For Papa, who I'd never see again. For Lampwick, Hurley, and Tonio. For Eugenio and Alidoro. And even for Serafina.

Something brushed my leg. I clung tighter to my rail. A gray fin split the water and circled closer. It looked like I wouldn't have to worry about drowning. A few more bumps and I started to get annoyed. Stop playing with your food and get it over with already. Then a fountain of spume burst into the air. Not a shark. A dolphin. He swam up close and fixed one eye on me. The white curve of an old scar over his eye made him look sly. I gasped, sucking in a mouthful of seawater and coughing. It was the same dolphin I had freed from the net!

"Ahoy, old friend," I said. "Are you here to make good on your promise?"

He chittered and nudged me again. I gripped his dorsal fin with numb hands, and we were off. To this day, I don't know how I held on.

● ● ●

Cold water sloshed up to my waist and retreated. I spat grit out of my mouth and pried an eye open, then immediately squeezed it shut against a hot needle of blazing light. The stabbing light turned out to be only a watery sun barely able to pierce clouds above a pebbly cove. I sat up and looked around.

The wreckage-strewn beach was a narrow strand with low gray surf, held in the arms of rocky cliffs. I didn't see a single person, alive or dead.

I also didn't see my leg. Shit.

I fell back onto the beach and pleaded with the sky. Take me now.

It started to rain.

I groaned and forced myself to get up on my hands and knees to look for the damned leg. I found it about an hour later, bobbing in the surf, shoe still on. I managed to grab it without swallowing more than a gallon or so of seawater.

It was wet and gritty, but once it was on, I felt more like myself. I stood and leaned on it to test its response. A little stiff, but given the circumstances, it was a miracle.

I found a trickle of fresh water at the cliff base and a bit of respite from the rain under an overhang and took the leg off. It was far too sandy to wear for more than a few minutes.

I figured I was in England, and given where we went down, Southampton would be to the east. If I could find a way up the cliff to a road, maybe I could get a lift there.

But then what? Go back to sea? At the thought of it, a crushing weight settled in my chest like an anchor. No. I was done with the sea. I thought it would make a man of me, but it was just more running away. Papa and Eugenio's father and the other men I knew at home were solid, honest men who found a trade, settled down and worked at it for life. They didn't go drinking and fighting their way around the world at random. Maybe it was time for me to settle down too. I didn't know how I could do that in my current circumstances, but the thought got me through a long, cold night.

· · ·

At dawn, my leg wasn't dry, but it was drier. I cleaned the sand out of the cup and strapped it on. Breakfast was clams dug up at the surf line. Smacking them between two rocks was a slow, messy business. I gave it up in favor of finding a way out of the cove.

If I wasn't going back to sea, if I was going to be a solid, hardworking man, I needed a job. I would look for work landside when I got to a town. No, not a town. A city. That's what I wanted. Someplace big enough to offer a man some opportunity.

I stood a little taller. You can look at just about anything two ways—even a shipwreck. I'd survived. It was like being given a new life. I could be anyone, go anywhere, do anything.

I'd get back on my feet, find a trade, and save some coin. I would go home as someone Papa would be proud of instead of a broken failure. If I could get out of this blasted cove. If there were stairs, I never found them. It took me until midday to scramble up a narrow path to the road above.

My enthusiasm for the new man I was going to be flagged a bit after a hard climb on a damp leg and an empty stomach, but a fellow driving a load of lumber stopped and gave me a lift. He was glad enough for the company.

"Where you headed?" he asked.

I shrugged. "Anywhere I can find work."

"Join the bloody queue, mate," he said. "What's your trade?"

"Ship's carpenter, but I'm looking to stay landside for a while."

He scratched the stubble on his chin. "Well, if you've any skill as a joiner, you might find something in London. That's where I'm headed."

London. Just the name sounded like ringing bells.

"London sounds good if you'll have me that far."

"Suit yourself, but it's an ant heap of a town. Pick a man to the bone if you give it a chance."

I entertained him with seafaring tales to earn my way. He gave me my first solid meal in what felt like weeks and a threadbare jacket with blown-out pockets.

• • •

He dropped me at a busy street corner in East London. We shook hands, and he drove on. The first street I walked down reminded me of the bustling ports I'd left behind. The hulls that rose on either side were brick instead of iron, and I walked on cobbles instead of planks, but like any big port, it teemed with people from all over the world, every one of them intent on some task or other. And it smelled as rank. Surely a spot buzzing with this much life was the very place to make my fortune.

I went into the first shop I saw. And then the second. And the ninth and the twenty-ninth.

If there was work to be had, no one was handing it out to bedraggled foreigners. My confidence started to fray around the edges, but I was by no means defeated. It had taken years to sink this low. It might take more than a day or two to get back up.

By the second night, I was ready to fight a rat for a crust of bread. I found my way to what the locals called a spike—a sort of one-night-only charity poorhouse where you could get tea, a slice of bread with margarine, and a dirty blanket to sleep on in exchange for your dignity.

The early thirties were not an easy time to become a self-made man, but I dragged myself to every door trying. In my lower moments, I cursed that driver for bringing me here, the dolphin for saving me from the shipwreck, and even Papa for carving me instead of throwing the log on the fire. But I kept putting one foot in front of the other. A job might be right around the next corner.

And it was. Though, as they say, be careful what you wish for.

I passed a narrow alley with soot-blackened brick walls that rose so high on either side, the sun would never shine on the pavement. You'd miss it altogether if you were just walking, but hunger sharpens the senses. A dim light about half a block down caught my eye. Maybe it was out of the way enough that others seeking work hadn't been there before me. The light was behind a cracked window set in an iron door facing the alley. A flaking sign beside the door read B.F. Shea & Company.

Inside, it was larger and busier than I expected. Workers, mostly women and old men, worked at a frantic pace, standing at long tables turning out—and I know this is going to sound crazy—marionettes. Where could they possibly find buyers for so many toys in such hard times? I didn't want to question it, though. They were busy and, by the look of it, not too choosy about the limitations of the employees.

The manager was a skinny, sour-faced man with an improbably round belly. He squinted up at me over the tops of his spectacles.

"Mr. Shea?" I ventured.

"'At's not me," he growled. He pointed to a slat of wood on his desk with "Grimble" painted on it.

"Excuse me, Mr. Grimble. I've come to see about work. Anything. Even sweeping up."

"Experience?"

"Fourteen years a carpenter's mate at sea, sir."

"Fair enough. Hours are six in the morning to eight at night, half-day off Sunday. Thirty-six shillings a week. Take it or leave it."

I took it. He bellowed, "Coldsnow!" and a moment later, a wizened walnut of a man shuffled over.

"Coldsnow, show young …"

"Pinocchio, sir."

"Show young Portfolio here to Crutchley's station."

"Yes, sir," creaked Coldsnow. "Come this way." He shuffled off without looking back. I caught up with him in a step.

No one looked up as I walked past the long worktables. Children ran carts up and down the narrow aisles dividing the tables, sweeping up a sea of wood shavings and collecting finished items.

"Crutchley's station," said Coldsnow, stopping at the end of one of the tables.

It wasn't so much a station as a patch of tabletop with a bin for incoming work, which was piled above my head, a bin for finished work, which was empty, and a spool of wire.

"What happened to Crutchley?" I asked.

"Sad story, that. Tragic," he said and walked away. I never did find out.

My job was puppet assembly. How fitting was that? Men at the table behind mine turned out bodies, arms, and legs on foot-cranked lathes. The heads came from a different table. Our table wired the pieces together before they were moved across the aisle, where women did the decorative bits and attached strings. A tired, gray-faced woman stood directly across from me, gluing on tufts of wool hair with bent and swollen fingers. She gave me a slight smile, and my eyes went watery with gratitude. It was the closest thing to a friendly gesture I'd seen since I'd gotten to London.

At the end of the first day, I was so stiff and sore, even my wooden toes ached. And there was still the matter of finding a bite to eat and a place to sleep. I asked Mr. Grimble if I might get my pay daily for the first week. He grumbled but handed over five shillings, marking it in his ledger with a surly scratch of his pen.

I found a room in an old, brick-faced home a few blocks away. The landlady, a skinny widow with a face like a melting candle, had divided once-spacious rooms into tiny cubicles with partitions so thin a light tap would put your hand right through. My room was elegantly furnished with an iron bed frame holding a thin straw mattress, gray sheets reeking of the former occupant's sweat, two threadbare blankets, and a chamber pot. For company, I had the coughs and snores of my neighbors through the partitions and parades of insects crawling up the walls and across the ceiling. But it was dry and paid for with money honestly earned, and I still had a few pence left over for tea, bread, and a bowl of watery soup. The comfort of a drink was a thing of the past.

B. F. Shea & Co. manufactured four different puppets: a harlequin clown, a red-coated soldier, a fair-haired princess, and a bearded king, all of which I was expected to assemble without mixing up the parts. It wouldn't do to put a clown's head on a king's shoulders even though real life did that often enough.

They were just mass-produced toys, but Mr. Grimble either cared a great deal about seeing them done properly or, more likely, wanted excuses not to pay us. Defective puppets were sent back to be fixed. Those beyond repair became fuel for the little stove that heated the factory. Lest we be tempted to increase the heat on cold days, ruined parts and lost time were deducted from our pay at the end of the week. If you were careless, slow, or unlucky, you could work a full week and come out owing money for the privilege. Many were so far in arrears they could never pay it back. And if they left without paying what was owed, a warrant was issued for theft.

Most of the men at the factory were either old or wounded in the war, like me. The women were widows or spinsters. Fiona, the woman who had smiled at me the first day, had a husband who had been so damaged on the Western Front he could scarcely do more than lie in bed and hurl abuse at anyone in range. His mother lived with them and saw to his needs during the day. Fiona's daughter, Claire, was one of the children who swept the floors in the factory. Claire was thin and pale as a ghost and had a hacking cough, but she was happy to work under the same roof as her mother and never complained. I found small treats for her when I could, but what she needed was a doctor.

My first efforts were clumsy and slow, but I soon got the rhythm of it and could turn puppets over to be painted at a respectable pace. While the mountain never shrank, at least it stopped growing.

It was miserable, tedious work that left my back aching, my fingers bleeding, my foot swollen, and my sight blurred every day for nine months. You might wonder why I stayed so long. Unlike Fiona, nothing kept me there. I could have gone back to sea, gone home, gone anywhere. But I was determined to prove I could be steadfast, dependable, and hard-working. A real man doesn't give up his trade just because it's tough. This wasn't a respectable trade, though. It was a millstone that pulled people in and ground them down. A day became a week. A week became a month. One month became nine. And before I knew it, I was as dumb and lifeless as the puppets I was making.

But it was also the puppets that kept me going. I felt a crazy sort of kinship with them. The first time I held a little wooden soldier's head in my hand, tilting it back to fasten it to his body, I imagined what we might say to each other if we had time to trade war stories.

One day when Mr. Grimble was occupied and no one was looking, I slipped a clown's leg into my pocket. It was just a little piece of turned wood and not even a good one. It had a gouge in it and likely would have ended up in the stove anyway. But if I'd been caught, it would have meant my job or my pay. No one stopped me on the way out the door, and I felt as smug as a master thief who'd pulled off a daring robbery.

Over the next few weeks, I thieved more: a cracked hand, a chipped foot, a bit of wire, a scrap of wool. In my room at night, by the light of a candle and the streetlamp outside my window, I slowly assembled two puppets of my own design. They became the comic theatre characters I remembered from home: wily Arlecchino and clever Colombina. I carved their faces with care. I made clothing for them from salvaged trash: shreds from a colorful circus poster, a lost glove found in a gutter, carefully cleaned and picked apart, tiny shards of broken glass—anything I could find. I traded errands and tobacco for paint with a street artist—a cheerful Yorkshireman with the unlikely name of Achilles. Achilles survived on the few shillings he earned each day painting the same likeness of King George on scraps of newsprint. He dragged around a useless foot crushed in a metal rolling machine.

I asked him about his name.

"Oh, aye," he said. "My da' heard the story about that fellow in the Trojan War as a lad and stuck me with the name in the hopes I'd grow up strong." He indicated his lamed foot with a wry tip of his head. "I reckon he never got to the bit about how it ended."

I spent the most time painting my Colombina. I gave her black eyes and tiny red lips. For hair, I trimmed my own dark locks and attached them to her wooden head a strand at a time with glue cooked up in a bottle cap over a candle. When

I was done and I looked at her, my heart thumped. I had made Serafina.

I thought about starting over, but I didn't. Somewhere along the way, the pain of losing her had become no more than a bruise I was hardly aware of unless I poked at it. I was still heartbroken, but that was my own fault for giving my heart to a near total stranger. Maybe it was time to let her go.

Arlecchino stirred complicated feelings too. He reminded me too much of myself—a clown, perpetually hungry for something he can't get.

Making my little troupe occupied the long nights; I had no goal or plan in mind. I hid them under a broken floorboard during the day.

They grew quite handsome in their own motley ways. The final step was attaching strings, and at last, I could meet my new little friends and find out what they wanted to do.

The first thing they should have done was sack me and find a new puppeteer. They constantly banged into each other and spent far too much time lying in an indecent heap on the floor while I untangled strings. With practice, I improved, and soon enough, they were able to avoid most collisions, but I still struggled to bring them to life.

Maybe it was a sign of just how beaten down I was. They began their puppet lives with the feeblest drivel imaginable.

I bounced Arlecchino a bit and gave him a low, gruff voice. "Hello, Colombina."

She replied in a ridiculous, high-pitched shriek. "Hello, Arlecchino."

"Shut up in there, will you?"

That was my neighbor.

I couldn't think of another thing for them to say anyway, so they wobbled their heads and hands about aimlessly until I gave up. But with enough time, even dumb marionettes will get over being awkward. My two little friends began to have whispered conversations and little dramas, some of them quite rude.

One night, Arlecchino turned to me and said, "I'm tired of being a puppet. I'd much rather be a real man!"

Colombina sniffed. "Oh Arlecchino, to be a real man, you must act like a real man and work all the time, like Pinocchio! No more of your tricks and games!"

Arlecchino considered this. "Working all the time is for suckers. If I were a man, I'd become king! And I would cut off the head of anyone who tried to make me work. Not yours, of course, my dear Colombina."

Colombina gave a little jump. "I would be so happy if you were king! Being queen would suit me very well."

"Criminy! Let a man sleep!" moaned my neighbor.

Night after night, Arlecchino and Colombina flirted and fought with each other. It left me sleepless and anxious about my sanity. I thought I wanted to be an honest working man, but maybe I was a sucker.

At work, I made more errors, and my pay, already scant, was reduced even more. I had to stop this before I lost my job. Arlecchino and Colombina would have to stay under their floorboard except for Sundays. But by Wednesday, the thought of them trapped in that suffocating space got the better of me.

When I let them out, they were so offended, at first they refused to talk. But they forgave me and put on a little drama in which Arlecchino buried a gold coin, believing it would grow overnight into a tree covered with gold coins. When the coin went missing (of course it did), Colombina scolded him soundly for being such a fool. I forgot myself and laughed out loud, to the curses of my neighbors on both sides.

One day, as I left for work, the landlady stopped me with a scowl. "I've had reports you've been entertaining in your room."

"I swear, I haven't!"

"There's them as heard voices. Even the voice of a woman!"

"I ... I talk to myself sometimes." It was a feeble explanation, but true.

"Happens again, you're out."

"It won't."

I swore I would get rid of the damn things before they made me homeless. But I didn't.

• • •

Summer arrived and we no longer froze, but every season has its miseries. Most of the windows were stuck shut, and the few that weren't did little to ease the suffocating heat.

In the middle of July, Grimble was sacked, and a new manager took over. Mr. Dove didn't resemble his name in the slightest. He was a tall, stiff-backed man with an unreadable face and dead blue eyes that never seemed to see us—only the work we did. He carried a cane, but not for support. He never raised his voice. Why would he? It would be like yelling at a hammer or a pot of glue. Behind his back, we called him Crow, Vulture, and worse, but quietly, since he had a freakish gift for appearing out of nowhere in front of your station. He instituted a series of changes. Our work areas were reduced in width to create more stations at each table. To squeeze in more tables, the aisles were narrowed so much we were at constant risk of being injured by tools wielded in too small a space. The children running with carts and brooms could hardly squeeze through the aisles. Sawdust and debris piled up to our knees. It attracted rats and insects and turned what little air we had into an unbreathable fug. Quotas were increased. Each station was given a number. I was ninety-seven.

It made no sense. The whole country was in a deep depression; businesses were shutting their doors, and laid-off workers went hungry in the streets. But B. F. Shea & Co. was busier than ever, though no more forthcoming with wages.

The princess, the king, and the clown were discontinued, leaving only the soldier. We were given new templates. His smart red jacket was now dull brown and his curling mustache shaved off. I tried and failed to imagine the children who would prefer these toys over the old ones. My nights began to be haunted by armies of grim youngsters putting armies of grim soldier puppets through endless grim parades and battles. I'd wake in a sweat, unsure if the drumming sound in my head was the echo of bootsteps from my dreams or my own heartbeat.

Day after day, we stood at our stations on legs that would barely hold us upright. Across from me, Fiona's knotted fingers curled into stiff claws, but somehow, like the rest of us, she managed to keep going for one more hour, one more day. Claire grew thinner, and her pale skin faded to gray. Her cough became a relentless, wet rasp.

On a sweltering August morning, the man next to me collapsed at his station and was carried out the door, unconscious, maybe dead. When another man replaced him less than an hour later, something in me finally snapped. He was a person, not a machine part to be replaced when it wore out. It was time to jump ship. I felt light-headed with relief. Why had I stayed so long? I wanted to put down my tools and walk out right that minute, but I owed more than I had saved, and Dove would have the police on me before I'd gone a block. I spent the rest of the shift making plans. I would keep working until the end of the week, collect my pay, and be far away before I was missed on Monday. I'd give the puppets to Claire. I just had to hold it together a little longer.

That night I looked around my room. I had so little to show for the months I'd lived here; most of it would fit in my pockets. Neither Arlecchino nor Colombina seemed to care that we were soon to be parted. Why would they? Puppets are meant to delight and goad, not hide in a dark hole. I took them to a building site a few streets away and hid them behind some loose bricks, with a plan to tell Fiona where to find them.

I got to work early for my last day. Fiona shuffled in several minutes late in a daze. She seemed to have shrunk overnight. Her hands shook as she fumbled with the wool, and the dirt on her face was streaked with tears. A clot of dread swelled in my chest. Where was Claire? She always came in with her mother. Always. I tried to catch her eye, but I don't think she even saw the work in her own hands, much less anything else. Dove was at the far end of the line, his back to me.

I dared a whisper. "Fiona!"

She gave an almost imperceptible shake of her head, not looking up from her work.

"You shouldn't have come."

She put down her work and looked at me. "And have the rest of us starve?"

Before I could answer, Dove appeared in front of her.

"Twenty-three," he said. "You're fired. Pay what you owe to Mr. Coldsnow on your way out." His flat, even voice somehow made the words seem harsher than if he'd screamed.

Fiona trembled. "Oh please, sir! I have nothing to pay you with today!"

"Then you'll be arrested as the thief you are."

She wailed in despair and reached across the table to clutch at Dove's coat. Dove stepped back and struck her with his cane. She staggered, and blood streamed down her temple. Red-hot rage filled me so full I was sure it must be shooting out through my eyes, ears, mouth, and every pore. Outside sounds drowned in the gale howling in my head. I came at him over the top of my workstation, swung him around, and slammed him back against the table edge, my face inches from his.

"Leave her alone, you rotting pig's bollock!" I roared.

Silence fell. Dove looked at me, and something in him shifted. His flinty blue eyes lit up with something like surprise.

"It's you!" he said.

He caught my arms in a steely grip and lifted me off my feet with shocking strength. Without another word, he carted me off as if I were no more than an armload of firewood. I managed to land a solid kick with my wooden leg. His grip loosened enough for me to pull away. I stumbled back against the table behind me. A spirit lamp used to heat glue tumbled off, splattering its flaming contents into the sawdust below. Flames spread instantly, but Dove didn't even seem to notice. His eyes were locked on me.

Thick, choking smoke, flaming cinders, and panicked screams filled the air. I looked towards the door, but the press of people trying to escape had already blocked it. The only other way out was the big cargo door in the back. I jumped up onto a tabletop, sending a cascade of puppet heads into the flames, and leaped from table to table, barely able to breathe for the smoke and flying ash. The door was padlocked. Dove would have the key, but there was no time to go back for it. Someone tossed me a hammer. I swung and nearly lost my balance as it clanged off the lock. I set my feet and kept hammering while others shoved at the door. At last, the lock gave way, and the door burst open. Workers spilled through, coughing and helping each other out.

By the time the fire brigade arrived, the building was engulfed in flames. I scrubbed the smoke out of my streaming eyes and searched for Fiona.

I found her, soot-streaked, blood-stained, and huddled by the corner, holding a rag to her temple.

What could I say that would mean anything? "I'm so sorry."

"Oh, love. It weren't your fault."

"If I'd just kept my mouth shut!"

"An' where would I be, then? With my little Claire soon enough either way, I reckon. But you should get away from here."

She was right. Whether it was my fault or not, I'd be blamed. I felt like a rat leaving her there, but what could I do to help? As usual, nothing. I gave her the coins in my pocket and ran. I risked stopping at the construction site to grab Arlecchino and Colombina from their hiding place. It was a stupid thing to do, but now, they were all I had. I didn't stop until long past dark, when exhaustion forced me to hide under a railway bridge for a few restless hours of half sleep, half terror.

5

I was on the move again before dawn. I passed by a church where I knew I could get a bite to eat, but I didn't stop, in case police were searching for me. I kept my ears open for news about the fire. On a street corner, I overheard some men talking about it.

"It was terrible, I heard," said one.

They all agreed it was terrible.

"Anyone die?" I asked, as if my interest was only casual.

"Nothing in the news of it yet but a fire like that? Some surely must have," said another. "Coppers lookin' for the bloke what started it. Hope he burnt up."

"Serve 'im right," someone added.

They all agreed it would serve him right.

An iron band squeezed my chest. I couldn't disagree with them. I kept going.

After a day or two of running and hiding with no sign that anyone recognized me, hunger got the best of caution, and I stole a roll from a bakery cart. But that was no way to stay alive. I had Arlecchino and Colombina. It was time for them to earn their bread. And mine.

When I was far enough from East London and hungry enough to risk it, I found a patch of pavement on a corner not already staked out by someone else, put out a tin can, and unwrapped my little troupe.

If you ever need to attract attention and stay invisible at the same time, I recommend a career in puppetry. The trick is for the puppets to be so alive that you're no more than a ghost, even in plain sight. I was jumpy and skittish at first; it's not easy to step into the light when your life depends on staying in the shadows. But my life also depended on eating. I got my rhythm soon enough, and we were off.

The story where Arlecchino is cheated out of his gold coin was a hit, and it expanded to include an angry innkeeper (Colombina) and a fairy (also Colombina) who rescued Arlecchino from various scrapes with magic spells. The two of them fought and flirted with each other shamelessly. They acted out tales of bandits and swindlers, shipwrecks and sharks, love and betrayal.

My first lodgings were in a room that held forty beds with scarcely a foot on either side. We were rousted out at dawn and not allowed back until dark. I slept in my clothes with my puppets and money under my coat, but it cost only eightpence and included a cup of tea and two slices of bread with margarine in the morning. I counted myself lucky; many didn't have that much.

In the mornings, my audience was mostly men on their way to work and children on their way to school. Later, it was jobless men, and women going to and from shops. Late in the day, the morning people were back, heading the other way. Even the local constable stopped to watch from time to time. My tin cup never sprouted gold coins, but copper was ready enough and rarely, silver. The children had no coins, of course, but they would sometimes leave me a button or a flower. Colombina thanked them as warmly as if it were guineas. Arlecchino became an ace at putting hecklers in their place.

• • •

By January, I moved up to lodgings with a hot meal and only eight beds to a room. I dressed my little troupe in fancier costumes and redid their paint. Life wasn't a breeze, but I was comfortable enough. Most importantly, I was putting away a bit of money for the future. My plan to become a new man had gotten off to a rocky start, but now things were turning a corner. Of course, the thing about corners is it's hard to see what's around them.

I had a new story where Colombina tricks Arlecchino into taking a bite of a magic apple that puts him under a spell. She then makes him do the most ridiculous antics. She had just ordered him to get down on all fours and chase his tail in circles, barking like a dog, when a man came around the corner. For a heart-stopping minute I thought it was Dove. But Dove was tall and pale. This guy was heavier and more muscular with dark hair. It was the way he moved—a stiff-backed, ground-eating stride—that gave me the shivers. Was he a cop? He wasn't dressed like one. A detective? He stopped a few meters away to watch, though he didn't seem to be very entertained. The man never so much as cracked a smile as I sweated and stumbled through the last minutes of the show. Very few coins dropped into my cup, no surprise, and my little audience drifted away quickly. Except for him.

He approached, fixing me with cold, blue eyes. The hairs on the back of my neck prickled. I tossed my things into my bag and rose to my feet, backing away.

He snapped out a hand and grabbed my sleeve. "Come with me."

I twisted out of his grasp and turned to run. He caught my bag and jerked me back, nearly off my feet. I let the bag go, tumbled forward onto the pavement, turning a fall into a somersault, and took off down the street.

When it was new, my wooden leg would have launched me like a racehorse, but both the leg and the rest of me had seen too much rough weather, and every bound threatened to send me careening down the pavement like a runaway wheel. I didn't need to look back. The sound of his feet hitting the ground in that steady, relentless beat told me he was close and getting closer.

I grabbed a lamppost and swung around a corner, scattering a column of schoolgirls and two nuns like geese. Around the next corner, a large, noisy crowd filled the street at the end of the block. Perfect. I ran right into it without slowing and pushed through.

The street opened onto a large public park that was mobbed with shouting people—a demonstration or rally of some kind. I kept going until I was in the thickest part before I stopped to look around. The cop, or whatever the hell he was, was nowhere in sight. It seemed like I'd lost him. But I'd also lost everything else—my money, my livelihood. Gone, just like that. Again.

Not far away a man dressed in black stood on a banner-festooned stage, ranting into a loudspeaker. My own breathing was too loud in my head to hear what he was bellowing about, but his outraged tone suited my mood. Someone shoved a flyer into my hands. On it was a picture of the black-dressed man waving a flag with an emblem of a lightning bolt in a circle above the words "British Union of Fascists." The muscles in my arms and back went rigid. Fascists? Here, too? I looked up and noticed arms raised in the familiar salute, many in black shirts. My head pounded. Didn't that just cap off a shitty day. I crushed the flyer in my fist and flung it to the ground. Then stomped on it for good measure.

It looked like about half the crowd were Fascists and the other half were there to protest against the Fascists. I had found my way to where the sides crashed like a stormy sea surging in rocky channels. I could do with a good old brawl right about now, and I took a moment to consider my options. Two red-faced men stood forehead to forehead, screaming at the top of their lungs. A middle-aged woman in a brown coat with a fur collar battered at a young man with her handbag and looked to be holding her own. A thug dressed head to toe in black thrust his flag into the face of an elderly Jewish man in a skullcap and long black coat, who fell back under the feet of the crowd. Rage bloomed in my chest, expanding into a blazing sun that felt like joy. I waded over, found the Jew, and pulled him to his feet. Then I turned to the black-shirted thug and punched him square in the face.

It had been fourteen years since I last belted a Fascist, and it felt great.

The screaming mob kept getting louder and more violent. They shoved and battered each other with fists, umbrellas, sticks, and anything that wasn't bolted down. Sirens wailed, and police on horses and on foot waded in, shouting and swinging truncheons. I had nothing more to lose, and it freed me. I punched another Blackshirt and laughed as he went down.

It was only a matter of minutes at most before I would have gone down, too. Dead or in jail. At this point, either was fine. But fate chose that moment to send one of those small miracles that make you think maybe God hasn't forgotten you after all.

The tide was turning in favor of the police, and the mob started clearing out. A hand landed on my arm and wouldn't let go. I swung around, expecting to see either a Fascist or a cop or the creep from before, but it was none of them.

Watery blue eyes peered at me from a dirty face under a mop of ginger hair. The face was familiar but so unexpected I couldn't place him at first. He shouted over the din.

"Woody!"

Only one person called me by that name. I blinked. "Lampwick?"

Rage melted into amazement. We hugged, and then I think he shouted, "Come on!" Or maybe it was me who shouted. We ran through the thinning crowd and ducked past the police who were shoving rioters into police wagons.

We kept going until we couldn't hear the mob anymore. We were both so winded it was another few minutes before either of us could get a word out.

"Lampwick! My God! What are you doing here?"

He was still bent over with his hands on his knees in a fit of coughing. "Long story," he wheezed. Then he pointed a finger at me. "You owe me money, by the bye."

The last coins in my pocket weren't near enough to repay the debt, but they bought us four meat pies and two bottles of beer.

"You got a room somewhere?" he asked. I shook my head. "Me neither. But I found me a sweet little spot we can go."

His sweet little spot was in a power station about a thirty-minute walk north, through a hidden gap in a fence and tucked into a corner behind some pipes outside the boiler house. It was sooty and noisy, but warm. We ate our pies and drank our beers and talked most of the night. Lampwick told me his story.

"Ah, Woody," he said. "Trouble and me is old mates, you know that. It was bound to get the best of me sooner or later. I took a shine to a barmaid in Cardiff, I think it was, and the bartender objected. Didn't know he was her old man 'til after I decked him and the whole place was in a proper dustup. Someone took a bad fall and woke up dead."

"How'd you end up in London?"

"Couldn't ship out after that, could I? Show my face in any port, they'd be on me like flies on a turd. My dad was a born Londoner, so I thought to look him up. Turns out, he already drunk himself into the grave. After that, I dunno. I just sort of got stuck here, you know how it is."

I did. "What would you do if you weren't stuck?"

He popped the last bite of pie into his mouth and chewed. "There's this old lighthouse back where my mum's from. It's in Germany on a spit of land stuck out in the North Sea like a wart on a witch's nose. Nothing but birds, sea, and salt marsh far as you can see. But there's a snug little cottage at the foot of it and no one to give you orders. My grandad took it over when he gave up whaling, and I used to go there summers as a lad. Someday, I'm gonna get there, and when I do, I swear, it'll take the German army to get me out."

Two minutes later, Lampwick was snoring. But I was restless, and the hours snailed by.

A small movement caught my eye. A cricket nosed around the crumbs from our pies. Now, crickets and me go back a long, long way, and I can't see one without getting pricks of conscience.

"Hey there, little fellow. What would you do if you weren't stuck here?"

It stood up on its back legs and grew larger and larger until it towered over me. I blinked and saw it wasn't a cricket, but Arlecchino.

"I'm sorry I left you behind," I said.

He snorted. "You didn't leave us. We left you."

"But why?"

"Why? Why? Because we want to go home!"

Colombina appeared beside him and scowled down at me. "Yes! We want to go home, and you won't take us, you selfish thing."

"I'm going as soon as I have some money. And a trade. If I go now, I'll just be a burden."

"Burden. Pffft!" sneered Arlecchino. "You don't care a fig about that. You're nothing but a plucked rooster too vain to be seen without your feathers." He danced around flapping his arms and crowing like a lunatic.

Colombina shook her finger at me. "Shame. Shame. Shame," she intoned.

Her final "shame" blended into the toll of a bell, and I woke up in darkness with a gasp. They were right. My shame about going home a failure was pure vanity. Papa didn't care if I was wood or flesh, rich or dead broke. Money and a trade wouldn't make a man of me any more than the army or adventuring had. Maybe nothing would. Maybe it was time to accept it. The supposed warrant on my head at home was an excuse to avoid facing the truth. I had a warrant on my head right here in England, and it hadn't chased me away. It was time to go home, and I didn't want to waste another minute.

I shook Lampwick awake. "What do you say we both get unstuck? Today."

He blinked at me blearily. "Today?" I suppose he'd been thinking of his lighthouse as a pipe dream for so long, going there seemed as likely as sailing to the moon. But then he sat up and grinned.

"I'm in. What's your plan?"

Plan? I hadn't gotten that far yet. "Have you ever stowed away?"

He winced. "Once. I got caught and lost a good bit of hide for it. I don't care to go through that again."

The days of keelhauling were gone, but a stowaway could still expect a flogging and a spell in the brig.

"Would you rather starve to death on this rock?" I asked.

"Maybe." He scratched his chin. "Ah what the hell. Let's give it a go."

As soon as it was light, we hitched a ride in the back of a lorry headed for Southampton. Lampwick knew of a sailors' tavern just north of the port. We found it easily enough. It was middle-of-the-day quiet, but a row of committed drinkers sat at the bar. In good times, sailors will stick a coin or two under the bar of a seaman's pub with a bit of wax. In lean times, you take enough to buy your first drink. Lampwick slipped his hand under the bar, felt around for a bit, and produced two shillings.

We shared our tale of woe, and as we had plenty of it, we soon had offers of assistance. When you're a seaman, you're a seaman first above any other nation, and a mate in a bind is your brother. We discussed it at length, but no one could think of a better alternative than stowing away. A passenger ship would be best. Easier to hide on, and several were in port, but all the boys in the bar were on freighters.

"What about Horst?" someone said.

Horst turned out to be a German mechanic who had signed on to a passenger ship sailing the next day for Amsterdam. Not his usual gig, but he wanted to get to a sister's wedding in Groningen. He agreed to meet us before dawn and sneak us aboard. From Amsterdam, Lampwick could make his way to Germany. I'd sign on to anything heading to Italy.

That night, Lampwick and I got to the appointed spot early. Lampwick jabbered nonstop about his lighthouse, but I hardly heard a word of it. My thoughts were on home and Papa. He could rest while I took care of him for a change. And if I ended up in front of a Fascist firing squad, at least I'd die in Italy. But hopefully not until after I made it up to Papa.

Horst got us onto the passenger ship, squirreled away in a closet, and off again in Amsterdam. It was all so easy—not more than six or seven close calls. What was Lampwick so worked up about?

On the dock, Lampwick and I parted ways. "Good sailing to you, mate," he said. "Stop in at my lighthouse if you're ever up my way. And bring that money you owe me."

At the shipping office, I talked my way onto a tramp heading to Civitavecchia as a deckhand.

I was going home.

6

I leaned on the rail as we pulled into port and let the air of home fill me out to the ends of eight fingers, two thumbs, and five toes. I swear I could smell coffee and vanilla, though anyone else would tell you it smelled like every other port: coal smoke, oil, and old fish. When we docked, my mates got me past the authorities in a crate, God bless them, and I stood on Italian ground for the first time in almost a decade and a half. I'd never been to Civitavecchia before, but it was unmistakably Italy. The blocky granite embankments and cobbled streets were lined with buildings the colors of ripe peaches and melons.

But the bright colors couldn't hide a darker truth. People looked hungry and fearful, the children silent and watchful. Armed militiamen were everywhere. I knew from reading the papers that Italy was even tighter in the grip of the Fascists than when I left, but it was a gut punch to see it.

I got myself out of town as quick as I could. I doubted anyone would recognize me now, but I didn't want to risk being stopped. I still had no papers and no one to vouch for me.

Outside the city, the air was as intoxicating as wine. I wished I had wings like Serafina's so I could breathe in more of it than my lungs would hold. I didn't have a coin to my name, but after a flat broke January in frozen London, a flat broke February in merely chilly Italy was a dream. I went home the same way I had left: shunning main roads, hitching rides when it seemed safe, walking when it didn't, and sleeping in fields. The closer I got to home, the faster I wanted to go. I had spent fourteen years away with hardly a thought. Now, one more day was too much to bear. Each landmark I passed—the henhouse where I'd scared a fox, the crossroads where a farmer gave me a lift—swept me backward in time. The wild youngster in me wanted to run full out, whooping with pure abandon. The more cautious adult in me didn't let him. But damn, it would have felt good.

As I neared my hometown, nerves dampened the urge to run. How changed was it? Would they still remember me? I stopped at a stream in the woods to clean up as well as I could. I didn't care anymore if Papa knew what a failure I was, but I didn't want to scare him to death. I stripped down, scrubbed my clothes, and hung them on a branch. I could see sunlight shining straight through them in places, but at least they wouldn't reek. While they dripped, I dunked myself in the cold water and scrubbed the top layer of the grime off.

I sat in a slant of waning sunlight, naked as a piglet. While I shivered myself dry, I imagined what Papa must be doing— bending over his workbench, putting his tools away in their proper spots, having a bit of supper and a cup of wine, feeding the scraps to the cat. Our old cat must be long gone by now. Did he have a new one? As the sun set, I gave up waiting for my clothes to dry and put them on damp.

Every stone, every fence post, every window brought back a memory. The fountain with the waterspout that was supposed to look like a lion but looked more like old Father Matteo still trickled greenly into its granite basin. The oak tree I used to sit under with Eugenio and Alidoro still stood on the hill. Maybe I'd go there tomorrow. The little triangular square at the center of the village had a new bench, but no one was sitting on it. Most people would be at supper at this hour. I recognized the grocer, Mr. Sabbatini, carrying the last boxes of vegetables into his shop before locking up. I was tempted to call out to him, but if he recognized me, he would keep me there for hours, and if he didn't, he might call the police. I didn't have time for either, so I skirted the square and started up the steep, narrow street to home.

Warm light, the clink of forks on plates, and snatches of conversation spilled from windows, each one nearly as familiar as my own. The aromas of long-simmered tomatoes, garlic, and sage teased my memories as much as my stomach. What was Papa having for supper tonight? I imagined his face, old and lined now, looking up, his fork dropping from his hand in surprise. Tears, embraces. Later, we'd sit by the fire with a bottle of wine and share stories. I'd take over running the workshop. I knew a fair bit more about woodworking than I had when I left. I could support the both of us. Who would bother us in this little backwater?

The Passerinis' house, next door to ours, came into view. My nose turned me toward the aroma coming from her window. Mrs. Passerini had made ribollita. It's just simple bread stew, but I swear, if I was dead in my grave, I'd get up for one more spoonful.

When I finally stood on my own doorstop, my heart hammered all the way to the ends of my hair. There was nothing to greet me but darkness and a padlocked door.

Not the faintest light showed around the edges of the windows, nor a wisp of smoke from the chimney. No chair scraped the floor in response to my pounding. I couldn't see a thing through a broken slat on a shutter. Was there something I could break the lock with?

The hair rose on the back of my neck. I snapped my head to the left just in time to catch a curtain twitch in a window next door. I went over and tapped on the door.

"Mrs. Passerini?"

Silence.

"Mrs. Passerini, it's me. Pinocchio."

The curtain twitched again. A moment later, the door cracked open and then swung wide, revealing a round little woman with a small, pointed nose and a kerchief holding back gray hair that had been black the last time I saw her. Her dress was still black, though.

Her bright eyes filled with tears. "Pinocchio! Is it really you?"

"Yes, it's really me."

"I swear I'd hardly know you! You're skinny as a stick! Come in and eat something."

"I'm fine. But I need to know what happened to my father."

Her expression darkened. "Eat first. Then talk."

"Please," I begged. "I have to know. Is Papa ... Did he ... "

She softened. "Your Papa was very much alive and well the last time I saw him. Come. Eat. I'll tell you what I know."

When an Italian mother is bent on feeding you, you might as well give in. And to be honest, when was the last time I'd had a real meal of any sort, much less a home-cooked one? She plonked an enormous, fragrant bowl of steaming ribollita in front of me. I polished off three bowls while she talked.

"He went away. He said he'd be back soon, and you shouldn't worry, but it was all very peculiar if you don't mind me saying."

My heart sank like a ship into the ribollita sea in my stomach. The last time he "went away" it was to look for me, and we both nearly ended our lives in the belly of an enormous fish. "How long ago was this?"

"How long? Oh dear, when was it? I know it was late summer because my peppers were getting ripe. I always give your papa a few jars. He loves them so much."

"Wait. Papa left six months ago?"

"Was it? No, it must have been the summer before because I remember thinking how he was going to miss my peppers a second time."

My spoon clattered into the bowl. This was no one's definition of back soon.

"Time just flickers by when you get to be my age! But it must be so. Gianni was here when your papa left, and he's been off at that factory almost a year now."

Gianni was her only living son since Rodolfo died in the war.

She huffed. "All the way in Bologna!" She fluttered her fingers in the air as if going to Bologna involved flitting there like a butterfly. "Young people these days! You forget about home. Do you want some more?" she asked, ladling ribollita into my bowl without waiting for an answer. "They must not feed you in the navy!"

"I wasn't in the navy."

"Well, whatever it was, your papa was so proud of you! He showed your letters to everyone. The places you went to! Oh, sweet Madonna! I can't imagine! And the money you sent … he couldn't have got by without it."

I winced at how few letters and how little money I'd sent. "Damn," I muttered.

Mrs. Passerini smacked the back of my head with her spoon. "No bad language, young man!"

"I'm sorry. Please just tell me what you remember."

"Well, it was not at all proper, I can tell you that. It came so late, when decent people were already in bed."

"What came late?"

"The motorcar!"

"A motorcar came here?"

"Can you imagine? It made the most horrible sound. Like a bear right outside my door! I was afraid to get out of bed, but Gianni looked out the window. He said a motorcar was outside! I couldn't have been more shocked if it was a bear! And in the middle of the night! So, I got up and looked too. It was so big! Who would believe it could even fit up our little street? Gianni wanted to go outside, but I begged him not to. Nothing good can come of a motorcar in front of your house in the middle of the night!"

"Did you see who was in it?"

"A driver in a uniform got out and opened the back door, and you won't believe it, a woman came out!"

"A woman?"

"At first, I thought it was you come home. Because of the size. I forgot you weren't a boy anymore. Silly me! But it was a woman. Good-looking, too." She scowled as if being attractive was a sin. "The driver knocked on your papa's door while she stood there like she was too important to do her own knocking."

This was getting stranger by the minute. As far as I knew, the only female Papa had ever talked to who didn't live here was the Blue Lady, and she was not the driver-needing type.

"If she had gone in alone, well, you can be sure I'd have a thing or two to say next time I saw your papa! Entertaining young women in the middle of the night! But the driver went in too. They were in there so long. When they came out, your papa had his things packed up. And then they knocked at my door! Yes, mine! Oh, I was shaking like a panna cotta. What if they wanted to take my Gianni too? He was all I had since my poor Rodolfo and his papa left us, God rest their souls. But it was Geppetto at the door. The other two were already in the motorcar. He said he was going away for a little while, and I shouldn't worry and would I look after the cat until he got back. I was speechless! Running off with strangers in the middle of the night, just like that, and all he could say was look after the cat?"

"Are you sure he didn't say anything else at all?"

"Oh! He left something for you." She jumped up and started rummaging through drawers and cabinets. "Now where did I put it?"

She found what she was looking for under a stack of linens in a basket.

"Aha!" She handed me a folded paper packet with my name on the outside in Papa's neat block lettering. "I knew I put it somewhere safe."

Inside was a heart-shaped wooden pendant on a leather cord. I read the note on the paper aloud.

"My dearest son, always follow your heart. It will never guide you wrong."

That was it? Follow my heart? Mrs. Passerini was rapturous. "It's like a poem or a line in a song!"

A letdown, more like. And peculiar. Papa was never given to poetry. But then, I hadn't seen him in a long time.

"Such a good man!" she rattled on. "Never a thought for himself. Only that you should be happy!"

Maybe he'd left another message inside the house. I hung the heart around my neck.

"I don't suppose he also gave you a key?"

"No. This is all."

I'd have to break in. I got up to leave.

She reached back into the basket and pulled out a key. "You'll be wanting this."

"You said he didn't leave you a key!"

"Well, he didn't! They just took off and left the house wide open! Wild animals or who knows what could have gotten in! So, I had Gianni put a lock on the door."

I thanked her and left before she could get out the biscotti.

The house was in a little disarray, but not enough to suggest a struggle. Mostly, it was just … vacant. The wooden bowl he had carved to look like a snail shell still sat on the table. In it were three dried brown knobs that might once have been apples. A dish and a spoon sat in the kitchen sink, and a few coins and crumpled bills were in the grocery money jar on the shelf. I wondered why he hadn't taken the money with him until I realized he'd probably left it for me. There wasn't much in the workshop. Most of his tools were gone. The little bedroom was neat, though it looked like mice enjoyed the cozy bed. My old cot stood folded up in the corner. A thick layer of dust furred everything.

I brushed off his old chair, sat in it, and rubbed my hands along the worn arms. Should I wait or try to find him? Papa had been gone a year and a half. He would never stay away that long if he could get home on his own. My foot tapped restlessly on the floor like it couldn't wait to go to the rescue. Where, you idiot foot? Last time I went searching for him, when I was still a wooden boy, I just took off, ricocheting around like a schoolboy's marble. This time, I'd be smart. Search the house for clues. Gather information. Make a plan. I'd go see Eugenio. It wasn't likely he'd seen the mysterious motorcar himself, but since his family farm supplied the whole area with wine and olive oil, he might have heard something. I yawned. Tomorrow. I fell asleep right there in Papa's chair.

I woke up early and busied myself getting the place fit to live in. Not because I needed a fit place to live; I was used to far rougher quarters. But Papa wouldn't want to see it like this, and I might as well get the place shipshape while I searched for clues. It was slow going. The place was littered to the rafters with memories.

I dusted the scarred workbench. My initials were still there where I'd carved them, along with the memory of the tanning I'd gotten for it. His stool was on its side, and I righted it, turning the worn side toward the bench. A couple of chisels and the same hammer I'd chucked at that damn cricket went back into their slots. I found the smooth spot on the wall where he'd patched the hole, too. I wiped soot off the old kerosene lamp with the blue glass base and remembered him reading to me by its light. I swept the floor and found a few tiny wooden gears among the sawdust and mouse droppings. They were a marvel of craftsmanship. Was this what was inside my wooden leg? What wonders had he learned to make in the years since?

In the bedroom, I shook out the quilt and dusted the little bookshelf. I fanned through the books one by one in case something was hidden in the pages. When I got to my old grammar book—the one Papa sold his only coat to buy for me—my knees buckled, and I sat on the bed. The weight of all those memories left me dizzy, and none of it gave me a clue about Papa's whereabouts.

I put my hat on and walked out the door.

As I entered into the square, two guardsmen on patrol rounded the corner at the far end. One of them was a boy so young his mustache wasn't even a shadow above his pink lip, but he carried a man's rifle. I ducked into Sabbatini's to avoid them. I bought some candied almonds and waited for Mr. Sabbatini to recognize me, but he didn't. When the guardsmen were gone, I left.

Soon I was in the countryside, feet crunching along the rutted lane of crushed rock that snaked into the hills. It had rained earlier, and water pooled in low spots, but the sun was out now and shimmering on new grass so green it made my heart ache. Cherry trees were just beginning to blush pink, and a few early bees were investigating. My heavy spirits drained away like the rainwater. Despite all my years abroad, I wasn't so changed that my bones had forgotten this place.

My steps were light by the time I rounded a bend in the road and the bramble-covered farmhouse came into view. It was too early for the roses to be in bloom, but by summer, the house would be hidden in a cloud of red and pink. It stood at the top of a rise surrounded by neat rows of vines and olives. A woman was in the yard, taking down laundry from a line. Could that be Angelina? A small child sat beside her on the ground.

I waved and called out as I approached. She bent and picked up the child, holding him close—a sign of how much times had changed.

"Angelina? It's me. Pinocchio."

For a moment, I was afraid she didn't remember me. But then she put down the child, ran down the hill, and threw her arms around my neck.

"I can't believe it!"

I tapped my nose. "You know I can't lie!"

She laughed. "Eugenio will be so happy to see you!"

I looked around for him.

"He's out trimming vines with Mario. Our son." She turned toward the house and shouted, "Stella!"

A solemn barefoot girl about eight appeared from behind the house.

"Go tell Papa we have a visitor!" Stella squinted at me with suspicion and ran off. While we waited, Angelina introduced me to three-year-old Silvio. He was shy until I offered him a candied almond, and then we were the best of friends.

When I saw Eugenio, I took him for his father. He had gotten thick around the middle and had streaks of silver in his curly hair. After the hugs and assurances that neither of us had aged a day, I told him I was hoping to learn something about where Papa might be.

"I'll tell you what I've heard, but I'm afraid it's not much." He clapped me on the back. "Eat first. Then talk." Some things are sacred. "Come. My Angelina is a magnificent cook!"

And she was. I ate until I was bursting. Cannellini beans swimming in green olive oil, penne with walnuts, spinach, and garlic, chewy farro heaped with fennel and broccoli, followed by pears and almonds. All of it grown right here. And, of course, several bottles of their Chianti to wash it down with.

Mario was a sturdy, dark-eyed thirteen-year-old who looked just like his father at that age. He was agog at my sailor's yarns and swore he would go to sea as soon as he was old enough. Stella was fair-haired, like her mother, and made sure I knew it was her job to look after the animals. She wished she could go to my North Sea beach and pet the dolphin. Silvio demanded a steady supply of candied almonds and made a sticky mess of them.

Eugenio gave me a pared-down version of the months after I left.

"Those of us who helped you and Geppetto had some trouble for a while after you left," he told me. "Wine barrels hacked open, kitchen gardens torn up. That sort of thing. We all knew it was Ludo's thugs, but what could we do?"

"I hope I can make it up to you."

He waved me off. "He had it coming. In any case, he's been off cracking heads in Florence for years now and hasn't come back once. Not even for his sister's wedding, the bastard. I don't think about it. Today's troubles are enough without adding yesterday's."

"How bad are today's troubles?"

He shrugged. "It's not good. But a barrel of wine and a spring lamb for the local commander buys a bit of peace." I was sure it was worse than he made it sound.

I asked about old friends.

"Not much to keep you here if you don't farm. Alidoro came home a couple of years back for his mother's funeral, God rest her soul."

"How is he?"

"He's doing well for himself at the railroad. He's a boss now. Got a wife and some kids in Milan. Only stayed here long enough to get things settled and then went right back."

When Angelina went off to put the little ones to bed, Eugenio and I settled in by the fire, smoking. I told him what Mrs. Passerini had told me.

Eugenio refilled his pipe and took a deep pull.

"We all heard about it, and everyone had a theory. Secret lovers, American gangsters. But I don't know of anyone who saw it firsthand besides the Passerinis. If you can find Gianni, he might know something. Or you could stay put. He might come home. Angelina and I would be happy to have you around anytime. We could use some help."

"He said he'd be back 'soon' a year and a half ago! I never should have left."

"It's lucky for him you did, since you're alive now to look for him. Which you wouldn't be if you'd stayed."

True, but maybe I didn't need to stay away quite this long.

• • •

I spent the next couple of days helping him with repairs and work around the farm. It would have been easy to stay another day and another and another, the way I'd done at sea and then in London. But that was the old me. The new me wished them well and left, loaded down with wine and food.

On the way home, I climbed the hill to the oak tree and sat looking out over the jumbled tile roofs below. I was no closer to knowing what to do than I'd been the first day. Maybe I would have to go to Bologna after all. Gianni wasn't likely to know more than his mother, but what other leads did I have? I'd have to walk or hitchhike. I was so sick of being flat broke all the time. I sighed and looked up through the branches of the oak. Lots of pale new leaves, but not a single gold coin.

I pulled Papa's note out of my pocket. "Always follow your heart. It will never guide you wrong." How vague can you get? Was it just him being sentimental, or was it a coded message? I tried rearranging the letters, but I was never good at that sort of thing. They just swam around in my head. I tried warming the paper with a match, but no hidden words appeared. I pulled off the pendant and looked at it closely. It was small—no bigger than a walnut from side to side and no thicker than an almond front to back. Could it be a puzzle box with a hidden compartment? Papa liked to make those. But I couldn't see any seams; nothing rattled when I shook it or clicked when I pressed it. As far as I could tell, it was solid wood. I hung it around my neck and dropped it inside my shirt, where it lay warm against my chest.

It was getting late, and the air was chilly. The evening star floated just above the rooftops. I wished for a sign, something to tell me what to do. Then I snorted at myself. I must have made a thousand wishes on that star, and what good had it ever done me?

At home, I made a dinner of Angelina's gifts and a bottle of Eugenio's wine and sat, absently rubbing the smooth wood of the heart between my thumb and forefinger. It gave me a little comfort to have something Papa had made for me. Not that I didn't already have an entire leg he'd made for me. And, come to think of it, my entire self.

Still rubbing the heart, I got up to take my glass to the sink, and when I turned, I felt the heart give a tiny pulse. I stopped. Then I laughed at myself. It had to be the pulse in my own fingers. But when I turned back toward the sink, I felt it again. I wouldn't have felt it at all if I wasn't holding it, but it was there. I pivoted in a slow circle. The heart was quiet until I faced north. Then, thump thump thump. I tried it three more times. Each time I hit north, the heartbeat came back. It was a compass! I laughed out loud. How clever was that? I'd gotten my sign. I should go look for him and not wait here. After all, only a traveler needs a compass. Message received, Papa. I'll follow my heart.

• • •

At dawn, the door burst open with a bang. I had fallen asleep in Papa's chair again but was on my feet in an instant.

A stupendous black mustache marched in, attached to the face of a lean, stiff-backed soldier who aimed his rifle at me with mechanical precision.

A moment later, a bull-chested man in a crisp black uniform and a patch over his left eye ducked his head under the door frame. Even after all this time, I knew the cruel face swelling above his tight, starched collar.

Ludovico.

"Ah, Pinocchio." He smiled, but it was the kind of smile that said, "at last my sworn enemy will meet his fate" rather than "welcome home, old friend."

Ludo had always been big, but he seemed to have grown even bigger. He walked up to me, and his right eye speared me like a bayonet. A white cord of scar tissue snaked across his left temple from the patch over his eye into his hairline.

"Go ahead. Have a good look. It's your own handiwork."

Before I could respond, a brick of a fist slammed into my stomach. I would have dropped to the floor if his other fist didn't catch me under the chin on the way down.

The last thing I heard was his satisfied grunt as he hit me again.

7

When I opened my eyes and got them focused, it struck me as odd to see two black boots standing on the kitchen wall. I followed the boots to the right until I reached the face of Mustache, who stood at attention between me and the sideways door. The room sorted itself out. I was lying on the floor, hands and feet bound with rope. Ludo wasn't in sight, and when I lifted my head to look for him, my neck immediately objected.

I shifted and squirmed, trying to find a position that didn't press a bruise directly into the floorboards. Sitting up took a long time and a great deal of swearing and struggle, but I didn't have anything else to do. From the angle of light outside, it was late morning.

I called to the guard. "Hey, friend."

He didn't budge a whisker.

"Ahoy there … um, what should I call you?"

Silence.

"Listen, I have to take a leak."

He was responsive as a stump.

"Come on. Help a fellow out? You can shoot me if I run off."

After half an hour of ignoring my squirming, cursing, and cajoling, he glanced out the window, then brought me a pot, untied my hands, and stepped back a few paces to point his rifle at me. If you've never tried to relieve yourself into a pot with your ankles bound and your head in a rifle sight, I can't recommend it. But I found myself warming to him. Ludo would have let me piss myself.

"Thanks, friend," I said after he retied my hands. "You know, I was a soldier too. Back in the Great War. Got this fine memento because of it." I banged my wooden foot on the floor. "Where did you fight?"

He didn't answer, but his eyes flicked to my foot for a second.

"There's a bottle of wine around here somewhere." I winked at him. "Play your cards right, and I'll split it with you."

Not a twitch. Now it was a personal challenge to get a rise out of him, and I spent the rest of the day entertaining him with my filthiest jokes and songs. I turned my bound hands into two puppets and put them through antics I could have been excommunicated for. He never uttered a word, though his face went bright red, and once or twice I think his lips tightened. I was impressed by his self-control. This was some of my best material.

The sun's rays across the floor grew long and gold before Ludo returned with a roasted chicken. He sat at the table and made a great show of sucking the meat off the bones, washing it down with my last bottle of Eugenio's wine while my stomach tied itself into knots of hunger and foreboding.

"Who told you I was here?" I asked.

He ignored me until he finished eating. He downed the last of the wine and gave a satisfied belch.

"Your old friend makes a fine bottle of wine, I must say." He winked at me.

"Eugenio? I don't believe it."

He shrugged. "Did you think no one would notice you were here? You're even stupider than your stupid father. At least he was smart enough to get out."

"Where is he? What do you know?"

"I don't give a dog's balls where he is. You should be more worried about where you are."

He wiped his hands on my father's tablecloth and stood. "Let's go for a ride."

The silent guard untied my feet and pulled me up while Ludo checked his pistol. Not something you want to see, as a rule.

I stalled. "Leave already? You just got here."

"I'm a busy man. Move."

Mustache marched me out the door. A small military vehicle sat in the narrow street. He prodded me in the back with the barrel of his rifle, and I was forced to tumble face-first into the back seat and wriggle upright without the aid of my hands. Mrs. Passerini was probably having a heart attack behind her curtains. Mustache drove. Ludo sat in the front passenger seat with his pistol pointed casually in my direction and whistled the Fascist national anthem. His good spirits were not contagious. I tried to talk him out of whatever he had planned.

"You don't have to do this. I'll leave the country. I promise. I've done it before. I know how."

He stopped humming and affably whacked me across the temple with the pistol. "Leave already? You just got here." He went back to whistling while sparks danced behind my eyelids.

When my vision cleared, I looked out at the achingly familiar countryside. Was this the last time I'd see it? By the time we stopped, it was dark. The headlights lit a weedy, rock-strewn field with a few red splashes of early poppies. Ludo ordered me out, and the three of us stood in the pool of light. Mustache kept his rifle trained on me from a short distance away, and Ludo tossed a shovel on the ground at my feet.

"Dig," he said.

Ah, forcing the condemned man to dig his own grave. Not a very original trick, but let me tell you, it's always fresh and new to the one doing the digging.

"How deep?" I asked.

"How deep do you want to be buried?"

"How about I stop when I see kangaroos?"

He waved the pistol at me. "Dig. I'll tell you when to stop."

The shelter of the trees beckoned from the edge of the field.

"Go ahead," said Ludo mildly. "Run."

When I didn't move, he aimed his pistol at my head.

"Run or dig."

I couldn't think of a good reason to go through the effort of either. It would end up the same, no matter what I did. But the heart begs for even one more minute, no matter how miserable. Who knows what might happen in a minute?

I dug as slowly and ineptly as I could. I fumbled with the shovel and stumbled around, pretending my leg was a greater handicap than it was, and kept talking.

"Ludo, come on. We were boys! It was just a brawl, and I regret how it ended. Truly." Not a lie. I regretted that I didn't finish the job.

Ludo lost patience and ordered me to stop digging, even though the grave wasn't deep enough to bury a cat.

"On your knees."

He aimed his pistol at my chest and smiled. "I've waited a long time for this day."

"I'm sorry about your eye. Take mine and we're even! An eye for an eye. That's fair, right? Biblical even."

His whole body stiffened with rage. "You think this is about my fucking eye? The sooner the world is rid of you and your kind, the better."

My kind? Shocked, I took a step back and nearly fell on my ass.

"Do you mean Blues?"

"Blues, yellows, purples. I don't give a shit what you freaks call yourselves. You think you're special, but you're not. You're abominations before God. Every damned one of you." He cocked the gun. "Making you pay for what you did to me is just a bonus. My only regret is that your blood will pollute Italian soil."

I couldn't contain a burst of hysterical laughter. Pollute Italian soil? Who the hell talks like that? "Tell you what, old friend. Let me go, and I promise I'll have myself shot in France. Or Germany. Name the country my blood should pollute and consider it done."

Ludo's jaw twitched, and his hand tightened on the trigger. I squeezed my eyes shut.

The deafening crack of the shot was followed by dreamlike silence. I felt nothing. Just floating numbness and gratitude that death turned out to be so painless.

But soon, I became aware of sensations: cool, moist air, the scent of dirt and crushed wildflowers, the chirp of crickets, pebbles digging into the back of my head. I opened an eye to the night sky. I sat up in my grave and looked around.

Ludo lay on the ground, motionless, dark blood soaking into the earth under his head. I gaped at Mustache in astonishment.

He grinned at me. "Been wanting to do that for a year."

When I still couldn't speak, he pulled open the top of his shirt and rapped on the bare skin of his chest. It rang with the sound of metal.

"Used to be a tin soldier."

The world tilted. Was anybody who they seemed to be?

He glanced at Ludo. "Give me a hand with this."

I scrambled out of the hole. We rolled Ludo in, shoveled dirt over him, and packed it down as well as we could.

"You should go," he said, dusting off his hands. "Get as far away from here as you can."

"And let you take the fall for this?"

He shrugged. "I shot him."

He headed back to the car.

"Come with me," I urged. "Maybe we can both get away."

He shook his head and started the engine. "I'll only have the Fascisti after me. But you … Keep your head down and head north. Don't stop. Don't go home. North."

He drove off, and I stood looking after him. What was that supposed to mean? Who was after me now? Why north?

The hoot of an owl startled me out of my trance. I left the mound of dirt covering my former schoolmate and tormentor behind and ran, stumbling across the rocky ground in the moonlight towards the cover of the woods. It was dark under the trees, and I slowed as much as I dared, praying I wouldn't step into a rabbit hole.

The far edge of the woods opened onto farmland, and I kept going. When I reached the cover of a large stand of tall, young artichokes, I dropped to the ground, bone-deep exhausted.

How many Blues were there? There must be a lot if Ludo considered them a plague. How could I not know this? But I hadn't been looking. The ocean looks like it's nothing but water until you start fishing.

I shoved those thoughts aside and sat up. Once again, I was on the run, on foot, with nothing but my clothes. I sighed. Every day, people everywhere take up trades, get married, settle down. How do they manage it? Why couldn't I? I made myself stand up before self-pity staked me to the ground. Papa was out there somewhere, and it was up to me to find him.

I stuffed my pockets with young artichokes and started north. Clouds rolled in, bringing a chilly drizzle, but it was easy to keep my bearings with the heart compass, even without the sun or stars. It seemed like magic. Of course, I had no idea how a regular compass worked, either. I knew it had something to do with magnets, but magnets are just more magic if you don't pay attention in school. I ate artichokes as I walked. They're better cooked, but you can eat the young ones raw. When they were gone, I stopped at an apple tree and refilled my pockets with last winter's withered apples. When I couldn't walk any further, I tucked myself into an overhanging embankment near a stream, piled leaves over me for cover, and slept.

I woke hours before dawn and started walking north again. I could go to Bologna, but I'd never had a chance to ask Mrs. Passerini where Gianni was working.

I decided to head for Milan instead. It was a lot farther than Bologna, and I had no idea if Alidoro would even be there. I imagined a railwayman was like a seaman—with a home port, but rarely in it. I couldn't think of another plan, though, and he'd always been a loyal friend. I felt a stab of guilt. Had I ever sent him so much as a letter?

I walked north, hopefully towards Milan, in as straight a line as I could. At a farm, I managed to pocket six eggs from the henhouse before the farmer saw me and chased me with a rake. By midday I was limping. Italy only looks small on a globe. I needed to find a ride. A motorized delivery van would be a good bet. Long-haul drivers were unlikely to be militia and, like the lumberman in London, might welcome a bit of company on the road.

Just after dawn, I came to a wholesale pork butchery. The sign on the side of the building listed northern Italian cities they served, including Milan. A heavy, middle-aged man sweated with the effort of lugging a crate to an open van parked outside the warehouse. When I offered to help, he looked me up and down.

"I can't pay you."

"A ride's payment enough," I said. He handed me the crate.

His name was Gino, and he was from a town not fifteen kilometers from my home. We did the obligatory rounds of "do you knows," and it turned out his brother's wife's aunt was the cousin of Mr. Sabbatini's son's mother-in-law. Now that we were officially family, he relaxed. I told him I was on my way to see a friend in Milan. Truth.

"Milan's the last stop on my route. If you spell me driving, we'll be there before dark."

We shook on it. I didn't tell him I'd never driven before, and thankfully, he didn't ask. How hard could it be? He took the first shift, and I tried to learn by watching and prayed he didn't have a stop in Florence. I had no idea if Ludo had told anyone who he was going after when he left, but Florence was his turf, and he was surely missed by now.

Gino did have a stop in Florence, of course. I pulled my hat down low and sweated like a cow passing a butcher shop, but no one stopped me. After Florence, Gino gave me the wheel and crawled into the back to sleep with the hams.

I stalled out a dozen times before I figured out how to change gears, and it was harder than I expected to keep the truck going in a straight line. Gino came up twice to swear at me. Once I got the hang of it, I liked it. I could do this. Why not become a delivery man when I got back? It was honest work, not too much on my feet. I'd have the freedom of travel without the homelessness of a tramp steamer, the stability of a steady job without a boss breathing down my neck. By the time we got to Bologna, I was half set to ask Gino if he needed a partner. He sent me back to rest and told me I could help myself to something to eat.

I took my time poking through the boxes. All of it smelled as good as anything I'd had at home. I was starving but didn't want to take advantage. I settled on a dry salami hardly bigger than my forearm. The meat was packed in tight with hay and newspapers, and I pulled out some of the papers to read while I ate. It made drowsy reading, for the most part— crop reports and last week's weather. I found a crumpled front page from La Stampa, a larger paper that carried some international news, and smoothed it out. The headline was something about the new chancellor stirring up Germany— a budding Mussolini with a silly mustache. There was a big photo of him giving a speech in front of a crowd in Berlin. But it wasn't him that made me drop the salami and sit up, heart pounding.

In the crowd stood a man in a flat cap and a rumpled jacket. His head was turned slightly away, and he was much older than the last time I saw him, hair whiter, shoulders stooped. But I would know him anywhere. Papa! No. Surely, I was mistaken. There were a million white-haired old men in the world. Even if he went to Germany—and that was hard enough to believe—I couldn't imagine what could get him close enough to the front at a Nazi rally for his face to be recognizable in a newsprint photo. I shook the cobwebs out of my head and looked again. I hadn't seen him in years, but I couldn't convince myself I was wrong.

A woman in a white hat stood next to him. She stood out from the sea of men in dark suits and uniforms, and she was the only one looking directly out from the picture. Was this the mysterious woman who had come for Papa? She was so familiar. Where had I seen her before?

And then I knew. I fell back against the hams in relief.

It was the Blue Lady.

Of course. She must have been the mysterious woman Mrs. Passerini had seen. It still didn't make sense. The Blue

Lady was so solitary, I'd only ever seen her when I was alone or with Papa.

If Papa was with her, he was safe. Or at least not kidnapped.

I carefully folded the newspaper and put it in my pocket. I pulled the little wooden heart out of my shirt and turned it north. The little pulse was steady. Follow your heart. I was going to Germany.

8

Berlin! It had to be a thousand kilometers away, over the Alps, and across at least one guarded border. By the time I got there—if I got there—they could be somewhere else. If it was even them in the photo.

But the pendant pointed north. Mustache had sent me north. I had a ride to Milan and Alidoro, which was more or less north. Alidoro, out of everyone I knew in the world, was the only one who might be able to help me cross the Alps. And now I had a destination. Fate was leading me.

After Parma, I sat in the cab with Gino for the last leg to Milan. He asked me where I was headed after Milan, and I confessed I'd gotten into a little trouble and planned to hop a freight train heading out of the country.

He nodded. It was a common enough story.

"Switzerland's all right. I have a cousin in Bern."

"Have you ever been to Germany?"

He spat out the window. "You couldn't pay me to go there. Those damned Nazi bastards are sucking up every good thing we've got while our own people starve. Have you seen those trains? Loaded down to the rails going north and light as feathers coming back. They won't stop until Italy is a hole in the ground. My family, we been in the business three hundred years. But I swear on my nonna's grave, God rest her, I'll feed my hams to pigs before they fill Nazi bellies. You suit yourself, but my hams ain't going to Germany, and if you ask me, neither should you."

I thought maybe Gino was going a little overboard about it. I mean, sure, from what I'd heard, this Hitler was a son of a bitch, but he couldn't be worse than Mussolini.

We were coming to a checkpoint, so I crawled into the back and hid under some sacking. I held my breath as officers opened the back door, but they settled for helping themselves to a crate of sausages.

It was late afternoon when Gino dropped me off near the Milan freight yard. We shook hands.

"Thanks for the ride."

"If you come back and need a job, look me up. I could use a steady man."

It was a satisfying moment, but I had to laugh. It might be the first time in my life anyone had called me steady.

I walked along the fence surrounding the freight yard, looking for a way in. It was too tall and exposed to climb. But others had been in the same fix as me, so I knew there'd be a way in, hidden from direct view of the street. I kept walking and tried to look like I had somewhere to be.

As I skirted a pile of rubbish, my eye caught a slight jog in one of the fence boards. It was so well hidden, you'd never see it if you didn't know what to look for. Some workmen were coming toward me, so I walked past it, looking straight ahead. As soon as they were around the corner, I doubled back, pulled aside the cut boards, and crawled through.

Inside, an embankment sloped steeply down from the fence to the bustling freight yard. I replaced the fence boards for the next lost soul, dashed down the slope, and made it safely to the back of a small shed. A roustabout might or might not turn me in, but a guard surely would. If I got caught, I had one ace to play.

A whistle blew, and the day shift men headed for the gates. I slipped in with the next shift streaming past and headed for the nearest train as if I was just getting to work too. A guard came around the back of a train a few cars down and squinted at me. I tipped my hat at him and ambled toward an open freight car door as if I did it every day.

As soon as he was gone, I stepped out of sight between two cars and breathed a sigh of relief. Before I could take a second breath, a voice behind me boomed, "Where are you supposed to be?"

I just about jumped out of my shoes. A hand clapped down on my shoulder and spun me around. The guy was big as a mule and looked stronger.

"Uh … can't find my crew, sir," I stuttered.

I was as scruffy as I'd ever been, but I knew how to look like I was on a crew. He didn't look convinced, but he didn't look unconvinced either.

"Who's your crew boss?"

Time to play my ace. "I didn't get his name. I'm new. But the boss guy, he'll vouch for me. His name is Alidoro."

"Never heard of him."

So much for my ace. He pushed me into the lane between tracks where a group of sweating men lugged a load of barrels up a ramp into an open boxcar.

One of them looked up. "Hey, Luca. You catch a rat?"

"Ciccio, you know someone called Al … Aldo …"

"Alidoro," I said.

I almost laughed. Ciccio is a pet name for a sweet little baby. This Ciccio had arms thicker than one of Gino's hams. I guessed he was the boss of this crew. "Only one around here by that name is the foreman."

"Yes! Yes! That's him. He'll remember me."

Ciccio folded his hams across his chest. "He's missing two fingers."

Without hesitation, I held up my left hand and folded down the fourth and fifth fingers. Ciccio nodded, and Luca relaxed his grip.

"He's away," said Ciccio.

Damn. "When's he getting back?"

"Do I look like I keep the foreman's schedule?"

"Please just let me stay until he gets back," I begged. "He'll vouch for me, I swear. Put me to work. See if I don't pull my weight."

One of the other men spoke up. "We could use an extra hand."

Ciccio hefted a hundred-pound sack of wheat like it was a loaf of bread and heaved it at me. I staggered under the weight but stayed upright.

"Just until end of shift. Your buddy gets here, and he don't know you, you got a date with the police. And don't think you can sneak off, either."

I spent the rest of the night loading crates onto a train they said was bound for Germany. They were all stamped F.T. Toscano – Bologna, but with no hint of what might be inside. One crate had a knothole. It was too dark to see what was inside, but my fingers encountered smooth rounded wood. Gun stocks?

"Don't finger 'em," said Luca. "Just load 'em."

I got on with the crew all right. Freight's pretty much the same, whether it goes by sea or rail, and so are the men who work it. They even shared their dinner with me, which I was grateful for as I was hungry enough to eat my leg. Either one.

I heaved the last crate through the door just after sunrise and was tempted to heave myself in after it, but the thought of seeing Alidoro again was enough to keep my feet on the ground.

Just as the shift whistle blew, a train rolled into the freight yard.

"There's your pal," said Ciccio.

Even before the train came to a full stop, Alidoro leaned out and peered in my direction. His mouth popped open.

I waved. He swung out and took a few steps toward me. "Pinocchio?"

"None other!"

He closed the distance between us in a few steps and lifted me clean off the ground. "Never thought I'd see you again, old friend."

For a minute, I couldn't understand why my face ached. Grinning that hard will do it.

"Come on. Let's go to my office."

The largest building in the yard was a vast open workshop filled with machinery and train parts, but one wall had been divided into offices. Alidoro's door had a little plaque with his name on it. My old friend had done well for himself. A large, messy desk dominated the small space. Filing cabinets crowded around it, and every flat surface was piled high with papers.

As soon as the door was shut, I couldn't resist a whoop. "Look at you, Mister Captain of the Company!"

He was older, of course, a little fatter, with a new air of solid authority, but he had the same warm eyes, the same slow, steady manner. He opened a file drawer and pulled out a sausage, a wedge of cheese, and a bottle of Chianti.

"Eat first, then talk."

We ate and talked at the same time. When the food was gone and the bottle empty, he got a bucket of clean water and lent me his razor and soap. He couldn't do anything about my clothes; he was twice my size. But just washing up made me feel like a new man. He opened a second bottle, and we settled down to serious talk. I showed him the newspaper photo. He'd never seen the Blue Lady himself, but he agreed that the man next to her looked like Papa.

"This picture was taken at least a week ago. He could be anywhere," said Alidoro.

"I know. But it's all I've got."

"Fair enough."

We moved on to logistics. Only one rail route operated across the Alps. From Milan, it crossed into Switzerland through Como and stopped in Zurich. From there, it was a short hop to the German border. Alidoro had the authority to hire crew, but there was a fair amount of paperwork around it. My best bet was to stow away in a freight car. He knew where the best spots were, and I had some experience as a stowaway. But it was risky; the border crossing swarmed with militia. If I got past that, the train didn't stop again until Zurich, but the cars were unheated. It had been a mild winter, and spring was warming early, but the higher reaches of the Alps would be icy. If I made it to Zurich without freezing to death, I'd be on my own to get into Germany.

Alidoro gathered some supplies: a box of matches and a candle, a small pocketknife, more sausages, and a bottle of brandy. He even dug up an old German rail map. I put the map, knife, and matches in my pockets while he wrapped up the rest in a heavy, mouse-chewed wool blanket.

"Get some rest. I'll come get you in an hour or so."

I made myself comfortable and waited, still warmed by wine, food, and the joy of seeing my old friend. He was instantly ready to offer whatever help I needed and never once chided me for not writing. I thought about everyone who had helped me along the way without asking a thing in return. Papa, the Blue Lady, Lampwick, Mustache. Even the dolphin. It humbled me. Had I ever been as good a friend to anyone as they'd been to me? I swore I would never neglect a friend again.

Alidoro roused me from a sound sleep. He handed me a heavy coat that was only three sizes too big and a wool scarf that smelled strongly of machine oil. I grabbed my bundle and followed him into the rail yard. Around us, men worked, steam engines hissed and huffed, brakes squealed, and no one paid us any mind. He checked the numbers on car after car against a list on a clipboard.

"Here we are," he said at last and slid the door open. "This train stops at the Swiss border and then Zurich. It splits there, and half is heading for Belgium, but this section goes to Stuttgart. Hide behind the crates and stay put." He reconsidered. "The German border guards are thorough. You might want to hop off in Zurich and look for another way across."

I tossed my bundle through the door and climbed in after it. "Come along? A bit of adventure?"

Alidoro laughed. "My wife would kill me."

He reached into his pocket, pulled out his watch, and held it out to me. I shook my head. "It was your father's."

He slipped the watch into my pocket. "He'd want you to have it. You'll need to get documents, and that's not cheap."

Someone called his name.

"Stay low and keep safe, my friend. And come back."

Alidoro slid the door shut with a solid thunk.

• • •

The car was full of wooden crates, but not the mysterious F.T. Toscano ones. The aroma alone labeled them cheese, and I silently thanked Alidoro again. I made myself a hiding place in the corner and practiced looking like cargo until the car jerked and began to roll.

The first crate I pried open was filled with beautiful rounds of pecorino, each nestled in straw. I could have fed myself on the smell alone.

I tossed cheeses out the door until there was enough room to curl up inside the crate. I was sad to see them go, but I couldn't leave them sitting out, and better they should feed Italian foxes than German Fascists. Gino would approve.

I lined my nest with the blanket, crawled in, and curled up like a dormouse.

When the train ground to a halt, I pulled the lid tight and prayed. Footsteps crunched on gravel outside, and the door slid open. Boots jolted the floor, and a flashlight beam swung around. Of course, my nose chose that moment to itch. I managed to hold off and timed my stifled sneeze with the squeal of the crate next to mine being pried open. He was close enough that I could hear his breath stop. I gritted my teeth and tensed for a fight if the lid came off my crate. But after a few sweaty minutes, he left and slid the door shut with a bang.

Forty-five minutes later by Alidoro's watch, the train jerked and chugged slowly up to speed. I pushed the lid open. Was I in Switzerland? I couldn't tell if the air smelled different, but it was definitely colder.

As the train labored up into the mountains, the temperature dropped. Cold air seeped into my crate, and I shivered even in my straw and blanket nest. I had matches and plenty of straw, but lighting a fire in a wooden freight car was a last resort. I tried to warm myself with memories of equatorial seas, tropical ports, and the charms of portside women.

Truth be told, there hadn't been many women since Serafina. Despite her cruel rejection, she still haunted me. Nothing could erase the heat of her body in my arms, the magical responsiveness of her wings, or the insistence of my heart that the truth was more complicated than it seemed. I wasn't sure if she'd turned me off women or ruined me for them. In my current situation, it didn't much matter which.

Alidoro could have mentioned the existence of a tunnel. The train plunged into thundering, sooty darkness that went on for what felt like hours. The cold eased a bit and I yawned, but I didn't want to risk sleeping and miss my stop—or miss waking up at all. I made myself get up, light the candle, and march back and forth along a narrow aisle between crates as I tried to decide what to do if the tunnel ever ended and I reached Zurich.

I was tempted to stay on the train and chance the German border. Stuttgart was closer to Berlin than Zurich, and I was sick of walking everywhere. But if what Alidoro said about German border guards was true, I'd be snagged like a fish in a net. On the other hand, I didn't have a clue what it was like on the ground between Zurich and the border. I could be just as exposed and be hundreds of kilometers farther from my destination.

It got so cold, I finally did risk a small fire, then thought better of it and put it out almost as soon as it was lit. I stomped around and did push-ups until I was exhausted.

When the train slowed to a clattering halt, I still hadn't made up my mind what to do. I was just about to poke my head out the door and have a look when I heard voices and footsteps. I hopped back into my crate.

I heard two men arguing. "… cases … get there today." Keep walking, I silently urged, but, of course, they stopped right outside my freight car.

"We can't just take them."

"It's just three cases. They won't miss it."

"Are you kidding? Those bastards raise hell if an i is short a dot."

"So what if some fat krauts throw a tantrum over some cheese? It's our necks if we're short in Metz."

The door rumbled open, and two pairs of feet thudded onto the floorboards. They grunted as they lifted a case—not mine. Then they picked out a second case—also not mine.

Just like in fairy tales, the third time was the charm.

Hands gripped my case, lifted it, and jounced me and my cheeses across gravel, across something quieter, like dirt or pavement, and then up a ramp and down with a thump. A few minutes later, a door slammed shut, and a truck engine rumbled to life.

Shit.

I was on my way to Metz. In France.

I pushed up the lid, thankful they hadn't piled more crates on top. Blades of light knifed through gaps around the tailgate of the truck. I climbed out, stretched, and took stock of the situation. In a rare lucky break, the tailgate wasn't latched. I rolled it up a bit and peered under. There was little traffic at this hour. Warehouses and factories gave way to a business district with shops and offices, mostly dark. I carved off as much cheese as would fit in my pockets, and when the truck slowed to make a turn at a construction site, I jumped.

I'd like to tell you I rolled and came up running, but the truth is, I was so stiff, rolling was entirely out of the question, and running wasn't much better. It was more of a topple followed by a crawl. Cheese makes reasonable padding, so I wasn't too bruised. The truck vanished around the corner.

I found a spot under a metal staircase and hunkered down to regroup. Alidoro's watch was still in my pocket, along with the German rail map, pocketknife, and the cheese. I'd left the blanket, matches, candle stub, and a quarter bottle of brandy in the truck. I was most sorry about the brandy.

I heaved myself to my feet, checked my pendant for north, and started walking. I've told you enough times about the joys of tramping cross country on a foot and a stump, so if you don't mind, I'll skip that part from here on out.

It was full daylight by the time the city gentled into farmland. I reached the sparkling, blue expanse of the Rhine the next day. The banks were lined with charming little farms so neatly tended I felt like I'd walked into a fairy tale. Like a fairy tale, the bridges were all guarded by trolls. Unlike a fairy tale, there was not one magic fish or swan to ferry me across for only the promise of my firstborn.

There was, however, an upside-down rowboat on the bank by a dairy farm. The farmer was in sight, tending to a herd of placid brown cows. I thought about asking him to row me across, but the only thing I had to pay him with was the watch, and I couldn't afford to part with it yet. After dark, I borrowed the boat and rowed myself across. I left it tied in plain sight on the far shore. It would be a loss of time for him to get it back, but not a loss of property.

German farms were very similar to the Swiss ones, though the cows were a darker brown. Their milk isn't chocolate, in case you're wondering.

I had some trouble following the map Alidoro had given me. I ran into a rather large and unexpected town and had to make a big detour to avoid it. The map was old, but I didn't figure even industrious Germans moved their cities around. When the sky cleared, I saw that the north star was west of where my heart pendant pointed. Not so reliable as a compass, after all. I made the mental adjustment, and things went better.

What I needed most was documents and a ride. I had the means to pay, but I couldn't trust strangers, and I didn't have a single friend in the whole country.

Or maybe I did.

• • •

That evening I passed a field on the outskirts of a town where a circus was packing up and loading cars onto a train. I remembered what Serafina had said about Blues in the circus. The people all looked normal, not a wing or a tail in sight, but that didn't mean Blues weren't there. They would probably hide or disguise their differences like she had. I took a few steps toward them but thought better of it and stopped. Why should I believe anything Serafina said? At best, I would make a fool of myself and, at worst, invite the wrong kind of attention. I kept walking.

But it kept eating at me. I knew she hadn't lied about there being other Blues. She was one, and so was Mustache. Even Ludo knew of enough Blues to think we were an infestation. I spent my whole life thinking there wasn't another living creature on the planet like me. And I'd walked right past a chance to meet more.

I was such an idiot.

I backtracked, but now it was just a littered field with no sign of where the circus was headed next. I searched for a poster—they often listed a series of stops—but all I found were candy wrappers, ticket stubs, and a pair of ladies' underpants. I'd have to chance going into a town to look for one.

Outside the next town, I traded my trousers and shirt for cleaner ones from someone's clothesline and found a quiet spot by a stream. I scrubbed down as much as I could and tried to shave with the pocketknife and cold water. Not something I recommend if there's any other option. The clothes were baggy, but times were lean, and I wasn't the only one cinching a belt. I hoped I looked normal enough not to attract attention. Or at least not terrify children.

The morning was gray and drizzling. Good. People would be more likely to hurry through their business with their heads down.

When I reached the square, a few people were out and about, though most businesses hadn't opened yet. I stopped in an alley and pretended to fuss with a shoelace while I had a look around. The clink of china and the glorious aroma of coffee wafted from an open window above my head. A butcher arranged sausages in his window across the square, and at the back of the baker's shop next door, a light popped on. Next to the baker, a construction fence ran to the end of the square, and I could see an assortment of flyers pasted to it. One of them was garish enough for a circus.

A boy on a bicycle rode past me and dropped a bundle of newspapers at a shop door. When I was relatively sure no one was looking, I snagged the bundle and perched it on my shoulder. I took a deep breath and strode forward, whistling a tune I remembered the German sailors liked to sing.

Two women rounded the corner from the opposite direction and stopped in their tracks when they saw me. One carried a baby on her hip. The other had a toddler by the hand. I smiled at them and tipped my cap.

"Morning!" I hoped my German accent was good enough.

They eyed me suspiciously, and I swallowed. If they raised the alarm, I'd have to run for it. But the toddler tripped on a cobble and skinned his knee. I was forgotten in the fuss that followed and made it past them. I dropped the bundle of papers in front of the butcher's and made a quick turn along the fence. I tore the circus poster off the fence as I walked past it, folded it, and stuffed it in my shirt. Now, for a quick exit.

A policeman walked into the square, making his rounds. He hadn't looked my way yet, and the corner was just a few paces away.

A noisy gang of young men appeared, maybe a dozen of them, all in brown shirts and carrying sticks and buckets. I took advantage of the distraction to duck around the corner out of sight. I should have kept going, but shouts of "Jew! Jew! Jew!" made me turn back.

They were gathered outside the baker's shop, chanting and pumping their fists in the air while two of them painted sloppy, blood-red swastikas on the storefront. Bile stung the back of my throat. They may have been wearing brown, but they were just as hate-filled and vile as the Blackshirts back home.

Heat surged down my arms and into my fists. I should go. This wasn't my fight. But I couldn't turn away.

One of the boys smashed the window. The baker, a stout, gray-haired man in a white apron, ran out and stood in the broken glass on the pavement swearing at the gang. I had to admire his nerve. They started shoving the baker from one to the other until he lost his footing and fell to the pavement. They closed in, shouting insults. Where was the policeman? He had been there just a minute ago. The few other people in the square stood and watched or turned away. The butcher was nowhere to be seen.

The sound of boots hitting flesh sickened me. Was no one going to help this man? A boot landed on the poor man's hand, and I heard the bones crunch, followed by his agonized howl. My hands were on the first boy before my feet knew they were running. They all turned on me. I knew a thing or two about dirty brawling and had the advantage of surprise and experience. It gave me the edge at first. But they were younger, better fed, and most of all, outnumbered me twelve to one. I was going to lose this fight. At least they weren't kicking the poor baker anymore.

At last, a policeman's whistle pierced the uproar, and the boys scuttled off like cockroaches. Before I could scuttle, a hand grabbed my arm and swung me around like a sack of potatoes.

It wasn't the same cop I'd seen earlier. This one was young, hardly more than a boy—smooth face, not even a shadow of whiskers—but with the strength and command of a man.

At our feet, the baker moaned. Blood trickled from his ears and mouth, his eyes were swelling shut, and he cradled his bleeding, ruined hand to his chest. The policeman didn't even glance down.

"You are under arrest." His voice was flat, emotionless.

"Officer, it wasn't me. It was those boys."

There had been witnesses, but now the square was empty and silent. Faces in windows vanished when I looked their way, though I could feel eyes watching as he marched me away.

9

When we were out of sight of the square, the officer stopped and shoved me against the wall. Then, he did a strange thing. He raised a hand and spanned my forehead with his fingers, and a strong, pulsing buzz shocked me—as if he'd touched me with a live electric wire. Was he wearing a battery of some kind? I didn't see any wires. I tried to twist away, but his fingers were a vise, his mouth a thin line of concentration. If it was a weapon, it wasn't a very good one. A bullet would be more effective.

If he hadn't been standing so close, I might not have seen it. Just above his collar, a thin white scar circled the smooth pink skin of his neck, exactly where a puppet's head would connect to a wooden neck.

A person could get such a scar in more than one way. But what if he was a Blue? He could be like Mustache—playing a role to survive. I took a chance.

"I'm a Blue!" I gasped. "Like you."

His eyes were cold, and his face showed nothing. Something about him seemed familiar, but it was impossible

I'd seen him before. The electric buzzing made it hard to think.

"I'm on your side," I said. "You can drop the act."

Still nothing. I must have been wrong. Maybe Nazis hate Blues as much as Ludo did. He finally gave up trying to irritate me to death with the buzz and shoved a pistol under my chin.

"Come with me," he said without emotion.

And then I remembered where I'd heard that voice before.

Dove. At the puppet factory, Dove had that same stiff look and flat voice. And the man who had chased me from my London street corner. Were all three of them Blues? It didn't seem possible, but they weren't regular people, either. Everything about them made my nerves itch. I needed to get away.

The wooden gate of a nearby alley swung open, and an elderly woman stepped out with a little black dog on a leash. She stopped and gasped when she saw us, distracting my captor for just a second.

I wrenched myself out of his grip and sprang toward the alley. A shot pinged off the wall over my head as I leapt over the dog, grabbed the gatepost with one hand, and pivoted into the alley, careening into a bin before stumbling forward.

Behind me, I heard screaming and a great deal of high-pitched barking. I mentally apologized to both the woman and her dog. Another bullet hit the wall near my ear, showering me with pinpricks of shattered brick.

A wall loomed at the alley's end. A dead end? No, there were low garden gates to the right and left. I caromed off the wall, vaulted over the gate to the right, and scrambled through backyards filled with laundry, startled housewives, wide-eyed children, barking dogs, and an elderly man gardening in the nude.

A gap in a fence led across railroad tracks, through brambles, and into a neighborhood with shabbier homes and dirt lanes, then on to fields of young vegetables and pastures full of sheep and geese. My lungs were on fire, but I didn't stop running until I got to the shelter of trees. Even then, I kept walking until my legs would no longer obey, and I dropped in a stand of tall weeds.

As I lay there, gasping, I tried to make sense of what I'd seen. What kind of creature was this stone-faced officer? And the two in London? Who had made them? It couldn't be the Blue Lady. I imagined an enemy the reverse of her: evil instead of good, monstrous instead of kind. Was this what Mustache meant when he warned me to keep my head down? Was this why the Blue Lady and Papa had come to Germany? Despite being overheated from running, I shivered. I couldn't stay here.

The poster rustled in my shirt as I sat up. I pulled it out and smoothed it flat. At the top, "Circus Fischer" arched over a drawing of a large green fish with a toothy grin leaping through a flaming hoop. Below it, acrobats cavorted, horses pranced, and a man and woman swung on a trapeze, all looking like normal horses and humans. A round-bellied frog in a top hat dipped a long tongue into an enormous stein of beer in the corner. A Blue or a fanciful cartoon?

A list of dates and cities was written in by hand at the bottom, as I'd hoped. It took some calculating to figure out what day it was now. They'd been here and gone two days ago and would leave their current stop before I could get there. But they had a date in Stuttgart a few days after that. I looked at my map. If I went straight there, I could probably make it in time. Did I still want to? I had no idea who I could trust anymore. But I'd never make it all the way to Berlin on my own.

• • •

I found the circus late in the afternoon on the last day of their stay. I've staggered aboard many a departing freighter with less time to spare.

Circus Fischer was larger and looked more prosperous than Serafina's circus back in France. The entrance of the big blue and yellow striped tent was kitted out like a maharajah's palace. Smaller tents, stalls, and wagons clustered around it like children at a candy shop window. I stood outside the entrance while people swarmed around me. I just needed to find a Blue. The right kind.

It wasn't easy. Plenty of outlandish characters wandered around, but costumes and makeup could account for any of them. A man as tall as a house turned out to be a normal human on stilts. Pictures painted on the outside of the "Living Wonders" tent showed a strongman with arms bigger than his legs, holding two enormously fat women over his head, one in each hand, while a snake with a boy's head coiled by his feet. Any of them could be Blues. Or it could just be a painting. I tried to sneak in but got shooed away.

A fence divided the public area of the circus from the back, where the performers lived. Inside, a man walked by with a bale of hay on his shoulder.

"Excuse me," I called. "I'm looking for someone."

He stopped and glared at me. "Buy a ticket."

"It's important. Life or death. I need to talk to the guy who looks a little like a frog." Circus posters aren't famous for accuracy, but it was all I had.

"Yeah, right. Now get lost before I call Dieter."

I assumed Dieter was the Alberto of this outfit. A face popped from the doorway of a nearby tent, round as a sunflower with blond curls peeping from the edges of a bright yellow headscarf.

"Why are you looking for Vrak?" she said in a high, fluty voice.

"I think we're ... related."

She stepped out and approached the fence. The rest of her was even rounder than her face. She was dressed like a farmer's wife in a billowing flowered dress and a long red apron that reached her ankles. My heart sped up. Was she a Blue?

"I'll handle this, Anton," she said.

The hay bale man grunted and moved on. She reached between the slats of the fence and took my hand in hers as if she was going to read my palm. But she hardly glanced at it, looking me straight in the eyes instead. Hers were enormous, long-lashed, bright blue, and baby-like, but something in them was old and penetrating. I didn't know what she was looking for, but she must have seen it because she softened.

"You're far from home, Sunshine. What kind of help do you need?"

She spoke with a Russian accent. I didn't know more than a few words of Russian, and most of them not suitable for mixed company, so I stuck with German.

"I have to get to Berlin. It's urgent. I don't know anyone; I don't have papers, and I'm broke. I'll do any work." I paused. Might as well go for it. "And I'm a Blue."

She smiled. "I know."

A clown leaned out of the tent—a tall fellow dressed like a caricature of a soldier.

"Matya," he called. "Showtime."

"I'll be right there," she answered without breaking her gaze from mine. "Come on, then."

Matya checked to see if anyone was looking and then pointed to where two fence sections met. I helped her push them apart enough to squeeze through. Backstage, pandemonium raged. I wanted to stop and take it all in, but we were only passing through. She gave me a front-row seat right by the curtained passage where the performers entered and left.

"Thank you!"

"No promises," she warned and vanished.

Tiered benches circled the perimeter of the tent, broken at intervals by aisles. A low rail and a track of neatly raked bare dirt separated the audience from a ring filled with the usual contraptions.

I looked up at the trapeze, and of course the first thing that caught my sailor's eye was the rigging. It was neatly enough done, but I would have tied it differently at the top. Before I could mentally rejigger the whole thing, the band blared to life, and clowns streamed into the ring.

The first was a clown with arms and legs so thin, a belly so round, and a head so bald you could easily imagine him seated on a lily pad. He had to be the beer-swilling frog on the poster. He waded into the stands, liberating umbrellas and hats from audience members and tossing them to other audience members.

The soldier clown chased after him, blowing a shrill whistle. His bright red uniform was trimmed with gold braid and his black mustache was waxed into elaborate, spiraled ends above an alarming set of enormous white teeth. In his haste to catch up to the thief, he constantly stumbled, knocking hats off men's heads and falling into the laps of pretty girls. Please, please be Blues, I prayed.

Matya waddled in with a wicker basket over her arm. A little white dog escaped from the basket, and Matya wandered around, calling for it, even when it was standing on her head.

The frog thief reached into a woman's handbag, pulled out an absurdly long string of sausages, and ran off, with the soldier and the dog in hot pursuit. As he passed Matya, she snatched the sausages out of his hand, opened her mouth wide, and dropped the whole length in.

She froze. Her eyes popped wide. The violin trilled. Her belly started to shake as if it was possessed by a demon. The drums banged and crashed in time with her contortions. Her skirt belled and fluttered wildly … and out came another chubby farmer's wife maybe half her size, sausages in hand! Had she been hiding under the skirt the whole time, or had she sneaked in when we were watching the thief?

This one waggled the sausages at the others like a worm on a hook, but when they tried to grab them from her, she twitched them away at the last second. They split up to come at her from different directions. When she saw she was trapped, she pulled the front of her bodice open and dropped the sausages down her ample bosom with a smug smile.

Then, *her* eyes popped, and *her* skirt bulged and ballooned. And well, what else? Another moon-faced farmer's wife no more than two feet tall and round as a persimmon crawled out wearing the sausages like a necklace. She strutted around, showing them off like they were pearls, until the little dog, now dressed like a Cossack, jumped out of the basket, got his teeth in the sausages and ran off with all of them in hot pursuit.

The audience was still howling when the lights dimmed, the band struck up a fanfare, and a spotlight speared the center of the ring. The man who strode into the light was head to toe what you want in a ringmaster: tall, with a military bearing, gray at the temples, broader in the middle than he might have been at one time, but still impressive. He wore a top hat and a smart blue velvet tailcoat with silver braid, and he carried a silver-handled cane. He introduced himself as Herr Fischer, our host for an Encounter with the Extraordinary.

Over the next hour, we were treated to horses, acrobats, dancers, an array of exotic animals, including cigar-smoking monkeys in suits, an actual ostrich, a sleepy lion, an elephant wearing a red-plumed headdress, and horses again. The final act was "The Amazing Flying Vogels" on the trapeze, "Fresh from Command Performances for Kings and Queens of the Orient!"

A man and woman dressed in tight-fitting gold costumes trimmed with fluttering swirls of red feathers swept into the ring to loud cheers from the crowd. They bowed to the ringmaster, the audience, and each other, and then climbed their ladders to a long drumroll. The man's upright pole wobbled a bit more than hers, and I eyed the rigging again. But they both reached the top and stepped out onto their tiny platforms. I put it out of my mind. They set up this apparatus every few days. They must know what they were about. The wobble could even be part of the act, to add a hint of extra danger.

The man reached up for his swing, but just before his fingers grasped it, one of the two tether lines snapped with a loud twang. The pole tilted and swung downward, to screams from the audience. The remaining lines held, stopping its fall to the ground, but leaving the pole swinging at a steep angle. The man would have fallen to the ground far below, but his foot caught a ladder rung, and he dangled, unable to reach the other rungs with his hands. Even if he had, the pole was too unstable to climb down—or up. Crew and performers gathered below and held the edges of a round net to catch him if he fell, but it seemed too small to do much good.

The unbroken tether line on the downward side of the pole was a slack loop of rope that swung back and forth. The circus vanished, and I was aboard ship, climbing up swaying shrouds in a gale to untangle a torn sail before it took down the mast. I could do this. I took a running leap from my bench onto the swinging rope and climbed it straight up to the top as it lurched under my feet. When I got to the man, he was clearly in pain but calmer than I would have been. Without momentum to keep me upright, the rope slipped from under my feet. I caught it with my hands.

"Grab onto me and hold on tight, mate," I said. "We're going for a ride."

He nodded and wrapped his arms around my neck. I hooked my arms and one good leg around the line and slid the two of us down the tether line to the ground in a long swoop. Circus workers met us with a stretcher, but he waved them off. He slung an arm around my shoulder for support, smiled through gritted teeth, and swept his other arm triumphantly to the audience in a grand flourish. His partner joined us for a bow, and then he shook my hand and nodded for me to bow too.

The crowd roared as we left the ring. Backstage, two people hustled the injured man away, and I stood in a daze as performers and crew crowded around, clapping me on the back and shaking my hand. In the tent, the ringmaster talked up the death-defying feat they had all just witnessed, as if it was part of the show.

When the excitement started to die down, I looked around for Matya. She stood off to the side, holding the little dog in her arms, eyes vacant, her mouth pursed in a tiny half-smile. The two smaller farmer's wives stood next to her.

"So ..." I began.

The littlest one tugged my trouser leg. "Follow me, Sunshine." She had the same fluty, Russian-accented voice and intelligent eyes as the big one. "Herr Fischer wants to see you."

She led me out the back of the tent, the two larger women falling in behind us. I gawked at the bustling yard. Horses, crew, and wagons blended into a confused mass with dancers, acrobats, and clowns still in bright costumes. Dogs and small children dashed around underfoot, while the ostrich stepped over them. I looked down at Matya's ... little sister? Daughter? What was she?

"How many Blues are here?" I asked.

"You saw most of them tonight. We lost poor Karl last week." I was curious to know what happened to poor Karl, but she went on. "One of the Living Wonders is a Blue and so is the costume mistress. Now, you were saying you need to get to Berlin?"

"Yes. Did your, uh, sister tell you?"

"She didn't need to. We may look like three, but we're all one."

I looked back at the other two women. They nodded and smiled like serene Buddhas.

"That must get confusing."

She rapped my wooden leg with a chubby knuckle. "You're in more than one piece yourself. Are *you* confused?"

"I doubt my old leg is running around under its own steam," I said.

"Are you sure about that?" She burst into a peal of laughter. Behind us, the other two tittered like birds. "Here we are."

Herr Fischer's carriage was decorated all over with intricately carved garlands. CIRCUS FISCHER was painted across the side in elaborate blue letters nearly buried in silver and gold curlicues. The door was bright red.

Inside, a small, curtained-off section separated an office from what must be living quarters. It was cramped but neatly organized. Papers and ledgers filled niches built into the walls. Herr Fischer sat at a small, antique desk writing in a ledger. When he saw me, he jumped to his feet and strode around the desk to shake my hand. He was one of those hearty, vigorous people who always seem to be striding around even when they're sitting still.

"I can't thank you enough for what you did tonight. Tremendous! I've seen plenty of tightrope acts in my day, but I've never seen someone run up a loose line like that! Where have you been performing?"

"Well, I ..." I wanted so badly to tell him I was a seasoned performer and could step right in, but I had a pretty good idea how that would end, even if I could get the lie out. My nose itched, just thinking about it. "Aboard ship at sea is all, I'm afraid. The man … is he all right?"

"Nothing broken, thank heaven. We'll be without our trapeze act for a few weeks, but it could have been worse. Much worse! I'm sure the Vogels will want to thank you personally. Can I offer you a drink? I could use one."

He was already pouring brandy into two glasses, and I wasn't about to turn it down.

We drank, and he looked me over. I straightened and tried to look like a good hire, though I was thin and scruffy as a dockside stray.

"Well, thank you again. Matya will get you a hot meal. It's the least we can do."

If I was going to make anything of this chance, it had to be now. "Please let me stay. I'll do anything you need to earn my keep. I'm sure I could turn the rope thing into an act."

He didn't kick me right out, so I kept on babbling.

"I know I'm just a sailor, but a circus isn't so different from a ship if you think about it. Both are on the move most of the time. Crew lives aboard; everyone has a job and answers to the skipper. And isn't that big tent of yours just so much canvas, rope, and wood?"

"But with more elephants, I imagine."

"How do you think the elephants get here?"

He laughed.

"Son, I'd like to help you out, but it takes years to build a good act, even with as fine a start as yours. And we have all the crew we can support at the moment." He paused. "We are short a clown since we lost poor Karl."

I mentally rubbed my hands. "People have laughed at me my whole life."

He folded his arms across his chest. "Make me laugh."

Just like that? I was flummoxed. What could I do? But then I remembered I was a seaman with a wooden leg. Pirate!

I stamped my foot onto the floorboards in my best pirate manner.

"Arrr!"

Well, that was hilarious. Now what? A brightly colored silk scarf hanging from a hook caught my eye. I snatched it and wrapped it around my hand and forearm to make a makeshift parrot. A single black dot in the pattern of the fabric would do for an eye, so I cocked it toward Herr Fischer with a mutinous squawk.

"Make you laugh? Orderin' me around, are you? No landlubber orders old One Eye Quill around. I'm the meanest parrot from here to Cape Horn."

"Hush, you!" I scolded the parrot. "He'll make you walk the plank. He's the captain."

"Is he now? Well, sink me in the drink! I'm beggin' your pardon, Skipper. If yer feelin' disrespected, t'weren't my doin'." The parrot leaned toward Fischer and whispered, "I'd make the scurvy dog behind me walk the plank if I was you. What kind o' man goes around with his hand up a bird's arse?"

Herr Fischer was kind enough to chuckle.

"Well, I can't say you're a clown," he said. "But I do owe you for what you did tonight. I can't put you in the show, but work up the pirate character, and we'll see how it goes."

"That's all I ask!"

"You could ask for more grog!" protested One Eye Quill.

• • •

Matya was still outside. All three of her. Herr Fischer gave instructions directly to the little one. She nodded. The other two mirrored the nod a second later. It was a little unnerving.

"Come along, Sunshine," she said.

She pointed out the sights as we went. Like a ship, the circus traveled with everything needed to keep things up and running. There was a carpentry shop, blacksmith, and sick bay. One whole section was set aside as a menagerie for the animals, so maybe it was more like Noah's ark. Like any ship about to leave port, it swarmed with activity. All around us, people and animals lugged gear.

I felt like I should pitch in, but above the stink of dung, sweat, paint, and tar, my nose detected food, and my stomach growled loud enough to be heard over the hubbub.

Matya laughed. "Let's feed your lion."

We stopped at the cookhouse—a big tent that held the kitchen and long plank tables and benches. A few small clusters of performers sat here and there, hunched over their dinners. I tried to peer at them without being too obvious about it. Matya grabbed two plates of sauerkraut and beans with a hunk of brown bread perched on top and handed me one. I followed her to a table at the back corner.

"This is us," she said, plunking her bottom down on the bench, with a bigger Matya on either side, each with her own plate.

I sat across from her and tried not to inhale my whole dinner in one swallow, but they emptied their heaping plates as efficiently as any sailor.

"Thanks for helping me out," I said when we came up for air.

"You helped yourself out. What you did tonight?" She belched delicately and tapped her temple. "Fast thinking."

"Thinking didn't figure into it much."

Two men showed up to carry away the seating, so we got up and walked toward the performers' carriages lining the perimeter.

"I've got to work up a clown act. Any advice?"

"Your new roommates will be full of ideas. Whatever you do, don't listen to them."

"I suppose it might be easier if I didn't look so normal."

She gave me that piercing look again. "Trust me, Sunshine, you're anything but normal."

"What do you mean?"

She ignored the question. "Here we are!"

The clown carriage was the last one. The side was painted with fanciful caricatures of the clowns—some I recognized and a few I didn't. Maybe one was poor Karl. Matya led me around to the back.

WeLcOmE to the ToYbOx was painted above the door, every letter a different color.

"This is our half."

She opened the door and waved me in. My first impression was that it was well named. The cramped space overflowed with a motley jumble of balls, costumes, hats, bottles, makeup tubes, cigarettes, mismatched shoes, and even a unicycle. I stood blinking until a portion of the jumble organized itself into two men playing cards on an upended crate.

"Say hello to our new clown," said Matya.

The taller one was the soldier from the show, now in undershirt and trousers. He jumped to his feet and tripped on the edge of the rug and tumbled, sending a bucket of multicolored balls zinging in all directions. Somehow he ended up on his feet, bucket in hand, and caught every single ball.

He tucked the bucket under one arm and gave me a wide, giant-toothed grin and a handshake that just about dislocated my shoulder.

"God's chompers, that was well done tonight! Well done!" he said.

The frog thief hopped to his feet as well. He wore a green brocade dressing gown that was frayed to a fringe at the bottom. "Yes, quite the feat, son."

"Bossman says he's to have Karl's bunk," said Matya.

Four eyebrows rose.

"No offense," said the soldier, "but you'll have to find another bunk. This area is for Blues only."

"Nothing personal, son," added the frog. "Rules."

Matya planted her fists on her hips and glared up at them. "He is one hundred percent Blue. Now be nice."

The eyebrows went up even higher. I showed them my little patch of wood, and they squinted at it as if it was an ant dropping.

"It's not much," said the soldier. "But our Matya has the gift, and if she says you're one of us, then that is what you are!" He gave a smart salute. "I am Armond. At your service."

The frog bowed his head regally, pressing a long, slightly web-fingered hand to his breast. "You may call me Vrak." He drew it out in such a long croak—Vra-a-a-a-a-kkkk—that it was hard to keep a straight face, which was surely his intent.

Armond fished a walnut out of a pocket and popped it in his mouth. The shell cracked between his big teeth like a pistol shot. Vrak winced but went on. "I'd welcome you to our humble abode, but I'm afraid this rattletrap only *aspires* to humbleness."

He flicked his tongue out and snagged a fly right out of the air. It was so quick I thought I must have imagined it. I looked down to see if little Matya had seen it, but she was gone, and so was middle Matya. Big Matya stood alone, stroking the little dog and rolling her eyes.

"Just ignore it," she said in little Matya's voice. "It only encourages him."

This was going to take some getting used to.

She held up the dog. "And this is Ivan." Ivan stuck out a paw, and I shook it.

Armond waved a bottle of schnapps. "A toast to the hero of the night, what do you say?"

"Hear, hear!" said Vrak.

Matya assembled an assortment of glasses. Armond poured. I sat on an overturned bucket and drank out of a tin cup that tasted faintly of paint.

"That rope walking trick was very clever. I look forward to seeing the rest of your act," Vrak said.

"If I tried to do that on purpose, I'd break my neck," I said. "I need to come up with a pirate clown act, and to be honest, I don't have a clue."

"May I inquire why you joined the circus, then?" asked Vrak.

I told them what I'd told Matya and sighed. "Maybe I should have asked to work with the crew. I'm used to hard work."

"Now, now, none of that, son," said Vrak. "You performed tonight in style when the moment called for it. We saw it and, more important, Herr Fischer saw it, too, or he would not have sent you to us. Nothing personal against the roustabout class. Salt of the earth and all that. But there's roustabouts and there's *artistes,* and the choice, once made, is final. Surely *artiste* is preferable?"

It was, absolutely.

"Show us what you've got," said Matya, settling in with Ivan and a tin of biscuits.

My mouth went dry. Nothing like pressure! I reprised the pirate act for them, but it was even worse than the first time. A long silence followed, which I can tell you is not as gratifying as the roar of applause.

"It's not … terrible," said Vrak at last.

"Perhaps with the right costume," said Matya.

"And a proper peg leg," added Armond, though he looked doubtful.

"I'll take you to the costume shop tomorrow," said Matya. "Ursula will fix you up."

"Don't fret too much about it, son." Vrak clapped a skinny arm around my shoulder. "We all start somewhere.

Why, I was once a prince, and I can tell you, it was a struggle to adjust to my lowered lot in life. Whereas you have nowhere to go but up!"

"Don't listen to him," said Armond, cracking another walnut. "He was a little wind-up frog."

"Frog *prince*," said Vrak and fixed a bulging eye on Armond. "Please, tell us what war you fought in, General Nutcracker."

Armond loomed over him. "As soon as you tell us what puddle you ruled, you bloated tadpole."

Matya snapped at them in rapid-fire Russian. I didn't catch all of it, but it was clear I didn't need to worry about language for mixed company. They went back to questioning me as if nothing had happened.

Armond refilled my cup. "Now, I have to know. Were you a real pirate?"

"I suppose it depends on how you define it. I sailed with some pretty dodgy outfits."

"And the leg. Shark?"

"Shell."

Vrak nudged Armond. "A *real* soldier."

Armond bristled, but before they could go at each other again, the carriage jerked. Vrak pulled a beautiful—and familiar—watch out of his pocket and opened it with a snap.

"Would you look at the time!"

I patted my pocket and found it empty.

Matya whacked Vrak. "Give the boy his watch back, you scoundrel!"

Vrak handed it to me. "Just a small jest, son."

I gaped at him. When had he taken it? How?

Matya handed me a bucket, a rag, and a sliver of soap. "Go wash up, Sunshine. You're a bit ripe. Even for us."

I looked around the cramped space.

"Outside with you. There's time if you don't take all night about it."

Outside, a long line of carriages was already hooked up to horses and underway, but the procession was slow. I managed to swab myself down and catch up to the Toybox before it was loaded onto the train. I couldn't do much about my clothes.

When I came back in, the others were already in their bunks.

Matya and Vrak each had a lower bunk, Matya's with a curtain for privacy. Armond had somehow folded himself into an upper and was already snoring.

"Early day tomorrow," Matya called from behind her curtain.

I looked at the remaining bunk. It was occupied by two top hats, three wigs, crumpled tubes of greasepaint, several empty brandy bottles, an alarming number of cigar butts, and a green concertina. I moved it all to the floor and climbed in. The ceiling with its flaking paint was a hand's width above my head. But I was in a bed. It felt like years since I had slept in a bed. I yawned.

A train on its tracks feels different from a ship at sea, more rumble than sway, but it works the same magic when it's time to sleep. I was nearly out when a question popped into my head I hadn't thought to ask.

"When are we getting to Berlin?"

"Not sure," came Matya's groggy reply.

"Four weeks, I believe," said Vrak.

I banged my head on the ceiling. "Four weeks?"

"Too early in the year to go that far north, son. You can thank the shitty economy we're on the road this soon."

I flopped back down. Four weeks! I could walk there faster. In the morning, I would thank them and be on my way. But with no papers and no money and no allies, I might not get there at all. If I stayed, I wouldn't have to walk the whole blasted way; I'd have a roof over my head, food I didn't steal. After a lifetime of believing I was alone, I was bunkmates with three actual Blues. Or five, depending on how you count. Was four weeks really that long?

For the first time since I jumped ship in France, the knots in my chest loosened. Surely that was a sign I should stay. Or maybe it was the schnapps. But what about Papa? The knots tightened. No, I would definitely leave. First thing in the morning.

Of course, I did no such thing.

10

When I opened my eyes, it was still dark, but the train had stopped. The others were already up and bantering with each other as they got dressed.

"Sleeping Beauty wakes!" said Vrak.

I hopped down. "Should I go see about a costume?"

"No time, son. For now, just try to stay out of the way."

There was no "out of the way" inside, so I stepped outside. It was chilly, but a springtime softness in the air promised a warm day. Roustabouts already had the baggage cars off the train and hitched to horses. I joined a line of yawning performers at the mess car and was handed a roll with butter and a mug of coffee. Some of them remembered me from the night before, and I had to keep explaining that I wasn't an aerialist. I eventually got routed around to where I belonged with the low-status clowns and concessionaires and followed them to the fairgrounds—a flat field surrounded by row houses and shops in a middling sort of town. My dreams of fame faded a bit when I learned my job would be selling sweets and balloons to the locals.

Teams of men and horses rolled the tent out flat on the ground, while other men swarmed over and around it, laying out poles, stakes, and rope. Raising the center pole was a major event saved for when Fritzi the elephant showed up with the parade. But I loved this part. It took as much coordinated effort as rigging any ship. I wanted to pitch in but remembered Vrak's warning. I wasn't sure if hawking candy and trinkets made me an artiste, but I didn't want to risk my place in the Toybox.

The sun was high when the performers and animals arrived in a big, noisy parade, tailed by flocks of excited children and adults. Emma and Ernst Vogel led the way, seated atop Fritzi like a maharajah and maharani in white and gold. Ernst's ankle was bandaged, and he would not be performing on the trapeze that night, but he looked grand sitting way up there. They were followed by the fancier carriages, animals, acrobats, musicians, high-status clowns, and dancers.

Horses and men, with the circus or hired on the spot, went to work pulling ropes, and the crowd cheered when Fritzi raised the center pole. The only one who had the whole day off was Fluffy, the lion, who slept in his cage, twitching flies away with his ears.

The public doesn't see it, but setting up the backyard is just as interesting. To me, at least. The menagerie, cookhouse, lavatories, and everything else needed to house a crew as large as any sailing ship were all squared away by mid-afternoon.

Matya found me and took me to the costume shop, a carriage stuffed to the ceiling with bolts of cloth, sacks of feathers, jars of buttons and spangles, and stacks of hats and wigs. Costumes hung from rods at the front and back. In the center of it all sat a woman at a sewing machine. She was compact and softly rounded in excellent places. Short, silky brown fur covered every bit of her body that I could see, which had me speculating about the places I couldn't see.

"Ursula, this is our new clown, Pinocchio," said Matya.

She put aside what she was working on and looked me up and down with predatory brown eyes. "Interesting." Her voice was low and a little growly.

"He's a Blue," Matya added.

I held up my wrist.

She squinted at it. "Well, isn't that cute!"

I felt like a grain of sand showing off to the beach.

"Do what you can with him," said Matya, and toddled off.

Ursula measured me with businesslike efficiency. Her fur, when it brushed my skin, was as soft as it looked.

"You got something in mind?"

"Pirate?"

"Fair enough. Haven't had one of those in a while."

"I used to sail a bit. And I have this." I rapped on my leg.

"Ha! I guess you *are* a Blue!" I let it go. Correcting people was getting tedious.

She dug through chests and boxes and racks. In a few minutes, she found a billowing white shirt without too many stains and holes; a green velvet frock coat worn shiny at the elbows; yellow and black striped pantaloons; scuffed black boots that only had holes on the bottoms; and an enormous black hat crushed on one side. She ordered me to put it all on and stood back, tapping a pensive finger on her chin. She added an ostrich plume to the hat.

"Better. But ..."

She pulled a heart-shaped pendant out from under her collar. It was like mine, but brass instead of wood, and it opened to reveal a tiny sewing kit. She extracted a needle, found a scrap of black fabric, and in a minute, I had an eye patch.

"There. Now that's a proper pirate!"

I swept my hat in a gallant bow. "My lady."

"Parrot would be good, but the closest we got is Tillie the Ostrich, and she's a bit testy."

"One moment," I said.

I poked through a basket and plucked out a bright scarf similar to the one in Herr Fischer's office. In a few twists, One Eye Quill was reincarnated.

"Avast, me beauty! They call me One Eye Quill," squawked Quill. "Prepare to be boarded!"

She threw her head back and laughed. Her mouthful of dainty, pointed teeth was a little disturbing, but I'd gotten an actual laugh!

"Good to meet ya, Quill." She turned to me. "Off you go now, both of you. Some of us have work to do. I'll come by the Toybox tonight, and we'll see what we can do about your parrot."

I stepped down from the carriage in my new getup with as much bravado as if it was my debut on the grand opera stage in Milan. A line of performers outside the door waited with expressions ranging from boredom to annoyance. A clown in sweat-streaked whiteface shoved a sack of sweets into my hands.

"Cover for me, would you?" he said. "I gotta take a piss."

And just like that, I was an artiste.

One thing I learned the first day is that a half-hearted clown is no clown at all. You might have the greatest act in the world, but if you're not all in, you might as well hang up your wig. I didn't sell a thing until I stopped wincing about how lousy I was and just went for it. I made fussy children walk the plank, pulled candy from ears, dueled with boys, and scolded Quill when he got fresh with the ladies. By dinner break, I was exhausted, still lousy, and sold out.

In the evening, I tried to help with props backstage but was invited to stay the hell out of the way. I learned the audience never sees the best part of the show. Herr Fischer's top hat went missing right at showtime, and he stormed around, shouting threats at anyone in earshot. It turned up in the monkey cage and had to be retrieved, repaired, and cleaned of monkey shit while the audience chanted for the show to start. When the bearded lady discovered one of the dancers oiling up the strongman—her husband—it took the intervention of the rest of the Living Wonders to avert murder. One minute before the human cannonball swept into the ring, she was still pinning dangling flame streamers to her costume and muttering a stream of blistering curses. The whole thing was a sweaty, smelly, preposterous melodrama. I loved it.

Later, when the last stragglers were gone and the circus buttoned down for the night, I hurried back to the Toybox. There hadn't been a chance yet to show my new friends the newspaper photo and see what they might know about the Blue Lady.

The Matyas were already there, lounging on their bunk, sharing a tin of butter biscuits. Little Matya offered me the tin. The other two Matyas also turned their wide eyes my way and blinked. If it sounds peculiar, it is. All I can say is, you got used to it.

Vrak and Armond came in a moment later. Armond had a bottle of brandy in his hand, and it was clear the two of them had a head start on us, drink-wise.

Once everyone had a glass, I was treated to a brutal thirty-minute critique of my first day's performance, only twenty-eight minutes of which deserved. They were just winding down when Ursula burst through the door, trailing bright feathers.

"Hand over the parrot," she demanded. "And some of that, if you don't mind." She nodded at the brandy bottle. Armond dug up another cup, wiped it out, and filled it. She threaded a needle from her locket and set about turning the scarf into a proper hand puppet. The Matyas nested themselves to make room. I'm too much of a gentleman to describe how that happens, so don't ask.

When everyone was settled, Matya gave me the perfect opening.

"So, Sunshine, what's in Berlin?"

"My Papa. Or he was. I saw a photo of him in the newspaper."

Vrak leaned forward and brushed a stray feather off my lapel. "In the newspaper! My, my. Is he someone important?"

Matya glared at him. "Hush. It could be a terrible tragedy, too."

"I don't think it's either. He was in the crowd at a political rally for that Hitler fellow."

"Does he support that bastard?" asked Armond.

"No! I have no idea why he was there. He would never even go as far as the end of the street if he could get out of it. I can't imagine what it would take to get him this far from home. There is one other thing I can tell you." I had no idea how they'd react. Maybe they saw her all the time and it wasn't a big deal to them, or maybe they'd forgotten her entirely. But my own heart fairly tap danced at the thought.

"He was with the Blue Lady."

The effect of my words was electric. They all sat up, talking at once and demanding to see the photo. Matya had to bang on a tray with a juggling pin to restore order.

I reached into my pocket for the newspaper and found it empty. I patted my other pockets but found only a few crumpled candy wrappers. The others immediately glared at Vrak, who played innocent until Matya smacked him. The folded newspaper materialized in his fingers.

I snatched it from him and unfolded it while they gathered around to look.

"So beautiful!" breathed Ursula. "Just like I remember her!"

Armond placed a hand over his heart and sighed dramatically. "That face. I'd know her anywhere."

Vrak pulled a monocle with no glass out of his waistcoat pocket and peered through it. "Indeed. I'd stake my kingdom on it. Son, no one has seen her in years. Most of us not since the day she made us and never at all in public. It must be something momentous, indeed, to draw her out of hiding."

"I know my Papa," I said. "It would take the end of the world to pry him away from home."

"Could it have something to do with the Manikins?" asked Armond.

"Manikins?" I asked.

"They're like Blues, but different," said Matya with a shiver. My pulse quickened.

"Murdering devils is what I call 'em." Ursula stabbed her needle through the fabric. "Ouch!"

"One of them got poor Karl," said Vrak. "Armond saw it happen."

"He just walked up to him and put his hand on his head like this." Armond spread his fingers across his forehead. Ice slid through my veins. "He must have had some kind of hidden weapon. Maybe something electrical. Karl's whole body jerked and shook. And then he just dropped. By the time I got there, poor Karl was dead, and the Manikin was gone." Armond buried his face in his big hands. "I should have stopped it."

Matya rubbed his back. "No one could have stopped it, doll."

"What are they? Where do they come from?" I asked.

"We don't know," said Vrak. "We have a theory that the Blue Lady has an enemy who is making Manikins the way she makes Blues."

"You probably haven't met any," said Matya. "We started hearing rumors about them last summer, but we didn't see one ourselves until poor Karl."

"I think I did meet one or two," I said. I told them about the Jewish baker and the Hitler Youth. They were as horrified as I was.

"Those bastards!" growled Ursula. "The Blue Lady should turn them all into toads!" She paused. "No offense, Vrak."

"You mark my words," said Vrak. "The Germans are going to regret making that brute chancellor."

"They're human bastards, though," said Matya. "Not Manikins."

"Right," I said. "It was the policeman who tried to arrest me. At first I thought he was a Blue. When he touched me, I felt the electric buzz, but not as strong as what poor Karl got."

"You're lucky to be alive," said Ursula.

Armond peered at the photo. "Look at that cold-faced son of a bitch. You don't suppose it's Hitler who's making them? It could explain why she's there."

Vrak scoffed. "He doesn't seem to have any trouble creating mindless followers the old-fashioned way."

Matya nodded. "I don't think it's him. The Manikins seem to hunt for Blues. Hitler's got bigger fish to fry. Why would he care about us? To him, we're no more than a few ants in the dirt."

"Then why go to his rally?" I asked.

"That's the mystery, son," said Vrak. "Of course, we'll help any way we can."

Armond stood and saluted. "I stand ready to go to battle for the Blue Lady."

"Stand down, toy soldier," said Vrak. "What we need is information. Let's keep our ears and eyes open and spread the word. If anyone else has seen her, we'll know quick enough."

"We Blues stick together," said Ursula, giving me a warm glance.

We Blues. It took my breath away.

One of the dancers poked her head in the door just long enough to yell, "Time to fish!"

Everyone grabbed coats and hats and ran out the door in a flash, leaving me alone and baffled.

Ursula stuck her head back in the doorway. "Come *on!*"

"Who goes fishing in the middle of the night?"

She gave an exasperated huff. "Do you ever stop asking questions?"

I followed her through the fence behind the carriages and into the shadows of the buildings at the edge of the fairgrounds where we caught up with the others. Armond led us through streets and alleys as fast as we could go while trying to stay quiet and out of sight. No streetlights lit our way or gave us away, but the moon was high and gibbous. Armond stopped and held up a hand. He sniffed the air. After a moment, I caught it too: horses.

He motioned for us to follow. We crept down a dark lane until we came to stables big enough for a dozen horses and looked around. No lights or signs of two-legged life, so we snuck inside and climbed the ladder to the hayloft. The horses shifted and nickered but otherwise ignored us. When we were settled in the hay, the others exhaled like deflating balloons.

"Funny place to go fishing," I said.

"In this case, we're the fish," said Vrak. "They call it a document check."

"In the middle of the night?"

Matya took up the explanation. "It's persecution. Stormtroopers sweep in and say they're looking for Communists, but it's an excuse to harass anyone they don't like."

"Which is anyone different. Jews, especially," said Armond. "But also, foreigners, deviants."

"Blues," added Ursula.

"Regular stormtroopers or …"

"We haven't seen stormtrooper Manikins ourselves," said Vrak. "But there are rumors."

"How long do we stay away?" I asked.

"An hour usually does it," said Vrak.

Ursula yawned and wriggled herself deeper into the hay. "This is a cozier spot than some."

For a little while, no one said anything. I leaned back and looked at the moon through the window.

"What's it like being able to pass as a normal?" Ursula asked me.

I swallowed a groan. I'd spent the first half of my life trying to prove I was human. Was I going to have to spend the rest of it trying to prove I was a Blue?

"I suppose I had it easier in some ways, but passing as a normal isn't the same as being one. Most of the time I feel like I'm just wearing a human body like a disguise."

"I never thought of it that way," she replied. "Maybe we're lucky to have our outsides match our insides."

"Maybe you can answer this. How is it possible that the same Blue Lady made all of us?" I asked.

"What do you mean?" asked Armond.

"Well, you and Ursula are German, yes?"

They nodded.

"Matya, you're Russian, right? And Vrak ... Hungarian?"

"Czech, though I'm impressed. I've been told my German is flawless."

Armond snorted. I forged ahead before they could get into another pissing match. "But the Blue Lady is Italian."

There was a brief silence.

"Son," said Vrak, "countries and languages are the creations of mortals. The Blue Lady is a being of magic. How could a mere line on a map contain her?"

I blinked while that thought worked its way into my head. It was so obvious I could have kicked myself.

Matya patted my hand and looked at me the way a mother might look at a dim but dear child. "Oh, Sunshine. Did you think only Italian toys wish to be real?"

. . .

When we got back to the Toybox, we were pretty sure it had been ransacked, though given its usual state, you might not be able to tell.

"Manikins or just normal Nazis?" asked Armond.

"Who knows?" said Matya.

Just normal Nazis. What a world.

We were all exhausted, but when I tried to sleep, ranks of stone-faced Manikins marched behind my eyelids. The thought of the gentle Blue Lady and my frail, old Papa taking on whoever was behind these monsters was horrifying. Then again, I shouldn't underestimate the Blue Lady. Turning puppets into people was more than a parlor trick. And Papa might be old, but the leg he made for me was still pretty damned incredible despite a decade and a half of constant abuse. Together they might not be so easy to stop.

Did they even need me to help them? What did I add that they couldn't manage to do on their own? I turned over and squeezed my eyes shut. I would figure that out when I found them. If I found them.

. . .

Morning came too soon, but we had a little more time before it got busy since the hard work of setup was done yesterday. We all sat together at the Blue table in the cookhouse, and I took advantage of the breather to bring up another matter.

"Do any of you know how a person might go about getting new papers?"

Vrak was all over it. "We deal with this all the time, son. You'll need an identity card and a work permit. I know a few people, but the best is a dry cleaner in Berlin—if you can afford him."

I reached into my pocket and pulled out Alidoro's watch, surprised it wasn't already in Vrak's hand. He peered at it closely, turning it over a few times.

"This is a fine watch. It will be enough. If we write to him right away, your documents should be waiting for you when we get there."

We spent the rest of breakfast concocting a false identity and profession for me to send to the forger along with Alidoro's watch. I would become Marco Costa, a construction manager from Florence visiting Germany to study building methods. I had enough carpentry experience to fake that if questioned.

• • •

In the circus, selling candy and trinkets was bottom of the barrel stuff, artiste-wise, but it seemed to be a popular job. I couldn't see why anyone was so keen on it until Vrak shed some light.

"You're not shortchanging?" he asked, incredulous.

He sat me down and gave me a lesson on palming coins that went way beyond pulling candy out of a toddler's ear.

"There's rules, though, son," he said gravely while I practiced. "Never take a coin from a child or a woman or the infirm or elderly. Only from someone who would not be undone by the loss."

Aside from the extra money, I liked the challenge of the game. Once I got to where I could palm a coin in half a dozen ways, I begged Vrak to teach me more sleight of hand. He taught me tricks but always left out the last little flourish that took it from trick to art.

"The only way to be a true master is to work it out for yourself."

One time, on the train between towns, he begged two walnuts from Armond and handed me one. He pulled a handkerchief out of his pocket, wrapped his walnut in a tight twist, and set it on the table.

"Put a mark on yours."

I scratched an X into the side of the nut with my pocketknife and dropped it into his palm. He held it up for everyone to see and then tossed it to Armond, who popped it in his mouth and crunched down. Then Vrak unwrapped his kerchief, and there was my walnut with my X on it! I went through bags of walnuts trying to duplicate it. He finally took pity on me and gave me a few hints, but even small children saw the switch.

Pretty much everyone had some kind of side hustle. Big Matya napped in the Living Wonders sideshow as Fat Sleeping Beauty while the other two told fortunes together.

"Can you really see the future?" I asked.

"Sunshine, there's no way to see something that doesn't exist. But I can see the present," she said, "which is a rarer talent than you might think and usually does the job."

"Can anyone learn to do that?"

"Maybe a little," she said. "But I have a lot more experience seeing inside than most people."

Armond's side hustle was simple but profitable. People put down money to see him crack or bend various things with his teeth. I swear I've seen him bite an oak plank clean in half.

I got on well with most everyone at the circus, but I felt a special kinship with the midnight fishermen—the Jews who worked in almost every capacity from the band to the crew; the Roma family who worked with the horses; the Living Wonders; and all the other outcasts who found a home here.

For circus people, the circus is your nation over whatever random patch of dirt you landed on when you were born or made. You might move from circus to circus, like sailors move from ship to ship, but your mates are always your mates. The few weeks I was there weren't anywhere near long enough for it to become my home, but it was long enough to want it to be. I had to keep rubbing the little heart around my neck, the way Greek sailors rub their worry beads, to remind myself I couldn't stay.

Maybe I'd come back when all this was over. I had to do something with my life. I was building a pretty good character as the Pirate, and if I could get the slack rope walking thing down, I had a great idea for a scene where I rescued a princess from a burning tower. Audiences would eat it up.

I rigged up a loose rope in the backyard and practiced on it, but I never made much progress. We had small children who could cross a tightrope on their hands, which was highly annoying.

"Maybe if you lay the rope on the ground," suggested Armond. He loved to mock my efforts. But I loved to drink his booze, so it was a fair trade.

"Don't listen to him, son," said Vrak. "What you need is motivation. Hang it thirty feet higher."

"Screw both of you," I replied pleasantly—then fell on my ass once again.

"Not everyone has my natural grace." Armond reached out to help me up, but when I pulled on his hand, he fell into one of his preposterous windmilling stumbles that landed him back on his feet as if nothing had happened.

"I'd like to see you do that with one leg!" I snapped.

He promptly executed a perfect tumble while holding one foot behind him. I gave up and left the rope to the children, who were getting the hang of it. The little brats.

As we walked away, Armond asked, "When you find the Blue Lady, are you going to ask her for a new leg?"

A new leg? Honestly, I don't know why I hadn't thought of it. But why not? And why not ask her to fix all the Blues? I had a sudden vision of myself as the hero of a grateful legion of flawless Blues. "I just might. You?"

He grinned wide and clacked his enormous teeth. "And give up these beauties? Not a chance."

"Oh, you should," said Vrak. "Cook could use more dinner plates."

"I pity you, Vrak. Truly," said Armond with a deep sigh. "Outside of fairy tales, no one wants to kiss a frog."

"Nonsense." He casually knocked Armond's hat off with a flick of his tongue. "There are some who would be desolate at the loss of my talents, and you know it."

Later, I asked Matya. She shook her head. "I like things the way they are. I am never lonely."

"One body to a customer works well enough for everyone else," I said.

"It would be like losing part of myself. I wouldn't be me."

I wanted to point out that I had lost parts of myself, and I was still me. But was I? If I never lost my leg, I might have stayed home, got married, had a family. I was as different from that version of me as I was from Matya. But wouldn't that also be me? It made my head pound to think about.

I was still musing about it the next day when Ursula waved me into the costume shop to drape the pieces of a waistcoat over my shoulders. She was always tinkering with my costume. Early on, she rigged up a proper pirate's peg leg, but it chafed and hurt like hell after ten minutes, and I refused to wear it. It gave me a fresh appreciation of Papa's skill.

I held out my arms while she pinned up the waistcoat. "Why do you think none of the Blues are changed all the way?"

"You don't know that. There could be a thousand perfect ones. It's the ones like me that end up in the circus. Where else we gonna go?"

"I'm not perfect, and I've been pretty much everywhere," I said.

"You count that pitiful patch of wood? What a princess."

"But if you could ask Blue Lady for a wish?"

"I'd wish for you to stand still so I can get this pinned!"

"Seriously, though."

"I like my fur. Don't know how normals aren't freezing all the time. Hold still!" She paused. "Maybe I'd wish for her to stay. I can't forget how she just stood there looking at me. She got this look on her face like I was a mistake or something. Maybe if I was perfect, she would have stayed."

She hadn't stayed for me either. Was a pitiful patch of wood enough to make me a mistake? "I'm sure she didn't think that."

"It was just for a second. Then she smiled and kissed me on the forehead and told me to be good."

"And just left you all alone?"

"No, of course not! I lived with an old seamstress who never had any children of her own. I had a roof over my head, and I learned a trade. Okay, that's good."

She helped me out of the waistcoat and tossed it on her sewing table. "I hated it, though. She wasn't mean or anything, and the work was all right, but I was so damn lonely. Can't go out with all that fur, young lady! What will people think? So, I sneaked out at night. And when the circus came, well, I learned there was a place for people who were too different for normal life."

Too different for normal life. That was it for me, too.

"I started out with the Living Wonders, but I hated all the staring. So, I started helping out in the costume shop, and now it's all mine."

She wrapped her arms around my waist from behind and pressed her warm little body close. It felt good. I knew she was interested in more than just talk, and I asked myself why I held back. She was a great girl, and it was beyond idiotic to still pine for Serafina. But I did.

"Tell me about her," Ursula murmured into my back.

Was I that transparent? I tried to protest, but she gave me a warning squeeze. "Uh uh. Think I'm stupid? Come on. Spill."

I spilled. The whole story. It was the first time I'd said one word to anyone about Serafina. When I got to the end of it, I felt scraped out, like a pot after the soup is gone. Ursula turned me around and put her face close to mine, forehead to forehead, nose to nose, eye to eye.

"Princess, life is like the circus. It doesn't ever stay in one place. You and your Serafina traveled together until she left. Now, you and me are traveling together until you leave. No sure things. No promises. When your circus moves on, you're on the train, or you're nowhere at all."

She pressed her lips to mine. I kissed her back and dipped my fingers into the soft fur under the hem of her blouse.

She nipped my ear with her sharp little teeth and growled low. "All aboard!"

11

Word about my Blue Lady sighting spread like the flu. There were only a few of us Blues at Circus Fischer, but performers and crew were always going from circus to circus looking for work. That had increased since the Nazis started shutting down Jewish-owned circuses. What we heard was both troubling and vague. Manikin sightings were on the rise. Blues were going missing or found dead. No one reported seeing the Blue Lady in person. Someone thought they might have glimpsed her in a newsreel at the cinema, but it went by too fast to be sure. The Vogels had been allies since the night I'd rescued Ernst, and they brought us a newspaper photo from a Blue aerialist at another circus showing the back of a slim, fair-haired woman in the crowd at another Berlin rally. It could have been her. Or it could have been anyone.

The closer we got to Berlin, the less time we had to think about it. Berlin was the big time for a small outfit like ours, and everyone was in a fever of preparation. If the right brass came and were impressed, it could be a fair wind in Circus Fischer's sails. For the whole week before we got there, the crew was busy around the clock repairing, painting, or polishing anything that could be repaired, painted, or polished. Extra practices and daring tricks kept the infirmary busy. Ursula vanished under a mountain of costumes that needed fixing or extra spangles or feathers. I tried to help her, but I was so inept with a needle she finally snapped her teeth and chased me out.

The approach to the capital brought other hardships, too. Especially for us night fishermen. There were more inspections, more uniforms in the stands, and more arrests. In Leipzig, armed soldiers dragged a man out of a matinee in front of his sobbing family and the entire shocked audience. Armond thought he saw a Manikin in Wittenberg, but he wasn't sure. If Matya had seen him, she would have known.

Herr Fischer floated the idea of pulling Vrak, Armond, and Matya from the show out of concern for their safety, but they swore to him they could hide in plain sight with costume and makeup tricks—like the harness Serafina wore to make her wings look fake.

We built extra hidey-holes. Some were tricky, like a false wall in the side of a carriage. Some were simple, like painting "Caution! Poisonous Snakes!" on the top of a large wicker basket. We wanted the Snake Boy to get in it, but he flat out refused. If you weren't near a hidey-hole when you needed one, you had to improvise.

I'd gotten into the habit of bringing Fritzi an apple from breakfast, and we were getting to be friends. I couldn't get over how neatly she plucked it out of my hand with her trunk. I didn't see the two Nazi soldiers come into the menagerie until it was almost too late.

I slipped inside Fritzi's enclosure and ducked under the half barrel she stood on during the show. Fritzi was a gentle old thing, but they didn't know that. I called for her to sit on the barrel and, wonder of wonders, she sat. Maybe I could be an animal trainer when I came back?

In a moment, the soldiers were outside Fritzi's cage. They sounded like the normal kind.

"Search the enclosure," one of them ordered.

"With that monster in there? You do it."

"It's just a dumb animal."

"Who could flatten me like a tank."

"I will report you to the commandant for cowardice."

A sigh and then the rattle of the latch. Fritzi, God bless her wrinkled hide forever, chose that moment to let loose a massive flood of urine that cascaded through the barrel staves and spread out through the dust and dirty hay on the ground. The soldiers' sniggers covered any sound of me gagging.

"Disgusting."

"I'm not going in there now."

"The new guy would do it without a blink."

"The Machine? Yeah. Cold as ice, that one."

"What does he want with those freaks anyway? Just shoot them all on sight is what I say."

"Right between their freaky eyes," agreed the other.

The Machine? Could they be talking about a Manikin?

I crouched in the puddle, listening, but heard nothing more. I had no idea if they'd given up, gone to get The Machine, or were lying in wait. I was about to pass out from the fumes when the elephant handler came back and offered Fritzi a treat. The look on his face when I crawled out from under the barrel would have been funnier if it wasn't me he was looking at.

"All clear?" I asked.

"All but the air around you."

I ran to the Toybox. It had been ransacked, and no one was there. Were they hiding, fishing, or taken? I changed out of my soaked clothes and went to look for Ursula. She was in the costume shop, snarling and sorting out the mess. When she saw me coming, she dropped an armload of satin and ran toward me, though she backed off when she got in sniffing range.

"Jesus, Pinocchio! Did you hide in the latrine?"

"In a way. Have you seen the others?"

"Not yet."

A dog barked, and a moment later, Ivan hopped in, tail wagging. He was the only one who was happy about the way I smelled.

Matya leaned in a moment later. "Oh, thank God you're safe! Did you hear? They arrested the Snake Boy."

My stomach dropped. "Oh no!" He was a good kid. "Manikin?"

"I don't know. Have you seen Vrak or Armond?"

We shook our heads. If my stomach had dropped any lower, I'd have needed a shovel to pick it up.

I washed up as well as I could. Then Matya and I put things back in some kind of order and fretted about Vrak and Armond.

They finally wobbled in, leaning on each other for support and reeking of beer. Matya was livid. "Really? We have a matinee in twenty minutes!"

"Stormtroopers," said Armond. "It was a narrow escape."

"We would surely have been apprehended if not for the refuge of a nearby drinking establishment," added Vrak.

"And you had to stay there and drink while the rest of us worried ourselves sick."

"There, there, little mother." Vrak patted her shoulder. "All will be fine."

Matya slapped his hand away. "The two of you!"

Armond sniffed at me. "It seems we're not the only ones who got pissed."

After the show, I told them what I'd overheard. Maybe The Machine was just a colder-than-average Nazi, but we didn't believe it. We'd had a close call with a Manikin.

Ursula borrowed Armond's razor and shaved her face and hands. She looked like a normal, brown-skinned woman, but it was so strange we begged her to grow it back.

She glared at us. "You only like me for my fur."

We apologized and promised we'd get used to it if that's what she wanted. But it itched her so badly, she gave up in a day, though it was weeks before she looked like herself again.

You might be wondering what plan I had to find Papa in a city of four million people. It's a good question and not one I had a good answer to. The best I came up with was to go to Hitler rallies and look for him there. One newspaper photo wasn't much to go on, but it was all I had. Aside from that, fate had led me this far. I'd trust in it to lead me on.

The day before we got to Berlin, Hitler flew to Munich. It was almost enough to make you think he wasn't such a nice guy. I decided to stay in Berlin as planned and wait for him to return. He had to come back sometime. Until then, I would lay low and try to find local Blues.

That night, the whole train stayed up late celebrating getting to Berlin at last. I drank too, but alone. Berlin meant an end to my time with the circus. Now that I had a taste of real family, being on my own again felt impossible. But Papa was real family, too.

• • •

The next morning there were so many hangovers, the cook served salted herring and gherkins for breakfast. It's a decent remedy if you can stomach it.

Herr Fischer was in a lather about the setup, but the worst thing that happened was that Fluffy wandered out of his cage and had to be lured back with the night's meat ration, leaving us a dinner of boiled cabbage and potatoes to look forward to.

The parade began as always, but to bigger and better-fed crowds than I'd seen elsewhere. The buildings lining the streets were bigger and heavier, too, as if Berliners believed the ground itself would fly away on the next breeze like a newspaper if it wasn't firmly held down. Our freshly painted wagons gleamed in the morning sun. Fritzi, white ostrich plumes billowing from her headdress, led the way from the train to the fairgrounds. Ernst and Emma Vogel rode atop her hulking shoulders, throwing candy and kisses to excited bystanders. Ernst still had a bandage wrapped around his ankle, but he would be on the trapeze that night. Horses pulled the wagons and animal cages, jugglers juggled, dancers danced, and acrobats tumbled. The band had worked their usual folksy waltzes and marches into something like hot jazz.

My papers weren't expected until night, so I still had all day with the circus. I knew I should make the most of my last day, but it all felt distant and blurred like I was outside a fogged window peering in. When I found my eyes welling up over a bucket of tent stakes, I went and ducked my head in the water trough.

Ursula dragged me off to one of the empty baggage cars for a private farewell, but even that made me sad.

"I promise I'll come back," I said.

She cuffed me playfully. "Don't you dare! I got your replacements all lined up."

Then someone was calling her name, and she had to go back to work.

Before the evening show, I wandered back to the Toybox to change into my street clothes. When I got there, the others were finishing up their makeup.

"Son, you look sorrier than the last fly at a bullfrog buffet," said Vrak.

"Hey, Sunshine," said Matya, handing me a large envelope. "This came for you."

My papers. My new identity card looked real enough. Marco Costa of Florence, Italy. The dark-haired man in the photo wasn't me, but close enough to pass a casual inspection. There was a work card identifying me as a construction supervisor and a letter of introduction in German. I silently thanked Alidoro again for the watch that had paid for this miracle. Vrak gave me a leather wallet to keep it in.

I looked around at my friends, and my eyes filled with tears. "I … I think I better go now."

"God's chompers! You'd deprive us of a proper celebration?" said Armond. He held up the bottle in his hand. "And I don't mean this swill."

"Indeed!" Vrak said, rising to his feet. "Every great venture deserves a bottle of champagne smashed across its bow, wouldn't you say, Mr. Costa?"

Matya planted her fists on her hips and glared at them. "After the show."

If I was staying for a party, I might as well go watch the show one last time. I needed to get used to being an outsider again, so instead of watching from backstage, I took a seat in the back of the stands. I'd left Italy with hardly a glance back. Twice! Thumbed my nose at the sea after fourteen years. But a few weeks in the circus, and leaving it felt like losing a limb.

The house was packed. Hitler Youth beetled up and down the rows, rattling their collection cans in everyone's faces. Plenty of uniforms were in the seats, but I didn't see anyone that looked like a Manikin. Vrak, Armond, and Matya had done such a good job with their costumes that even I found myself wondering if they were Blues. Their routine was a hit, as always, and no one stopped the show. The musicians struck up the fanfare, and Herr Fischer strode into the spotlight, looking unruffled and confident as ever.

I spent most of the show scanning the audience for Papa or the Blue Lady, as if my mere presence would magically draw them here. Afterward, I sat like a sack of sand until the tent was empty.

As I trudged away, I stuck my hands in my pockets. My fingers hit something with a sharp corner. It was a card with a picture of a cat's paw print on it and underneath, the words DIE KATZENTATZE and an address. I flipped it over. Nothing on the back.

Who had slipped the card into my pocket? Who even knew I was here? It could just be a come-on from a bar, but I didn't believe it. A rush of excitement tightened my skin.

The others were waiting for me in the Toybox. The glasses were out, and Armond held a bottle of champagne in his hand. He pulled the cork with his teeth.

"Show-off," said Vrak.

Armond ignored him and filled my glass. "Where will you start?"

I handed him the card. "This was in my pocket. Someone must have slipped it to me in the tent."

"The Cat's Paw?" said Armond. "It sounds like a club. Are you going to go?"

"Absolutely."

"Be careful," said Matya.

"Maybe I should go with you," said Armond. "In case it's a trap."

Poor Armond. He wanted so desperately to be worthy of his soldier's uniform. I understood. Who knew better than me what it's like to feel like a fraud? I slung my old rucksack over my shoulder and shook my head.

"I've got this," I said. Famous last words.

• • •

My new identity card felt like armor. I mentally dared every cop I passed on the street to stop me so I could test it out. But of course, none of them did. I even asked one for directions, and he was politely helpful, the son of a bitch.

I found the address at the end of a quiet street lined with hulking apartment blocks. It was so dark I had to light a match to read the number. Chips and peeling paint showed the door had a colorful history but let on nothing about what was on the other side. I straightened my jacket and rang the bell.

The man who answered had on so many layers of moth-eaten sweaters, he resembled the door. I held up the card.

"Blue or normal?" he asked. He looked like a normal.

"Uh … normal."

"Two marks."

"What if I'd said Blue?"

"Then it's free."

I decided it was better to pay up than show my hand before I knew more.

At the end of the hall, a hand-lettered card in a tiny brass frame nailed to the door read DIE KATZENTATZE BUCHHANDLUNG. A bookstore? I put my hand on the worn brass handle and pushed the door open.

It was a bookstore, in the sense that there were books. But it wasn't like any bookstore I'd ever imagined. Books filled shelves up to the ceiling, spilled out of umbrella stands, and were stacked on every step of a spiral staircase except for a path in the middle. Tucked between the books were taxidermy birds, rodents, and reptiles, and jars of unidentifiable pickled things. Enameled vases sprouted dusty feathers, palm fronds, swords, and even an African spear. Leering masks, lace fans, clocks, and dolls hung on the walls. Wine bottles and glasses crowded every remaining horizontal surface.

The rest of the floor was taken up with Blues. Everywhere I looked. Fifty? A hundred? The babble of conversation almost drowned out the operatic warbling from a gramophone.

A gray-whiskered man with a towering pair of white rabbit ears and shoulders as broad as two of me shoved a glass in my hand. He wore gold hoop earrings and a white satin evening gown that strained to contain his hairy chest.

"First time?" he asked.

"Yes. I'm supposed to meet someone."

"Aren't we all!" He laughed, and when his ears wobbled, I realized they were fake. He wasn't a Blue at all but a normal dressed up like one. I looked around and realized that most if not all the people I'd taken for Blues were normals in costumes. I'd seen clubs where the boys dressed like girls and the girls dressed like boys. But I'd never imagined a club where humans dressed like Blues. I was the most normal-looking guy in the place by a good margin. Was I the only actual Blue?

I squeezed into an empty spot next to a moth-eaten stuffed polar bear in the corner and tried to get my bearings. In the center of the room, small groups were deep into heated debates. The corners and nooks held couples. I didn't see any that looked like Manikins.

I searched for a familiar face or an unfamiliar face searching for a familiar one. Was there anyone here I'd seen in the audience at the circus? I wished I'd paid more attention. I wouldn't find out standing by a bear, so I took a breath and waded in, listening for clues. Everyone seemed to be a normal, and a lot of the talk revolved around politics and the sharp increase in Nazi brutality under the new chancellor. At least this crowd didn't seem to be in favor of it.

I finally did meet a Blue. His head was on a spring, but he'd hidden that under a scarf and was passing as a normal dressed up like a tin soldier. We exchanged names, and I told him I thought someone was looking to meet me here.

"Watch out. There are some crazy stories going around lately."

I asked him what he'd heard. They were the same rumors I'd heard before. He hadn't seen anything himself.

"Do you think it's true?"

"Trust me. It is."

He shook his head. "As if things aren't bad enough these days with just Nazis."

I picked my way downstairs. It was just like upstairs but with the addition of the remains of a feast eaten down to pools of gravy and a smashed carrot on a table in the middle of the room. In one corner, a crowd gathered around a pale teen who had bent his body into a tight pretzel with his legs passed in front of his shoulders and tucked through his armpits. He waddled around on his hands while people gave him sips of their drinks and tucked money in his pockets. I wouldn't call that normal, but he wasn't a Blue, either.

"You ever think about trying out at the circus?" I asked.

"Too much work. I make more in one night here than I could in a month anywhere else."

No one seemed to be looking for me here. Someone had given me the card for a reason. Where were they?

Back upstairs, the large cuckoo clock on the wall struck one, and a tiny naked woman popped out and ran around the track pursued by a tiny but impressively endowed naked man.

I found an unoccupied corner between an orgy tableau of taxidermy mice and a tureen of glass eyes and settled in to wait. I'd wait all night if that's what it took. I had nowhere else to be.

The party settled into a quieter phase. Committed debaters huddled in twos and threes, and couples canoodled in dark corners. I rested my head against the tureen and tried to see the bright side. I was no worse off than I was before I'd found the card.

I must have dozed off because I was startled awake by a hand on my shoulder. I peered up at a tall ginger-haired man in a finely tailored, brown wool suit. Beside him stood a short, burly man with bushy side-whiskers and a tweed flat cap. They looked vaguely familiar.

"Please excuse me for disturbing your reverie," the tall one said in Italian. "But are you, by any chance, Pinocchio?"

I blinked at them in disbelief, scrubbed my eyes because I had to be dreaming, and blinked again. They were still there. I leapt to my feet, ready to punch both their lights out.

12

If you read that book about my wooden boyhood or my boyish woodenhood, you might remember those two thieves, Fox and Cat. They weren't a fox and a cat in real life, of course, but the comparison suited them well enough. I'd come into a bit of money—not gold coins as it says in the book, but more money than I would see in one place again for a long, long time—and when they couldn't get it from me by thievery, they got it by trickery. Now, impossibly, they'd found me again, more than a thousand kilometers from home. How? And why?

"Please," said Fox. "May we have a word?"

My gut told me there wasn't a word he could say that I should believe. But why had they come all this way? How had they found me? I wasn't that naïve little puppet anymore. I knew a thing or two about liars, whether their noses grew or not.

I lowered my fists. "Well?"

"If you don't mind," said Fox. "It's not something we can speak of openly. Would you be willing to step outside for a moment?"

I sighed and followed them out the door. The rain had stopped, but pre-dawn fog gave the air damp, cold fingers. I stopped and crossed my arms.

Fox glanced around. A drunk lolled on the pavement nearby, but he wasn't paying us any attention. He leaned forward and spoke in a low voice.

"There is an urgent situation involving people known to you. I can't say more, but you must come with us right away."

"Right away," echoed Cat.

I snorted. "How stupid do you think I am?" I turned and started to walk away.

Fox said, "Without our assistance, you will have a hard time finding your father."

I swung back around, grabbed his lapels, and got right in his face. "What do you know about my father? Tell me what you've done to him, Fox, or I swear to God, I will knock your teeth right through the back of your head."

"Please. We are not your enemy nor your father's. We're here to help. The Blue Lady sent us."

He was lying, of course. But how did they know about the Blue Lady? How did they know Papa was missing? How did they know I was here looking for him? I wanted to just kick both their asses and be done with it, but what if they knew something?

"Why should I believe you?" I asked.

"Naturally you are skeptical. We completely understand. Which is why we brought proof. Mr. Cat?"

Cat pulled off his left glove and held his hand in the lamplight. I froze.

Plenty of people had wooden bits and pieces since the war, including me. Cat had not lost his hand in the war, but because of me. If you believe the book, I bit it off with my wooden boy's teeth in revenge for cheating me. That's preposterous, of course. I only bit him hard enough to break the skin, and then it festered. But that memory is not what stopped me. The wooden hand he wore fit his wrist like it had grown there. Its glossy curves were so natural I expected it to be warm and soft as flesh to the touch. Every joint, down to the last pinkie knuckle, was perfectly and almost invisibly articulated. And it was new. He flicked the fingers and they moved easily, making a sound like castanets. Only one person could have made that hand.

I rounded on Fox and slammed him against the brick wall. "Where is he?"

"There's no need for violence," said Fox. "We can take you to him immediately."

"Not a chance. You bring him here."

"I'm afraid that's impossible. As you know, these are dangerous times. Both your Papa and the Blue Lady herself have been forced into hiding."

I thought of the Manikins and the Blue deaths and disappearances. I knew the Blue Lady had a powerful enemy. These two might be liars, but that hand was no lie. It was absolutely Papa's work. And it wasn't stolen, either; the fit was too perfect. That didn't mean they'd gotten it honestly. But it did mean they'd been in more than casual contact with him. And recently.

I had to go. It was infuriating, but what else was I going to do? Wander around Berlin asking strangers if they'd seen an old man or maybe a woman who used to have blue hair? I had to go. But I'd keep my eyes open this time.

Reluctantly, I let go of Fox. He straightened his jacket. "I admit our first meeting was unfortunate. We deeply regret any inconvenience you might have experienced because of it."

"Regret," echoed Cat.

"Inconvenience? You hung me in a tree and left me to die!"

He looked me up and down. "You seem to have recovered well enough."

"No thanks to you."

"Pinocchio, please. Let's not rehash the past. Your father and the Blue Lady are most anxious to be reunited with you, and there is no time to waste."

"Let's just get this farce over with."

They led me past blocks of buildings wedged so close together there wasn't room between them to slide a knife blade. Fox stopped in front of one of them and flipped through the keys on his key ring. I looked up at the dark-eyed windows. Was Papa behind one of them? Fox found the key he was looking for and let us into a dusty, unlit lobby with a staircase on either side and a sour-smelling mop and bucket in the corner. We didn't go up either staircase but straight through the opposite door into a central courtyard. A padlocked shed stood in a corner. Fox opened it with another key. Cat dragged the door open, ducked inside, and rolled out a motorcycle with a sidecar that had seen a lot of terrain but looked well-cared for.

"Wait a minute. They're not here?"

"It's a secret location," said Fox.

"You expect me to just get in and go with you to some secret location?"

Fox sighed. "I can't make you believe me. It's your choice. I won't keep you. I'll just have to tell your Papa we did the best we could." He turned away.

"Oh, come on, this has gone far enough! I'm not going to fall for your lies this time. What are you really after? Do you want mon—Ow!"

I felt a bee sting and swatted my neck. When I turned, Cat was there with a hypodermic in his hand and an apologetic expression on his face.

"You goddammed bastards!" I took a swing at him but staggered and missed. My head was rapidly filling up with fog.

• • •

I woke up cotton-headed, dry-mouthed, and wedged into the sidecar. A deep, thrumming roar rattled my teeth. We were stopped at a railroad track where a freight train thundered past, car after car after car. The sun was high in a pale blue sky. The air held a brisk chill, and dense pine forest lined the road on either side. Were we in the mountains? I must have been out for hours. I struggled to climb out, but my legs might as well have been logs.

"Ah, you're awake," said Fox with a smile. "Almost there."

The last train car passed. Cat gunned the idling motorcycle and swung out alongside the tracks. He drove with surprising skill for someone who didn't seem able to string more than two words together. We drove in the same direction the train had gone.

The forest grew denser. Soldier-straight trunks crowded closer to the tracks. Moss and ferns furred the ground between clumps of old snow. The track joined up with a river. We didn't pass a single crossing or house. I was still trying to shake the fog out of my head when we rounded a bend, and a large compound of low block buildings dominated by a single round tower came into view. A prison? Bile burned the back of my throat, and I choked it back. Shit. Instead of searching for Papa in Berlin, I'd let myself be delivered into captivity.

The tracks led through a massive iron gate into a courtyard in the center of the compound where the train had stopped. Men unloaded wooden crates and carried them into a stone building dug right into the mountainside. No one stopped us or even looked our way as we rumbled past. Cat veered sharply into an open garage and swerved to a practiced stop where a young soldier holding a rifle waited. Cat and Fox hopped off, and I pushed myself out of the sidecar, torn between wanting to throttle them and wanting to run. I couldn't do either.

My good leg buzzed like it was full of angry hornets. I collapsed on the ground, cursing, and by the time I struggled to my feet, Fox and Cat were nowhere in sight. The soldier gestured with his rifle for me to follow him. I managed, though my knees tried to buckle with every step. The garage was spacious and neatly swept. Solid, stonework walls were stacked high with pallets and empty crates. At the back, three concrete steps led up to a heavy timber door with iron fittings. We went through it and down a corridor of the same stone, painted a cheery sky blue, to a metal staircase spiraling up and down. I followed him up to the first landing. He knocked, opened a door, and gestured me through. I stepped into a small, tidy office, and the door clicked shut behind me.

A slender woman at the desk stood and turned. My heart raced, and tears stung my eyes. I tried to speak, but I couldn't remember how to exhale.

It had been almost twenty-five years since I'd last seen the Blue Lady. Her blue hair was now nearly white, and instead of tumbling over her shoulders, she wore it swept back along the sides of her head like swan wings, but aside from that, she had hardly changed. A thousand imagined reunions never even came close to the joy that lit her face now. She took my cold hands in her warm ones.

"Pinocchio." Her voice was low and musical and as full of warmth as I remembered. It nearly brought me to my knees. "Thank you so much for coming."

She spoke in the Tuscan Italian of my youth, and even though I was a grown man, I wanted to lay my head in her lap and weep like a child.

"What is this place?" I asked when I could form words. "Are you a prisoner?"

"Hardly! I know it must look alarming, but I assure you it's all for our safety."

"Is Papa here?"

A furrow creased her smooth brow for the briefest instant, and my throat tightened. "He's away at the moment doing important work." She squeezed my hands. "He'll be so excited when he hears we've found you at last. I know he'll hurry back as fast as he can."

I was disappointed, but a day ago, I had no idea how I would find either one of them. This was a definite step forward. "You could have picked better messengers to come after me."

She smiled. "Those two may be rascals, but they've known you almost as long as I have, and they have unique skills. I don't think anyone else could have managed it. You're not easy to find, you know!"

That was true. I'd made a career of being hard to find.

"None of that matters now," she went on. "You're here, and we can move forward at last!"

"Move forward with what?"

"Good things! The best! I can hardly wait to tell you all about it! But you've had a long journey, and you must be hungry and tired."

She led me up the spiral staircase. At the top, she unlocked a door and led me into a cozy room. Glossy little tables covered with lace doilies flanked a long settee upholstered in blue with yellow flowers. A fire crackled in a cheery hearth, and a clawfoot tub with a stack of white cotton towels beside it hugged one corner. I must have looked like a country hayseed, with my mouth hanging open at the sight of a bathtub, but most of the baths in my life had involved a bucket of cold water, and even those were rare enough.

She laughed musically. "Take as long as you like. There are clean clothes in the cabinet. I have some things I must do, but I'll come back in a few hours, and we'll have a good, long talk." She squeezed my hands again, and I swear she had tears in her eyes.

After she left, I filled the bath with steamy water, unstrapped my leg, and hopped in. I refilled the tub three times and went through an entire cake of soap before the water stopped turning gray. I shaved and then sat on the edge of the tub, cleaning as much grime as I could off my leg and oiling its pocked surface.

The clothes in the cabinet were far better than any I'd ever had. White button-down shirt, gray wool trousers, waistcoat, and jacket—they all fit perfectly. The tie defeated me, but I put on the swank tweed flat cap and admired myself in the mirror. Not too bad!

I was still posing when the door opened and a soldier brought in a tray with a silver cover. He placed it on the table and left without a word. When I lifted the lid on the tray, I found a full meal: an actual steak, pink in the middle, mushrooms, white beans with sage and garlic, warm bread with butter, a bowl of sugared strawberries, coffee, and a little pot of cream. I finished every bite, then ran a finger through the gravy on the plate and licked it off. I felt like a new man.

The door opened, and I jumped to my feet. She stepped in.

"Well! You look refreshed!" Once again, her smile reduced me to a tongue-tied boy. She sat on the settee and patted the cushion beside her. "Come sit. I'm sure you must have a hundred questions."

A thousand was more like it, and they tumbled around my head until the first random one popped out.

"When you changed us—the Blues—why didn't you change us all the way?"

She tilted her head sympathetically. "It might seem strange to you, but even magical beings were young once. Everyone struggles and learns. It's always been my hope to bring you all back and complete what I started."

"I don't know about the others, but it's been twenty-three years for me."

"That must seem like a long time to you. But now that you're here, it will all be done very soon."

I didn't care about the patch of wood on my wrist. It would be nice to have my leg back if that was possible. But my most unfinished parts didn't show—the puppet boy that lived inside my human skin and kept me apart from others, refusing to be either fully human or fully Blue.

"You look troubled," she said. "Tell me what it is, and I'll try to help you."

"I don't think even your magic can fix me. I'm …" I choked up, and the words I needed fled. "Not unfinished. Broken? Separate?" I put my hand over my heart, hoping she'd understand.

Her smile spread across her face like the sun returning after an arctic night. "Yes! Oh, Pinocchio. Yes, that, most of all! The only thing that truly matters is what beats in your heart and the unbreakable bond that connects us."

For a moment, I felt unbalanced. Like I was teetering on the edge of a cliff. Then I was lifted by wings of hope that carried me up and up and up. That was what I was missing. The bond.

When I looked at the Blue Lady again, she had tears in her eyes, and her face was grave. She stood, walked to the window, and looked out. "I'm so sorry for how much you and the others have suffered, but I promise I'll make it up to you. To all of you. For years, even I didn't understand what was missing. Why should I have this amazing gift, this power, only to use it to turn toys into living beings? It seems silly if you think about it."

It hadn't seemed silly to me, but maybe it would to living beings created the usual way. Or however she had been created.

"It took many years, but God finally revealed his greater purpose for me. It still humbles me every time I think about it." She turned, and her beautiful face was fierce with passion. "There is so much pain in the world. Suffering and hatred and loneliness without end. Not just you and my other children, but everyone, everywhere. We are barely past a terrible war and are already on the path to another that will be even worse."

I thought of all the boys from home who had died in the war. I thought of Snake Boy and poor Karl and the Jewish baker. I thought of the Fascists, the Nazis, the Manikins. Evil was eating up Europe like a plague of rats.

"What if I told you there is a way back to Eden, where everyone lives in perfect peace and goodwill? And what if I told you it was in my power to make it happen?"

She looked in my direction, but her eyes were so full of her vision of the future, I doubt she saw me at all.

My mouth dropped open. "You're going to save the world? All by yourself?"

"I'm not all by myself. I have you."

I couldn't hold back a bark of laughter, but it turned into coughing when I saw she was serious. "Me?" I sputtered. "I can't even save myself!"

"I know it sounds mad. But hasn't that always been God's way? An ordinary person is called to an impossible task, and somehow miracles happen."

She sat next to me and gave me that heart-melting smile. What did she see in me? I suppose Moses thought he was just a regular guy, didn't he? I shook it off. I had to put a stop to this nonsense before I started believing it myself.

"I hate to disappoint you, but you've got the wrong guy."

"My dear Pinocchio. You are more special than you know. If you think about it very hard, you'll understand."

I shook my head. I could think about it very hard for a hundred years and still come up not special. Especially not in a world-saving way.

"Let me show you."

She pulled a chain out from the collar of her blouse. A golden pendant about the size of a walnut dangled from it. At the turn of a tiny latch, it popped open, and she tipped the contents into her cupped palm. A blue jewel, smooth as an egg, glowed from its cloudy interior with a gently pulsing light so mesmerizing, I felt sure I knew what blue sounded like. When I bent closer, I saw that the surface was etched with nearly invisible lines and swirls that could have been writing or the scuffs and scars of great age.

"I call this precious jewel the Heart of God."

The Heart of God. Its power pulled me toward it the way the North Star draws a compass needle. I wanted to dive into its lagoon depths headfirst.

"You've seen its light before. Do you remember?"

The last day I had seen her—the day she made me real—blue light had cascaded from her hands. I never saw a jewel, though. I always thought the light came from her.

She took my hand and held it above the jewel in her palm. She hesitated, hands trembling, and took a shaky breath.

"I have never let anyone even see it before, much less touch it. I must warn you, it's very powerful. But it won't harm you, I swear. Do you trust me?"

I nodded.

"Close your eyes."

I closed my eyes. She brought my hand down, clasping the jewel between our palms. The instant my palm touched the jewel, the darkness exploded. A blinding blue sun blasted through me with explosive force. The breath was torn from my lungs, and I feared my body would fly to pieces. I jerked my hand away, breaking the connection, extinguishing the sun. The jewel went flying, hit the floor with a crack, and rolled under the table. She dived after it and came up clutching it to her chest, panting wildly. Strands of pale hair clung to her damp, flushed face.

She closed her eyes and slowed her breathing. "Give me a moment."

A moment? I might need a year. She got to her feet and left the room, shutting the door behind her.

I tried to catch my breath. Powerful didn't begin to describe it. And she held it in her hand as casually as you'd hold a plum. But there was something else threaded through all that energy. I couldn't shake the feeling that it *knew* me. I shivered. I paced the room, splashed water on my face, took deep breaths. I reminded myself I was safe. This was the Blue Lady. The one who had sheltered me through my wayward youth, who gave me the gift of life, who Papa trusted enough to leave home for.

When she came back a few minutes later, she was smiling and composed, though she looked a little tight around the eyes. She sat down and looked at me with concern.

"Please forgive me, Pinocchio. I've become so used to the Heart of God that I forget how truly strong it is. If you're willing to try again, I can put myself between you and the Heart of God, to protect you. Will you give me another chance?"

She showed me the jewel in her right hand and held out her left hand to me. I hesitated.

"It's all right. I promise."

I touched her hand with a fingertip, ready to pull it back. Light filled my head. The jewel still blazed bright, but it seemed tamed. She wrapped my hand in hers and pulled me down to sit beside her. I closed my eyes. Threads of light flowed from the jewel, through her and into me, turning our bodies into a swirling river of pulsing light. The current was strong, but I could swim in it without drowning.

"Is that better?"

"I think so."

"Now, look outward, away from the Heart of God."

I tore my attention away from the blue sun and was surprised to see that we were in the middle of a dazzling sweep of stars, more stars than a moonless night at sea. They glittered against velvet darkness in every direction.

No, not stars. Stars are frozen and distant. These lights were suspended around us like sultanas in a cake, some far and others close by. And these stars weren't frozen; they trembled and winked. The closest ones crept across the sky, or whatever the darkness was.

"Every point of light is a living soul," she said.

"It's beautiful!"

"Yes, it's beautiful, but not as beautiful as it could be. Do you see how each one is unconnected to the others? You told me yourself you feel separate and broken. You've been wandering your whole life without direction or purpose."

Yes, yes, and yes.

"Nearly everyone lives this way—blind and alone, believing emptiness is all there is because it's all they've ever known."

I was one of those wandering stars, lost in the coldness of space. I shivered, and she squeezed my hand.

"Keep looking. What else do you see?"

I didn't see anything at first. But then I noticed that a few of the stars seemed to have faint tails, like fine blue threads. Those threads led back to the pulsing blue sun.

"Some are connected to the jewel," I said.

I couldn't see her smile, but the warmth of it radiated through our joined hands. "Those are my precious doves who are bonded with me through the jewel. It took many years and many failures, but I learned. When the Heart of

God beats within you, it's impossible to be alone, impossible to be lost, impossible to make a wrong step. Everything and everyone you need is there for you. That's what I want for all of you."

"I still don't see how I fit in."

"So far, the only way I can save them is in person, one by one. They are spread out too far. Finding them and bringing them to me is far too slow. I can't bear to think how long some will have to suffer and wait. Some I might never reach at all. But with your help, that will change."

"How?"

"Just hold my hand and watch."

She gathered light into herself and sent it flowing from her along a thread to a star that pulsed at the far end. A cobbled street lined with small shops overlaid the stars like a cinema projected on the sky.

"We are looking through the eyes of one of my doves."

A girl hurried by. She was wrapped in a shawl, her head down. We followed her, and I heard footsteps on cobbles.

"Sylvie," said the Blue Lady. Her voice was doubled by a lower one.

The girl froze.

"Don't be afraid. I'm here to help you." She spoke in French. Was this a street in France?

The girl looked back over her shoulder. She was a Blue. She looked like a normal girl, maybe fifteen or sixteen years old. Her pretty face was covered with fine white fur except for a small, pink nose. Her gray eyes were wary.

"What do you want?" she whispered.

"My dear child," said the Blue Lady. "I may look different from when you last saw me, but you know me, don't you?"

Sylvie's mouth popped open, and she nodded.

"Come closer, dear."

She hesitated, then shyly stepped forward. A hand extended toward her—the Blue Lady's? The dove's? Mine?—

and touched her forehead. Sylvie stiffened; her eyes went wide, and she gasped. Just for an instant, she tried to pull away. Then joy suffused her face and she relaxed, standing straighter, taller.

"Is that better?" asked the Blue Lady.

Sylvie smiled. "Yes."

"Do you see that we will always be together now?"

Sylvie nodded. "Thank you."

The scene vanished, and I was back in the sea of lights. Where there had been one light connected to the jewel by a slender, pulsing thread, there were now two threads. Beside me, the Blue Lady glowed brightly, and the warmth of her joy poured into me like wine.

"I couldn't have done that without you," she said.

"I didn't do anything!"

"How do you feel?"

I was tired but also curious. What part had I played? "Are you going to connect me?"

She paused. "Not yet. You're not the same as the others, and I want everything to be perfect."

I still didn't know how I was different, but I couldn't deny that the jewel had treated Sylvie more gently than it had me. If the Blue Lady wanted to practice first, I was good with that.

She squeezed my hand. "Shall we try another?"

We flew through another thread. A dark-haired family sat around a campfire at dusk, horses and a wagon nearby. They looked like normals, a Roma camp perhaps. One of the men rose and approached us, suspicious. His tanned face was deeply lined, and gray streaks silvered his black hair, but he was strong and carried himself with the air of a leader. He said something harsh in a language I didn't know. A threat or a challenge.

The Blue Lady replied to him in his language, and his eyes widened in surprise. They chatted for a moment, and he relaxed his guard. Once again, "our" hand reached out for his forehead. His entire body spasmed and twisted; his eyes bulged and his mouth gaped wide as he struggled to breathe. His knees buckled, and he started to fall. I never saw what happened next because the Blue Lady let go of my hand, and the man, his family, and the entire bright universe of the Heart of God was snuffed out like a candle.

I fell back on the settee as if I, too, had been snuffed out. It was a minute before I could focus my eyes again. I looked for the Heart of God, but she had already returned it to the pendant and snapped it shut.

As soon as I could speak, I asked, "What happened to him?"

She dropped the pendant inside her blouse and stood. "He's fine. Don't worry. And please don't blame yourself."

Blame myself? "I don't understand."

"I will explain everything. I promise. But right now, I have business to attend to, and you need to rest."

As soon as she said it, I realized she was right; I was as empty as a bottle of whiskey on the last day of shore leave. But she wasn't even slightly worn out. She was so radiant I could almost see the blue glow even without the jewel.

I didn't want to sleep; I needed to think about what I'd seen. But the room ebbed away and carried me with it. The last thing I remember was the soft click of the door.

• • •

The smell of food roused me from a dreamless sleep. I had no idea how long I'd been out, but when I opened my eyes, the Blue Lady stood in the doorway, a tray in her hands. She set it down on the table.

"Hungry?" she asked with a smile.

I was ravenous. She lifted the cover, and steam billowed out. A large plate overflowed with golden ribbons of pasta tossed with ham, garlic, and tomatoes, all of it snowy with cheese. There was also a bowl of olives swimming in oil and fresh herbs, roasted asparagus with pine nuts, a full loaf of warm bread, and a bottle of Chianti. I fell on it like a starving wolf while she watched with a motherly smile. When I was done, I sat back, a little abashed.

"Sorry you had to witness that."

She chuckled. "I thought you might appreciate a taste of home."

I looked at the ruins of dinner. "I don't know why I'm so hungry. I haven't done anything but sit or sleep since I got here."

"You worked harder than you know. Perhaps harder than you've ever worked in your life."

"What did I do?"

"You," she paused, "added your strength to mine. It's hard to explain except to say that the Heart of God chose you like it chose me."

I'd had that feeling the first time I'd touched it—that, somehow, it recognized me. I found it unsettling, but it didn't seem to bother her. Maybe you get used to it, or magic beings were better equipped to deal with it than blockheaded Blues.

"The man, last time," I said. "He was a normal. I thought we were looking for Blues."

"I don't believe I ever said that," she said. "It's easier to start with Blues, of course, since we have a natural connection already. But there will never be peace in the world until we can help everyone."

It made sense. How many Blues were there? A few hundred? But something about it made me uneasy.

"Do you think it might have gone better if maybe you explained it to him or asked first?"

"Most people are like children who refuse a sweet because they've never tasted it before. It's so much simpler to experience it than explain. You saw Sylvie, didn't you? As soon as she tasted it, she knew it was good."

"But what if she tried it and decided it wasn't for her?"

She paused. "I'd be sad. But I would release her if that's what she truly wanted."

"Did you release the man? Is he all right?"

"Of course." Her brow furrowed. "It's true that didn't go as well as I hoped. But it was only our first time working together. I'm certain it will go better this time. If you're willing to try again. We can keep to Blues for now."

When we joined hands, I saw the strands of light right away; the threads connecting the souls to the Heart of God seemed sharper than before. Maybe she was right; we just needed practice.

We connected three Blues in quick succession, one in Italy and two in Germany, but not anyone I knew. It went well in each case, and they all seemed happy about it, though each one drained a little more out of me while she burned brighter than ever.

"One more, and then we'll stop," she said. "A human this time, if you feel up to it."

"Are you sure it's safe?"

"All great ventures carry some risk, don't they? And this is the greatest venture of all."

She cast out along a thread.

We were in an office with cream walls and gleaming dark woodwork. A map of Germany with pins in it hung on a wall to our right, and above the desk straight ahead was a framed portrait of some general. "Our" reflection overlaid his in the glass: male, fair skin, fair hair.

A dark-haired man sat at the desk with his back to us. He was absorbed in paperwork and didn't seem to be aware we were there. The Blue Lady didn't speak this time. She paused a moment, gathering light and power. I felt chilled and light-headed. We crossed to the man in a few quick steps and laid a hand on his forehead from behind. He jerked upright. Tendons stood out white against the ruddy skin of his neck, and the pen in his hand snapped, spattering ink across the page. I was afraid he would collapse like the Roma man had. But the Heart of God seeped in and filled him up. His chair creaked as he relaxed.

Our hand stroked his brow. "How do you feel, my child?"

"Wonderful!" he replied.

He turned to look up at us.

I shot to my feet, pulling my hand from her grip and shutting off the magic world.

The man at the desk was Germany's newly minted Nazi Chancellor, Hitler.

13

I staggered back, trying to get my head around what I'd seen. "That was—that—he—"

The Blue Lady beamed up at me. "Yes. We did it! You and I!"

"But how—I mean, you can't just walk into Hitler's office."

"One of my doves infiltrated his guards months ago, in the hope of a moment like this."

"Can we please do Mussolini next?"

She laughed. "We will get there soon enough. Don't you realize what we've done?"

I blinked at her. "Stopped the Nazis?"

She waved a hand as if the Nazis were a cloud of gnats. "We saved a *human* soul. Now the real work can begin!"

I should have felt excited, right? If she could turn Hitler into a good guy, maybe the idea that she could change the world wasn't as crazy as it seemed. But something was off, and my brain was too fogged to figure out what.

She was speaking, but I didn't hear a word. She stopped and patted my hand.

"You poor dear. I will leave you to recover your strength."

A wave of fatigue swept over me so strong my knees buckled. She leaped up to help me back to the settee and brushed the hair back from my forehead with gentle fingers while sleep pressed down on me like a mountain of wet sand. I had to fight it. If I kept on sleeping away the time between sessions, I would never have a chance to think.

I sagged back and let my eyes close but dug my fingernails into my palms. After I heard the door click, I counted to fifty then rolled to the floor and pushed myself up on trembling, kitten-weak arms. I gripped the arm of the settee, dragged myself to my knees, and then stood. The floor pitched under my feet like a ship's deck, and my head filled with buzzing bees. I leaned against the wall until the room steadied. Then I moved along the wall, opened the window, and let cool night air blow away more of the fog. I marched around, swinging my arms and taking deep breaths.

Everything she said was true. The world was a troubled place that could use a little peace and love. Maybe she was right that we were like children who didn't know what was good for us. God knows, most people could be counted on to do the wrong thing, left to their own devices. Including myself. But what was the value of doing the right thing if it's not your choice? If you make a puppet drop a coin in a beggar's cup, it doesn't make the puppet charitable.

My eyes started to close, and I shook myself. Why was I sucked dry while she left our sessions blazing with energy?

I wasn't going to find any answers here. If I could explore on my own, talk to one of her doves, maybe I could get a handle on what was going on. In the sessions, I had sensed some of them were close by, perhaps even inside this compound.

I splashed cold water on my face and looked in the little mirror on the wall by the tub. I half expected to see my wooden face looking back; the Blue Lady made me feel like a child who wanted his mama. But a man's face looked back from the mirror. I smoothed my hair back and squared my shoulders. I was about to turn away when a flash of memory tugged at my brain. I took a step back from my reflection. And another. And then it clicked. The face I'd seen reflected in the glass of the portrait above Hitler's desk came back to me. I'd seen that smooth, blank expression before.

It was the face of a Manikin.

My heart banged against my ribs like a hammer hitting an anvil. I was hallucinating. Mistaken. Too tired to think straight. The Blue Lady made people good and happy. Like me. And Sylvie. And Hitler, for God's sake! How could changing him be anything but good? Manikins were bad. They electrocuted Blues with their fingers. Like they'd done to poor Karl. Like they'd tried to do to me—

Like she had done to the old Roma man.

Every atom of oxygen in my body burned away in a flash, and I gasped for air. I had no proof of anything. Yet. Were the men working in the yard when I'd arrived normal men? Or were they Manikins? I was too distracted at the time, but now would be a very good time to find out. I headed for the door.

It was locked.

I looked through the keyhole, but something was blocking it. Under the door, I saw two shadows that might have been boots. A guard?

"Hey there!" I called. No answer.

I knocked. "Hello? Open the door!"

Still nothing. Maybe it was only something that looked like boots. A chair or a washstand. Right. The Blue Lady locked my door and set a washstand outside it. That made perfect sense.

I rattled the handle. "Come on, man! It's urgent!"

Was there something I could use to break the handle? I picked up a lamp and hefted it in my hand. The base might do, but then what? Fight an armed guard with a lamp?

As I set it down, something on the floor glinted in the light. I knelt and picked it up. It was a flake of glass about the size of a fingernail and not much thicker. It had razor-sharp edges, though. If the guard stood very still, maybe I could scratch him to death. I almost tossed it aside, but when I pinched it between my fingers, it pulsed. I looked at it more closely. Even though it was such a thin piece, it had a blue cast to it. Had it chipped off the jewel when we dropped it? I held it tightly between my fingers and closed my eyes, but the darkness behind my eyelids was just regular darkness. No lights, no sense of vast space. It was either too small to be of use, or the Blue Lady needed to be there, or it was just a bit of glass. I tucked it into my wallet and looked around.

How was I going to get out before she came back? The window was small but big enough to squeeze through. I leaned out. My room was near the top of the tower, at least four stories up. Smooth stone walls stretched below. It was still too dark to see anything that might serve as a foothold, but the sky to the east was thinking about sunrise. A shadow to the left might be a drainpipe, but it was out of reach. There weren't enough towels to make a rope, and looking out the window every two minutes wasn't making a ladder appear.

When it got lighter, I saw a narrow ledge a few meters below. I'd have to hang from the windowsill, let go, and drop down to it. There would be no going back, and a long fall if I lost my balance. I'd have to leave my rucksack behind. Even if I could get me and it out the window, the weight of it might throw off my balance, and if I dropped it out first, the sound might alert someone on the ground.

I was thankful for the new clothing, which was sturdy wool, and for its pockets into which I tucked my wallet, pocketknife, matches, and the contents of a candy bowl. I yawned loudly and made a show of snoring for the guard's benefit. Then I quietly pulled a chair over to the window and eased myself out feet first. If you think that's easy, try to do it with a wooden leg sometime. Silently. But no one burst in to stop me as I hung from the sill, working up the nerve to let go.

A little voice in my head accused me of going off half-cocked, which I almost certainly was.

I let go anyway.

My toes caught the ledge and I wobbled, scrabbling at the stonework with my fingers. By a miracle, I found just enough depth between the stones to dig my fingertips into and steady myself. When the hammering in my chest slowed, I eased over to the drainpipe and used it to slither down to a second ledge about a story below. Several bolts popped loose, and the pipe pulled away from the wall, but I made it to the ledge, and no sirens went off. I looked down. No more ledges and still too far to jump. Going further on the drainpipe was out of the question; I was lucky to get as far as I did. A rumble below told me the big doors were opening. There would be people in the yard soon, and someone was sure to spot me. I crept along the ledge to a window below the one I'd climbed out of and peered in. It was the office where the Blue Lady had greeted me. Neatly stacked folders sat on an open rolltop desk along with a teacup, a stand holding several pens, and an inkpot. The chair was pushed back from the desk as if she had recently gotten up out of it. No one was in sight.

It was such a normal office that I started to doubt myself again. Was I stupidly risking my neck over nothing? Was this the best thing to happen since the Garden of Eden? Or the worst? Whatever it was, I needed answers I wasn't going to get from her.

I pulled my sleeve over my hand and broke a pane with the butt of my pocketknife, using the rumble of a truck engine starting up to cover the sound. I plastered myself to the wall, out of sight of anyone coming into the office to investigate, as if they wouldn't notice the broken glass. When no one came looking, I unlatched the window and climbed through. The top folder on her desk was open. It looked like shipping orders, a thick stack of them. But they just listed numbers of crates, not what was in them. I tried the drawers, but they were locked.

In the stairwell, voices echoed, but not close by. I slipped out and headed down to the ground floor, back down the corridor I'd come in through, and listened at the door to the garage. It was quiet, so I opened it a crack and peeked out. No one was in sight, and even the sounds of activity I'd heard earlier had stopped. Where was everyone? A pair of guards walked into view. They were tall, straight-backed, blond, and moving in perfect lockstep with each other. Manikins. I was sure of it.

I retreated to the stairs and headed down. Maybe there was another way out. The block walls soon gave way to solid stone, then to rougher stone that wept ochre tears. This whole place must have been a mine at one time—and not a small one. It was bigger than it seemed on the surface, but I guess that's how mines usually work.

The stairs ended at a dank corridor so narrow I could lay my hands flat on the walls on either side. Not that I wanted to—they oozed with slime. A bare bulb hung every twenty paces or so. Pipes and wire conduits were bolted to the walls, and it only took banging my head on overhead knobs of rock three or four times before I learned to crouch. Water puddled on the floor below a wooden walkway that was spongy and slick under my feet.

At every light bulb, I passed an iron door. But each one only led to a tiny cell carved into the rock, and they were empty aside from an occasional ragged blanket, dented cup, or candle end. Who had been kept in these cells? Where were they now? It was possible they hadn't been used in a long time, maybe years. Or they could have held prisoners recently. My stomach knotted.

Beyond the last lightbulb, the passageway stretched into darkness. I groaned. I had left a perfectly cozy room—voluntarily and with great effort. I could be having one more hot bath, one more plate of pasta, one more snooze by the fire. One more soul-draining round of turning innocent people into mindless sleepwalkers.

The cell directly by the last working light bulb was larger than the others, and I stepped inside to look around. Light from the tunnel lit a small wooden table and a cot in the corner. When I pulled away the thin mattress to see if anything was under it, something small plinkety-plinked across the floor. I felt around with my hands until I found it and took it out into the light. It was a tiny wooden gear, no bigger than a chickpea—identical to the one I'd found on the floor of Papa's workshop.

What in the name of God was going on here? Had Papa given this to the poor soul locked in this miserable cell? Had he been here himself? The Blue Lady had said he was away, but was he? The weight of the entire mountain over my head seemed to press down, crushing the breath out of me.

I pocketed the gear and forged on into blackness, feeling my way along the clammy wall until my hands found the end of the corridor. There was one final door, and I prayed it would open to something other than one final cell. It opened with a heart-stopping screech of rusted hinges, but it let in a promising draft of warm, dry air. I opened it only far enough to squeeze through.

I stood on a suspended ironwork walkway running along the wall of a vast, roughly circular chamber. Electric sconces high on the walls cast only dim light, and the farther reaches vanished into blackness. Echoing creaks, rumbles, and clatters rose from the chamber floor, but I heard no voices.

Something close by was putting out a lot of heat. I crept across the walkway to the railing and looked down. A Manikin was feeding empty crates into the glowing mouth of an enormous furnace to the right of where I stood and maybe six or seven meters below. Beyond that, a wide ramp led upward into darkness.

Below to my left, water ran in a channel toward the back of the chamber. Water might lead to an exit. An enormous wooden waterwheel, black with age, hung above the channel. Some of the baffles on the wheel were broken or missing, and the whole thing looked like it hadn't been used in years. Cables looped from the top of the waterwheel into the shadows.

Manikins pushed large hand carts piled with crates around the central area of the floor, which had an odd, bumpy, grid-like look. As my eyes grew more accustomed to the dim light, the hair on the back of my neck prickled, and my mouth went dry.

The floor wasn't bumpy. It was entirely filled with orderly ranks of identical wooden soldier puppets.

It could have been thousands. I knew what they would look like close up because I had made hundreds with my own hands: simple wooden forms with painted-on faces and uniforms and a plain black stick for a rifle. They were no more than knee-high to the Manikins who were unloading puppets from the crates on the carts and setting them up in columns. Other workers collected empty crates and carried them to the furnace, but a mountain of crates was still piled around the perimeter. Were they empty or still full of puppets?

Though I heard no signal, the crew stopped working and stood at attention. A door opened onto the walkway nearly across from where I stood, and the lights grew brighter. I slipped into the shadows. Two uniformed soldiers stepped out and took up positions by the door. They saluted when the Blue Lady stepped through and walked to the railing.

She wore a spotless white jacket and skirt that somehow looked softly feminine and severely military at the same time. Her pale, beautiful face seemed bathed in light—a single rose on a battlefield. She raised her arm over the heads of the soldier puppets like the pope giving a benediction. But her hand was fisted, and I knew what was in it.

A blue haze formed around her fist. It grew brighter and denser until her hand vanished in a ball of pulsing light. A low thrum that made me clutch my head to keep it from coming apart rose until the ball of light burst outward and cascaded down, washing through the ranks of puppets like a ghostly sea. In the light from it, I saw that the chamber went back even farther than I'd thought.

The puppets writhed and stretched and grew to human size, popping and cracking like pinecones in a fire. Bare wood became soft with flesh and then hard with muscle and smooth with skin. Hair sprouted on scalps; eyes opened. Paint peeled into crisp uniforms complete with red swastika armbands. The sticks became gleaming rifles.

Once the transformation was complete, the blue sea drained away, leaving every one of them standing shoulder to shoulder, back to chest in a solid mass of perfect Nazi soldiers. Alive. Not one of them moved, but it wasn't the stillness of lifeless wood. It was the stillness of absolute discipline.

The Blue Lady gazed out over them for a long moment. Then she nodded.

My ears popped as ten thousand lungs filled with air for the first time. And, as one, these newly made soldiers—these Nazi Manikins—raised their right arms and roared, "Heil!"

The sound was volcanic. It erupted through the chamber and pushed me to the wall. I crawled back and peered over the railing in time to see every one of the new soldiers raise his left leg at the same instant and march toward the ramp in perfect time. Every eye stared straight ahead; every foot hit the floor as if part of a single machine. The thunderclap of their feet on the floor rattled my bones in a beat I'd felt before.

It was the pulse of the Heart of God.

I stood frozen until a small disturbance caught my eye. One of the new soldiers groped blindly, his head still a knob of painted wood. Another swung his fists and scuffled with his neighbors. Still another stood rooted to the spot, buffeted by the others marching around him.

Guards plucked them and others out of the formation and herded them to an open area near the furnace. When they were done, some twenty defective soldiers stood in a ragged line.

A few moments later, guards herded in half a dozen others. These weren't Manikins. They were humans: an elderly man and woman, a younger man, a boy not older than ten who clung to the man, and two Blues, one with pale fur, the other green-scaled. They were all thin and filthy, dressed in rags. The guards lined them up with the defective soldiers.

The first Manikin in the line had no outward defect, but he trembled in fear. One of the newly made soldiers approached him and spread his fingers across his forehead. His body jerked and shook so hard that if he'd been made of wood, he would have shattered into splinters. But after a moment, he snapped to attention. The Blue Lady smiled. He joined the ranks marching up the ramp.

One by one, the soldier went down the line. Out of twenty Manikins, fourteen joined their brothers marching out. Six lay where they fell, at least two of them twitching. He moved on to the Blues and the humans. The Blue with fur screamed until the soldier abandoned the effort and left him on his knees, moaning. The elderly couple fell almost at once and lay in a motionless heap. The child collapsed on the floor but crawled to his knees after a few moments, shaking violently. The green-scaled Blue and the young man were "saved." That's what she would have called it. I grieved for them as much as for the others.

The Blue Lady turned away while a guard led the successfully altered man and Blue away. Other guards heaved the "failures" into the furnace.

I couldn't begin to make sense of what I'd seen. Not even the horrors of the battlefield had shaken me so hard. The floor seemed to slip away from beneath my feet, and I clung to the railing to keep from falling to my knees.

I knew the exact instant she saw me. The impact of her furious eyes was like a physical blow. That was a mistake on her part. When she'd acted like a mother, it had reduced me to a child. But now I knew she was the enemy. Cold rage knifed through me, sharpening my senses. I was aware of guards moving towards me along the walkway from both directions and the last rank of new soldiers gathering below, but my eyes were on her. I leaped up onto the railing, aching to fly across the chamber and tear her to pieces.

Instead, I vaulted toward the waterwheel. I barely caught the side of it and scrambled to the top. My hands slipped on moldy wood, and my foot broke through a rotted baffle. I hung on and crawled to the top, where the cable stretched slackly above the rushing water toward a mass of gears and chains at the back of the chamber. My weight on the waterwheel made the cable sway—the way the trapeze tether line swayed the night I joined the circus.

I pushed to my feet and leaped onto the cable. It swung wildly, pinging as strands snapped under my feet, but I kept my balance and ran. Near the back wall of the chamber, the canal cascaded down into a black hole. There was only one way to find out how far down it went or what was at the bottom.

At the last second, I spied a small door in the back wall below. A stairwell, perhaps? It was that or fall into the black pit. I leapt from the cable, scrambled to the door, jerked it open, and threw myself through it. I slammed it shut and felt around in the darkness for something to jam it with. My fingers found a crate, and I shoved it under the door handle. It wouldn't stop them for long.

I lit a match and saw a cord hanging from the ceiling. I pulled it, and a bare lightbulb flicked on, casting dim, yellowish light on a random collection of junk.

It was a closet.

14

I shoved toward the back of the closet, pushing aside buckets and crates filled with greasy tools and machine parts, coils of rope and mounds of chains. There had to be a way out—a hidden back door, a vent, a drain. I'd try a mouse hole.

A door off its hinges leaned against the back wall. It resisted for a few seconds when I pulled it and then gave way, sending me reeling backward a few unbalanced steps before I managed to fling it aside.

Behind it was not the exit I was praying for but a tall, blond, fully armed Nazi soldier.

We stared at each other for a moment, and then he knelt and held out his rifle to me.

"I surrender," he said.

"I think you have this backward."

"I'm defective."

"Defective?" He looked entirely human.

"I cannot receive orders."

It took a second, but I got it. No thread connected him to the Heart of God; the Blue Lady couldn't tell him what to do. He wasn't a Manikin. He was a Blue.

Behind us, fists pounded on the door.

"I should have surrendered immediately." He looked down and whispered, "But I did not want to burn."

Fair enough. I didn't want to either.

The corner of an axe blade smashed through the door, sending splinters flying. I had a sliver of an idea. And less than a sliver of time.

· · ·

When the closet door burst open and the doorway bristled with rifles, my hands were up, my Nazi Blue's rifle barrel jammed into the back of my head.

"I have apprehended the defective," he said.

One of the guards looked me up and down and curled his lip. "Disgusting."

I didn't like to think so, but I let it go.

"Make way," my Nazi barked with impressive authority.

They made way, and he marched me forward. As we neared the blazing furnace, I started to have second thoughts. No, I'd left second thoughts behind some time ago and was now up to at least fourth or fifth thoughts. He was too good at this. Had I just been had? I tried to look back, but he struck the side of my head with the gun barrel hard enough to put me off a second try. The furnace's heat was too close on the left and the waterway's cool dampness too far to the right.

"Halt!" he commanded.

The Blue Lady looked down at me from her platform. "Oh, Pinocchio. What am I going to do with you?"

"You're going to let me go."

"I'm afraid that won't be possible."

I had to act before she realized my captor wasn't following her orders. I felt the gun pressed against the back of my head. I moved my head to tap the barrel once, twice—

And leapt toward the canal. Several crates toppled into the cold water along with me, and I grabbed one. A second splash told me my Nazi was right behind. At least, I hoped it was him. The current swept us toward the back of the chamber.

I didn't hear her give orders to stop us, but why would I? She didn't have to open her mouth or even twitch a finger to command every Manikin.

I kicked forward to where the water vanished into roaring blackness. As I flew over the brink, the crate spun out of my hands, and the stamp on the side came into view: B.F. SHEA, LONDON.

We plummeted in a weightless tumble that ended with a bone-shaking plunge into a larger, faster channel. I came up choking.

We shot down a steep chute into a tunnel, and I struggled to keep my head in the small gap between the water and the ceiling. When the tunnel narrowed, I lost even that slim air space, but it widened, and the water level dropped before I drowned. I gasped for air and heard a cough nearby a second or two later. I couldn't see a thing, but this darkness felt bigger. Were we in another chamber or a wider channel?

A glimmer of light appeared ahead.

Daylight? Given my luck so far, it was probably a smelter. We were in a mine, after all. Even if it was the exit, there could be a gate across it, or there could be a hundred-foot waterfall or man-eating Nazi sharks. If it was an exit, I had to assume armed guards were nearby.

I snagged my companion's sleeve and yelled over the rush of water.

"When you get near the exit, dive down. Stay as deep as you can!"

The water was high and fast, nearly filling the tunnel. We glanced off the far wall as it took a curve, and bright sunlight rushed toward us. I took a deep breath and plunged as deep as I could, which wasn't as deep as I would have liked.

An instant later, sunlight shafted through the water.

I kept to the center of the channel where the water ran fastest and waited as long as I could to come up for air. When I finally surfaced, gasping, I heard a single gunshot.

I looked around for my accomplice.

A body bobbed to the surface downstream, face down and motionless.

Shit.

I swam to him as fast as I could and flipped him face up. I couldn't tell if he was breathing. Was he dead? He didn't appear to be shot. I hauled him to the more sheltered shore and dragged him just far enough up the bank not to slide back in. He was heavy for a newborn. I rolled him onto his side and pounded his back.

I was about to give up when he spasmed and retched. About a gallon of water gushed out of his mouth and nose, and he took a wheezing gasp of air.

"We have to get to cover," I said as soon as his eyes fluttered open. "We're sitting ducks here."

Without hesitation, he pushed himself up on his arms and crawled up the bank, still gasping for air. By the time we got to the trees, he was on his feet. The man had just drowned. If all the Manikin Nazis were this tough, it was bad news.

He shook himself like a dog, and water flew. His rifle was slung across his shoulder, as soaked as we were. It would need to be cleaned before it was ruined, but we couldn't stop here.

"Are you up to walking?"

"I don't know. My body is shaking. I think it must be one of my defects."

My mouth fell open. He was so new he had never shivered.

"You'll feel better when we get moving."

We were in a pine forest, slanting steeply toward the south, if my wooden heart compass was working. The duff of winter's leaves was spongy, and green shoots pushed through a thin crust of old snow. I had no idea where to go, so downhill seemed as good a plan as any. He fell in beside me.

"Did you hit your head?" I asked as we walked.

"No."

"What happened when you came out?"

"I dived down deep when I saw the exit."

"Yeah. And?"

"I followed your order."

"But why didn't you come up? Did you get caught on something?"

"You gave no order to come up."

I tried to think of a reply to this but only opened and closed my mouth like a beached carp. If all the Manikin Nazis were this stupid, it was good news.

I gave him my name and asked his.

"I don't have access to a name."

Don't have access? "What the hell does that mean?"

He frowned. "I believe if I was not defective, I would know the designation assigned to me."

"Right. Well, you need a name."

"I will accept any name you choose," he said.

Not a chance. He wouldn't last a day if he had to rely on me to tell him when to piss. He had to learn to think for himself, and this was as good a start as any.

"Pick your own name."

"Yes, sir."

"And don't speak again until you can tell me what it is."

Hopefully, that would shut him up for a while. I needed to think.

Who was this Blue Lady? I couldn't connect what I'd just seen with the one I remembered. Was she an impostor? But she knew things only she, Papa, and I knew. I pushed it aside. All that mattered was what was she going to do next—and what could I do about it?

The Blue Lady had been making Blues for a long time— she'd made me almost twenty-five years ago. But the first Manikin appeared only in the last year. She said she could only make them one at a time, in person. Until I showed up. I had no idea what juice I added to the pot, but it was strong stuff. In our first session together, she used one of her Manikins to take control of that poor Blue, Sylvie.

By our second session, she was able to take over a human—Hitler himself, no less—a normal with no previous connection to her or her magic at all. That was her true goal all along. Sylvie and all the Blues were just a stepping stone. She didn't care about the Blues. We were just practice for the main event: controlling everyone.

The only way to make "everyone live in perfect peace and goodwill" was to turn every person on Earth into a Manikin—a mindless body unable to choose his or her own path.

Whatever it was she sucked out of me, she kept. It explained why I felt so drained after each session. I'd just seen the proof of it when she used Manikins to change those prisoners without me. The ones who survived. Even with the appalling failure rate, if each one who lived could make more, and if each one of those could go on and make more, it would spread faster and be far deadlier than the Spanish Flu. But when it was over, she'd have her toybox full of playthings. Her Eden.

What the hell was I?

I shuddered so violently I had to grab a tree branch to keep from curling up into a ball on the ground. What would she be able to do if she had me for a third session? Just hold out her blue stone and turn the whole world into her puppets, the way she'd brought her Manikin army to life? I couldn't give her that chance. Should I ask the Nazi to shoot me? That would stop her from using me any more than she already had.

Before I did something rash out of panic, I counted my footsteps, one foot in front of the other the way we did in the army, until I was calm enough to think it through.

The suicide gambit was always open if it came to it. But staying alive was probably the better option. She might hold off on launching her plan if she thought she could still get her hands on me. Once I was gone, she had little to lose even if she left half the people on Earth dead. I hadn't found Papa yet. He might know more than I did. And if I was dead, I couldn't warn anyone. As long as there was any hope at all, I had to try. But how?

Should I go to the authorities? I could imagine how that would go. At best, they would lock me up as a lunatic. The only ones who might believe me were my friends in the circus. I tried to count the days since I'd left them. They would be in Frankfurt in a day or so. I didn't want to draw trouble their way, but they were already in more danger than they could imagine.

I nearly jumped out of my skin at the crash of branches nearby. My companion already had his rifle in his hands, on full alert. There was a flash of antlers, the thump of hoofs on duff, and then it was gone.

"It's just a deer," I said.

"Is it a threat?"

"No." My stomach rumbled. "Delicious, though."

Her soldiers were surely hunting me right now. I picked up the pace.

What would she do? In my head, I saw Manikin Nazis swarming out of the mine like ants, laying their buzzing hands on everyone in their path as they went. Leaving a trail of death as the army's numbers exploded.

Pinning humanity's hopes on a pitifully small group of clowns in Frankfurt felt useless, if I could even get that far. It was the longest of shots, but it was all I had. Of course, it would help if I had any idea where Frankfurt was.

We came to a village out of a fairy tale—timbered cottages with roof slates like fish scales. My first instinct was to skirt around it, imagining Manikins around every corner. The Blue Lady could see us through a Manikin's eyes. But two points of light going cross-country by themselves would stand out, too. If we passed through towns and paralleled roads, she might lose track of us. In a crowd, we'd be two grains of salt in a sugar bowl.

• • •

I looked at my companion. I must have assembled a thousand of those damned soldier puppets myself. I could be his dad. I'd seen him go from sad, orphaned duckling to ruthless Nazi in an eye blink, but now he just seemed blank.

"Thought of a name yet?"

He hung his head. "This is not something I am able to do." Duckling then. "I should have burned. What purpose do I have if I cannot follow orders?"

"You followed orders pretty well when we escaped from the closet," I pointed out.

"Escorting prisoners is a suitable task for my rank. I can access the protocol when commanded."

Access the protocol? What did that even mean? And God help him if I was his commanding officer now.

If he was going to have a name, I would have to give it to him. I sized him up. Like the other Manikins, he was tall and fit with close-cropped, blond hair and blue eyes—the ideal Aryan. I was tempted to saddle him with a name like Giuseppe or Mordecai. But it seemed cruel. He wouldn't get the joke anyway. I went with the first German name that popped into my head.

"How about Hans?"

He stood a little straighter if that was possible. "Thank you, sir."

"Okay, Hans. Let's find some cover until the moon comes up."

"Cover" didn't mean much under the circumstances, and Hans showed no signs of flagging, but I needed rest, and he needed to see to his rifle before it got too dark. We moved farther from the road and hunkered down in a dense cluster of trees against the side of a boulder with a slight overhang.

He took the rifle apart and began cleaning and oiling the pieces.

"Is it ruined?" I asked.

"The rifle was wet for longer than optimal, but I believe it is not ruined."

"What about the bullets?"

"I cannot determine that at this time. If water has penetrated the casings, they will not fire."

"How much ammunition do you have?"

He emptied his pockets and the leather pouches on his belt. The one that held his rifle cleaning kit was large enough to hold a fair amount of ammunition, but there was only one five-bullet clip. With the clip in the rifle, ten in all. Or maybe none if they were wet. His belt held a bayonet clip but no bayonet. It must have come off in the river. He had no sidearm, compass, or even a knife. Far less than I'd carried in the Italian Army. But we'd had a bit of a war going on then. Hans' other pouch held basic rations: potted meat, a waxed paper packet of pale mush that might once have been biscuits, some small, dried sausages, a round tin of hard chocolate, and a soggy pack of cigarettes.

"No beer?"

"I'm sorry, sir. I'm sure it's because I'm defective."

I had to stop making jokes.

"Hans, listen. You can't go on thinking you're defective. You're just different."

"But I don't feel ..." He struggled for the words and finally just pounded his chest with a rhythmic beat.

He wasn't connected to the—I couldn't call it the Heart of God. I didn't believe God had anything to do with something so evil.

"The thumpity-thump?" I asked. It was all I could think up at the moment.

"Yes! I know I should feel it. But I do not."

"So? I don't either, and I hope it stays that way."

I took one of the sausages and divvied up the biscuit mush.

He frowned. "Who tells you what to do?"

"I tell myself."

He pondered this for a moment, then rejected it. "This is not possible."

"Sure it is. Everyone I know does it that way. You're just not used to it yet."

He went back to cleaning his gear.

"Listen," I said. "You're better off. Really. Do you think the non-defective soldiers are having fun like we are? No. They follow orders every minute. Day and night. No leave, no time off. Just more orders."

He smiled wistfully. "I would like that. Not knowing what to do makes me feel shame. You could order me to go back."

"Order yourself," I said, and his face shut down.

Poor chump. I almost felt sorry for him. I pried the candy out of my pocket. It had solidified into a single, lint-covered mass. I broke it in two and gave him half.

"You can do it, you know. Who gave you the order to hide in the closet?"

"I don't know. It is more proof that I am defective."

"No, it's proof you're not an idiot. Look, Hans, if you want to go back, go back. If you want to stay with me, stay. Or we can part ways and you can go anywhere you like. But I'm not going to make that decision for you."

He went all blank again.

"Oh, to hell with it. You want an order? Fine. Go to sleep!" I remembered my botched order earlier. "But wake up in four hours. And wake me up too."

A moment later, he was gently snoring.

I don't know how I slept, but I must have because Hans shook me awake.

"Four hours," he said.

I dragged myself to my feet and brushed leaves and twigs off my rumpled clothes. Hans was tidier than seemed possible for someone who'd been pulled out of a river a few hours ago. The sky was clear and the moon bright enough to silver the ground. I shivered in the frosty air.

Hans stood at attention, awaiting orders. My first order was to beg a cigarette. He used his flint to coax enough of a smolder out of a dry leaf to light it.

"It would be helpful to have a map." I sighed.

Hans straightened. "This is within my capabilities."

"What? You have a map?"

"It is something I can access."

I had no idea what that meant, but all right. "How far is it to Frankfurt?"

"Two hundred seven point three kilometers to the city center."

I blinked. Well, that was a neat trick. I sent a silent prayer to Papa to hold on, wherever he was.

"Lead the way!"

He saluted smartly, poor lad. He was looking to me for direction, and I was looking to him for protection. We were both in deep water.

15

Heavy mist rose at dawn, leaving us dripping. I chafed everywhere, but nothing seemed to annoy Hans. He gazed wide-eyed at rotted logs and hopping sparrows as if they were wonders. Oh, to be just one day old again!

The mist burned away with the sun. The last traces of snow were gone, and we walked all day through stands of spruce, oak, and birch. I had Hans fill his pouches with fiddleheads and morels elbowing up through the shaggy duff. They'd extend the few rations we had left when we stopped.

I quizzed Hans, trying to get a better handle on what he could and couldn't "access." He could do most things you'd expect a soldier to do if ordered and could see to his own basic needs on his own.

"Couldn't that mean you're connected after all?"

"If I was, I would feel it. Here." He slapped his chest in the heartbeat rhythm. "I would know what my mission is."

"But how do you know anything at all?"

He sagged. "If I were not defective, I'm sure I would know the answer."

I left off questioning him. We weren't getting anywhere, and it made him so wretched it seemed mean to keep at it. Instead, I told him about the Blues we were going to meet. He frowned in confusion when I hopped onto a slanting log to act out how I ran up the rope the night I joined the circus.

"That is a fallen tree," he said.

"Just imagine it's a rope."

"But a tree is not a rope."

"I was acting."

"Is that the same as lying?"

"No! Acting isn't lying. You're not trying to fool anyone. Everyone knows it's just made up."

I did a little Charlie Chaplin bit, using a stick for a cane. I tipped my imaginary bowler and waggled my eyebrows.

"That's acting, see? An actor's whole job is pretending to be other people, and they get paid good money for it. Everyone knows it's not real, but people still love going to the cinema. You see the whole story on a big screen right in front of your eyes, and you can feel like it was you marching into battle yourself or fighting the villain or falling in love."

I don't know why I thought I could explain cinema to a two-day-old puppet Nazi in back-of-beyond-nowhere Germany who didn't know a joke from a poke in the eye. It was like trying to explain cake to someone who's never tasted sugar. But it took my mind off Manikins for a bit.

"How does the actor know what to do?" he asked.

"Well, there's a script. That's all the words the actors are supposed to say written down. And there's a director who … directs."

Mercifully, he stopped asking questions, and we walked in silence until late afternoon.

A rabbit hopped into view, and I ordered Hans to shoot it. There'd been no signs of pursuit all day, and we needed to test the rifle. And eat. Without hesitation, he pulled the bolt, aimed, and pulled the trigger, but it only clicked. I stopped him after the third try. The bullets must be wet. The rabbit was gone, and we were down to seven shots. As if seven bullets would fend off an army any better than six.

We built a small fire and tucked the fiddleheads and morels into the coals along with the tin of potted meat. They got a bit scorched, but they weren't too bad. We shared a wedge of chocolate, smoked another cigarette, and tried to get a few hours' sleep.

Just as I was dozing off, Hans announced, "I would like to be an actor."

"What? Why?"

"If I was an actor, I would have a script and a director so I would know what to do."

• • •

We rose with the moon a few hours before dawn. I scrubbed my face with cold water, combed my hair with wet fingers, and brushed the worst of the dirt and creases out of my clothes. Breakfast was one wedge of chocolate, water, and a cigarette.

It was still dark when the trees gave way to pastureland. Despite the lure of eggs in the henhouse, we circled wide around a small farmhouse with a light glowing in a window and a blue tendril of smoke curling out of the chimney. I waited for first light and climbed up a wooden ladder into a hunter's blind for a look around. Sheep streamed out of a barn in the distance. Beyond them, more hills. We'd never get there on foot. Especially mine.

I climbed down. "Is commandeering a vehicle something you can do?"

He thought for a moment. "I believe so if you order it."

All right then. We needed a fast car, not some pokey farm rig. That meant we needed a highway, not this country road. I started to climb back up to scan the area again but remembered my walking map.

"Hans, how far to the nearest highway that goes to Frankfurt?"

"There is such a highway 19.4 kilometers to the east."

Amazing. We reached it by midafternoon and hid in some bushes on the southbound side. There wasn't much traffic—a few farmers trundled by in horse carts, and an occasional underpowered flatbed truck chugged past. We retreated further into the bushes when a military transport passed. I couldn't tell if they were Manikins or regular soldiers.

Finally, a car approached at a good clip. The deep growl of the engine promised plenty of muscle. It wasn't obviously military or police. Or at least no flags or wailing sirens. I fought back a wave of nausea and gave the order.

"Commandeer that car."

Without hesitation, Hans stepped into the road, planted his feet apart, and held up his hand. The car rolled to a stop, and a heavy-jowled man in a business suit leaned out the window to scowl at him.

"What is this?"

"Your vehicle is required," said Hans without emotion. "Please step out."

Red crept up the man's face from collar to shiny crown. "And leave me stranded here? I will not."

"Your vehicle will be returned to you."

"Take someone else's car. I have important business in Nuremberg. On behalf of the Reich."

"Refusing to cooperate with a military requisition is a criminal offense. Do you wish to be arrested?"

I didn't know if that was true, but Hans said it with such cool authority, the man nearly bought it. Nearly.

He huffed and glared for a bit. Then his eyes narrowed. "Let me see your orders."

Hans raised the rifle to his shoulder and pulled the bolt. "Step out of the vehicle."

The man set his jaw and held his hand out with the confidence of someone used to being obeyed. "Not until I see your orders." He was calling our bluff.

Hans was not moved. "If you don't leave the vehicle at once, I will shoot."

The man revved the engine. He had nerve; I'll give him that. "Find another chump. I'm reporting you to the—"

The rifle crack cut him off. He jerked backward and then slumped, head and arm hanging out the window.

Shit!

I ran to the car. Blood streamed from a bullet hole in his forehead and down the door onto the road.

"The ammunition appears to be functional," said Hans.

"You killed him!"

"I followed orders, sir."

"I didn't order you to shoot him!"

"You ordered me to commandeer the car. He was preparing to leave."

Ordering people around seems like it ought to be easy until you try it. My heart climbed into my head and tried to escape through my ears. I knew how it felt; I wanted out, too, but I was in it up to my eyebrows and had nothing to gain from standing in the road with my mouth open. I swallowed and squared my shoulders.

We dragged him into the bushes. I pulled out his wallet. We had just murdered Jürgen Gross of Hanover. I left him the wallet but removed a sheaf of banknotes. I felt terrible about it, but the money wouldn't do him any good at this point. Hans wiped off the side of the car with a scarf he found in the back seat. God rest you, Jürgen Gross.

My head was still throbbing when I fired up the engine and stepped on the gas pedal. I tried telling myself it was justified; what was one life when millions were at stake? But my conscience wasn't having it. I'd screwed up again, and this time someone was dead.

"You might as well get some shut-eye," I said.

Hans was asleep in a minute, and I was alone with my thoughts. I was officially a terrible person and grossly unqualified to be in charge of a dangerous innocent like Hans. I felt responsible for him. He'd saved my life, and he'd never survive on his own. But he was like a car with no driver. Everything was there under the hood except any way for the wheels to know which way to turn. Unfortunately for him, I was at the wheel. And so far, I was doing a piss-poor job of it.

After a few hours, I was so tired I started seeing double, and when I couldn't decide which highway was the real one, I pulled over. Hans hadn't so much as twitched. I hoped driving a car was something he could do.

I woke him up. "Drive us to Frankfurt. That's an order."

"Yes, sir."

Not only was driving something he could do, but he did it better than me. I rummaged around and found a heavy leather briefcase behind the seat. I pulled it onto my lap and unhooked the brass latch.

From the papers inside, it seemed Herr Gross was a weapons contractor building something large and complicated for the military. At least we hadn't murdered a doctor or a priest. Along with his papers was a thermos bottle of sweetened coffee, a ham sandwich on thick brown bread, several hard-boiled eggs, an apple, and a large wedge of cake wrapped in waxed paper. I split it all with Hans and we polished off every crumb while I tried not to think about the wife who had baked the cake and packed the lunch. I imagined her at home, unaware her dear husband was lying under a bush instead of at his Nuremberg appointment. Did they have children? Had he been missed yet?

I found a half-full flask of schnapps under the seat and took a long pull on it, sighing as the familiar heat spread through my chest. It wasn't enough to melt the cold knot of guilt, but with the steady rumble of the engine on top of the ordeal of the last few days, it was enough to lull me to sleep.

"Wake me when we get to Frankfurt."

• • •

I woke to silence and darkness. The car was stopped by the side of the highway. Hans sat gripping the steering wheel, staring straight ahead.

"Why are we stopped?"

"The fuel has run out," he said.

"Why didn't you wake me?"

"We have not arrived in Frankfurt."

Breathe in. Breathe out. Breathe in. Breathe out.

"And how far are we from Frankfurt?"

"Twenty-seven point four kilometers from the city center."

We pushed the car off the road and down an embankment where it would be out of sight. It was time to ditch it anyway. Our weapons contractor would surely be missed by now.

We hitched a ride the rest of the way in a dairy truck. The driver was all in for the Nazi Party, so he was overjoyed to be of service to Hans. We made it to Frankfurt, no one died, and we got a free bottle of milk each, but the price was twenty-seven point four kilometers of listening to him crow about how Hitler was going to purge Germany of Jews, Communists, and every other kind of filth.

He insisted on driving us all the way to the fairgrounds, even though it was far past his destination.

"It's my honor. For the Fatherland."

He probably would have driven us right down the aisle of the main tent if we'd asked, but I stopped him as soon as the black silhouettes of tent peaks came into view. It seemed wise to stay out of sight until we knew more.

It was late, past midnight, with a steady rain that was trying to be sleet. The circus was straight ahead on the far side of the fairgrounds, but the direct path was across an open field. Staying out of sight meant a long, winding detour around the field and down one dead end after another. I pulled up my collar and shoved my hands in my pockets. Whatever happened to spring?

We finally found a road that opened onto the field, and peered toward the back fence from the shelter of a building. Aside from the few security lights along the fence, the circus was dark and quiet. No surprise, given the hour and the weather. The carriages were lined up, just like always, with the Toybox at the end. I swallowed a lump of emotion. It had only been a few days, but it felt like coming home after the war. A lone figure patrolled the fence. Probably Dieter, poor bastard. I was eager to be back among friends but froze at the sound of a footstep in the shadows behind us. We flattened ourselves to the wall.

A lamp in a window two stories up was the only light, and the alley was nothing but black shadows. Had I imagined it? No. There it was again. A scrape. A rustle. Then a tall silhouette stepped around the corner. A tall silhouette with a flat, beaked head atop a long neck.

"Tillie!" I whispered to the ostrich. "What are you doing out here?"

She should have been tucked away in the menagerie. Not a good sign. Tillie peered myopically in our direction and then lowered her head to pick at some trash on the ground.

I started toward the fence as Dieter was heading away. But when he passed a light, I saw a Nazi arm band. It wasn't

Dieter. Off to the right, a second figure came into view. Both walked in a steady, matched beat. Thumpity-thump. I ducked back into the shadows, heart hammering. I was too late.

The signs were there. The circus was completely dark, and it should have tipped me off. The circus was *never* completely dark. There was always something going on—a late party, a sick animal, breakfast crew clattering pans. It wasn't just dark. It was dead. Where was everyone?

At the back end of the alley, Tillie continued to scuff around. Hans leaned close and whispered, "Sir, the Tillie creature has been replaced by a person. Male, one-hundred ninety-four centimeters in height, approximately seventy-eight kilograms in weight."

I glanced back but couldn't see anything. "Is it a Manikin?"

"I cannot determine that."

"Whoever it is, restrain him, but don't shoot unless I tell you to." I was learning.

"Yes, sir." He moved quietly toward the back of the alley.

A moment later, I heard the commotion of a struggle. I winced. Even if it wasn't a Manikin or policeman, I was starting to worry we'd attract unwanted attention.

Then I heard, "God's chompers, let me go!"

I gasped. "Armond!"

"Pinocchio? Save yourself! I can't hold him off."

"Hans! Let him go!"

Then Armond himself emerged from the shadows, tugging down the sleeves of his jacket—the most welcome sight I'd seen since Berlin. He wasn't quite as happy to see me. He looked from me to Hans and back again.

"It's kind of a long story," I said.

"Just skip to the part where you order Manikins around."

"Hans isn't a Manikin. He was supposed to be one, but it didn't take. He's a Blue. One of us."

Armond did not look convinced.

"Did you feel an electric shock when he touched you?"

"No." His tense shoulders loosened a bit, but he still looked doubtful.

"Hans," I said. "Give Armond your rifle."

Hans handed it over without hesitation.

Armond's mouth dropped open, then snapped shut with a clack. He aimed the rifle at Hans and gestured for him to step away.

"I came to warn you," I said. "There's some bad stuff coming"

Armond snorted. "You're a little late. The bad stuff got here yesterday. I guess it was the day before yesterday now. Every one of them looked like your friend here. They were definitely Manikins. And they were looking for you. We barely escaped."

"I'm afraid there's worse bad stuff on the way. Where is everyone?"

"Hiding. We got a warning from the—" He glanced at Hans. "Let's just say it was a lucky stroke because otherwise none of us would have got away."

"I got here as soon as I could. I can explain everything, but not here."

Armond nodded. "Come with me."

He guided us through crooked streets and alleys, keeping Hans in sight but far enough ahead to be out of range of a quiet conversation. He leaned close and whispered.

"There's an underground resistance. Well, it's more underground than resistance at this point. Blues, and even some human allies. Looking for all the Blues they can find to warn them and provide safe hideouts from the Manikins. That's who warned us."

A Blue underground! Maybe there was hope after all.

"I need to contact them."

"Not a problem. As a matter of fact, they're looking for you, too. You're a popular guy."

I was baffled. "How could they know I'd be here?"

"They had some information that you might be." They did? "In fact, they sent me here tonight. Intercepting you was my first mission." He sighed with satisfaction. "Ah, Pinocchio. I pray the underground grows into a true resistance. I was made to be a soldier! A real one. Marching into battle instead of a circus ring. Medals on my chest instead of pies in the face."

"I doubt there's much of either in a resistance."

"Even better. To be in the trenches, serving my people instead of some preening general. What are medals compared to that?" He clapped me on the shoulder. "Wait 'til they see you! My first mission and it's a smashing success!"

He leaned down and whispered, "We even have a safe house."

A few minutes later, he pulled open an iron gate and led us into a weedy, overgrown churchyard. We made our way through squelching mud, to a small, crumbling brick mausoleum. I looked at it in dismay. A safe house had conjured up images of warmth and food.

"This isn't it," said Armond. "I can't just walk you—and especially your friend here—into the safe house without getting clearance. They'd bite my head right off! And I'd deserve it. Wait here."

He strode off, taking the rifle with him, while we made ourselves as comfortable as we could on a damp stone bench. At least we were out of the rain. For the first time, I looked at it from their point of view. A stranger appears out of nowhere, makes himself at home for a few weeks, disappears, and a few days later, the bad guys descend. And then he turns up with an enemy in his pocket. Hell, he should have shot both of us on sight. That he didn't was a testament to the trust they put in Matya's gift.

Hans sat quietly. I leaned into the wall at the corner and closed my eyes.

• • •

The next thing I was aware of was a hand shaking my shoulder and a woman's voice.

"Wake up!"

I peeled an eye open and was blinded for a moment by bright light. A few blinks later, the light became an electric lantern. The woman holding it wore a long, dark coat and a hat that cast her face in shadow. I looked for Armond, but she was alone. This must be the underground contact. I shook the cobwebs out of my head, stood, and stuck out my hand.

"I'm Pinocchio."

"I know," she said, and her voice prickled the hairs on my arms.

She pulled off her hat, and the sight of her face filled my chest with the frantic beating of wings. In a startled, impossible moment, my heart flew back to another lantern-lit space, in another country. In another life.

Then it slammed back to the dripping mausoleum and the cold weight of three heartbroken years. What chain of chances brought her, of all people, to this spot on this night?

"Serafina!"

16

She was thinner than I remembered, and there was something hard about her—not cold like when she kicked me out. More like she'd grown a shell. But she was just as achingly beautiful, and my skin went hot despite the damp chill. She smiled sadly.

"I'm sure I'm the last person on earth you expected to see," she said. "I know you must hate me."

Did I? I thought I'd left both hate and love behind. Now, I was burning up, and I couldn't tell which it was. Either one would have to wait.

"All I need to know right now is can you get me to the under—"

"Shh! Not here!" She flicked her eyes toward Hans.

"He's not one of them. He's just a Blue like us. I promise."

"You can't be sure of that," she said.

I gritted my teeth. After everything that happened, she just appears out of nowhere and starts telling me what I know and don't know?

"He's saved my life half a dozen times in the last three days. I'm sure. And I'm not going to give him the heave-ho for you or anyone."

She looked back and forth between the two of us, still doubtful.

I put my hand on Hans' shoulder. "He could be the key to understanding what's happening and how to stop it."

"That's true." She paused. "I still need clearance before I can let him in the house. Until then, there's a shed out back. It's not much, but it'll keep the rain off. We can give him blankets and food. Does he eat?"

"Yes, he eats!" I snapped. She was making it easier for me to decide how I felt about her. "And he hears and speaks, too!"

She flinched, and I felt a flash of satisfaction. She hadn't minded making me flinch once upon a time.

"I'm sorry. I deserved that." She looked so genuinely abashed, I had to beat down a flash of sympathy. How much had she changed in three years? She turned to Hans. "Until you're cleared, you'll have to stay in the shed. Will you cooperate?"

Hans looked at me. I nodded.

"I will cooperate," said Hans.

"All right then," she said. "Follow me."

To the ends of the earth, said my traitorous heart before I could shut it up. To slap some sense into myself, I replayed how Serafina and I had parted as she led us on a winding route through alleys, passages, and dark streets. It had to be dawn by now, but the clouds were so heavy, you wouldn't know. No one said a word the whole way. Not out loud, anyway. In my head, the questions were nonstop. How big was this underground? What did they know? How in God's name did Serafina end up in it? And how was I going to keep both oars in the water when she could still capsize me with a glance?

I looked down to see if I could see her wings. Her coat was long enough to brush her heels, but I thought I saw the very tip of one. My breath hitched, and I cursed myself for even thinking about it.

She stopped in front of an unremarkable house on an unremarkable street.

"Wait here," she said to me. She turned to Hans. "Follow me."

Hans looked at me and I groaned. "Do what she says. I'm not the only one who can give you orders."

She led him into the alley that ran between the house and the one next to it.

The house was dark except for a thin wedge of warm light through a gap in the heavy curtains. It should have been as inviting as a knife in a hot pie, but my stomach was in knots. My friends' world had just been turned upside down, and now I was about to turn it inside out.

Serafina returned and rapped a staccato pattern on the front door. A latch rattled and the door opened a crack.

"Jutta, I hope you have room for one more," said Serafina.

The door opened further as Jutta, a large woman wearing a starched white apron and a breathtaking scowl, gave me the once-over. Her scowl deepened, which I wouldn't have thought possible. She grunted and made way for us to enter. I sucked in a breath and edged past her.

The cluttered kitchen was too warm and close after so much time outdoors. Shelves stacked with crockery filled the walls above the sink, and a large iron pot bubbled on a coal stove set into a brick fireplace. A big slab of a table, heavily gouged and nearly black with age, took up the center of the room. An assortment of mismatched stools and chairs surrounded it. The only light was kerosene lamps.

And there, out of sight of the door, stood Armond, Matya, Vrak, and Ursula in a tight cluster. So much had happened since I last saw them, it felt closer to a lifetime than a week.

Armond grinned like he'd pulled me out of a hat, but that was mostly due to his success on a covert mission. He started to move forward, but Vrak put a steadying hand on his arm. Ursula leaned towards me with damp, shining eyes but didn't move her feet. Matya looked tired and even paler than usual. They all looked tired. Only little Ivan, tail wagging, seemed unreservedly delighted to see me.

Matya stepped forward, took my frozen hands into her soft, warm ones, and looked into my eyes with her fortune teller's gaze. Whatever she saw there filled her eyes with tears, but I also saw welcome. She squeezed my hands tightly.

"You've done the right thing, Sunshine."

"I thought you couldn't read minds."

"I can read your heart."

The others relaxed, trusting Matya. Ursula ran forward and pulled me into a tight bear hug. She trembled in my arms, but I couldn't tell if it was from distress or relief. I only had more distress to deliver.

Vrak clapped an arm around my shoulders and led me to the table. "Son, you look more worn out than Armond's jokes."

Over their heads, I caught Serafina looking my way. She turned away and busied herself with gathering food and blankets, and then quietly slipped out the door.

Ursula followed my gaze and gasped. "*That* Serafina?"

I nodded, and her arms dropped. I wanted to sink through the floor.

Jutta plonked a steaming bowl of soup in front of me. "Eat," she commanded.

The others had already eaten, but Armond poured drinks around, and they peppered me with questions. I stalled.

"Let's wait for Serafina to get back."

"Yes," agreed Matya. "Eat up. You look half-starved."

The soup was mostly sad shreds of cabbage floating in broth. I vowed that if I ever got back home, I would never eat another bite of cabbage as long as I lived. Matya sawed a thick slab of bread off the loaf that sat on the table, smeared it with butter, and ordered me to eat it. I took an obedient bite. It was good. Dark, heavy, and sour. I downed it in three bites. After a second slice, the gale of anxiety that raged in my head quieted enough that I could hear what they were saying. I worked through most of the loaf while they caught me up on what I'd missed in the week I was away from the circus. Serafina had come and warned the Blues to run just as the Manikins showed up. The underground she was part of seemed to have some idea of what was going on—I was relieved to know that—but it was sketchy. No one had any idea where Herr Fischer or the rest of the troupe were. By the next night when Armond came to look for me, the circus was abandoned.

"If they've just been taken in for questioning, they should be released soon," said Vrak without much conviction.

I prayed someone was feeding the animals and that Fluffy the lion wasn't enjoying the same kind of liberty as Tillie.

Serafina came in a moment later and the conversation stopped. She conferred quietly with Jutta while Ursula shifted in her chair and darted glances her way from under half-closed eyes. I looked away from both of them. There's only so much a man can deal with at one time. Jutta put her apron on a hook, wrapped a woolen shawl around her shoulders, and hung a basket over her arm. She looked at us like she was an exhausted mother robin and we were a nest of giant, open-mouthed chicks and walked out the door.

Serafina was all business. She sat down at the head of the table and dived right in. "Here's what I know. The Manikins have been around in small numbers for more than a year, but something has changed in the last few days. We're seeing more, a lot more. They're traveling openly, dressed as Nazi soldiers."

"Are they … what are they doing?" I asked.

"We don't know. The ones who came here were looking for you."

"No attacks?"

"None that we've heard of."

I felt light with relief. Maybe she wouldn't launch her plan without me after all.

"Anything else?"

She took a deep breath and blew it out. "We know about the Blue Lady. That she is making the Manikins."

The Blues looked at me in misery, the hope that I would deny this slander clear in their eyes.

She turned to me. "What can you tell us?"

My mouth went so dry, I thought my tongue would crumble to dust if I spoke. I reached for my glass and took a long pull.

I talked for an hour without stopping while Vrak refilled glasses.

My friends still resisted the idea that the Blue Lady was behind it all. I didn't blame them. I'd seen it with my own eyes, and I still found myself wanting to make excuses for her. I resisted the temptation to downplay my own role in creating the current situation. They questioned everything. For once, I wished I had my old wooden nose. If you've ever been known for telling lies, you know how maddening it is not to be believed when you're telling the truth.

"It's not that we think you're lying," said Vrak. "But what if you're mistaken?"

"Perhaps it's someone pretending to be her," said Matya.

"Could you have been drugged?" suggested Armond. "Or under a spell?"

"Maybe we've been under a spell from the start," I said. "Why do we all feel such intense love whenever we think of her?" I looked around the table. "Was she ever actually loving? She made us and then just left. Even a sparrow stays around to feed her chicks."

"We're not the regular sort of chicks," Vrak pointed out. "It's not like we needed her to bring us worms." He looked a little wistful at the mention of worms.

Even clear-eyed Matya tried to justify her. "She had so many children. You could hardly expect her to be as attentive as a mother of just one."

"Why have child after child after child?" I urged. "Could it be that when we didn't turn out perfect, she dumped us like so much scrap?"

"Maybe *we* didn't," said Ursula. "But what about you?"

"I'm the least perfect of all! She wanted me to be a good boy: obedient, selfless, truthful, and hardworking. She wanted a Manikin."

"But kill us?" said Matya. "How do you explain what happened to poor Karl?"

"The Manikin wasn't trying to kill Karl. He was trying to fix him."

"God's chompers, why? Why go through so much trouble for a few Blues?" said Armand. "Surely there can't be more than a few hundred of us!"

"It's not about us," I said. "She wants to fix everyone. Spread it from one to the next to the next until every human man, woman, and child is in her control and unable to ever do anything wrong again."

"Can she do this?" asked Serafina. "Change humans."

"She changed Hitler."

There was a pause while they absorbed this.

"Well, that's not good," said Armond.

"It seems to work about half the time."

"What happens when it doesn't work?" asked Vrak.

"Mostly, they die. Like Karl."

"Half die? My God," said Serafina.

The clock on the wall was the only sound for a long, horrified moment.

"If she's really that cold-blooded," said Vrak, "what is she waiting for?

"She may be waiting to get her hands on me," I said. "In which case, someone should put a bullet in my head right now."

The room fell silent.

"Would that stop her?" asked Ursula in a small voice.

Would it? In my heart, I didn't believe anything would stop her.

"I wouldn't count on it."

"There's another possible explanation for the delay," said Serafina. "What if she's moving them into position first?"

"What do you mean?" asked Vrak.

"Her lair is in a remote area with low population. It doesn't make sense to attract attention too soon. Having control of Hitler makes it easy to deploy the Manikins quietly to densely populated cities. Then, when she gives the command, it would spread too fast to be stopped."

If that was true, it might buy us some time.

"Where's your Nazi buddy?" asked Armond, looking around. "Maybe he knows something."

All eyes turned towards me. I told them about Hans, doing my best to show him as the innocent and heroic Blue he was. They were instantly on his side.

"He seemed decent enough to me," said Armond.

"That poor boy!" said Matya. "Sitting in a cold, wet shed, while the rest of us are in a warm kitchen."

Ursula crossed her arms and shot Serafina a look. "If he was in here, we could keep an eye on him."

"It's not up to me." Serafina pushed back her chair and stood. "I'll try to get an answer as soon as possible, but until then, he stays in the shed. Headquarters is about fifty kilometers south of here. It's not safe to travel by day, but I will arrange for a car to take us tonight. Until then, I suggest you get some rest and be ready to go as soon as it's dark."

She touched my arm. "Before I go, will you ... can we talk? In private?"

Vrak and Armond already had their heads together, talking in low voices. Ursula examined her fingernails with elaborate casualness. Matya looked from Serafina to me and gave a tiny nod. I pushed my chair back and stood.

Serafina picked up a lamp. I followed her down a narrow, creaking staircase to a storage room crammed with boxes, broken chairs, sacks of dry beans and flour, a crate of cabbages, tools, scrap wood, and old plumbing fixtures. We picked our way through it to an old, peeling wardrobe that sat against the far wall. She opened the door and pulled out the back panel to reveal an opening into another room. You would never know it was there. She stooped to step through, and I followed.

We were in a sizable basement room fitted out like a proper hideaway. A stack of thin mattresses sat in a corner with worn blankets neatly folded on top. Several mattresses and blankets had been pulled off the stack for use by the others, no doubt. A small table in the middle of the room held a worn deck of cards, a chipped ceramic water pitcher shaped like a mouse with its upturned mouth the spout, a matching cup painted to look like a crouching black cat, and a bowl of walnuts. A blanket hanging from the low ceiling partitioned one corner into a small cubicle with a faucet that dripped into a bucket beneath it. All the modern conveniences. Several small rectangular niches near the ceiling might have been basement windows at one time but were sealed under so many layers of paint I couldn't tell if it was night or day.

"Pinocchio." Serafina's face had lost its hard-shell look, and her eyes glistened in the lamplight. I looked away. I couldn't let myself fall for those eyes again.

"I need to explain—" she began.

I held up my hand. "I don't need explanations or excuses or whatever it is you're about to say. Just get me to your headquarters, and you won't have to see me again. It was a long time ago. I'm sure you've moved on."

"I haven't!" She took a step toward me, but when I stepped back, she stopped and scrubbed her face with her hands. "There hasn't been a day in the last three years that I haven't wished things could have ended differently. That night in the boathouse—that was real. You showed me that a man could be decent. That I could be free. That I could have love."

"And the next day in your carriage? You were pretty convincing."

"I had to be! Maestro Grillo, the ringmaster, he was in the closet with a gun, listening to every word."

"If he was so dangerous, why did you go back?"

"Like I told you then, I thought it was safe. I only needed a few things, and I had some money stashed away. It would have taken ten minutes. He was drinking that night. And when he drank, he always slept like a dead man."

"Except that one night. How unfortunate."

She reached a hand toward me. "Please. Just hear me out."

"Try telling the truth, and maybe I will."

"This is the truth! The man you beat up for me—you remember him? He went to the Maestro and told him what happened and he waited up. I never saw him so angry. He threatened to shoot me, but I knew he wouldn't. I was his golden goose. He might knock me around, but he needed me up on that wire every night. But you … I never should have agreed to let you come looking for me. I might have slipped away later. But of course, you came. I got down on my knees and begged him not to kill you. I promised I would do anything he asked. He smiled, and I knew it was going to be something terrible, but I didn't care. Whatever it was, I would do it." She stopped and took a gulping breath. "He said, 'Make him hate you.'"

The room reeled, and my vision filled with buzzing dots. I sank into a chair. She had done a bang-up job of it. But what was I supposed to do with this revelation? Was she acting then? Or was she acting now?

She sat too and touched my arm. I jerked it away.

"I'm so sorry. But there's more."

"More?" It came out as a screech. "I threw away three years of my life trying to get over you. Do you think you can tell me a story and it will all be fine?"

"No. I know it's too much to ask, and I accept that. But I wanted you to know. And you need to know what happened after you left."

"After you drove me away."

She inhaled as if she was going to deny it but looked away and spoke softly instead. "I never performed again. He tried everything to get me up on that wire, but I wouldn't do it. He kept me locked up for months and months. He threatened all kinds of violence. He beat me, starved me. When I still refused to perform, he sold my body to a parade of men. I wanted to die."

"Yet here you are."

She took a shaky breath. "In time, I was no use to him even for that. Late one night he came and dragged me to a van that was waiting out back. I didn't resist; wherever it took me or whatever might happen when I got there, it couldn't be worse than where I was. But before I got in the van, he said he wanted to give me something to remember him by."

She stood, raised her hands to the collar of her long coat, undid the buttons and laid it over the back of her chair. She was just as beautiful in practical black trousers and boots as she had been in circus spangles. Tears spilled down her face as she reached back and spread her wings out with her hands.

I tried to breathe, to speak, but my throat squeezed shut. Her glorious butterfly wings hung in shredded tatters from her back, their shimmering colors dull and nearly lifeless. They trembled and wheezed slightly as her breath escaped through slashed veins. Attempts had been made to sew them up, but they were ruined. It had to be excruciating. Whether I believed her whole story or not, this was real, and rage at what he'd done to her scorched me with such blazing intensity, it was almost more than I could contain.

When I didn't say anything, she dropped her wings. She wiped away her tears and put her coat back on, fumbling with the buttons. When she looked up again, her face was composed. The shell was back in place. "It's all right. There's another reason I'm telling you all this. It has to do with everything that's happening now." She looked away. "There were others in the van. Three Blues and two normals—a pair of orphaned children."

I buried my face in my hands. I wanted to beg her to stop. I knew where this was going. This was how the underground knew so much. The blood pounding in my ears was loud, but not loud enough to drown out her voice.

"All those Blues who came and went from the circus? They didn't just move on. He sold them to her. To the Blue Lady. He only kept me because I made him rich."

In a strange way, it steadied me. It was one thing to go off half-cocked against one bastard. But this was so huge, I had nowhere even to aim a punch.

"They put me in a cell. It was cold, and water dripped down the walls. I don't know how long I was there. I was in so much agony; it felt like centuries, though I suppose it was weeks. Sometimes I heard others crying or calling for help. When they took me to her, I was so happy. I thought I was saved! But she never spoke to me and only watched while her Manikins put their stinging hands on me. It was worse than the pain of my wings, and it went on and on. I thought it would kill me, but it didn't. They dragged me back to my cell. I refused to eat, hoping to die before they came to try again."

I shuddered. Now I knew what those cells had been used for. Dear God, how many had ended up in the furnace? Were others still trapped there in cells I hadn't found? Was Papa?

She went on. "The next time my door opened, it wasn't a Manikin. It was prisoners. Blues and normals. They told me they were escaping! I was weak, but they wouldn't leave me behind. It was a long, hard journey, but we helped each other. People we met along the way helped us too—Blues and normals. That was the start of the underground."

I leapt to my feet and clutched her shoulders. "Did you see ... was one of the prisoners an old man with white hair? A normal?"

"That's what I've been getting to! The one who led the escape knows better than anyone why the Blue Lady must be stopped. He stayed to be our leader. Even though he only wanted to go home. To wait for you."

I gaped at her, speechless, and she smiled.

"Your Papa will be so happy to see you!"

17

If I was still a puppet, my head would have spun right off my neck and caromed around the room like a top. The years of running, weeks of searching, and days of horror were still there, but pushed to the edges to make room for one bright miracle. Papa was safe, and I would see him tonight.

I bounded up the stairs toward a cheerful babble of voices and a sight as unexpected as any I could imagine. Serafina came up behind me a few seconds later and gasped.

Armond was on one knee, hands clasped, gazing up rapturously at Hans, who stood on a stool, decked out in Jutta's big apron, with a kitchen towel draped over his head like long hair. Vrak, Ursula, and little Matya shouted instructions and laughed, and the big Matyas just laughed.

"Put your hand on your breast and look up," said Vrak. "As if beseeching God himself."

Hans laid one hand over his heart and raised his eyes to the ceiling just above his face.

"See it in your head. *Feel* your heart breaking," said Vrak. "Now, try again."

"O Romeo, Romeo! Wherefore art thou Romeo? Deny thy father and refuse thy name."

"Better …" said Vrak, though he was being kind.

Hans saw me and grinned. Grinned! I'd never seen him smile before, and for a second, I wasn't sure it was even him.

"I am learning to be an actor," he said.

"I can see that," I said.

When Serafina found her voice, she was livid. "I told you he was not allowed inside!"

Matya planted her fists on her hips. "I looked in his eyes, and I know he is safe."

Serafina sputtered for a moment. "You *what*?"

"Dear lady," said Vrak. "If our Matya looks in someone's eyes and declares them safe, you may be sure they are safe."

"She has the gift," added Ursula, and we all nodded.

Serafina threw up her hands. "What's done is done. Tonight, Pinocchio, Vrak, Armond, and I will go to headquarters. Ursula and Matya will follow tomorrow night."

"What about Hans?" asked Ursula.

"And Ivan?" added Matya.

Ivan sat up like the good boy he was. Hans was a good boy too, but with a towel on his head and standing on a stool.

"Ivan will be safest with Jutta for now. Hans is not my decision." Serafina grabbed her hat and opened the door. "Wait downstairs. Get some sleep if you can. I'll be back by dark."

She met my eyes for a moment. My heart thumped. When I turned, I caught Ursula watching me, and Matya watching Ursula. I stifled a groan. Dealing with an army of deadly Nazi Manikins seemed easier than figuring out what to do about the women in my life.

● ● ●

In the hideout room, Hans was asleep in a minute, as usual. The rest of us sat around the table and tried to play cards, but the jack of spades was missing from the deck, Ursula was too restless to sit, and my head was still spinning. We gave up. Armond tried to beat his previous record of juggling nine walnuts at once. He made it to seven, which was still impressive. Then he and Vrak went back to drinking and talking in circles, rehashing theories about the Blue Lady's plans, and getting nowhere. Ursula prowled the room like Fluffy at dinnertime. When I couldn't stand it anymore, I got up and stopped her with a hand on her arm.

"Listen, Ursula. I had no idea Seraf—"

She rounded on me and slapped my hand away. "We have no idea what happened to anyone at the circus, the Blue Lady turns out to be an evil witch with an evil army, Adolf Goddamn Manikin Hitler is running the country, we're trapped in a windowless room and can't do a thing about any of it, and you think this is about *you*?"

Ouch.

Matya appeared with a woolen blanket in her hands. "Ursula dear, we had to leave without our things, and it's cold out. Do you think this would do for scarves?"

Ursula snatched the blanket out of her hands and retreated to a corner, pulling her little sewing kit out from inside her blouse. God bless Matya. She was always so self-contained. Literally.

"Hey, Pinocchio," said Armond, "We've got a few more questions for Hans. Let's wake him up."

I didn't think it would help, but it was better than standing there smarting. We woke him.

"Just close your eyes and concentrate," said Vrak. "Can you sense any others? What are they doing?"

"I cannot help you," he said. "Since I am defective, I cannot receive orders or communicate with others."

"But you must know more than we do," he persisted. "Can you at least make a guess?"

Hans frowned. "Guessing is inefficient and unproductive. If every cog in a machine has to guess which way to turn, the machine will break, and no one will know what it was meant to produce."

"We should try to get some sleep," said Matya.

Everyone retreated to their corners, but my head was too full for sleep. I understood what Hans meant. When I was a sailor, I followed orders and never spent a minute thinking about how the ship stayed afloat or where it should sail next. But there was a crucial difference: the skipper might be able to tell me what to do and when to do it, but in the end, doing it was my choice, and no one could *ever* tell me what to think.

Jutta came down in the late afternoon with a supper of sauerkraut, peas, and potato dumplings in gravy. I forced it down, where it sat in my stomach like ballast. Ursula made a show of sitting close to Hans and ignoring me. I suppose she assumed I would run right back into Serafina's arms, but she was wrong. What Serafina had told me, if it was true, cast everything in a new light. But three years of grief and anger at her betrayal stuck to me like tar, and I couldn't just wash it away.

• • •

Serafina strode into the hideout room, shaking raindrops off her coat.

"Help me move these," she ordered, indicating the stack of mattresses.

We dragged them aside, revealing an iron trap door set into the floor.

"Well, that's handy," I said.

She nodded. "Every good safe house needs an escape hatch. If you have any weapons, bring them. Armond, you take the rifle."

Armond saluted. "Yes, sir! Ma'am!"

"The rest of you, cover this up and stay put. I'll come for you tomorrow night." She pulled aside the hatch to uncover a dark opening about a meter across that let cool, rank air into the room. "It's a little smelly."

She swung herself onto the ladder and disappeared into the hole.

Vrak looked down with a grimace.

"Go on, Pollywog," said Armond. "Think about all those tasty flies."

"I hope you get termites," said Vrak as his head vanished into the hole. Those two.

I went last. When the lid clanked back over the hole, Serafina switched on her electric lantern. We were in a brick-lined sewer tunnel, on a slick, sloping walkway that ran beside a murky channel. It was more than a little smelly; the stench was thick as grease. I kept my thoughts on Papa and held my breath.

The vaulted ceiling was low enough at the sides that even Serafina had to duck. We passed several ladders leading up to the surface but didn't meet anyone. Any workers would have gone home for the night. Serafina led us through the maze of tunnels. No one fell in, though I won't say we didn't have any close calls. Armond whacked his head three times and nearly fell in twice; I don't think he was pretending more than once. We finally came out through a culvert into a wooded area and took a moment to breathe air that was still ripe but at least didn't feel poisonous.

A narrow path led through pines. Wet mud sucked at our shoes, and the rain was mixed with flakes of snow. Snow. In April. One more reason to prefer Italy.

Thankfully, it was less than a kilometer to a clearing where a car waited, engine idling, needles of rain glittering in the headlights. The driver stood at attention beside the car. The minute I saw him, my scalp crawled. Nothing I could put my finger on, but something wasn't right.

Serafina didn't seem to notice. She strode forward. "Otto! Thank God! Let's go."

He opened the front passenger door—thumpity.

The back passenger door—thump.

Turned to face Serafina—thumpity.

Raised his arm toward her—thump.

I lunged forward, shoved her out of the way, and slammed Otto against the side of the car. The instant his hands touched me, I knew I was right.

"Manikin!" I shouted.

The others cried out as I grappled with Otto, but he never said a word. He was strong, and every time he touched my skin, the electric thrum burned like wasp stings.

"Armond!" I gasped. "Shoot him!"

"I can't get a clear shot!"

Otto got a grip on my face and a powerful jolt blazed through my temples. Vrak and Serafina moved in, but I warned them off. "No! Stay back!" I wrenched my head back, twisting and straining to pull free. His nails tore my skin, but I kept pulling.

I was almost free when a steely finger slipped into my left eye. Something burst in a white-hot arrow of pain. I howled.

The next minutes felt like shattered glass, each splinter bright and sharp, but the whole fractured and confused. We pieced it together later.

A heavy blow knocked me free of Otto's hands. It was Armond.

I remember falling in the mud, clutching my ruined eye, and hands under my arms pulling me away while Armond battered Otto with the butt of the rifle, roaring like a madman.

Otto got a hand on the rifle butt, and instead of pushing it away, he jerked it back, pulling Armond off balance. That was all the opening he needed.

His free hand shot out and caught Armond's face. Armond's back arched and his body jittered, arms and legs rigid as tent poles. The rifle dropped from fingers splayed like stakes. Vrak and Serafina circled, looking for a way to get to him. Vrak got a hand on Armond's arm, but the electric jolt flung him back.

Armond was bigger and taller than Otto, but Otto held him up easily with one hand. He scanned the clearing until he found me.

A blue glow sparked in his eyes, and he shook a scolding finger, as if he wasn't electrocuting a man with his other hand. "Pinocchio! You've been very naughty!" It was Otto's voice, but the Blue Lady's lilting Italian and feminine posture. "You never could behave. Always running off instead of doing the right thing."

I fought back nauseating pain. "Why do you even care? You got what you wanted from me."

"There is so much more you have to give. God himself chose me for this mission, and so it must go on even without you. But many more will die who might have lived. Because of your willfulness."

Even after everything I'd seen, her scolding made me feel like a naughty little boy. The searing pain in my eye made it hard to think. A second pulse thrummed behind the throbbing of my own heart. It was the heartbeat of the blue stone. I was sure of it. Somehow she was forcing herself into my head. I pushed her out with a shudder.

She clucked. "You're a spoiled child, thinking only of your own selfish desires, never the greater good. Be a man, for once." Otto's hand gave the helpless Armond a little shake. "I'll even let your friend go."

I crawled to my knees. If I could make her stronger, more might survive. How many more? Would a quarter of the people on Earth die instead of half? And what kind of life would the survivors have?

A gunshot cracked. Otto fell back against the car, releasing Armond, and crumpled to the ground.

Serafina held the rifle. "Otto was my friend." Her voice was choked with angry tears.

With no one supporting him, Armond teetered wildly on his feet, windmilling his arms clownishly like I'd seen him do a hundred times. Then he found his balance and straightened. Blue light bloomed in his eyes.

He glanced down at Otto's body and prodded it with a toe. "Such a waste." Then *she* narrowed his eyes at me. "Now, are you going to be a good boy and come home, or are you going to continue to make things worse?"

It was already worse. She was wearing my friend like a suit.

She raised Armond's hands and turned them this way and that as if seeing them for the first time. "Your friend was ready to sacrifice his life for you. And you won't do one little thing for him?"

My gut lurched, but I shook my head. If there was any chance at all to stop her, I couldn't do it. Not even to save Armond.

She grinned wide. "My, what big teeth I have!"

She raised his right wrist to his mouth and bit down with a sickening crunch. No normal human could have done it, but Armond's huge teeth were easily up to the task.

Vrak keened and fell to his knees beside me.

Serafina pulled the rifle bolt, aimed, and pulled the trigger, but it only clicked. She popped the cartridge with shaking hands. There was just one more bullet.

With a final snap, Armond's severed hand dropped into the mud. She waved his wrist toward Serafina, who was aiming again, and drops of blood hissed on the hot glass of the headlight. "Go ahead. It won't change a thing."

Serafina fired, but the bullet whizzed over Armond's head.

Vrak retched beside me, and my own stomach heaved as the Blue Lady raised Armond's left wrist to her mouth.

Armond's left hand fell not far from the right, fingers curled to the sky. The Blue Lady grinned at us through Armond's dripping face. She spread the ragged, bleeding stumps of his arms out in a grotesque parody of a casual shrug.

"You can't hurt me, you know. But I assure you your friend feels *everything*."

I pushed aside my own pain and surged forward, but Vrak grabbed my arm.

"Wait," he croaked in my ear.

Wait? Wait for what? But then I saw it. Armond's skin was waxy and gray. She tried to take a step forward but staggered drunkenly sideways. He was weak from shock and blood loss.

Fury flashed in her eyes, and Armond's knees buckled. She tried to catch herself on the car, but without hands, she slithered to her knees.

"No matter. I've already won."

The blue light in Armond's eyes blinked out.

He curled up in silent agony, cradling his wrists against his stomach.

Vrak ran to Armond and gathered him up in his arms, sobbing. He turned to me. "Why? Why didn't Otto change you?"

His words were a fist to the gut. It should have been me. I turned away and vomited on the ground.

The rest of that night faded into a haze of pain. I remember someone wrapping bandages around my eyes, a long ride in the car, the wet dog smell of river water, a boat.

Rocking on the water was familiar and soothing, and by the time we hit the other shore, the world had become distant and muffled. I remember hands pulling me out of the boat, low voices, endless stumbling in the dark across wet, uneven ground, the creak of a gate or door, and then smooth stone underfoot and cool air that smelled like rain coming after a long dry spell.

• • •

I woke to darkness and quiet. I brought my hands to my face and felt dry bandages. Two warm, callused hands gripped mine, and the smell of wood shavings and pipe tobacco filled my head.

"Papa?"

"It's me, son." His voice broke, and we held each other in a tight embrace. It was a long time before either of us could say another word.

If I live to be a hundred and fifty, I'll never understand how I could be pulled by such extremes of grief and joy at the same time and not be ripped right in half. I'd found him at last. But the cost was unbearable.

We lost Armond not three days later.

During the war, I'd seen what can happen to a body in the aftermath of injuries like his, even with proper medical care. The medic, a plump, rosy-cheeked Blue named Gretel, did what she could for him. Vrak never left his side. When Matya and Ursula arrived, they nursed him around the clock, too. But infection outran their efforts, swarming up his arms like an invading army and leaving fever, delirium, and ruin in its wake.

We buried him under a walnut tree in the woods near the banks of the Rhine, serenaded by spring birdsong.

By that time, I was recovered enough to walk there myself. My eye was lost, but the wound was clean and healing well. The pain had diminished from stabbing to drumming.

Ursula, tears wetting the dark fur on her face, laid an armful of wildflowers on his grave and retreated to Matya's arms.

Vrak looked like he'd aged twenty years. He stepped forward on shaking legs. "Armond …" It was several minutes before he could go on. "Armond, you were my first and best friend. More than a brother. We fought like dogs, and there were times I wanted to throttle you, but I wouldn't have missed a minute of it. You were the best clown I ever knew, even though all you wanted was to be worthy of your soldier's uniform." Vrak saluted while tears streamed down his face. "You were always more than worthy. God's chompers, you are a true hero."

Matya, Ursula, and I gathered him in and hugged him tightly. Matya looked at me, pain and pleading in her eyes. "There is no more sunshine until this evil is gone from the world."

I nodded. In some way I still didn't fully understand yet, this was my battle to fight. I forced my clenched jaw to open and made a promise I had no idea how to keep. "I won't let him down."

On the way back, Papa walked by my side. He seemed smaller, beyond the normal shrinking of age—like something inside him had been compressed, leaving his skin too loose over a flinty core.

The Blues were flintier, too. They no longer tried to make excuses for the Blue Lady. She was the enemy, and this was war.

That night I dreamt that Serafina walked toward me with her wings whole and spread wide. I reached out, but my own hands were torn away at the wrists, and twisting, thorny branches sprouted in their place. They caught her wings and tore them, and the more I tried to untangle them, the worse it got. I woke up gasping.

When morning came, it was like wartime anywhere— bottle up your grief, shove a cork in it, and get on with the fight.

• • •

Papa led me to his quarters deep in the maze of ancient tunnels. Some of the tunnels ran right under the houses and cobbled streets of a town I hesitate to name. Who knows when they might be needed again? But there were older tunnels that went much farther, and this is where we hid. Unlike the Blue Lady's mine, the walls here were dry and the floors dusty. They had a generator, but it was mostly used for the radio. Kerosene lamps supplemented the few electric lights.

We turned at an archway that led down a few steps to a large, low-ceilinged chamber. Planks and crates served as workbenches, tables, chairs, bookcases, and bed. Tools, wood, pots of glue, jars of screws and nails, coils of wire, half-built contraptions of wood and metal, and piles of papers covered in notes filled every surface. A hat and coat hung from a hook on the wall beside a map covered with pins and pencil marks. The air was fresh; there must have been a vent to the surface nearby.

"Home, sweet home!" said Papa.

He moved notebooks and empty plates from an upended crate to another teetering stack and invited me to sit. I sat, still not quite believing that he was right there in front of me. More than once, my throat tightened when I thought of how long I'd stayed away.

He knew some of my story from Serafina, and he'd spent hours talking to Hans, who fascinated him. But he wanted to hear it all again, directly from me. Especially the parts where I was in the jewel's starry universe. When I was done, he buried his face in his hands.

"If only I had stayed home!"

"Why did you go?"

"She said she needed my help. I would have done anything for her."

"It was the same for me," I said.

"Without her," he went on, "I never would have had you! And God forgive me, I did work out the template for her wooden soldiers before I found out the truth and refused to do any more. I'm so sorry." He sighed. "I didn't know it at the time, but I was mainly there as bait. She was fishing for you all along."

"But how did she think I would find you? The first rule of fishing is to drop bait where the fish are."

He reached out and tugged on the little wooden heart around my neck. "I'm afraid I helped with that too, though now I wish I hadn't."

"Your compass? How could that help?"

"Compass?" He laughed. "I guess in a way it is, but not to find north. It points to the jewel."

"How could I know that? Your note wasn't exactly helpful."

"She insisted that secrecy was critical. I couldn't tell you right out in the note. We were heading north, so you'd be going the right way. And when you figured it out, it would have led you right to me if she and I hadn't parted ways. I waited as long as I could," he said. "But those poor people. I couldn't let her keep on torturing them. When I saw a chance to escape, I took it."

"What the hell is the jewel anyway? I always thought the Blue Lady was just, you know, magical. Herself."

He refilled his pipe, poking a splinter of wood into the lamp flame to light it with. The little face on the pipe bowl was carved so that the eyes glowed when he drew on it.

"She was just an ordinary girl who lived in our town when I was a lad. Wretched little thing, mother dead, father a mean drunk. When she went missing, everyone assumed she ran off with some boy. I didn't see her again until she came to us not long after I carved you. By then, she had the jewel, and it had changed her. I didn't believe it was the same girl at first; she'd hardly aged, and I was getting to middle age. She was most interested in you. When she told me she could make you a real boy, I didn't ask too many questions. Having you for a son was my heart's desire."

"Where did she get the jewel from?"

"I didn't know until I came to Germany with her. There'd been a storm the night before she ran away. She told me she found the jewel buried inside a lightning-split oak. Who knows how it got there? Maybe the tree sprouted right over it and grew up around it. It must have been inside that tree for a long, long time. Maybe a thousand years."

"What is it?" I asked.

He puffed thoughtfully for a moment. "She believes it's a token—proof that she was chosen to do God's will. But I think it's a machine of some kind."

"What, like a car?"

"More like a radio. One person controls the broadcast, but any receiver can pick up the signal. Her Manikins are receivers."

And now she'd learned how to turn receivers into broadcasters? No, that wasn't quite right. There was still only one broadcaster, but the receivers acted as relays. And they could make more relay receivers. And those could make more. And those—my head throbbed.

"The things it can do are miraculous!" Papa said. "I suppose her explanation makes as much sense as mine."

"I still don't see how I figure in."

"You don't? Think about it," he said.

Him too? I opened my mouth to tell him I was sick of riddles. But then I knew. "You carved me from that tree!"

"The very same. The stone didn't just change the Blue Lady; it changed the tree it was inside of all those years. Of all the Blues, you are the only one who was already alive before she changed you."

No, surely he was wrong about that. I searched my memory. Had any of them ever talked about their lives before the Blue Lady came? I couldn't come up with a single time. They'd been toys or puppets, and then, alive. I always thought of my former self as a puppet too, but was I? I never needed anyone to move my body or give me a voice. I might have been made of wood, but I had a mind of my own even before I had a head. Was I really the only one? My heart sank a little. Just when I thought I'd finally found my own kind.

"That tree ... all that wood. There could be others."

He shook his head. "Gone. I went looking, but there'd been a fire. Nothing is left but this little wooden heart. And you."

"Why did she leave Italy?"

"She had to. She got careless, making all these Blues and then just leaving them when they didn't turn out the way she wanted. The Church took notice. The police. People got scared."

Or homicidal, like Ludovico.

"She kept moving. The jewel gave her languages and power. She could go anywhere. She was in Germany when she made her first Manikin, and she's been here ever since. Getting ready for this moment. You were the last piece she needed."

"Why didn't she just turn me into one of her Manikins? She's had plenty of chances. Then she could just order me to do whatever she wanted. Am I immune or something?"

He gave a long sigh. "I wish you were. She doesn't dare connect you and the stone. The power you experienced when you touched the jewel? It's because it's like you, or you're like it. You would take it over, and she would lose control of it."

"Well, there's the answer! If I can get it away from her, I'll just take it over and fix everything!" Thoughts of all the good I could do swarmed my head.

"No!" he cried. "It's far too dangerous. We do have to get it away from her, but you mustn't use it or even touch it directly. I should have said it would take *you* over. You've seen what it did to her. You'd be lost forever."

"We're all about to be lost forever! She's set on turning every living person on Earth into a Manikin or furnace fuel!"

"And she was just a young, inexperienced girl." Papa gripped my arms tightly. "What would it do with you?"

I knew he was right. The Blue Lady believed she was doing good and fixing everything. Could I trust myself to do any better? Look what a great job I'd done giving orders to Hans. The world would probably be a smoking ruin by the time I got through with it. But, oh, I wanted to try.

Serafina stuck her head in the door. "Hitler is going to speak on the radio."

18

The radio was housed in a side chamber at the end of a long, upward-sloping corridor. A vent in the vaulted ceiling allowed an antenna wire to pass through to the surface, where it was hidden in a tree. When we got there, the small room was already crowded. Aside from Vrak, Matya, Ursula and me, Papa had a core crew of five running the operation there. Four were Blues, but the radio operator was a strapping, freckled human teen named Rolf. He was one of the normals Papa liberated in his escape, and he was utterly devoted to the cause after witnessing what the Blue Lady had done to his parents.

Near the entrance, Vrak and Matya slumped against each other as if either one would collapse if the other stepped away. Ursula clenched her fists and looked like she wanted to crush something. Hans stood by the wall, waiting with endless patience for someone to tell him what to do. And I had the first glimmerings of a plan.

It wasn't much of a plan. In fact, it was almost certainly a flat-out disaster, and I prayed to God we wouldn't need to use it.

It's disappointing how often God does not answer prayers.

There was a crackle of static after the radio announcer switched over, and then Hitler began to speak. This was his first public address since the Blue Lady had changed him.

He began with his usual rubbish about Treason and the German Farmer and the Scourge of Bolshevism. Blah blah blah. Had he managed to break free from her? No. As he spoke, his voice fell into a hypnotic and familiar rhythm. If I could have seen him pounding on the podium, I'm sure it would have been in perfect time.

Thumpity-thump, thumpity-thump.

Toward the end, he spoke less about Marxists and armies and more about law and order. The one thing we were waiting for he delivered at the end.

"I call on every loyal German! Come to Berlin on the First of May. Join your brothers and sisters at a rally—the biggest rally the world has ever seen! There, we will begin a new era! A new world! A new future!" Thumpety. Thump.

May Day. Less than two weeks away. After the speech, the announcer gave more details. The rally would be held at the Tempelhof Airfield to accommodate the million or more people expected to show up. That had to be the day the Blue Lady would give the order for her soldiers to begin turning humans into Manikins. With that many people all in one place, it would create so much chaos and spread so fast that there would be no way to stop it.

In the chamber we used as a mess room, we gathered around the long table. Papa stood at one end of it and looked around at us. "Well?"

"Do you think she'll go to Berlin?" asked Serafina. "She could give the command from the safety of her hideout."

"She could," I said. "But my guess is she'll want to witness her big moment in person."

"I think so, too," said Papa. "Now, how do we get the jewel?"

A long, uneasy silence followed. When I couldn't put it off any longer, I took a deep breath and laid out my idea. A longer silence followed. Several people opened their mouths and then shut them again.

Finally, Serafina spoke. "It *could* work … if we could locate her exactly."

"I can't get her exact location," I said. "But I can tell what direction she is from me."

"We might be able to improve that," said Papa. "I have some ideas."

"I can sew disguises," said Ursula.

"I will do anything you ask," said Matya.

"Wait a minute," said Gretel. "If we touch it, will we end up in its power?"

"There's no way to know for certain," said Papa. "She shouldn't be able to command it once we get it away from her. I don't know for certain if it can act on its own or if it needs someone to direct it. Try not to touch it directly. If you can't avoid it, then be careful not to wish for anything. Pinocchio, don't you touch it at all."

"That shouldn't be a problem," I said. "She keeps it inside a locket."

Everyone nodded and my chest tightened. God help us, we were actually going to attempt it.

"We have Otto's car," said Bernard. Bernard was a Blue who had been a wind-up cymbal-clapping monkey. He still had a long tail, but thankfully, no cymbals. "I'd feel a lot better if we had backup transport."

"Hans and I hid a car off the road outside Frankfurt," I said. "It might still be there."

Papa nodded. "We'll send Hans and another driver to see if we can retrieve it."

"What do we do with the jewel once we get it?" asked Ursula.

Using it ourselves was out. Destroy it? We didn't know if it *could* be destroyed or what the effect might be. All the magic it had done might be destroyed with it, which would be fine as far as the Manikins were concerned, but it would be the end of all us Blues too. It would be a last resort.

"What if we drop it at the bottom of the sea?" Gretel suggested.

Everyone bent over the map on the table. The sea was a long way from Berlin.

"Due north is closest," said Bernard.

"We have contacts in Hamburg," said Papa. "They might be able to arrange a boat."

Bernard scoffed. "Hamburg is a huge port. It'll be swarming with militia. You can't just get on a boat."

"I was a sailor for fourteen years," I said. "If there's one thing I can do, it's get on a boat."

It went around like that for a while until Rolf piped up. "My Uncle Franz has an airplane."

Nine jaws dropped.

"He's a farmer now, but he used to be a barnstormer. Near Itzehoe."

We all looked back at the map. Itzehoe was near the coast, about sixty kilometers northwest of Hamburg.

"Does he still have the airplane? Does it still fly?" asked Papa.

Rolf shrugged. "I don't know."

"Well, let's find out," said Papa.

The discussion went on, and assignments were given. Then Papa turned to me. "Let's go."

• • •

In Papa's workshop, we experimented with different ways to pinpoint the Blue Lady's distance as well as direction.

"Try holding it in your mouth," said Papa.

I put the heart pendant in my mouth and closed my eye.

"Still nothing," I said.

He sighed.

"Maybe we should let the others have a go," I suggested.

"You're the only one with even a sliver of magic in you."

A sliver of magic! How could I forget? "Wait here."

I ran back to my cot and fumbled through the pockets of my jacket until I found my wallet. I emptied it and shuffled through the papers. I wish I had known I'd never need them; it would be sweet to return Alidoro's father's watch to him. I opened each document and set it aside. I shook the wallet, holding it open wide. Was it lost? I ran my fingers inside along the seams and felt a sharp edge wedged into a corner. I carefully freed it.

The tiny chip of the blue jewel I'd saved from the tower room glittered on my fingertip.

Back in the workshop, Papa took it to the light and examined it closely, turning it over and over.

"Will it help?" I asked.

"I don't know," he said. "This is the first time I've seen a piece of it directly. I can't feel anything." He handed it back to me. "Can you?"

I pinched it between my thumb and forefinger. I felt the faint buzzing pulse but saw no points of light or filmy threads when I closed my eye.

"Nothing useful. I think it's too small."

"Try holding it together with the wooden heart."

The pulse was stronger, and when I closed my eye, I saw a faint wash of blue. Progress!

"It may need more direct contact. Try putting them in your mouth," he suggested. "But whatever you do, don't swallow that chip!"

I did as he asked, and the blue haze grew stronger. In the direction of the wooden heart's pulse, the glow was denser, like a faraway lighthouse through heavy fog. But I still had no sense of how far it was. Maybe I should swallow it. That would get it deeper inside. But it wouldn't stay there. I spat the pieces into my palm and wiped them off on my sleeve.

"There's just not enough," said Papa.

"Isn't there some of the wood in my leg?"

His head shot up. "Of course! It's been so long I forgot! Let me see it."

I rolled up my trouser leg, and he knelt to look at it closely. He ran his fingers over the rough surface and moved the ankle joint this way and that.

"So crude," he murmured.

"Are you kidding? It's a miracle."

He stood. "Please take it off."

While I unstrapped it, he soaked strips of cloth in a bowl of wet plaster to make a cast of my stump. While that was drying, he rummaged through piles of junk stacked against the wall.

"Aha!" He held up an ancient pair of crutches. The look on my face must have been pitiful. "None of that, son." He popped the cast off my leg and handed me the crutches. "Off you go, and don't let anyone disturb me."

He was already hunched over my leg on his workbench when I hobbled out. No need to warn anyone not to disturb him. It would take the ceiling falling down to disturb him, and maybe not even that.

Everyone was busy, proceeding as if my plan was sound instead of desperate. Disguises had to be obtained, fitted, or sewn, transport arranged, messages sent, routes and rendezvous points debated, roles practiced, new identities created.

I would go to Berlin as a blind Great War veteran longing to hear my Führer speak, with Vrak and Matya as my parents. Hans would be our driver. Contacts in Berlin arranged a rendezvous spot in a warehouse just to the west of the airfield.

Serafina was everywhere, helping everyone. The more I saw of her strength and character, the more I kicked myself for how I'd reacted to what she'd told me in the safe house basement. I wanted to apologize, but she was always running. Sometimes I was sure I felt her eyes on me, but when I turned, she was always heading away or talking to someone.

We got word that Uncle Franz did indeed have a small airplane. It hadn't been flown in years, but he would fix it up. Rolf would head straight to the farm in the other car with Papa, Ursula, and Serafina and wait for us. Serafina could drive in a pinch, but they knew another driver who was first-rate and sent for him.

Ursula was in her element. She took over a storage room and set about sewing and ordering people around. Gretel joined her. She wasn't a seamstress, but she'd trained as a medic and knew her way around a needle well enough to satisfy Ursula. The two of them became inseparable.

For Matya, Ursula found a matronly brown wool suit and a felt cloche suitable for a proper German hausfrau. Her German was better than mine, but she still had a Russian accent.

She sniffed. "Being a fat woman is disguise enough. No one will see me or listen to a word I say."

A fake mustache and beard did quite a bit to hide Vrak's facial oddities, if you didn't look too close. A waistcoat buttoned across his round belly made him look comfortably well off. He hobbled around for us, leaning heavily on a cane. The act was nearly perfect. Until he shot out his tongue and snagged a fly midair.

"You're going to have to not do that," I said.

He sighed. "I don't even like them, really. Nervous habit."

We were silent for a moment, and the absence of Armond floated between us as solid as an iceberg.

"You were right," I said. "It should have been me."

"No, son," said Vrak. "I'm sorry for what I said. If it had been you, we'd have no chance at all now. It's just that Armond and I ... we were very close. You understand?"

Vrak dropped his face into his hands and shook with low, croaking sobs. There was nothing I could say. I put an arm around his shoulders and cried with him.

• • •

I tried to perfect my German accent, but in the end, we added "mute from head wound" to my disabilities. Ursula had found an old infantry uniform and an impressive collection of medals, including an Iron Cross. Dark glasses, an eye patch, and a white cane finished off the disguise.

"Dark glasses *and* an eye patch?" I asked.

"Why just be blind when you can be blind and mysterious?" I was fine with it. My eye was still sore enough that even the small amount of protection the patch gave it was welcome.

Then, with typical Ursula bluntness, she asked, "So, are you and your butterfly pollinating the flowers or what?"

"No!" I don't know why I thought we couldn't have both a battle to save the world *and* unfinished relationship business. But honestly, after the reaming she gave me in the safe house basement, it soothed my vanity a little to think at least a bit of it was about me.

"I know how you feel about each other," said Ursula.

"Maybe you can tell me because I sure don't."

"Oh, come on! Both of you light up like neon signs whenever you see each other."

"We do not!" I was probably guilty as charged. But did she?

"Then what about you and me?"

I looked at her. She was strong and feisty and funny. Back in the circus we were good together. But until I could turn off my neon light for Serafina, it wasn't fair to Ursula. I was resigned to ending up alone.

"I'm sorry," I said.

She sighed. "It is what it is, Pirate. But if it doesn't work out, don't think you can come running back. Bears have long memories and sharp claws."

Then she jabbed me with a pin.

Later, I passed Serafina in the corridor. In public, she wore her long coat. But here, she was always in trousers, boots, and a shirt with the back ripped out for her tattered wings. They hung behind her like battlefield flags, and every time I saw them, my heart spilled over with grief. She rounded on me.

"Stop looking at me like I'm some wounded puppy. They're no more useless now than they ever were. It's not like I could fly before!" She was lit up, all right, but not in the way Ursula meant. "Don't you have anything better to do?" She stormed off.

The problem was, I didn't. And I wouldn't until Papa was done with whatever he was up to. For the moment, I wasn't much use to anyone. I was healing well, but if I worked for more than a few hours, my eye started to feel like it was full of sand. And on crutches, I was useless even to fetch and carry.

One other person had almost as little to do as me. Hans did anything he was asked to do, but the others were still a bit leery of him. And if you weren't careful in your instructions, you could get some pretty random results.

I found him in his usual corner of the mess room, staring into a cup. He'd developed an absolute passion for coffee with a spoonful of wood ashes stirred into it. I poured myself a cup without ashes and managed to carry it without spilling more than half.

"Don't look so happy," I said.

He sighed. "Forgive me. It is not my intention to look happy, as I am not."

"It was a joke." When would I learn? "What's eating you? And by that, I mean, what's on your mind?"

"It troubles me that I don't know what will happen."

"It troubles all of us, my friend. You get used to it."

"But it also troubles me that it troubles me. I was made to be part of a system. I should not have these thoughts. It must be part of my defect. When I heard what happened to Otto the driver, at first, I was curious. Maybe I could be fixed, the way he was. But then I would no longer know you. And when I saw what happened to Armond … I should not have a feeling about it—against the Blue Lady. But I do."

"You should absolutely have a feeling about it."

"Do you think that she—" He scrubbed his eyes with one hand. "No, it is impossible."

"What?"

"Do you think she might also be defective?"

I barked a laugh and then felt bad about it. This was serious stuff. "What makes you think she might be defective?"

"I have been thinking about her plan to make everyone in the world part of the thumpity-thump. For a long time, I didn't understand how this could be bad. But now I see that other people are not like me. They are made to choose for themselves, so it is right that they should choose this also. In her plan, there is no choosing."

"Hans, you're made to choose for yourself too. The very first thing you did in your life was a choice."

He paused. "I don't think it was a choice in the way you mean it," he said at last. "It was without thinking. Like blinking when something is in your eye. Your kind of choosing takes much thinking. And every minute, there are more choices to be made. It goes on and on and there is no end. How do you know the right choice?"

"We don't. You learn as you go. Sometimes you learn from the people around you. Parents, teachers, friends, enemies. Sometimes you just think things through until you figure it out. Sometimes you make mistakes and hopefully learn from those. It's called being human."

He was silent for a long time. Then he asked, "Am I human?"

I looked at him. He was such an odd mix of bits and pieces. But he wanted to understand the world and his place in it. He wanted to do the right thing and be useful to the people around him. He made mistakes and got confused and he tried to learn. What more was there?

"Yes," I said. "You're human."

• • •

Early the next morning, Papa came to get me.

The end of his workbench was cleared except for two bundles wrapped up in cloth. Papa never could resist making Christmas gifts of things. One of them was leg-shaped. He handed me that one first.

I expected it to be my old leg with a new cup, all polished up, but it wasn't. It was a new one, and I'd never seen anything like it before. I stared at it, open-mouthed. Aside from the foot, which could wear a shoe, it looked more like a machine piston than a leg, with a gleaming steel shaft rising from the ankle joint.

It didn't have any straps. Papa showed me how to fit a tight, rubber sleeve over my stump and fit that into the cup at the top of the leg. I was sure it would never stay on until I stood and put my weight on it. It worked like a suction cup, and each step renewed the vacuum. It hung on like a barnacle until you turned a nut to let air in.

"Give it a try," he said

I took a step. Then another. And then six more. It was stronger and more responsive than my old leg. But where that one had been wild and rowdy, the power of this one was steady and controlled. Maybe it would help me feel steady and controlled too.

Papa gave me some time to practice and made adjustments. I took it off and put it on a dozen times. I ran, jumped, spun. I decided it was Christmas, after all.

"There's more," he reminded me.

I unwrapped the small package and found an eye looking back at me—a disturbingly lifelike one, down to the brown iris that matched my own and the tiny veins. Lamplight glinted off the pupil.

"That's the chip," he said. The rest is wood from the tree. I pieced it together from your heart pendant and some of the wood from inside your leg. If you're wearing it, maybe you'll be able to see more."

"How could you make all this in a week?"

"I just made the eye this week," he said. "I've been working on the leg for months. Hoping for this moment."

He examined my eye socket. "How does it feel?"

"It hurts like a bastard. But it used to hurt like ten bastards, so that's something."

Of course, I hadn't tried putting anything inside it so far. It took a few tries, a lot of swearing, but eventually, it went in, and it only hurt like five bastards. Maybe six.

You never think how your eyeball feels in its socket until it's not your own eyeball. Then just try thinking about anything else.

"What do you see?"

I closed my good eye and tried to concentrate, slowing my breathing and pushing past the red throb of my own heartbeat to a blue fog. Then a flicker at the corner of my eye. I turned my head and "stared" at it straight on. It's not that facing it mattered—this wasn't seeing in the same way that your eyes see—but it helped to think of it that way. A brighter blue dot floated in the fog. Nothing like the blazing sun I'd seen when I was with the Blue Lady. It throbbed, but not in time with my heart.

"I can see it!" I hoped it couldn't see me.

"Can you tell where it is?"

"I'm not sure. It has a … a place? A distance? But I have no idea how I would point to it on a map."

"Let's find a map."

When Papa was right next to me, his glow was distinct, but if he moved away his light blended into the general blue fog. As I got used to it, I began to see places where there didn't seem to be any clouds at all and places where the clouds were thick.

"Those must be cities," Papa said.

Of course. Densely populated areas versus empty countryside.

He laid a map of Germany on his workbench, oriented to the compass. We painstakingly matched the clouds in my head with cities on the map. Frankfurt was brightest and closest; Berlin was an enormous fog bank in the distance. I stuck mental pins in every spot we identified and slowly built a map inside my head.

A burst of excited voices filled the corridor, and a minute later, Bernard poked his head in the door with a wide gap-tooth grin. "Driver's here."

We followed him out the door. The new driver was surrounded by the others.

Rolf looked up. "Oh, here's Pinocchio."

The driver turned to face me, and what was left of my vision went red. In an instant, we were both on the ground with my hands around his neck. "Spy!" I bellowed. "Cat, you goddamn spy!"

Hands pulled me away and Papa shouted. "Stop! What's going on here?"

"Get him out of here! He's a spy!"

"Yes," said Papa. "But he's our spy."

"What? And you believe him?"

Cat sat up, mopping a scrape on his forehead with a handkerchief. "Geppetto was kind to me even before you was a real boy. Even though I didn't deserve it. I know you don't believe it, and I can't say as I blame you, but it's true."

"Liar!" I bellowed.

"Calm down, son," said Papa. "Cat's as loyal as they come."

I snorted. "And what about Fox?"

"No, not him," said Cat. "He was never loyal to no one but the highest bidder."

Hearing Cat suddenly speaking in full sentences didn't make me trust him more.

"You don't know it, but you owe Cat your life," said Papa.

"He handed me to the Blue Lady!"

"That was Fox. Weren't nothing I could do without giving away the game," said Cat.

Some game. "So, when did you supposedly save my skin?"

"When you come out of the mountain holding onto that crate. Did you hear a shot?

"You missed."

"That I didn't," said Cat. "Fox was taking aim at you, but I took aim at him first. That bullet hit the mark true as any I ever shot."

I shook my head to try to clear it. "You killed Fox?"

"It was Cat who told us to look for you," said Papa, helping Cat to his feet.

I rubbed my throbbing head. "You could have sent a car."

I still didn't trust him, but it wasn't up to me. Cat and Hans left to see if they could fetch the defense contractor's car. Everyone went back to work. I went back to staring at the map. We'd drawn an X on the spot where the jewel and presumably the Blue Lady's hideout sat. It was in the Harz Mountains between Berlin and Hanover. I was getting better at judging locations in my head, but it was slow, tiring work.

Cat and Hans came back with the car. Ursula put the finishing touches on our disguises. Inside the cuff of my jacket, I found Armond's name embroidered in red thread. As if I needed a reminder of what was at stake. Our false identity papers arrived. I felt like a different person. One named Günther Schmidt. I bid Marco Costa a sad goodbye. The pieces were falling into place.

Except for one. The Blue Lady still hadn't budged from her lair. We decided we'd wait as long as we could but head to Berlin anyway and hope for the best. It was damned annoying.

• • •

Most of the entrances to our tunnels were under homes in the town and were protected by locked gates, but a forgotten one opened into the forest far from any building or road. We hid the cars there for loading and final checks. I was headed there when I saw Serafina in the entrance, alone and standing still for once, lost in some private thought. The sun behind her blurred the edges of her body and made her look like she was dissolving into the air. The shell she wore to shut me out was gone.

And I saw what I'd been blind to. She didn't wear a shell to keep me out. She wore it to keep her own pain in. On that terrible day three years ago, she wore it to save me, and the thought of the strength it must have taken almost brought me to my knees. Could I have been that strong for her? At the safe house, when she opened up to me, I'd shut her down and stuffed her back inside. I felt a hot rush of shame. Now, in this unguarded moment, I saw through it to a heart more aching and broken than my own. I had never known how deeply one person could love another. Until now. When it was far too late.

We were leaving in a few minutes, and the odds I would ever see her again were slim at best. If I let her go without telling her what was in my heart—what I now knew for sure—my silence would be the biggest lie of my life. Even if I was wrong. Even if she rejected me again and I was the biggest chump in the world. If I died tomorrow, I'd die the way I lived: telling the truth.

When I called her name, she startled. But then she came to me. I took her hand and led her up a short stairway with a blind wall at its end. It was one of many like it in the tunnels, leading up or down to nowhere. Maybe there were other tunnels or rooms hidden behind those walls, but I never found out. This one was just big enough for the two of us.

I took a breath and just blurted it out before I lost my nerve.

"Serafina, whether I live another day or a hundred years, whether you still care about me or you hate my guts, I want you to know that I understand what you did for me that day and why. I can't even imagine what it cost you—what it continues to cost you. You don't have to answer. I don't expect anything. I've been a complete ass, and there's nothing I can say or do to make up for it. I just want you to know I love you. I loved you from the first minute I saw you, and I will never stop loving you."

She put her fingers on my lips to stop me from going on. "The most I ever hoped for," she said, "was your forgiveness."

She replaced her fingers with her lips, and electricity leaped between us just as strong as the first time. Her body melted into mine, and her wings, even as damaged as they were, shivered against my hands. I didn't need a blue thread to know our connection was real and unbreakable. If we survived, I would never let her go again.

Far off in blue-fogged darkness, the jewel began to move.

I held Serafina tighter. "It's started. It's time to go."

She gripped my head in her hands and looked into my eyes fiercely. "You better come back to me."

I wished it was a promise I could make. Hands clasped tightly, we walked out into the sunshine.

The others were already there. Ursula gave us a once over and then squinted as if our neon lights were so bright, they hurt her eyes. But she smiled and gave me a thumbs-up. It might have been another finger.

"She's heading toward Berlin," I said.

Cat saluted and slid into the driver's seat of his car, Rolf beside him. I hugged Papa tightly. Another impossible goodbye. I had only just found him. He got in the rear seat with Ursula on one side and Serafina on the other, and they were gone.

Vrak, Matya, and I climbed into our car. Hans shut the doors and started the engine. Anxiety burned a path from my stomach to the roots of my hair. What was I leading them into? We would have to get past thousands of soldiers without being recognized. Maybe tens of thousands, many of them hunting for me, specifically.

Papa had tried to reassure me. "A big crowd is your best cover. Like hiding a stick in a woodpile."

And the Blue Lady was holding the match.

19

It seemed like the whole country was on the road. The weather was fine, and flag-waving patriots filled nearly every car and bus. It turned my stomach.

Late that night, we camped just off the road when Hans needed his few hours of sleep. I offered to drive, but a blind driver might raise a few eyebrows. We all needed a break from sitting, and the smaller Matyas appreciated a chance to stretch their legs. I walked restlessly, testing my new leg, watching the blue stone move towards Berlin, and thinking about Serafina.

In the morning, a steady drizzle spattered the windshield. We napped in the car as much as we could, but not as much as we should. Matya taught us a Russian song with pornographic lyrics, and we sang it for an hour straight. Hans turned out to have a sweet baritone voice, and when ordered to translate from Russian to German, he did so with unflinching accuracy.

"What other tricks do you have up that Nazi sleeve of yours, son?" asked Vrak. "Anything useful?"

"I don't know," said Hans. "There are many protocols I can only access if ordered."

"I order you to give us a list of protocols," Vrak tried.

"I don't have access to a list."

Matya said, "Perhaps some protocols are best left unaccessed."

We stopped at a café for lunch, though we didn't get out of the car until I scanned the area for Manikins. I made a show of twitching and mumbling as I tapped around with my cane. I felt a little guilty about pretending to be a wounded veteran until I remembered that I *was* a wounded veteran. While we ate, regular Nazis evicted Jewish families from their apartments across the street, throwing furniture and dishes from the windows to shatter on the pavement. My fists clenched with the itch to go paste them, but we had to sit there and nod while the café owner crowed to us about how the country was getting cleaned up at last. When I couldn't take it anymore, I pretended to have a seizure, and we left without finishing lunch.

The closer we got to Berlin, the heavier the traffic became, but we were still on track to arrive there by nightfall. We'd stopped singing or even talking; the only sound was the rumble of the engine. I held the map in my lap and focused on the stone. I could place it more accurately now, somewhere near the city center. The mist of other souls was brighter too, and clumpier. I couldn't separate one person from another, but the busy streets and squares were rivers and pools of light.

The sun came out, and a rainbow appeared over the fields to the east.

"That's a sign of good luck, right?" I said.

A moment later, something under the car hood clanked and the engine died. Shit!

Hans rolled the car to the side of the road and stopped. Vrak groaned, and Matya pressed her lips into a tight line.

We all got out to have a look. I knew pretty much nothing about automobiles. We'd carried them as cargo sometimes, but there wasn't anywhere to drive them aboard ship. It didn't stop me from wanting to look.

"You're blind and shell shocked, son. Act it," said Vrak. So, I stood there with my cane, eye patch, and dark glasses and gaped open-mouthed at nothing while trying to peek at the engine through the corner of my eye.

"Can you fix it?" Matya asked Hans.

"Perhaps, if I am ordered to."

"Hans, I order you to fix the engine," I said.

He bent over and poked around in the beast's oily guts. He searched through a box of tools and parts, consulted a manual, and returned to poke at the engine some more. After a few moments, he straightened up.

"To fix the engine will require obtaining a part," he said.

A large, sleek Mercedes with military insignia on the door panel pulled up next to us. A Nazi officer leaned out the window. From the amount of hardware on his uniform, I pegged him somewhere in the neighborhood of general. My heart banged so loud in my chest I was sure he could hear it.

"Engine trouble?" he asked.

Vrak nodded sadly. "I'm afraid so, sir. And we were so hoping to hear our beloved Führer speak tomorrow."

"Oh, that's a pity," said the general.

Why would someone like him give a pfennig about people like us? It made me edgy, but Vrak was warming to his role. He slapped a fatherly hand on my shoulder. I flinched.

"I am most heartbroken for my poor son. When he heard our Führer speak on the radio, he stood to attention, saluted, and said 'Heil Hitler!' First words from his mouth since he was so grievously wounded serving his country in the Great War."

I stuck out my arm and garbled, "Heil Hitler!" They all Heil Hitlered back.

The general took me in, from my dark glasses and cane to the medals on my chest. "He couldn't speak before? Not at all?"

"Not one word since Verdun. Wounded in an ambush by the damn French. Bullet went straight through his head. It was a miracle he survived at all."

Matya gave a mournful sob and dabbed her eyes with her handkerchief.

"But hearing him speak those two words. That was the true miracle." I cringed, but Vrak was into it now, and there would be no stopping him. "Can there be any more proof that Germany is blessed by God Himself? If the mere sound of the Führer's voice on the radio healed my precious son's voice, we believe that being in his actual presence will bring back his sight or even cure him completely."

Matya crossed herself.

The general listened to this complete tripe with great interest. He rubbed his chin and then seemed to come to a decision. "Don't worry, son," he said. "The Fatherland is grateful for your sacrifice. We'll get you to the rally."

"Heil Hitler!" I honked and saluted again.

"Heil Hitler. Well done, lad." He turned to Hans. "Soldier! What seems to be the problem here?"

A discussion ensued that involved words like ignitioned magnetos and sparkling carbonators and maybe flywheel valves, but I couldn't possibly tell you exactly what it was. What it boiled down to was that fixing the engine required obtaining a part.

"Hmmm. Everything in Berlin will be closed for the rally," said the general.

Matya sobbed and buried her head on Vrak's shoulder.

"Now, now, little mother," said the general. "We can't have our brave warrior miss a chance to be healed by his Führer! You will come with me!"

"Oh, we couldn't possibly impose on you," said Vrak. "I'm sure you have much more important business."

"Nonsense! I won't hear of it!"

Vrak bowed. "You are too kind."

And just like that, we had a ride to Berlin.

Introductions were made and our things transferred to his car. The general kissed Matya's hand and chuckled when she blushed like a starstruck schoolgirl and peered up at him through her lashes, clinging to his hand. When he wasn't looking, she wiped her hand on her skirt.

The general moved to the front seat, and the three of us climbed into the back. I'm afraid that my blindness caused me to accidentally knock the general's hat off while I was being helped in. Twice.

The general turned to Hans. "Soldier, you will remain with the car. I'll send my driver back with the part tomorrow."

Hans saluted. "Yes, sir."

And just like that, we had no way to get *out* of Berlin. Hans had been given a direct order to stay with the car, and we had no chance to give him a different order. Vrak and Matya both stiffened beside me. If I had another seizure now, it wouldn't be fake.

Herr General was in a great mood, and Vrak entertained him with wildly extravagant tales of my heroism in battle, sparing nothing in describing my gruesome injuries. Apparently, I earned my Iron Cross when I single-handedly saved my entire unit from a deadly French ambush while suffering from a freshly ventilated skull. The general made him repeat three times how I sat blind and mute for fifteen years until the Führer's staticky words entered my ears.

I Heil Hitlered at the right moments, but I vowed if we were still alive after this, the first thing I was going to do was throttle Vrak.

After that, the general preached about all the great things Hitler would do for Germany now that he was Chancellor.

"The Jews, Communists, defectives and degenerates, the French, they're all the same. Oh, there may be some small differences, but in the end, it all amounts to the same thing: filthy swine who want to destroy Germany. Well, not anymore, eh?"

We couldn't do a thing about it but nod and try not to vomit.

We entered the city after dark. One thing I can say in favor of traveling with a Nazi general: we sailed right through checkpoints. Crowds thronged the streets, drinking and singing. Flags hung from every lamppost, and the parade route was already barricaded. The jewel glowed in my head like a blue pearl in the gray oyster of Berlin's city center. I couldn't place it exactly without checking a map, but she was not more than a few kilometers away. It made my skin crawl, and Matya squeezed my hand. The mist all around us pulsed with Manikins, though I didn't see any with my regular sight.

The general waved an arm out the window at the teeming streets. "Berlin!" He turned in his seat, took my hand, and shouted at me as if I was deaf, too. "Son, I know you can't see it yet, but this is the greatest city in the world."

"Heil Hitler," I sputtered.

Vrak said, "We are in your debt, Herr General."

"Good, good," said the general. Then he nailed Vrak with cold eyes. "And now I will tell you how you will repay that debt."

All three of us froze mid-breath. Of course, there was a price. And I was one hundred percent positive we weren't going to like it.

"I've been called to a meeting at the Reich Chancellery tonight. Top-level brass. Very top." His voice went conspiratorial. "Between you and me, they've gone a bit soft lately, all this talk about peace and such. They're losing touch with true German grit. But if they meet this brave boy who sacrificed so much and still loves his country so deeply that just the sound of his Führer's voice restored his speech? If they witness a miraculous healing firsthand? Why that ought to slap some life into them!"

I wanted to climb screaming out of the window. Of all the Nazi generals in Germany, we got the crazy one.

Vrak choked for a second before he found his voice, and I prayed he wouldn't deploy his tongue out of nervous habit. "Herr General … It's … it's too much. We're just ordinary folk."

"Nothing to worry about. The Führer himself had humble beginnings. Your son is a decorated hero!"

"But we've been traveling for two days. My son needs to rest."

The general considered this for a moment, then dismissed it with an airy wave of his hand.

"Nonsense! After the terrors of Verdun, a simple meeting is child's play." He turned to me and shouted, "Don't you think, son?" He punched my arm, then nodded to Matya. "But of course, you'll want to freshen up. Where are you staying? My driver will take you there and wait."

"Oh, can you recommend a hotel?"

"What? You haven't reserved a room? You'll never find one now. But don't worry! You will be my personal guests. You must be starved, and our cook makes the best Schweinshaxe in the country."

My stomach chose that moment to rumble loudly.

"There, you see?" exclaimed the general, slapping the back of the seat. "A good German stomach in need of a solid German meal. And then, a miracle!"

We would need one of those.

"Heil," I said, but "Hitler" came out as a squawk. Matya managed a smile, though her knuckles were white on the handle of her purse. Vrak bowed his head and said nothing.

• • •

The general's house was a typical Prussian fortress of heavy, gray stone and black iron railings. The driver leaped out and opened the door for the general and then for us. Vrak and Matya helped me out. We hung back, but he waved us forward. I tapped my cane and made sure to stumble several times on my way up the steps. Maybe if I was pathetic enough, he'd change his mind about taking me along. No such luck. He helped me up the steps himself.

"Very soon, you won't need that cane!" he bellowed.

Frau General was a large, pillowy, gray-haired woman in a flowered silk dress and pearls. Her mask of hospitality slipped at the sight of us, but she pasted it back on pronto.

"Please do come in," she said and turned to snap orders at several maids.

Inside, the house smelled of beeswax, lemon, and roast pork. On a gleaming entry table, photos in polished silver frames clustered around a vase of fresh lilies. Above them on the wall hung three large, matched paintings in gilt frames: on the left, Jesus gazed down; on the right, Mary cast her eyes heavenward; and in the center, Adolf Hitler stared straight into our souls.

She led us to an upstairs bedroom to freshen up and told us that dinner was over, but she would have a light supper laid out for us when we were ready.

The curtains, bed cover, and chairs were done up in a matching floral chintz that seemed to vibrate if you looked at it too long. A large, framed photograph of the General and Hitler shaking hands hung above the bed. On the walls, the Jesus and Mary theme expanded to include paintings of angels guarding red-cheeked children. Some of the angels wore red arm bands.

Matya closed the door. Vrak collapsed in a chair and mopped his head with his handkerchief. He looked up at Matya. "What did you pick up from him?"

"He's terrified, desperate," she whispered.

Hitler had not appeared in public since the day we changed him. But I could imagine what was going on behind closed doors. If he'd been trying to convert those around him, there'd be more and more people acting strange and a lot of mysterious deaths. Rumors had to be flying like gulls around a garbage scow.

"He probably thinks he's been called in for some kind of purge," said Vrak.

"He's not wrong," I said.

"He's desperate enough to grasp at straws. Even the idea that he can avoid being purged if he brings the right tribute," Matya said. "That's you."

I groaned. "She'll be over the moon."

Vrak sat up. "What if the Blue Lady is at this meeting? It could be a chance to get the jewel now instead of waiting until tomorrow. We could skip the whole mob at Tempelhof."

"Why would she be at the meeting?" asked Matya.

"She has to be somewhere. Puppet Hitler will be there, right? What better place to be than at the center of power?"

Matya pulled the map of Berlin out of her bag and unfolded it on the bed. "Can you see where the jewel is?"

I found the Chancellery and tried to place what was in my head on the map. "Very close. She could be there, but I'm not sure." It made my skin itch to be this close. Could she sense me? She wasn't making a beeline our way, so maybe she couldn't. Or just hadn't looked yet. She did have a few other things going on at the moment and no reason to think I'd be here.

"If she's there, we'll have to try," said Matya. "What else can we do?"

Climb out the window? Convince the general not to take us along tonight? But what if fate was offering us this chance and we passed it up?

"Supposing she's there, and supposing a miracle happens, and we get our hands on the jewel," I said, "how do we get out? What do we do with it?"

What was Hans doing right now? How long would he wait there? Until he starved to death? If we managed somehow to get the stone and drop it in the sea, I swore I would come back for him. If we didn't, then it didn't matter for any of us.

"One catastrophe at a time," Vrak said.

When we came downstairs, the general greeted us with a bottle of wine and a grin. He filled our glasses and raised his.

"To the Fatherland!"

I saw the fear Matya had seen in his face. All his to-the-fatherland bravado was a brittle mask stretched over a solid core of panic.

Frau General's idea of a light supper made me wonder what actual dinner might be. A colossal platter of steaming pork sat at the center of the lace tablecloth surrounded by bowls of boiled potatoes glazed with rich brown gravy, glossy sauerkraut, white asparagus swimming in hollandaise, and thick slices of white bread.

Some people can't eat when they get too wound up. I'm the opposite. My nerves were a furnace that needed fuel. Matya piled up my plate, and I waded in like I hadn't eaten since Verdun. I had developed my opinions about German cookery on circus swill, but this was a revelation. I pushed food onto my fork with my fingers and licked the gravy off them. I fumbled around for my glass and knocked it over twice.

The general's wife kept her smile plastered in place, but it was getting thinner around the edges by the minute. Herr General tapped his fingers restlessly on the table and gulped wine until the maid came in and announced that the car was ready.

He drained his glass and stood. "Time to go!"

I shot to my feet and flung my arm up in salute, sending a drop of hollandaise as far as Frau General's startled face. "Heil Hitler!"

• • •

The car was polished to a mirror shine. The driver opened the rear door for us, and the general rode in front again. His earlier cheer was pasted on even more firmly than before, but I didn't need Matya's gift to see the grim despair underneath. The ride to the Reich Chancellery was silent, tense, and short.

I closed my eye and concentrated on the thumpity-thump. We were heading right towards it, and this close, I could see faint wisps radiating out from it into the pulsing mist of life surrounding it. My stomach flipped, and I regretted eating so much supper.

The wide, flat front of the Reich Chancellery, with its towering, square pillars and symmetrical ranks of windows, looked more like a prison than a seat of government. Floodlights lit the outside like flames. The throbbing glow of Manikins filled the inside. At the center of it all, the jewel was a fat, pulsing spider.

We stopped in front, and two armed guards opened the doors. All three of us got out, but the general stopped Vrak and Matya. "You may wait here," he said.

"My son is blind," said Vrak. "He needs us to help him."

"We will provide any assistance he requires," said the general. "And God willing, he will walk out on his own."

Shit.

One of the guards took my arm in a firm grip. I stumbled on the smooth pavement, but he held me up. "There are ten steps directly ahead," he informed me.

At the top, more armed guards opened the massive doors.

On the fifth step, I tried the only move I could think of. With a choking groan, I stiffened, jerking my head to the side, crabbing my arms, and arching my back. I'd done the seizure act at the café yesterday, but this was a new audience. I fell, forgetting we were on steps. The tumble was painful but impressive, and I added spitting and drooling to my twitching.

The guards jumped away as if I might be contagious, and the general gaped in horror.

"My baby!" screamed Matya.

"He's having a seizure!" cried Vrak. They caught on quick, I'll give them that. In a moment they were kneeling by my side, clutching my arms while I writhed and foamed.

"What should we do, sir?" asked a guard.

Beads of sweat popped out on the general's forehead, and his collar seemed to have shrunk around his neck. A party of officials approached from inside the Chancellery, and one officer stepped forward.

"Ah, General. You're here at last. The Führer is waiting for you." The officer glanced down at us. "What is this?"

The general gave up. I suppose he finally realized that I was more of a liability than any possible use as tribute. "They are nothing," he said.

He squared his shoulders, turned away, and walked up the steps to his fate with his head high. I almost felt sorry for him. Almost.

When the doors closed, I recovered from my seizure, and the three of us ran to the shelter of the crowds mobbing the leafy paths of the Tiergarten, two streets away.

We spent the rest of the night there, trying to keep to the thickest crowds we could find. It was a good strategy; half the city was there, and the Manikins were mostly elsewhere. We strolled through the gardens, bought beers from a sidewalk vendor, agreed with other strollers that yes, the scent of night jasmine in the Tiergarten was especially lovely this year, and generally tried to blend in.

"I suppose the general won't be sending that engine part to Hans tomorrow," I said.

"One catastrophe at a time," Matya said.

No one bothered us, even when we fell asleep on a park bench, leaning against each other.

• • •

It was still dark when we set out for the Tempelhof airfield, but the city was already—or still—humming. Vrak wanted to take the U-Bahn subway, but Matya felt too closed in. We had to wait for several trollies to pass before we found one with room for us.

The closer we got to the Tempelhof district, the more jammed the streets were. Chartered buses were arriving from every corner of the country, festooned with banners for various unions, regiments, and hometowns.

Tempelhof was not like central Berlin. Little wood-frame houses lined residential streets, all very neat and tidy. We stepped off the trolley into a heaving mass of excited, chattering, singing, chanting people. The gates wouldn't open for hours, and I was already sweating through my shirt. I'm sure Vrak and Matya were edgy too, but they were more experienced actors and hid it better.

Like ourselves, thousands had come to Berlin on their own rather than with a group, creating quite a bit of chaos while soldiers attempted to sort us out for the march onto the field. We attached ourselves to a group of disabled Great War veterans with their families. At noon, a military band struck up a patriotic song, and the gates rolled open.

The terminal building was reserved for important people. Regular folk like us were herded through large gates in the perimeter fence that led directly onto the airfield. It took hours for everyone to stream in, and the band never stopped playing.

When we got to the gate, I clutched my cane and shuffled in with Vrak and Matya at my sides. Our fake IDs were good enough. One hurdle down.

The field already held more people than I had ever seen in my life. Soon, it would be more people than anyone here had ever seen in one place. The odor of unwashed bodies, sausages, tobacco, alcohol, and farts jangled my nerves as much as the rumble and hiss of too many voices. Even if I closed my eye to escape the visual stew, I couldn't escape the pulsing light of Manikins throughout the crowd. I rubbed Armond's embroidered name inside my cuff to steady myself; I could almost read the letters with my fingertips.

After we were inside, it was still a long walk. We had bet on disabled heroes getting preferential treatment, and that paid out pretty well. We got a decent spot—not all the way up front with the bigwigs, but we could have been a kilometer from the stage.

At the front, armed troops stood shoulder to shoulder behind a low wooden barrier. Behind them, a platform big as a freighter floated above the sea of heads. In the center of that, a white-painted staircase climbed to a speaker's platform high as a crow's nest. Everyone would be able to see their Führer. Behind the platform, swastika banners at least double the podium's height snapped like sails in the breeze.

We scouted the exits. The main terminal curved along the edge of the airfield to the left of the stage. Windows were spaced evenly along the side of the terminal facing the field with a pair of large glass doors at the center. Armed soldiers lined a corridor from there to the stage. We eased our way in that direction, trying to get closer but not so close as to attract attention.

As the crowd grew, so did the number of Manikins. We had tried to calculate how many there were, based on what I had seen in the underground chamber and what Papa knew. There might be as many as five thousand, and most of them would be here. If a million people showed up, that was one in two hundred. The Blue Lady could be looking through the eyes of any of them. I could see the closest ones individually by their pulsing light and tried to maneuver us away from them. Even with my new leg, my stump was starting to ache, and there was nowhere to sit. Not far away, a woman fainted. Vrak and Matya stood on either side of me like doting parents and clutched my arms. It was too noisy to speak. Nothing more to say even if we could.

The light of the blue jewel was now moving along the parade route towards the airfield. I just needed to stay out of sight until she was here. Until she stepped through those doors herself.

Then it would be time to stop hiding.

20

The start of the rally was weirdly like the start of a circus show, if the circus had dozens of giant floodlights instead of a single spot, a hundred trumpets instead of a five-piece combo, and an audience of a million instead of a few hundred. The stage and the towering banners behind it blazed like flames against the darkening sky. The glass doors of the terminal opened, and men filed through the corridor of armed guards to the stage.

What did you call humans who were chained to the thumpity-thump? It didn't seem right to call them Manikins. They weren't manufactured creatures with no past. They had lives, families, jobs. Were their memories erased? Locked away? Screaming to get out? It didn't matter what we called them. What did matter was that every single one of them walked with the same heartbeat rhythm. Including our former host, Herr General.

When a man in a uniform walked to the podium and began to climb the steps, I stopped breathing until spots danced in front of my eyes. Matya tugged on my arm, and I tried to loosen up. It wasn't Hitler. Like any circus, they'd warm up the crowd with some lesser acts before bringing out the headliner. I forced myself to take slow breaths. The Blue Lady was close. Nearly here.

The first speech ended to roars of approval. The second speaker climbed to the podium. My arms cramped, and I realized I'd been clenching my fists. Matya and Vrak stood beside me, for all the world like a proud mama and papa, but they twitched with every cheer from the crowd.

She was inside the terminal now.

Time to move closer to the terminal doors. No one in that crush wanted to be jostled any more than they already had been, but I acted like I was about to be sick, and they got out of the way. We skirted around two Manikins and reached a good spot—close enough to have a clear view of the doors but with a few rows of people between the guards and us— just as the third stuffed uniform droning on at the microphone saluted to cheers and climbed down.

She was moving along the corridor.

There was a pause, and I could feel the crowd hold its breath. The band struck up the national anthem, and they pressed forward, pushing us closer to the front. Hitler strode out on the stage and climbed the stairs to the platform. To anyone else, he was a man walking up some stairs. To me, it was unmistakable. Thumpity-thump, thumpity-thump. At the top, he paused and then raised his arm in salute. A million arms shot up.

"Heil Hitler! Heil Hitler! Heil Hitler!" The earthshaking roar went on and on.

The movement of the jewel stopped. What if she didn't come out? I quivered with tension, and Matya patted my arm. Stay cool.

All eyes were on the stage. Even the soldiers guarding the path from the doors to the stage watched now that their escort duties were done.

I closed my eyes and saw the jewel—a small, bright star suspended around her neck. But something was off. I touched my chest where the locket should be. The jewel was lower. Had she put it on a longer chain? I looked through the windows of the terminal, searching for her.

And there she was, watching through a window, making no move toward the doors.

She was still beautiful, but whatever spell had drawn me to her before was reversed; my heart recoiled. She wore a black coat and hat, head held high, hands thrust in her pockets. The jewel was not on the chain around her neck. Of course. It wasn't in the locket. It was in her hand, ready to be used.

I needed to let Vrak and Matya know, but the crowd was still chanting and roaring too loud for me to make myself heard. I turned and looked into Matya's eyes, hoping she would see. She nodded.

They vanished into the crowd to do their part.

It was time for me to do my part.

I closed my eye and reached out to her with all the power I could muster from my mind, my wooden eye, and whatever ghosts of magic lurked in my body. Would it be enough?

The faintest wisp of blue threaded toward her like smoke. I knew the instant she sensed it. I felt a tug, like a fish on a line, but which of us was the fish? I opened my eyes. She had stepped right up to the window, and stared directly at me, her eyes arctic.

The line connecting us snapped taut. I was the fish, and she set her hook.

She moved to the next window and found me again. And then the next one. Hitler began to speak, but he was drowned out by her voice sizzling inside my head like wind through dry reeds. "Why did you come?"

I stumbled. I was only supposed to distract her. I wasn't expecting to have to *talk* to her. I couldn't lie. And I couldn't give away our plan. I made my mind as blank as I could and shouted my thoughts at her. Maybe if I was loud enough, it would distract her from the truth. "Look at all these people! How many will die so you can enslave the ones who survive? Half? Three quarters?

"Enslave is a harsh word. I only want what's best for them."

"If I come back—if I let you use me—will more of them survive?"

She moved to the door and pressed a hand against the glass. I felt her pull on me, drawing me toward her. "Yes. Together we'll be stronger."

She'd be stronger. I'd be a husk.

"I can't let all those people die." Not a lie, but would she take it the way I wanted her to?

A soldier opened the door for her. She stepped through and beckoned to me.

"Hurry." Her voice was urgent in my head. "There's not much time."

She needed her hands on me. I couldn't stop my feet from moving as she reeled me in, but I went as slowly as I could, using the crowd to block my path. She pushed impatiently through the line of guards, ordering people out of her way.

Matya stepped into view from between the two men closest to her, stumbled, and bumped against her. The Blue Lady shoved her away without even looking at her. And that was enough for Vrak. He stepped forward, as if to help Matya. I didn't see him take it, but the Blue Lady's voice vanished from my head, and the line connecting me to her broke with a sharp snap that sent me stumbling backward into the man behind me. Vrak and Matya melted into the crowd.

The Blue Lady's hand flew to her pocket, and her mouth fell open in a scream that I didn't need to hear to know was bloodcurdling. She dove into the crowd after them.

A rustle swept through the crowd like the wind ahead of a storm. On the podium, Hitler broke off mid-sentence. He signaled to an aide who ran up the steps. Was he free of the Blue Lady's control? I couldn't wait around to see. I turned my back to the stage and started for the gate we'd come in through. People peered toward commotion surrounding the jewel and those closest started closing in around it. For a moment, I thought she was still controlling things, but it was probably just nonmagical rubbernecking. Anyone coming through those doors was important—part of Hitler's inner circle. And in a crowd like this, it wouldn't take long for anyone nearby to be drawn into a chase, whether they knew what it was about or not.

More people craned their necks to see what the flap was about, and I stopped too. The plan was for me to stay clear of Vrak and Matya and head to the rendezvous point. But every time the jewel's movement stopped, so did my heart. Through a brief gap, I caught sight of Vrak in the grip of soldiers who were trying to wrestle him to the ground. Just before he went down, he tipped his head far back, opened his mouth, and his long tongue shot out. Hundreds of eyes watched the jewel fly in a high arc from its tip, catching the light for a frozen moment, and then it dropped down—right into big Matya's open mouth. She clamped her jaw shut and swallowed. There was nothing stealthy about it. This was pure theater.

The crowd around them roared and converged on them. I groaned aloud as they both vanished from sight.

I felt a hand on my arm. I turned and found myself facing a German officer.

"Are you all right, soldier?" he asked. "Do you need help?"

"The gate," I managed to say. He nodded and started clearing the way, still holding my arm. I was a blind war hero with an iron cross on my chest. Wherever I needed to go, someone would see that I got there.

Once I got outside the gate and rid myself of helpers, I slipped into the shadows of a dark shop across the street, and watched the jewel's slow, zigzagging route in my head. If it started moving the wrong way, I would go after it. What did I have to lose? But it kept moving my way.

What seemed like a hundred years later, little Matya, alone, crawled out of the crowd right between a boxy matron's legs. The woman, caught up in the end of Hitler's speech, only glared.

Matya pushed herself to her feet, disheveled, hair plastered to her sweaty face, but she had the stone. I ran to her and scooped her up like a child and held her tightly.

"The others?" I asked.

She shook her head and buried her face in my neck.

Another one and two-thirds of my friends were gone. The loss hollowed me out. We knew the odds going in, but knowing the odds is never a comfort at the time; it's a story you tell yourself later. If I let myself think about it right then, I'd drown in grief. I forced myself to walk.

We had stopped the end of the world. For the moment.

The only thing that mattered now was to keep it that way. The Manikins could be dealt with later. With no one to give them orders, they'd be no more dangerous than Hans.

I threw away my cane and dark glasses and carried little Matya while she wept on my shoulder. I don't know how I reached the rendezvous spot. I was so numb with shock I couldn't feel the pavement underfoot.

I counted seventy paces down the alley to the door and found it unlocked, as promised. An electric lantern hung just inside the door, also as promised, and I switched it on. When I put Matya down, she curled into a silent ball with her face buried against her knees. We were in a small storeroom filled with tools and greasy machine parts. Two fuel cans stood just inside the door, along with a canvas bag of food and water. I sent a silent prayer of thanks to the underground.

It was time to deal with the next catastrophe.

I hadn't expected Hans to be here with the car, of course, but it was still a blow when he wasn't.

I sat next to Matya and put my arms around her. I was nearly overcome by grief myself, and I had only known the Blues a few weeks. For her, they were her oldest friends, and the other two Matyas were more than friends, more than sisters, more than a leg or an eye. And now they were gone, amputated. And Vrak! How could the world not have him or Armond in it and still keep turning? I rocked her in my arms like a child and wept with her. For her. For Vrak and Armond. For everyone I had ever lost.

When our tears subsided a bit, Matya pulled her handkerchief out of her blouse with the jewel tied up inside and gave it to me. Even through the cloth, it sent tendrils of power fizzing through my veins. It wanted to connect to me, and it would have been so easy to let it. I could fix everything. But Papa's warning killed that idea, and I pushed the tendrils away.

If we couldn't drop it in the sea, it was only a matter of time before someone else got their hands on it. The Blue Lady. Or someone worse.

I knew what I had to do.

I stood and searched the storeroom for something to do it with. A heavy sledgehammer leaned in a corner. That should do the job. I placed the jewel, still wrapped in the handkerchief, on the cement floor and measured the distance with a practice swing and tap.

Matya, curled up against the dirty wall, might be the last thing I saw. She looked up at me and nodded.

I took a deep breath. And swung.

The sledge struck the jewel dead on with a bone-shaking ring. But when I lifted the hammer, the stone wasn't flattened. I unwrapped it. Not even a crack.

It almost sucked me into its blue depths, but I shook it off.

I set it directly on the floor, being careful not to touch it with my bare hand, and tried again, grunting with the force of my swing.

The jewel spanged off the wall above Matya's head and ricocheted around the room but was undamaged aside from a tiny chip. It shouldn't be this hard. A piece had chipped off just from dropping it on the floor of the tower room. Maybe it was like a diamond that would come apart only if it was struck at just the right angle. I'd just have to keep bashing it.

I froze at the sound of a car turning into the alley. Headlights speared through the crack under the door. Wheels crunched on gravel and came to a stop outside. The engine thrum was too loud and powerful to be our car.

I wrapped the stone in the handkerchief and jammed it in my pocket, then stood just inside the doorway, gripping the sledgehammer in sweaty hands. A car door clicked and creaked. I heard footsteps, and the door creaked open.

"Pinocchio?"

"Hans?"

"Yes. It is Hans. I have a car."

The sledge fell from my hands and clanked on the floor.

He did indeed have a car. A big, gleaming Mercedes idled in the alley. I gaped at it and at him. How had he done it? I'd have to ask later.

"Let's go," I said.

Hans moved the fuel cans to the back of the car. Matya tried to get to her feet, but she was trembling so hard I just picked her up and packed her into the back seat along with the bag of supplies.

Hans eased the car out of the alley and headed east— obeying all the traffic laws.

When we got to the highway, I said, "We're gonna have to pick up the pace, mate."

He pressed his foot down, and the car leaped forward. It had some serious juice. Soon, Berlin was behind us, an open road was ahead of us, and I took what felt like my first breath in a year.

We'd done it. We'd done the impossible. But our losses were heavy. Armond was gone. And Vrak and two of the Matyas. I looked back at Little Matya curled up in the back seat. How could she get over such a loss?

After the chaos of the last days, the silence in the car seemed strange.

"So, Hans," I said when the silence went from strange to oppressive. "It looks like you gave yourself some orders. How did you manage it?"

"I waited for the general's driver to return with the part. He didn't arrive before the time I would need to make the repair and go to the rendezvous."

"How did you get around the order to wait?"

He paused. "I made a cinema. In my mind. With you as the actor playing the general and me as the actor playing the soldier."

"And that worked?"

"No. I didn't know what the script might say in this situation. But I remembered that sometimes, orders are given at one time that are meant to be carried out at a later time instead of immediately. Waiting is a standard protocol that I have access to. I thought perhaps I could use an order you gave to me in the past at this later time."

"And that worked?"

"No. You have given me many orders that did not help solve the problem. Like 'when you see the exit, dive down deep' and 'shut up and go to sleep' and 'shoot the rabbit.' But one order was 'commandeer that car.'"

I whooped. "And that worked!"

"No. You ordered me to commandeer *that* car—the one that is now broken. Not just any car."

"How did you get around that?"

"You and I talked about how my first act in life was an order I gave myself. Choosing to hide so I wouldn't burn. I thought very hard about how that was possible. I think it has something to do with natural reflexes, which I do possess. At that time, I believe I acted on my natural reflex to survive. If I could feel enough fear, perhaps I could trigger that reflex again."

My head was spinning.

"Did *that* work?"

"No. I could not make myself feel enough fear. I believe the part of my brain that has thoughts cannot access the part that has feelings."

"So, what did you do?"

"The thinking part of my brain made another cinema in my head to show the feeling part of my brain what would happen if I failed to arrive in time. Then I commandeered a car."

I was thunderstruck. He didn't even know how remarkable he was. Then I commandeered a car. Holy Mother of God.

"Congratulations, Hans, my boy. You're officially a human!"

Hans smiled. "I think I like being a human."

I laughed. "Enjoy the feeling it while it lasts."

I was so caught up in talking to Hans that I hadn't been paying too much attention to anything else. The highway was dark, and the lights of Berlin were fading behind us. When I closed my eyes, the brightest thing by far was the jewel in my pocket. It so overshadowed everything else that I almost didn't notice. Once I did, I couldn't believe I'd missed it.

We were being followed.

And by "followed" I don't mean a car or two in the rearview mirror. In my head a spear of light sped towards us along the highway from the bright glow of Berlin's millions of lives. It was pointed right at us and moving fast. Narrow at the tip, but wider and denser as more and more joined the chase. And it pulsed. All of it. It must have been one hundred percent Manikins.

"How fast can this car go?" I asked.

21

The car shot forward. I scanned around. No other lights, Manikin or normal, streamed towards us from other directions. So far.

How were they following us? I had the jewel, and I hadn't given any orders. We figured the Blue Lady would be able to *see* the jewel; she was still connected to it by her own thread. But she shouldn't be able to *use* it without having it in her hand. If she could, that would be bad. But if she could use the jewel without touching it, the number of Manikins should be exploding. It wasn't, as far as I could tell. I exhaled. A little. Maybe she could order existing Manikins around, but not make new ones. Or maybe the Manikins were just driven to follow the jewel themselves, like radio receivers still tuned to the station after the broadcast stops.

If she could still give orders, she could order Hitler to call up regular troops. Our planned route through Hamburg felt like a trap now.

"Hans, what's the best route to our destination that doesn't go through cities?"

He reeled off highway numbers and road names that meant nothing to me. I cut him off.

"Just take the fastest route that doesn't go through Hamburg."

"There is a route that will add approximately twenty-three minutes to our travel time."

We had at least an hour head start and were still pulling ahead. Could we risk it?

"What about fuel?"

"Refuel in seventy kilometers."

I shoved the jewel deeper in my pocket as if that would hide it.

"Let's do it."

The countryside was so dark, it was hard to know which eye I was seeing with. Reaching under my eye patch to adjust my wooden eye didn't make a difference. Any speck of light could be a person or a lamp. My heart jumped into my mouth when a cluster of lights appeared in the road ahead. Roadblock? No. Cats' eyes lit up in our headlights. They bolted when we got close.

I was ready to bolt out the window, watching the Manikin army eat up the ground we'd gained while Hans filled the fuel tank. And I just about bolted out of my skin when we came to a washed-out bridge and had to backtrack several kilometers toward our pursuers.

By the time we finally bumped off the lane onto Uncle Franz's land at about three in the morning, I was so worn out and wound up, I couldn't tell if the lights I was seeing were cats, Manikins, headlights, or hallucinations. The farm buildings were looming silhouettes. Our headlights swept across a large barn and just behind it, a trim stucco and timber farmhouse.

The farmhouse door opened before we stopped. Serafina flew down the steps and into my arms. This was what I had wanted my whole life. It was everything I needed in this minute. Her warmth melted the knife edges off the iceberg in my chest and I held her close, wanting to merge our bodies inside a single skin.

Papa's voice intruded. "Do you have it?"

Merging would have to wait. I pulled the handkerchief out of my pocket and spread it open. The jewel glowed softly, and I could feel the immense power of it trying to snake into my veins. Could the others feel it? They stared at it, speechless for a moment.

"You did it!" breathed Ursula.

"Vrak and Matya did it," I corrected.

They looked hopefully toward the car.

I shook my head. "Little Matya's in the back. She's going to need a lot of help. The others ..."

I didn't need to say more. Serafina's arm tensed around my waist, and she buried her face against my chest. Ursula clapped her hands to her mouth, but it couldn't stifle her moan. She ran to the car. Papa's face aged another ten years in seconds, but he was steady as a rock. I straightened too. We had to keep our heads a little longer.

I wrapped the stone back up. "There's something else. We were wrong about one thing. I don't think she can make Manikins, but she can still order the ones she's got. There's a whole Manikin army coming after us."

Everyone froze and Serafina's fingers dug into my arm.

"How much time do we have?" Papa asked.

I checked their progress. "I can see where they are, but I don't know how long it will take them to get here. Maybe an hour? I sure hope that plane is ready."

Inside the barn, Cat was bent over the open engine of a small biplane. He gave me a genial salute with a greasy wrench. Alongside him stood another man. He had gray hair and weathered skin but looked hale enough with broad shoulders and a straight back. Papa introduced him.

"This is our pilot, Gustav."

"Where's Uncle Franz?" I asked.

"I'm sorry to say that he took ill this morning and went to the clinic in Hamburg," said Gustav. "He asked me to fill in for him. But don't you worry. I've been flying as long as old Franz. Almost done here."

The plane had two seats, one in front of the other, and had seen better days. Some of the patches on the wings had patches. The paint on the sides had mostly flaked away, revealing bare wood. I reminded myself we didn't need to go far. We didn't even need to make it back, though I would prefer that.

I pulled Papa aside. "How well does Rolf know this guy?"

"He said he and his uncle are in the same flying club. Is something wrong?"

"I'm just jumpy." I rubbed the back of my neck. "If this doesn't work, it's over. I already tried to smash it."

"Don't give up, son. I've been thinking over what you said. The Blue Lady may not be giving the orders to the Manikins."

"What's driving them, then?"

"Now that Hitler is free, he likely wants it for himself. The Blue Lady can see where it is, and he can give orders the old-fashioned way. After that, it's a chase to see who gets to it first."

That was a cheery thought.

"It still doesn't explain why it's only Manikins after us. Why not just call out the whole German army? They could have headed us off a dozen times by now."

Papa shook his head. "They can't. The next person to touch that stone rules the world. Would *you* trust any human to hand it over once he had it? I doubt they trust the Manikins much more. They're along for backup, but I bet you they don't let a single one of them get in front."

Gustav called out, "She's as ready as she's gonna be."

Cat and Gustav pushed the big barn doors open, and we all helped wheel the plane out. It wasn't heavy, but the ground was rough and muddy.

Gustav started the engine, and it roared to life.

"Which seat is mine?" I asked.

He rubbed his chin. "Well, this old girl doesn't have as much get up and go as she used to. Might not make it to the coast with two. Best let me drop it for you."

"I have to do this myself."

He pulled out a pistol, cocked it, and pointed it at me with a rock-steady hand. Even the crickets froze and held their breath.

"You sure about that?" he said.

"Do you even know what it is?"

He shrugged. "Not really. But certain people seem to want it pretty bad. I'd say it's worth having. Now be a smart boy and hand it over, and I'll be on my way."

We stared at each other. I didn't blink—on the outside. Inside, I was blinking like a signal light. Hans stood frozen by the car. Had I ever given him an order he could use in this situation? "Shoot the rabbit" probably wasn't close enough. If we survived this, I was going to spend some time giving that boy as many orders as I could. He needed material.

A heartrending wail rose from behind the house. Gustav smiled. "That'll be young Rolf learning what's become of dear Uncle Franz."

"You son of a bitch!" I roared, taking a step toward him.

Gustav lowered his aim to my leg and fired. The bullet glanced harmlessly off the metal shaft with a loud ping. He wasn't expecting that, and it threw him for an instant. I took advantage of it.

"Do you see how powerful the jewel is?" I asked. I had to get this right. I was skirting the edge of truth and rubbed my nose to hold off the sneeze. "Don't make me use it on you."

For a second, I thought it was going to work. But he shifted the gun toward Cat without even looking away and fired. Cat jerked backward with a gasp. Ursula and Papa caught him as he crumpled to the ground. Then he aimed it at Serafina.

"Go ahead. Use it on me."

I sagged and pulled the handkerchief out of my pocket.

"Don't give it to him!" Serafina cried.

Gustav's hand didn't waver. "Let me see it first."

I untied the handkerchief, revealing the glowing blue stone. His mouth dropped open, then he snapped it shut and held out his hand. I tied it up and dropped it into his palm. He stuffed it in his pocket and vaulted into the cockpit. The plane rolled across the field, took off, and disappeared into the night sky.

Serafina flew at me and gripped my shirt, spitting mad. "How could you just give it to him?"

"Who said I gave it to him?"

I pulled a rag out of my other pocket and opened it to show them the jewel.

Ursula burst into peals of laughter. "You switched it! Vrak would be so proud!"

The others looked from her to me in confusion.

"So, the pilot has …" Papa began.

I flipped up my eyepatch. "A very nice but used wooden eye."

"But when did you …"

"Magicians never give away their secrets."

They mobbed me with hugs.

"All right, now what?" asked Papa.

Without the eye, I couldn't see where the Blue Lady, Adolf Hitler, and their Manikin army were anymore, and I didn't dare use the jewel even for that. But it didn't matter. Wherever they were, it was too close, and our plane—along with our whole plan—had vanished into thin air. Literally.

Plan or no plan, plane or no plane, all we could do was keep ahead of them as long as we could and pray for a miracle. Cat was badly injured but still alive. We carried him into the house while Hans refueled the car and checked the magnetos and thingamabobs. Papa and Ursula would stay with him, Little Matya, and Rolf. Serafina flat out refused to be left behind.

"You need backup. I can drive a car, and I can shoot a gun."

I polled all the nerves in my body, and the vote was unanimous to lock her away in the safest place I could find. But my brain knew better than to keep arguing with Serafina when she'd made up her mind. Especially when she was right.

There was no time for long goodbyes, even though these goodbyes were probably final.

Serafina and Ursula hugged each other warmly. I turned to Papa, hardly able to bear leaving him yet again. He wrapped his arms around me and patted my back while I clung to him.

"Do what you can, son."

"I will," I said, but they felt like empty words.

In the car, Hans waited for an order. The army was coming from the south. The sea was about forty kilometers to the west, but we didn't know where we might find a boat and didn't have time to wander around looking for one. Until I could think of something better, we'd head north and hug the coast. I pointed.

"That way."

Hans immediately put the car in gear and bounced across the open field toward the road.

"Take coast roads, but don't get us trapped," I said.

Serafina leaned out the window and looked back. "I think I can see them!"

Far behind us, a few needles of headlights speared into view as they rounded a curve. Then, a lot of them. If Papa was right and Hitler and the Blue Lady didn't trust anyone but themselves to touch the jewel, they'd be at the head of that parade. I forced myself to unclench my jaw before I cracked a tooth.

"How far is Denmark?" asked Serafina.

"One hundred forty-seven kilometers," said Hans. Serafina blinked in surprise.

We'd never make it to Denmark. Even if we did, it wouldn't change anything. We needed a destination. With a boat. But I'd never been here before, and I didn't know this coastline.

We rounded a bend in the road, and this time the beams of our own headlights swept across a sea of young wheat with tips frothy and pale as whitecaps. A memory floated at the edge of my brain, just out of reach. And then I had it.

"Hans! What are the nearest lighthouses?"

"There are two." He named them and the distance to each.

"Which one is on a spit of land that looks like a wart on a witch's nose?"

"I don't have access to information on the anatomy of witches," he replied.

I scrabbled through papers, looking for the map, and tore it in my rush to unfold it.

"I need a light!"

Serafina found a box of matches and lit them one after the other while I scanned the map. The North Sea coast does look like a witch's profile, and the nose is witchily long and crooked. I gave Hans the order.

I had little hope we'd get there in time. No hope if anything went wrong.

And something always goes wrong.

● ● ●

Dawn pinked the sky behind us when we reached the turn to the coast. The plowed fields on either side of the road were flat and yellow as a kettle of polenta, well-peppered with squabbling seabirds. I smelled salt and the eggy tang of marsh. We'd kept a lead on the army, but where was the sea? Where was the lighthouse? It should be in sight by now, but it wasn't.

The horizon crept closer but stubbornly remained an even green line with no hint of a lighthouse. Could we have taken a wrong turn?

"It's a dike!" shouted Serafina.

I have no idea how she knew it, but I should have known it. I had sailed the North Sea before. The land in front of us looked like the horizon, but that was an illusion. It was the top of a long, grassy, man-made embankment. The far side would slope down to a shallow salt marsh that went on to the horizon before reaching deep water. There wouldn't be more than a raised track across it to the lighthouse and maybe not even that much if it was high tide. I didn't expect to find anything solid enough to drive a car on.

Hans pulled to a stop at the bottom of the dike. We piled out and ran to the top. The marsh swept outward in front of us, iron gray and black in the early light. And there, on a low rocky rise: the red and white spire of a lighthouse.

The tide was high. I couldn't see a road or even a raised footpath leading to it. There probably was one at low tide. But the marsh wasn't submerged. Seawater ran into narrow channels cut into dense turf.

The turf would be spongy, but we should be able to walk on it, hopping across the channels. Behind us, I could make out individual vehicles bumping across the fields. The trucks would have no more luck than us on the marsh. They'd be on foot too.

"Is that a tank?" asked Serafina, shading her eyes with one hand.

"Yes," said Hans. "It is a Neubaufahrzeug tank armed with a turret-mounted 7.5-centimeter gun."

I swore. "Where in the hell did they get a tank from?"

The tank stopped in the road while men swarmed around it. They were strapping something to the top of it. "Hans, what are they doing now?"

"I cannot determine that."

We turned and ran along the top of the dike to the point closest to the lighthouse.

A few cottages lined a lane on the inland side, but I didn't think they'd be much help. People around here might supply the lighthouse but would wait for low tide to do it. A man came out of one of the houses with a crate of milk bottles and fixed it to the front of a bicycle. He hopped on and rode along the path at the bottom of the dike, oblivious to the horde bearing down on him from the east. His hat blew off in a strong gust, and he watched it sail into the sky.

Serafina gasped. "We can use my wings!"

"Your wings?" What was she talking about?

She started undoing the buttons on her coat. "Hans, get the bike!"

Without hesitation, Hans ran toward the man and relieved him of his bike.

Serafina dropped her coat and took a deep, deep breath. Her wings lifted as the veins filled until they were fully spread. My mouth dropped open.

"How?"

She grinned. "Ursula."

"Ursula?"

"We had to do something while we were waiting for you."

With the rising sun behind her, I could see the fine lines where the rips had been neatly stitched together. Only Ursula could have done such painstaking and intricate sewing. Even torn and repaired, they were astonishing, wide and elegant as a butterfly's. It was nothing short of a miracle. But I didn't see how they were going to help us.

"But you still can't fly, can you?"

"No, I can't fly," she said. "But you can sail."

22

Could it work? I tested the wind.

When Hans came back with the bike, I told him to head up the coast and find somewhere to wait for us to come get him. If we weren't there by nightfall, he was to go back to the farm and report to the others.

It took a moment for Serafina and me to get situated on the bike. I sat in front, and she crouched behind me, feet on the frame, arms around my chest, and wings folded back out of the way. I itched with impatience to go; on top of the dike, we stood out like targets. But we'd only get one chance to set sail.

I could hear the deeper roar of the tank engine behind us above the sound of trucks and screaming seabirds.

"Ready?"

She gave me a squeeze, and I stood on the pedal, giving the full power of my new leg to the downstroke. I rode as hard as I could along the top of the dike to build up speed, waiting for the right moment.

I watched the birds. When they swept up into the sky on a gust of wind, I counted to three and turned the wheel, shouting, "Now!"

Serafina spread her wings, and we whooped as the wind caught them. The bike surged down toward the marsh. I wouldn't want to tack this way, but with the wind at our backs, it might just do.

Normally, it would be impossible to ride a bike across soggy, matted vegetation, but her wings gave us just enough extra speed and loft to skim across the turf and clear the channels we couldn't avoid. The lighthouse loomed closer, but the water also grew deeper and the turf wetter. I glanced back. Cars and trucks lined the top of the dike, and the tank came into view.

"Look out!" shouted Serafina.

I swung my head back around. We were heading right into a wider channel.

"Fly!" I shouted. I gripped the handlebars and pedaled with everything I had. She swept her wings up and down with as much force as she could. The tiny amount of extra lift kept us from crashing straight into the channel but wasn't quite enough to clear the far side. We hit the bank and tumbled into the mud.

I looked back again and groaned. The tank and whatever was on it splashed into the shallow water on wide treads. I prayed for it to sink, but it churned forward, leaving a wake of shredded marsh. Soldiers on foot streamed down after it.

We left the bike and crawled the last few yards through sucking mud and seawater.

Serafina fell behind. I reached for her, but she waved me off.

"Go!" she screamed.

I scrambled onto the rocks surrounding the lighthouse and got to my feet. My muddy shoes slithered on the stone steps leading up to the door. I pounded until it swung open to a familiar, glowering face.

"All right, all right. Where's the bloody fi …" His mouth dropped open. "Woody?"

I leaned against the door frame, panting. "Hey, Lampwick."

His face split in a wide grin. "Well, I did say you should drop in if you were in the area, but most folks wait for low tide."

He saw Serafina over my shoulder and raised a shaggy eyebrow at me.

"No time to explain. We need a boat," I said. "Right now!"

"In trouble again, lad? Well, I could use a break from this brick pecker. I'm in." His laugh cut off short when he saw what was headed our way. "Holy hell!" He grabbed his hat and a knapsack off a peg by the door. "Let's go."

The three of us ran down the rickety dock to a small skiff and hopped in. I cast off the line while Lampwick started the outboard. The water was shallow and weedy, but the boat handled it well, if not speedily. At this rate it would take hours to reach deep water.

When we were underway, Lampwick looked back and whistled. "What the hell have you been up to, Woody?"

I gave him the barest bones of it, and to my great relief, he believed me. Or at least pretended to. The tank stopped near the lighthouse, and soldiers unstrapped the thing from the top and started assembling pieces. It was a boat. Of course, they had a boat.

"Artillery would be quicker," said Lampwick.

I shook my head. "They can't risk losing the stone."

"How far do you need to take it?"

"Anything they can dredge is too close. It's got to be deep." Outside the boat, weeds drifted just below the surface.

"That'll be quite a ways out. It's a puddle for miles."

They were in the water now. Their boat was long and streamlined. A powerful outboard motor churned the water behind it. A soldier sat at the tiller, and at the bow, I could make out two others. They had to be Hitler and the Blue Lady. Papa was right. Neither one of them would let anyone else near it. Which one of them would end up with it? I assumed they each had some kind of dirty trick planned to keep it from the other, but that wasn't my concern right now. I looked out to sea. The darker line of deeper water was only a thread on the horizon.

A gunshot snapped my head around. Hitler stood at the bow, pistol in hand. The Blue Lady crouched behind him, her face a mask of rage.

"There's an old revolver in my bag," said Lampwick.

A second gunshot sent splinters flying from the gunwale. Serafina dived for the bag.

"Can you go any faster?" I shouted.

"Going as fast as I can," said Lampwick.

"How deep is it here?"

"Up to your ears, I reckon."

I couldn't drop it here. They would have it in no time.

A third shot struck the hull near the waterline, and we started taking on water.

A flash of gray caught my eye to the side. Too small for a boat. Did they have torpedoes? No. It was a fish leaping in our wake.

It swam closer, close enough for me to see the scar curling above his eye. My dolphin! How had he found me all the way here?

I looked back toward the lighthouse. The shore was black with Manikins. Hitler and the Blue Lady were close enough that I could see that their eyes weren't on me. The stone in my pocket was their polestar. My heart plummeted. Even if we dropped it in the middle of the ocean, they would always be able to find it. All our plans were useless. We were beaten.

"Thanks, old friend," I said to the dolphin. "But I don't think you can save me this time."

The stone pressed against my thigh. It called to me. My hand dipped into my pocket.

Papa's warning echoed in my ears. If I started using it, I wouldn't be strong enough to let it go. I had a lifelong history of giving in to temptation, even when it wasn't magically induced, and it never ended well. It would control me like it controlled the Blue Lady until someone stole it from me like we'd stolen it from her. But what choice did I have? If I failed now, it was over. Over for Hans, who was only just figuring out how to be human. Over for Papa and Alidoro and Ursula. Over for everyone else in the world. Over for Serafina and me.

I looked over at Serafina and Lampwick, who were screaming at each other about bullets. I wanted to scream too.

A fourth shot whizzed past, grazing Lampwick's shoulder, and he let out a stream of curses. It shook me out of my stupor.

What if Papa was wrong? Wrong about me?

We'd been apart my entire adult life. In his mind, I was still that scatterbrained puppet, that reckless teen. But I wasn't a kid anymore, and I hadn't been a wooden boy for twenty-three years. Had I *ever* been a puppet? God knows, no one could make me do what I didn't want to do, even when it was in my best interest. I'd been free to choose my own way from the first minute of my life to this one. I might have a different body now than when I was new, but didn't everyone? All my life I'd been trying to become something I always was. Myself.

At this moment, the one thing I never wanted to be—the only one like me in the world—was the only thing that mattered. Would it be enough?

I stopped fighting the stone's pull and gripped it in my hand.

Lightning blasted into my body a thousand times stronger than what I felt with the Blue Lady. I understood why she called it the Heart of God. What else could contain this much power? Crackling fingers of it dug into my head, looking for a way in. Lines of pulsing light streamed outward from the jewel to thousands of Manikins, a few Blues, and a handful of humans. And her. The Blue Lady was snared more tightly by the stone than anyone. Tangled threads of power laced throughout her body like the roots of the tree she had stolen the jewel from. She struck out at me through them, raging, demanding, threatening, clawing to wrench the stone out of my grasp. I'd made a terrible mistake. Papa was right. It was too much. Too much power to control. Any wish I had, any order I gave, would flash instantly through those lines. The stone would not only obey my commands, it *needed* my commands—make things, do things, change things. The world was a vast toy box full of abandoned toys itching for someone to play with them. It was even more than that. The small blue stone I held in my hand was only one tiny point in a vast web. It went on and on, connecting to other points, other stones, other worlds. If I gave a single command, it would never let me go. But how else could I end this?

A memory swam up out of the depths. A long-ago brawl in a bar in Marseilles and Lampwick saying, "When all else fails, lad, pull the damn plugs."

I clenched my hand. I held my breath. And *pulled.*

A blinding nova of blue fire burst out and spread in every direction. Ropes of light whipped and coiled like eels gone mad, scorching my skin from the inside. At any second, I would fly apart and never come back together again.

Then, a line snapped. A pop, a flash—and a Manikin was free. Then another. And another. Until the continuous snapping of connections breaking was brighter and louder than fireworks on a thousand New Year's Eves. Until only the Blue Lady was left. Her voice howled and shrieked inside my head. She clung to her connection, fighting me with everything she had. I pulled again. Harder. No pop and flash this time. The stone's tendrils ripped out of her body with a deafening screech like steel girders giving way. Then silence.

She was gone.

I floated in darkness. Then the outside world rushed back, filled with chaos and shouting. The jewel was a cool, dark egg in my hand, its blue glow reduced to the smallest spark deep inside.

A gunshot pinged off the outboard motor, and it sputtered and died.

Hitler's boat rammed ours, tipping it sharply and knocking Lampwick into the water. The Manikin at the tiller of Hitler's boat was no longer steering; he sat immobile, staring into space. Just behind him, the Blue Lady floated in the water, face down. Despite everything, I felt a pang of sadness at the sight of her. In a way, she was a victim too.

Hitler, screaming at us in a frothing, purple-faced rage, reached for our gunwale with one hand and tried to aim his pistol with the other, struggling to keep his balance in the rocking boat. The stone slipped from my fingers into the water that had collected in the skiff. I scrabbled for it.

Serafina swore nonstop as she shoved bullets into the ancient revolver.

I came up with the stone in my hand and looked out to sea. My dolphin streaked toward us, skimming under the surface like a gray torpedo. Come on! I urged.

He leaped into the air over our bow, and I flung the jewel. It arced high, glinting in the sun.

The dolphin plucked it out of the air as neatly as Armond ever caught a juggler's ball. And with a splash, he was gone.

"Take it as far as you can!" I called.

I nearly fell in after him as the boat was rocked by another gunshot, this one so close and so loud I thought I was hit.

But it was not my body that tumbled back, landing heavily on the boards beside me.

Serafina! No!

I turned and crawled to her, my heart in my mouth.

She lay half-submerged in the bottom of the skiff, eyes staring up at the sky. I grabbed her arms and pulled her up.

"Serafina!"

She blinked and looked over my shoulder. Then she grinned at me and pointed, Lampwick's revolver still in her hand.

"I told you I could shoot!"

I turned. Hitler sprawled lifeless across the gunwale, blood streaming into the water.

The boat rocked again as Lampwick tried to climb in. We gave him a hand and then took stock.

On the shore, soldiers stood like statues or wandered at random. Some sat down where they were. Some simply walked away.

"What the hell did you do?" asked Lampwick.

"I unplugged the lot of them."

23

We couldn't sit around congratulating ourselves. The human authorities weren't there yet, but they would be soon. We swapped boats, leaving Hitler's body in the skiff. We found Hans on the beach and dropped off the former Manikin soldier who had driven the boat. He stood there looking like a lost puppy until we pointed him towards his mates and sent him off. Lampwick motored us to an inlet he knew where we could hide the boat.

"What are you going to do?" I asked him. "You can't go back to the lighthouse."

He looked off toward the horizon, then grinned. "Go to sea, of course. I was never meant to sit in one place anyway."

• • •

It took several days for Serafina, Hans, and me to make our way back to Rolf's farm. It was a happy and sad reunion. We'd done the impossible. But Armond, Vrak, and two of the Matyas were gone forever. Little Matya was still crippled with grief. It looked like Cat would recover, but he couldn't be moved for a while. Hans and Ursula decided to stay and help them and Rolf. Papa, Serafina, and I wanted nothing more than to go home to Italy.

I won't go into the details of that journey. It was long and filled with a lot of running and hiding. But with most of the country in chaos, no one paid much attention to a few strays. I was with Papa and Serafina, so I remember it as a happy time. Sometimes we traveled with circuses. We learned that Herr Fischer and most of the company were freed after questioning in Frankfurt, but Circus Fischer was closed. Maybe for good.

The night we crossed the border into Italy, helped into in another boxcar by a railway man who knew Alidoro. Papa—at Serafina's insistence—spent the whole trip telling the most embarrassing stories about my youth.

Later, when Serafina was asleep in my arms, and I was yawning, Papa said, "When you were a boy, you used to fret that you weren't really human. It kept you up nights. I never could convince you that you were. Does it still eat at you, son?"

"Not anymore," I said.

"When did you finally know it for sure?"

"Never. I still don't know," I said. "How do you know you're human for sure?"

He opened his mouth several times. Then he shrugged.

"Don't worry about it," I said, closing my eyes. "It doesn't matter at all."

• • •

What happened in Germany after we left isn't my story to tell. Oh, those Nazis threw themselves around for a while, but with Hitler dead and Stalin licking his chops over Poland, cooler heads took over, and it was a good thing. Who knows what would have happened if the Germans hadn't allied with France, Britain, and America against the Soviets? But that's all stuff you can look up in any history book.

The poor Manikins were lost lambs. Hans and Ursula stayed in Germany and took on the work of getting them sorted out and settled. The few normals and Blues who had gotten plugged into the thumpity-thump went back to being normals and Blues when they got unplugged.

After Papa, Serafina, and I got settled in at home, we sent for Little Matya and brought her to live with us. None of us ever got over losing Armond, Vrak, and the two Matyas, but it was the worst for her by far. We did what we could for her, but she mostly just sat and stared out the window.

Papa and I expanded the workshop and did all right making prosthetic arms and legs, though with all the magic wood gone, none quite matched the level of mine.

Cat came back too, when he recovered, and turned out to be a decent enough fellow. Eugenio hired him to work at the vineyard and never had a problem with him.

About a year after we got home, a large crate arrived from Germany. I had no clue what it could be, but from Serafina's smirk, I was pretty sure she did. When we opened it, Ivan the dog popped out, tail wagging. After that, Matya perked up and started looking after Papa.

They've both been gone for many years now. We still have Ivan the Fifth. All of them were just as smart as Ivan the First, except Ivan the Third. He was dumb as a brick.

We never had any children of our own. None of the Blues did, as far as I know. We'll all be gone soon. Alidoro passed about ten years ago. He used to come home at Easter, and we'd meet Eugenio up on the hill under our oak tree and drink a few bottles of wine. Eugenio's gone now, too. His grandson runs the farm, and his kids come and see us.

And I've still got my Serafina.

In fact, that's her calling us to dinner and it's not wise to keep her waiting.

Let me just add this: You can believe what I've told you or not, but you'll notice I didn't sneeze once.

THANK YOU FOR READING PINOCCHIO'S GUIDE TO THE END OF THE WORLD

I hope you enjoyed reading the tale as much as I enjoyed writing it. As an independent author, every review matters; please consider reviewing the novel on the websites of major retailers, your blog, or Goodreads. And please! Tell your friends about *Pinocchio's Guide to the End of the World*.

If you'd like to stay in touch, head on over to my website, evamoon.net, where you can find news about upcoming projects, my original music, videos, and free stories and articles.

ACKNOWLEDGEMENTS

The two people I most particularly need to thank are my husband, Mike Gordon, who listened with endless patience as I stumbled through the many twists and turns and dead ends; and my friend, John Rutherford, who not only helped me figure out what the blue stone really is, but followed me tirelessly and without complaint on a frantic ten-day research trip to Germany.

There are so many others I want to thank: Kathy Klein for her above and beyond critiques; Andrea Monticue and Eric Gordon for their feedback; Tony Sell for his help with the sailing bits; Arne Zaslov and Pepper Kaminoff for their circus expertise; Kim Donald Houde-Martens for his hospitality and entre to the after-hours bookstore party in Berlin; Wiebke Göbber and Herr Hilpke, tour guides extraordinaire at Rammestein Mine and Oppenheim, respectively. Thank you, Jonas, for letting us in and giving us a tour of your circus in Berlin even though it was closed for the season, and we were just two foreigners peering through the fence.

I am indebted to the whole team at Allegory editing: Christine Pinto, Amy Holm, and Elena Hartwell. Thank you, Penny Orloff, for being you.

And of course, my greatest gratitude is for Carlo Collodi, who created the original, immortal Pinocchio.

ABOUT THE AUTHOR

Eva Moon's original plays have been staged across the U.S. and in the U.K. Her solo show, The Mutant Diaries: Unzipping My Genes, is available streaming on Amazon. She has written award-winning screenplays, released five music CDs, and her work has appeared in the soundtracks of multiple feature films. Eva is a former Huffington Post blogger, a community arts activist, and sings in 15 languages, including English. *Pinocchio's Guide to the End of the World* is her first novel.

She lives in Redmond, Washington with her husband and two naughty cats, hikes in the beautiful Pacific Northwest mountains, and loves to swim in lakes that are far too cold for normal humans. More at <u>evamoon.net</u>

CPSIA information can be obtained
at www.ICGtesting.com
Printed in the USA
JSHW080231230223
38109JS00001B/2